"If thou gaze long into an abyss, the abyss will also gaze into thee."

—Nietzsche

"Abyss: The primeval chaos. The bottomless pit; hell. An unfathomable or immeasurable depth or void."
—*The American Heritage Dictionary*

You're holding in your hands one of the first in a new line of books of dark fiction, called Abyss. Abyss is horror unlike anything you've ever read before. It's not about haunted houses or evil children or ancient Indian burial grounds. We've all read those books, and we all know their plots by heart.

Abyss is for the seeker of truth, no matter how disturbing or twisted it may be. It's about people, and the darkness we all carry within us. Abyss is the new horror from the dark frontier. And in that place, where we come face-to-face with terror, what we find is ourselves. The darkness illuminates us, revealing our flaws, our secret fears, our desires and ambitions longing to break free. And we never see ourselves or our world in the same way again.

CRITICAL RAVES FOR
KELLEY WILDE

THE SUITING

"A skilled writer who has produced an engaging novel. . . .
He handles the idea with wit and energy."
—*Publishers Weekly*

"A quick read—rollicking along on Wilde's clean prose
style. One can sense his enthusiasm for his craft on every
page." —Charles de Lint, *Mystery Scene*

"Highly readable. . . . An excellent choice."
—*Library Journal*

"Just the right touch of madness. . . . [Wilde is] an author
to watch." —*The Buffalo News*

MAKOTO

"Enthralling . . . Oriental eroticism and thunderbolts of
violence." —John Farris

"Not just another horror novel! . . . [Wilde's] prose style
fits the story perfectly—it's as sharp and as polished as a
samurai sword, and just as dangerous."
—Rick Hautala, author of *Winter Wake*

"A talent that is all too rare. . . . A remarkable novel, full
of subtleties and compelling force. Brilliantly drafted!"
—Lisa W. Cantrell, author of *The Manse*

"One of Wilde's particular talents is getting inside his characters' heads. Whether it's a dream, a cocaine high, or a
slooow torture scene, his expert streams of consciousness
and incredible sound effects put you right there."
—*Fangoria*

MASTERY

"Untamed, unpredictable prose—that's the trademark of Kelley Wilde. He writes like a bucking bronc, and each time out of the chute the Wilde man keeps improving. He's got the *moves*!"
—Rex Miller

"A surrealistic thriller . . . giving the whole concept [of vampires] at once a whole new interpretation and a sense of historic sweep. The most unforgettable train ride since Agatha Christie booked the Orient Express."
—Tyson Blue, author of *Cemetery Dance*

Mastery

KELLEY WILDE

Illustrated by Olivia

A DELL BOOK

Published by
Dell Publishing
a division of
Bantam Doubleday Dell Publishing Group, Inc.
666 Fifth Avenue
New York, New York 10103

ISBN: 0-440-20727-4

Printed in the United States of America

Published simultaneously in Canada

September 1991

10 9 8 7 6 5 4 3 2 1

OPM

For John Farris, with thanks for those Thanksgiving dinners.

And Herb Caen, "Mr. San Francisco."

ACKNOWLEDGMENTS

Special thanks to Ms. Pat (Duricka) Kelly, of Amtrak, for sponsoring the cross-country trip that got this novel on the right track.

To the crew of the *California Zephyr*, for turning a research excursion into the trip of a lifetime.

To my agent, Lori Perkins, for believing when nobody else did.

To Jeanne Cavelos, my editor, for refusing to let go until the book in the heart was the one on the page.

And to Frank Bellavia, a landlord with a heart of gold.

I stare, but I am new here.
—Tom Wolfe

Though they abhor its destructiveness, those who lived through 1968 are still hooked on the energy, prisoners of their old freedoms. They may feel safe, but they are sorry. For they were born, born to be wild.
—*Time* magazine

Things got wider in the Seventies. . . . All we remember is a kind of pervasive spreading, thickening, broadening . . . and, next thing we knew, it was 1980 and the expanse of our lapels mocked us cruelly.
—*Spy* magazine

When San Francisco had it, no one ever had it like San Francisco had it.
—Herb Caen

BOOK ONE

DECEMBER 31, 1985

I

"Mastery," the tall one said.

The horror began in East Soho, New York, at midnight, with that single word.

Eleven caped Europeans had gathered in a warehouse loft with their selected prey. They'd come from England, Italy, France; Romania, Germany, Sweden. They'd come from Greece and Portugal, and from three smaller countries whose names, for some, were still hard to pronounce. They'd crossed the world to hear the word that joined them as a group of Twelve. Or had, until tonight.

"Mastery," they echoed, waiting to begin.

A sudden crack of thunder brought wails and half-mad jibberings from the bodies that hung from the wall.

For longer than most could remember, these parties had started precisely at twelve. None of them had ever missed —indeed, the rules proscribed that—although each accepted that change was the Rule . . . that on this or on any Performance his place in the circle could somehow be lost to one who stood outside it. (The missing one, blond Austin Blacke, had shown *that* in 1960 the night he joined the Twelve.)

Still, they'd been together for twenty-five years as this particular dozen. And despite the cold perspective their superior natures had brought them, they were not wholly free of—attachment?

"Welcome," said the tall one, the one they knew only as Malcolm.

Now, *he* had been of the Twelve from the start. Not even

Romaine, joined just fifty years later, could match him in strength or in cunning. And even the youngest, the *difficult* Blacke, had bowed to the difference between them: Malcolm's genuine love of the Classics . . . his blazing faith in Mastery.

Without it, what were they but mortals who'd died?

And so they stood on the rim of the clock Malcolm had drawn on the floor. Brooding on Blacke's absence—tonight of all nights, their first time in New York, his home town. Observing small Blacke touches: yellow Happy Faces pasted on the stakes and crosses . . . the casket's satin lining half covered with posters of Elvis . . .

Change was the Rule, yes . . .

and Time was a river . . .

and, yes, they would find a new twelfth before long. . . .

Still, it was a matter devoutly to be wished that no further changes should happen tonight.

Dark was the Night that had taken poor Blacke. That extreme American.

Eleven alabaster faces shone in the moonlight that fell through the cracks with the snowflakes that floated around them. The group circled the rim of the clock with their eyes, each gauging the changes since they had last met.

All eyes, in the end, turned to Malcolm: the picture of Power itself.

Were they pale? Indeed, they were; their countenances lit the room. But beside Malcolm they had the sick color of flesh. Since Paris, 1980, his skin had grown utterly, beautifully white, as if he were sculpted from marble or bone.

Yet his Classic features were infinitely flexible; capable of an astonishing range of gradients of thought.

Now, the loft Blacke had picked was as large as a field. Yet Malcolm's voice, serene and soft, sailed like a lazily spiraling pass.

"Beautiful," he murmured. "So beautiful to see you grow. Soon you will show us the skills you've developed in the past five years. Real power shows most clearly, though, when it is most relaxed. So, by all means, *do* relax. But, in your quest for Mastery, never forget for a moment the midgets of the Night."

One long hand with shapely nails directed their eyes to the window, through which flickered neon flashes from some tavern far below.

"Amateurs who *chew* the wrists! Vulgarians who *tear* out throats!"

"Imposters!" cried the ten as one.

They understood his anger well. The ranks of Imposters were growing each year.

But Malcolm felt this in a way they could only hope to know.

"Mastery starts with control of the blood: with the quality of its progression . . . the style and sensibility that it is taken *with.*"

The tall one bowed to the baby-faced Swede who'd been with them twenty-nine years. "We were all *most* impressed with your Performance in Paris, my boy."

Ingmar bowed, too deeply. It was still impossible, after five Performances, to remember how little he knew.

One required a monstrous degree of control, even on the First Performance, over jaws and lips. Too weakly and the flow congealed into an unpleasant pudding. Too strongly and one ended with the mood shot to hell, a great splash in his throat.

The first thing to learn was to sip it, just so.

And so he had. And progressively so. Until his Fifth Performance, when he'd switched from wrist to throat.

How well he still remembered:

the twin scratchlike puncture marks below the young girl's jaw . . .

her sumptuous paste-white complexion, a faint touch of rose on her cheeks . . .

If Ingmar could have framed the girl, in his pride he might have. But the Night required no such souvenirs. If one failed to remember, he would not survive.

The Swede turned to the shapes hung on hooks from the wall.

The men and women kicked and thrashed in crudely fashioned harnesses, screamed at the slashes of tape on their mouths.

His glance settled on the eleventh, a last-minute find in Times Square.

(One *look* at that jacket—with "Rhodes" on the back and two Golden Gloves on the heart—and Ingmar's heart had nearly stopped. *This* would be a Sixth Performance worthy of them all!)

The boy regarded Ingmar with a horrified expression. The Swede floated over on fog feet. Hooked one finger in the strapping. Lifted him, smiling—a feather, no more. Then lowered him smoothly and purred.

"Would you like to come into our circle now, please?"

Wails and thrashings from the wall. Taped whimperings and choked-in cries. The Swede floated backward and took the boy with him. A circle of two that the sounds could not touch.

"You really must be comfortable. Why don't you slip out of that straitjacket, please?"

The Swede remembered London. Austin, harnessed just like this, had had the same spellbound expression. Had he been faking the trance all along? How, if not, had he managed the kick that shattered Leonard's spine?

Ingmar wondered if *this* one was skilled with his feet. He studied the young man intensely. Careful, though, not to diminish the spell. Faint shadows flickered, fading even as he probed:

the face of a girl with blond ringlets and Hollywood I-Love-You eyes . . .

Christmas scene: a well-trimmed tree . . . the boy and the girl singing carols . . .

Not even the ghost of a plan there.

"There's no need for formality. You really must feel free. Relaxxxx. . . ."

The Swede beamed and the snugly laced harness opened and dropped with a sigh.

"That's good. You've made us all feel so much more re-laxxxxed . . . But wouldn't you like to remove that gold cross? It really is distracting you. You know that, don't you? Good boy."

The spirit was willing. The hands took a week. But with a

lift from Ingmar's eyes, the chain rose and fell with a soft golden plink.

"Yesss. Oh, yes, that's very good. Now, wouldn't you like to just slide it away? You really could, just use your foot. Ohhh, that's *very* good!"

The boy's shoulders relaxed, sinking into themselves, then rose in slow and rhythmic heaves.

"Yesss. Dear boy. You're ready now. You're ready, so ready, to join us. You needn't breathe so quickly now. You really needn't breathe at all. Others might find that surprising—"

More horrified thrashings and wails from the wall.

"—but there is only one thing now that you find surprising. And that is that you worked so hard . . . and that it took so very long . . . when you could have been here with us all along . . . been here with us . . . where you belong . . . for you have so longed to be with us . . . and to finally . . .

"wholly . . .

"re-laxxxxx!"

Malcolm sighed behind the Swede. And Romaine whispered "Exquisite!" The Swede sent a signal to François, his second, who slipped a volume from under his cape and opened the book to a page that he'd marked.

"Brother Ingmar's rendition of 'Pulsebeat.' From *Dinner with the Vampire*."

A murmur of approval rippled all around the clock.

For with the Performance of this Classic scene one moved from the basics to the soul of Mastery.

François paced it perfectly, gazing up at signal points to recite from memory.

" '. . . And so, with infinite patience and craft—children of the centuries of nights I had been borne to—I advanced, I advanced—do I say I *advanced*?—no, rather did I float on clouds to this missing part of me! I did not move, he did not stand. One moment there was distance—or, rather, say there seemed to be—and then distance was lost as the lost part was found."

François looked up and there Ingmar was, caressing a pale, tender sliver of throat in the moonlight that fell through the cracks with the snow that floated not on but around him. François half-forgot himself . . . until Malcolm sent him the gentlest *nudge*.

" 'Now, dear boy,' " he continued. (The vampire had, by this scene, been talking for three hundred pages. Which made for a rather long dinner by even the clocks of the Twelve.) " 'Do my teeth still trouble you? My eyes—are they too . . . cold for you? Or is it the unearthly pallor of my ivory complexion? This is all, rest assured, very well and natural. But you may also rest assured—I beg you, relax. . . . Do have more of the veal. . . . You know I'm not going to eat you. . . . Oh, dear, are you quite sure you have enough paper?—I say, it is all very well for you to feel the things you're feeling now. But if you had been standing *before* me . . . the long-lost part that had come home . . . If you had taken *your* place in the Night and seen the moonlight's side of things . . . your hunger would have matched our own. Mine for completion, yours to belong, a perfected particle in the undying progression. On that night the teeth that disturb you tonight would have filled you with anticipation. And more and more you would have felt how painfully unnatural . . . and infinitely *lonely* . . . that the pulse in your throat should not be one with mine.

" 'Did he reach out then? Or did I? And how many angels can dance on a pin? And which comes first, the chicken or . . .' "

François recited from memory now, his voice a deep purple that rivaled the prose. The Swede half-bowed. The boy rose in his arms. The Frenchman shuddered as they joined.

" 'I felt my body pressed against the body pressed to mine. And then the arching of his back, in the fit of ecstasy, drew me closer as I leaned, drawn to the power that drew us in tow.' "

"Music!" Malcolm murmured.

And François, beside himself, continued. " 'Together we were locked and drawn in slow rocking movements that hypnotized us half as much as the force of the sucking itself.' "

"Oh, yes!" someone—Romaine?—cried out.

And Malcolm whispered, "The sucking itself . . ."

" 'Then it came, at last the Sound. I heard the dull insis-
tent roar. And then the pounding of a drum, as if the
Mother of us all—O Goddess! Beauty! Mother Night!—were
coming toward us slowly through a forest as dark and as lush
as her soul . . . pounding and pounding one great mighty
drum. And then a second, still greater and deeper.' "

François rocked with the Swede and the boy. He was
vaguely aware that he had dropped the book. He watched
the Swede become the boy and felt drums of desire in both
of his eyes.

" '. . . the Boom-ka-da-Boom! of his heartbeat with mine
. . . of my heartbeat echoing his heartbeat echoing my
heartbeat echoing his . . . and yet all so exquisitely timed
and *together* that there were no echoes at all!' "

"Perfection!" someone cried—Alfonse?

"Yes!" Malcolm sighed to the beat of the drum.

The Performance could have stopped there.

And, as it happened, should have.

Suddenly the freight lift sounded its shattering blast.

And the Swede wholly snapsevered the neck.

II

Their watchman had only been doing his job.

But that had meant nothing to Ingmar, whose Sixth had
been so cruelly torn that he tore the man to pieces.

Malcolm gave the strap a tug, shutting the lift's clamshell
gate.

Mad Ingmar scarcely noticed, engaged as he was in the
corner reducing the pieces to bits. While the moonlight still
fell through the cracks with the snowflakes that fell not
around now but on him.

From the lift, just before it descended, Romaine cast a
troubled glance.

"Patience," Malcolm said. "You shall not miss your Performance. Go now and watch carefully. And, by the Night,
if you *see* him . . ."

Romaine nodded solemnly, then dropped with a joltshudderbuzz.

Malcolm stood facing the lift for some time. Folding and folding the note in his hands.

His own Sixth—in Venice, so many years ago—had been accomplished, but nothing like Swede's. What a magnificent balance: of relaxation and control . . . precision and abandon. Stamina was everything. The most skillfully taught, the most sure to succeed, could be betrayed on any Night by some error in the blood, some failure to digest. Where were they now, the proud ones who'd been neither as swift nor as strong as they'd thought? Was he not the sole survivor of the original Twelve?

From below he heard the whistle that signaled Romaine was in place.

He turned slowly and leveled his gaze upon the figure at his feet. A most disturbing puzzle.

"Well, my friend, your untimely arrival has caused us no small inconvenience."

The bloodied figure glowered back. His expression was even more baleful than when he'd arrived on the lift, slung over the poor watchman's shoulder. "A present, Sirs, just come by cab."

Malcolm held up the note he'd squared into a speck.

The prisoner strained against the handcuffs locked behind his back. Sounds of hog-tied cycle boots thumping on the floor. Black leather jacket's rustling. Gray eyes—as piercing as Austin's—raging through punched swollen lids. Bristling spikes of coal black hair ready for takeoff like porcupine quills. Hooked nose smashed to add a new twist to the seemingly permanent sneer.

Oh, a bad one, this one.

Mad and bad and dangerous. And chosen very well.

Malcolm gave the note a flick. Then sent sparks flying from the tips of his extended fingers. The note danced and popped in the air, disappeared.

A pleasant but useless display of his pique. The paper was gone, but the words crackled on.

For Malcolm on his Forty-first.
Sorry I couldn't be with you tonight—but, frankly, you
guys bore me.
      Blacke

Malcolm leaned over just slightly.

The biker raged at the cuffs.

"Dear boy, before the night is through, you'll wish our friend Austin had kept you. Ingmar, of course, needn't worry you much: he'll be busy for hours there stripping those bones. Romaine was quite *red* when he left us, it's true; but for now he is out of the way. That leaves the eight to think about, all of them rather unhappy. And then, of course, there is myself. And, just between the two of us, I'm feeling *very* annoyed."

The biker bolted a foot off the floor before Blacke's work undid him. He fell back hard, head bouncing.

The eruption itself was surprising. But, to Malcolm, more so was the wolfish flash of white.

He said "My, my," and wondered just what Austin Blacke had brought him.

"Dear boy, you mustn't think that way. It isn't *you* I'm annoyed with at all. Sincerely, your teeth are amazing. But imagine the nerve of that—*upstart,* dropping you off here like yesterday's trash. Not even thirty, and thumbing his nose. I should have known. I should have. You see, that's the *thing* about Austin, dear boy. Always the show-off. The *cowboy.* At his First Performance, he was fooling with the Second. At the Second, with the Third. And, of course, he had to add some little twist every time. You know, just to make it his. I suppose that's the thing in the Colonies, yes? Something you've all simply got in your *blood.*"

The biker's sneer looked almost like a smile. Malcolm matched it, eager now to show this one the works.

"Well, American blood's a bit tangy, you know . . . but rather tasty in its way."

He gathered a bunch of black buttery leather in one ivory fist. Then started to raise the man in a dead lift.

But—

Curious . . .

How could it *be?*

His arm actually started to quiver.

Impossible.

He knew this.

Why, he'd mastered the dead lift before Swede was born. And Ingmar—a baby!—had done it tonight, easily, with just one finger.

And yet—

The seed of a low rumble bloomed in his back.

Concentrate. . . .

Concentrate!

You will not flex your arm.

You *won't.*

That's not the way to Mastery.

Lift now . . . straight and clean . . . and light . . .

not with your arm but your

mind . . .

Use your

MIND!

The tall one thought of liquid nights and the lightness of young girls at menses and glorious Performances that he had seen and given.

He felt the lightness coming home.

Easy now.

That's the spirit.

You were thinking of Ingmar, poor Ingmar, that's all.

You were thinking of Austin, his treacherous—

(Whooooofffff!)

The white noise of effort had not quite escaped. But the labor to check it had cost him.

The tall one felt the others' eyes.

The weight,

the dead weight,

he held in his fist tormented and exhausted him. But the strength of the Twelve rippled through him.

Two hundred years.

Two hundred—

Tons!

When, at last, their eyes were level, he hoped no one heard his pained stoppings for breath.

"I'm going to enjoy you . . . boy. For all his *cowboy* antics . . . Blacke does have, undeniably, a certain sense of . . . style."

Malcolm lifted him higher, a foot off the floor, then started crossing in long, liquid strides.

When the biker saw where they were headed, his lips rounded in a small "Oh."

"I suppose you'd prefer a nice . . . harness." Malcolm smiled ferociously. "But, you see, it's . . . Party Time."

He lengthened his arm, somehow, straight out and up.

Then slammed the body on the hook, clean through the leather, and then through one lung.

The biker screamed; kicked, twice; slumped, tamed and stupefied.

"Enjoy the Performance . . . you dear naughty . . . boy."

III

Across the room the woman wailed as Diogenes showed her the stakes.

Mortals.

The tall one slipped into the coffin, inhaling the satin that stopped at his hips. Under the weight of his elegant legs, Blacke's posters teased and crinkled. They seemed much less amusing now, although the evening *had* gone well.

Garcia's Performance of "Mirror" (his Ninth)—a fine reflection of real growth.

And Gruber's Eighteenth, "Cross Me"—done almost to a T.

And "Hammer," Romaine's Thirty-first—could any Imposter *conceive* such a thing? To play it straight, as Romaine had, the Classic Movie Death Scene: lips drawing back over castanet teeth, nose shrunk to a couple of black gaping holes . . . irises doing a frenetic jig while bones shot through parchmented skin . . . And then, *then,* at the Moment itself, to *snap* the reel into reverse. And rise, refleshed, triumphant—one's partner a jumble of bones at one's feet.

Mastery! Oh, Mastery!

And on and on around the clock.

But no Performance had been what it might have, if not for young Austin. The *cowboy.*

Well, his Performance would fix *that*— if only she'd get on with it. He heard her scrambling through the stakes and half-wished that Adolph would tell her: Any one at all would do or not do just as nicely.

Holy water, crucifixes . . . Child's play to such as he, who had been of the Twelve for so long.

Sunlight? Nothing to it: Drop your pulse just half a beat for every degree above sixty.

Decomposition? Right up to the Moment . . . if you looked out for your heart.

The heart was the Law even they could not break.

And "Stakeout" was the Great Divide that none of them had crossed.

For two hundred years the old dream had remained: a progression of Performances that went on for all time . . . each one greater than the last. But even at the very start, *this* they had *known* was beyond them.

The tall one had outlived them all. He had accomplished miracles that they had not imagined. But always he'd stood humbled and confounded by the Law. Its terrible simplicity.

Malcolm smiled.

Simplicity.

The woman went to pieces in the corner, as if struck.

The stake—dropped—clattered, rolled.

He heard the thump of knees on wood, the high squeal of some alien prayer.

Heard the dropped stake rolling back, silk's rustling as she was raised to her feet.

Felt a soft breeze as Adolph and she started sailing across, while the biker just hung there and hung there and watched, looking more bored than alive.

(Watch me, dear boy. Closely now. For you're in the hands of a Master.)

The woman looked into the casket and shrieked. Her hair, which had taken dictation so well—Subject: Senior Power Play—shot out in desperate scribblings. Her face was as pale as the tall one's—but *his* veins seemed to run with milk and all *she* looked was drained.

Bald Adolph enveloped the woman in a lavender murmur as smooth as his dome.

"My dear, there's no need to be frightened. In one way we are just like you. The heart. The thing you must consider is where—"

He gave her no further instructions.

The tall one sent a look so short and filled with bugged malevolence that Adolph scuttled, crablike, back to his spot on the clock.

The woman looked, back and forth, from Malcolm to the stake. The one she had chosen was admirably sharp. But her cow's eyes were faithless and fearful.

If she'd had *ears*, she might have caught the subtle shifting of the beat.

Simplicity.

The heart itself.

Don't break the Law.

Just move it.

He felt it push against the ribs. He emptied his mind of the woman, the stake. He emptied his heart of all thoughts of the Twelve. He emptied the room of mad Ingmar and the riveting absence of Blacke. All that remained was one lavender thought: Simplicity . . . *Simplicity* . . . He took this thought inside his heart. It made him feel so small and light. It refined and simplified. Until the puzzle grew so pure it slipped through the cage of the ribs. To have lived to have done the world's simplest thing!

The woman whooped with all her soul as Adolph started reading . . . from *the* book by Old Blackbeard of Bangor.

" 'Ay-uh! Ay-uh! Ay-uh! *Christine* thought. Blind faith had *carrie-d* her this far. But now *the shining* moon illumined the hideous leech in his crypt. And her thoughts turned to Freddie

" '(the Cheerios® Kid)

" 'who would always Romero the night in his Keds®, half of him craving an Oreo®, the other half crying for blood.

" 'Her breath came out in little puffs. The kind made by smokers who smoke *Salems*® (lots). She raised the stake above her head!' "

And so the woman tried to.

Malcolm steadied her hands with a lavender look. That much he would do for her. He felt something close to compassion itself. He might have diverted the stake from the X her own heart was so set on. But even then, even so, how could she ever reach him? His heart had truly gone out of its way to welcome

and embrace

the point

of absolute

Simplicity.

Old Blackbeard came aroaring out of Adolph's mouth.

" 'Ay-uh! She was scared all right. But she'd parked her Isuzu. And now this was *it*. *The stand* had already been taken, tonight at *four past midnight*. And though she was in *misery* with the thought that this might be *the dead zone*— to never feel Steve's kingly touch on her great *tommyknockers!*— she struck hard and screamed—

                        OOOOOOOOOOOOOOOOOOOOOOOOOP!
             o
            o
          o
        o
       o
      o
     o
    o
   o
  h
w

The cry began low Orson Welles and ended Prince-falsetto. It had come from nowhere and everywhere at once as the stake descended. It raised the tall one half out of his coffin. Dropped the woman like a stone. And stunned the nine, who looked over at Adolph, who stuttered and looked up at Ingmar flywalking the wall to safety.

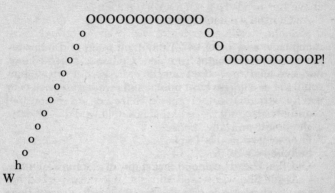

The second cry shattered the windows, thundering off at the end.

The sounds were so alien, wild and weird . . . they filled the room so totally—that none had been able to figure the *source*.

Silence for two seconds. Three.

Stillness, total, in the room.

Four seconds. Five.

The tall one slipped his left leg from the coffin. Held the pose a second.

Six.

Then slipped out the other.

Seven.

Easy now. Simplify.

Two hundred years behind you.

Eight.

Freeze the clock . . . a strobe-lit flash: the woman, heartstopped, at his feet . . . eight pairs of eyes around the rim and none of them believing this or knowing what to do . . . Ingmar, perched above the lift and staring bug-eyed at the wall . . . Follow his eyes to the ten empty hooks and

the half-dead biker hanging there . . . just hanging there
and hanging there, eyes closed . . . and yawning, was he,
what was—

WHOOOOOOOOOOOOOO-
OOOOOOOOOOOOOOOOOOOOOOOOOOOP!

Helltrain roaring through the night miles and miles below them. Floorboards rumbled. Ceiling cracked. Snowflakes, dusted, blew the scene at the speed of moonlight.

It had been longer than most could remember since they
had felt afraid. Together, they'd collected twelve hundred
years of Nights. But the eyes that now followed the tall one's
were almost mortally spooked.

For the sake of the Twelve . . .

For the love of the Night . . .

Malcolm took two proud first steps, sparks bursting from
his eyes.

On the third step courage snapped—if only for a moment
—as:

the biker's eyes snapped open . . .

the steel cuffs snapped behind his back . . .

the straps around his feet exploded in a vicious scissoring
that snapped back hard against the wall.

He landed lightly enough on his feet; screaming, though,
and agoneyesed.

What he'd left on the hook, red and steaming, should
have stopped him with some sense of loss.

Instead, he made that—*sound* again. And it seemed to fill
him as it filled the whole room. And the tall one could see
the pain fading . . . the rumble of the floorboards charging up the man's legs to his shoulders . . . the old cold
coming back to those gray eyes again . . . that *smile* . . .

Malcolm gave him the latest in Masterful looks, but took a
small step backward. The second step was just as small. But
not the third. And not the fourth. And not the ones that
followed

as the biker started *changing*.

Oh.

What *had* dear Austin brought them?

IV

Midway through the changing, he understood the Beauties best.

Perched as he was for this instant, seeing at once from without and within, the logic and *simplicity* rocked him in his soul.

Of course their front quarters were shorter! Of course their claws were useless! Nature, in designing them, had had a one-trap mind. They were made to go in low, to snap at and feed on the first thing in reach. From the slope of their backs to their powerbull necks: all parts interlocked to steel the only weapons Beauties had . . . the only ones they needed:

the heartstopping incisors and canines . . .

bone-crushing third pre-molars . . .

great scimitar curves, the carnassial sheathes, for cutting tough tendons and hides . . .

At first glance, a Beauty's mouth was a jaggle of Cuisinart blades. One wondered how the mouth could *move* without some grievous loss of face. But here, now, *understanding* settled in the teeth. And one knew instinctively which to use for what: wombs, legs, arms, ribs, spines, hair, skulls . . . Hell, one took everything on the menu—and then ate the menu itself.

The pain was the worst when the changing began. The very sounds would make him scream: bones popping . . . spine snapping . . . sinews squealing like parboiling rats . . . teeth exploding everywhere . . .

Seconds in, control and cunning rallied to his side. He found that he could split the pain with flashes of past changes and visions of Beauty to come. But he could not escape just yet the pain of the loss of his self. He would burn to preserve just enough to *be* there.

Midway through, the loss became the glory of the act: Beauty, sprung more free and whole with every part one lost.

To dare to disappear like *this*!

He wanted to *tell* them, but words were beyond him. He

felt the words flurry and melt like the snowflakes that fell now not on but around him:

Look at you—just look at you! The Great Masters. What a joke!

Look at you standing there, ruffling your capes, so pleased with all your grand Techniques . . . your tired blood . . . your dead ideas . . .

Look at you there in your safe little circle, serving up the same old Classics year after year after year. You make me sick. I want to puke, just being in this room with you.

You clubby fools! You boring fucks!

You can't imagine what it's like . . . to go into a seizure from the force of some idea. Something new and bold that *no one's* ever had the balls for. You can't imagine the nerve that it takes. Or the shock that it gives to one's system. To die, like this, for Beauty.

Watch me.

This is *really* wild.

Here I am.

Whoops—there I go!

Chattering around the rim as the change completed. The sounds did not escape him. (At night across an open plain he could hear mosquitoes' wings.) But words, this far into Beauty, were useless information. He took in the tones instead. Gleeful risings in the pitch.

"A wolf?"

"I don't believe—"

"A *wolf*?"

The Beauty started to circle the clock.

"That maniac's sent us a *werewolf*!"

Loose as a goose now, with long loping strides. Throat aching to make just one Beautiful sound.

"No, wait," the tall one said. "It's not a wolf at all. It's— Noooo!"

The Beauty circled, missing nothing. Not distracted in the least by useless information.

"Surely not!"

"My *word*—how droll!"

The Beauty continued its circling lopes, taking it in, taking all of it in:

the contemptuous chatter that followed his moves . . .

the words repeated again and again, like fat cats swatting summer flies . . .

"A hyena!"

"A *hyeeena*!"

Laughter all around the rim.

Everybody so relaxed.

The Beauty stopped. Its ears went flat. Its snout dropped a couple of inches. It almost growled, despite itself. For of all things difficult, silence was hardest of all. On solitary strolls, the sheer joy of existing would fill the night with bumptious whoops. In the frenzy of feeding, its trumpet-screech solos could be heard for miles. Still, the Hunger, as the Beauty knew, was sometimes served by silence best. And though its throat was aching, the Beauty watched and waited.

"This one's *mine*," the tall one said.

The Beauty watched and waited.

Kiss-calls from the tall one.

Cat-calls from around the rim.

The price of stillness was too high, and yet the Beauty did not move.

The tall one waved and widened his stance in an aggressive posture.

Good meat there between those legs.

"Here, boy!"

Kiss-calls.

Giggles.

(Ohhhhhhhhhhhhhh.)

Giggles. Theirs.

Giggles. His.

The difference was that his went on as he sprang, snapping, for the meat.

V

The commotion was worse than the carnage: an awesome cacophony of screams and manic giggles.

The creature snapped and shook its head. And the tall one looked down at the hole in his crotch . . . where a part of himself he'd been fond of had been.

The next scream never cleared his lips.

The creature rolled him over and sank its snout into the seat of his pants, bulldozing up through the anus.

Around the clock the others watched.

There were Rules. There had to be.

And there were reasons for the Rules.

And that was why they did not move. Assuredly, that was the reason!

They heard a dreadful plopping sound as the head giggled out with its goodies. Giggle. Scream. Giggle. Scream. The creature flipped the tall one, ignoring the last futile snappings of fangs, to plunge unerringly down to the heart.

Finished, it sat there licking its chops, finely sugared with feces and innards.

High in the cobwebs, Ingmar thought that one eye had winked. At him. This was, of course, ridiculous.

The creature yawned. Lazily stretched up onto its hind quarters. And then started changing again.

Except—

When the change was completed the biker was gone. And along with the biker the Rules.

"YOU!" cried the nine as one.

And Ingmar, all too visible, fell to the floor with a shriek: "It's Blacke!"

"Hi, boys," Austin drawled. "You sure throw one helluva party."

A GATHERING
OF PASSENGERS

I DODGE

 "Mister Drake will see you now."
(Fat Man . . .
Pivot . . .
Father . . .
Peace . . .)

"Excuse me? Yoo-hoo! Are you there?"

The mantra dissolved in a vision of pink—a translucent bubble that ended with a cheery pop.

Suzy giggled and did what she did best of all: just sat there looking terrific. Twenty years old and a 38-D.

I fingered my lovebeads and walked to her desk. Gave her the latest in By-the-Bay grins. Felt the sway of gold-gray curls and peachfuzz barely on the chin. They didn't seem to cut much ice here in the Big Apple. But, though one time was as good as another to me, I knew something the Big Apple didn't. The Sixties would be coming back in a Nineties sort of way. And it's just good business to be the first in line.

"You know," I said, "I'd give anything to have been that last bubble you blew."

"Don't you wish."

"I'd even trade my old posters from *Hair*."

Suzy laced her fingers behind the streaked, spike hairdo.

"You're kinda cute," she said sadly. "But you're, like, a dinosaur."

"You ever tried it??" I asked.

"What?"

"Brontosaurus sex?"

Suzy stretched, superbly. "Like I said, you're cute but . . ."

"Yeah."

The Yellow Pages on her desk weighed a good five pounds. I snatched them, curled them just for show, and went in to meet The Man.

"Sit down, Mister . . ."

"Dodge," I said, as if he needed reminding. He was holding my card and he'd already dished out half of my retainer. I was here to get the rest . . . expecting, as usual, trouble. For some reason, my clients seldom paid up without a fight. I'd made a kind of game out of it, which helped me avoid thinking about why it happened with such consistency.

I set the Yellow Pages on the visitor's chair—an inch or two short for a tall man to enjoy a good eyeball discussion. At five-eight (with insoles) I don't enjoy many of those on my feet. I sat and squared off for the closing with William Thornton Drake III.

Who was older than I was, by maybe two months, and had done lots with the headstart. The desk and chair were solid oak. And *there* was a hairdo no hands were allowed in. This was a Powerful Man.

I said, "So, Bill, what's shakin'?"

"Well, *Dodge,*" he answered, "the bottom line is this. I've read your—*report.* I should sue you for fraud. What are you smiling about?"

"Aren't you gonna mouse the card?"

He arched one eyebrow, glowering.

"Everybody always does." I clasped the lovebeads to my throat, made those swooney eyes. "That's the part I really like. You just pick the card up like a mouse by the tail and set it down way over there by the phone. That registers *extreme distaste.*"

Drake gave the card a flick that sent it flying at my nose. I caught it without blinking, in a smooth nimble blur of one hand. The move surprised him. I had a few more.

I pointed to the folder at the end of the soccer-field desk. "Now, let's play the Hrumph Game!"

"And what might that be?" Drake said. Droll. Getting back into the spirit.

"You know, with the—*report.*"

His arms were longer than I'd imagined. He reached one hand clear to the end zone and slid the file back to the net.

"Oh, yeah," he said. "I know. This is where I open it. And start flipping through—like this?"

"That's it!"

"How are my eyes? Should I open them wider?"

"No, no, the wide is cool. A bit more, though, on the glower—yeah!"

"So," *glower,* "I just flip. And when I come to something—"

"That really flips you out!"

"All I do is hrumph?"

I nodded, lovebeads clicking. "Yeah! That's just the way they do it, Bill! Then they read it back to me and that's the part I like the best!"

"You like to hear what you've written?"

"I do! Come on, let's play the Hrumph Game!"

Drake flipped a couple of pages ahead.

" 'December 28th,' " he read. " 'Followed subject to East 67th, where he then slipped into Myrtle's and took a seat at the counter. Quick exchange ¹etween himself and the night girl Eleanor: "The usual, Frank?" "You got it, El—and tell them to *deep*-fry the fries!"

" 'Subject lit into a cup of black coffee from a weeks-old pot. He looked around, on the sly, and slipped a pack of Winstons from his attaché. Chain-smoked three before dinner arrived: a burger so raw and so greasy the fries were swimming on the plate.

" 'Subject proceeded to TGIF, where he ordered a cold jug and chaser.

" 'Trailed subject to the men's room. Waited discreetly outside a few secs, then took a breath of smoke-filled air—and moved in for the kill.

" 'Now, as a San Franciscan, I have—necessarily—a very open mind. As, I hope, a gentleman, I know some things are sacred. Still—' "

For a second I thought that he might not go on. Sometimes they make me do that, ask them to continue.

Drake played the game like a trooper, though, and polished off the paragraph.

" '—an army fed on beans for months couldn't have rivaled the sounds or the stench. From the end stall, the cordovan wing tips beat out a tortured tattoo, punctuating anguished farts and nauseous jets of foul decay.' "

Drake slammed the file on the desk. Ground his teeth so hard I thought he'd spit out a mouthful of ivory dust.

"Here it comes! The Why-You Game!"

"Why, youuuu," he bellowed.

"Yes! Oh yes! You've got it, Bill!"

Well, granted, the game has a charm all its own. And it should never be rushed. But my train was leaving in twenty-four hours and I didn't have all day.

"YOUUUUU—" he started, all over again. Power hands gripping the edge of the desk so hard I thought the oak would crack.

I'd played the game so often now—lately, only one in ten just paid—that, honestly, few things surprised me. But William Thornton Drake surprised me with what he did next.

He started laughing like crazy. No lowdown Power chuckle, this, or mellow one-lung ho-de-ho. The man *exploded* on the spot. And I began to wonder for the first time if The Trip—

"WHY, YOUUUUUU—!!!"

Drake began *screaming* with laughter. The oak chair rattled and rocked on the tile beneath the inch-thick carpeting. The screams turned into screeches then. And, offhand, I couldn't recall ever seeing a face that shade of crimson.

"YOUUUUUU . . . REALLY ARE A HOOT!"

Say what?

The seizure stopped abruptly. Not exactly on a dime, but within a couple of seconds Drake was able to dab at the tears in his eyes.

"Dodge," he managed finally. Intimate now, right down

to the shorts. "You're gonna have to excuse me. But Jesus, I couldn't resist! Jack Gallagher phones me from Frisco, you see. He says, this guy's terrific, Bill—but listen, he says, trust me. You *gotta* play the mouse game. So here's what you do . . ."

When I spoke, the O'Tooleian tenor sounded stiff and squeaky.

"You don't mean . . . Uh . . . Naw . . ."

"Hell, Gallagher heard it from Thomas, who told him he'd heard it from—"

"Right! Okay!"

Drake produced an envelope from his inside pocket. It looked thicker than the first. "Here, no hard feelings, eh?"

I took it, half-expecting some mad joke-buzzer he'd palmed to go off.

"Don't worry, it's all there," he said.

A casual dignified flip-through showed about five hundred extra.

I fingered my lovebeads and gave him a look.

"A bonus for a job well done."

You can't imagine my surprise. The first half of my retainer was usually paid with a tolerant smirk; the second, more often than not, with a snarl. See, what I was doing *was* rather New Wave. I trailed key executives whose work had not been up to snuff. I recorded their actual diets . . . then offered counter-diets based on Intestinal Light: proper Food Combining—no more starch with protein—with scattered snacks of nuts and fruit. The results, I promised, were stunning and would spread throughout the firm: upgraded performances, reduced absenteeism, lowered insurance premiums . . . In fact, I guaranteed this, if they tried it for a month.

I'd never been asked for a refund.

But no one had offered me extra.

I wondered why.

Drake told me. "Look, I don't give a good goddamn if he eats burgers à la mode and goes home to a bottle of Screech. But the son of a bitch has been after a raise, along with a full partnership. I can't sack him for that. I can sack him for this."

"Jesus Christ," I whispered. "How?"

"You mean you didn't know? Hell, Gallagher got rid of Harlan that way. That's how Thomas showed Weinroth the door. Insurance liabilities. And it holds up in court."

My emotions were, shall we say, mildly mixed. On the one hand, I felt I'd been had good and proper. On the other hand, business was business, and business would pay for The Trip. I felt I'd betrayed the Life College. Then again, my Ph. D. had arrived by mail. The money was dirty. But, oh, it was crisp.

My feet could not move fast enough. My fingers fumbled with the knob.

But always leave 'em laughing, eh? I winked at Drake and roared:

"WHYYYYYY, YOUUUUUUU!!!!!"

Then I lickety-split, leaving Drake on the floor, an emptied shell of a Powerful Man.

I shut the door behind me. Suzy looked over her shoulder, something resembling a twinkle in her much masacara'd eyes.

On the couch where I'd been sitting, the to-be-sacked Frank Casey was darkly engaged in a game with his thumbs.

He was one of those young happy warriors who should be wearing helmets with their brawny custom suits. He wasn't accustomed to losing the ball. Or feeling the thing just deflate in his paw like the bubble that popped as the intercom buzzed.

"Mister Drake will see you now," Suzy purred to Casey.

He lumbered up. Great pops of knees. He was bigger, much bigger, up close than he'd seemed. He crossed the room in a couple of strides, rolling his neck and his shoulders. I stepped aside, discreetly, wondering if he'd made me. He passed, though, threw his shoulders back, and went in to meet The Man.

Suzy swiveled in her seat. "Don't worry. He's a pussycat. Besides," she said, *"I'll* never tell. That is, on one condition. Mr. San. Fran. Cis. Co. Dickkk."

I said, "I'll bout a-think it."

Suzy blew a bubble. She popped it gently with a nail, then slid the finger in to catch the collapsing membrane. She swirled her finger a couple of times, like coning cotton candy. Then stuck the finger in her mouth and sucked it clean to the bone.

Suzy slipped me a card with an address she'd typed. The number looked vaguely familiar. But then, I was in the Numerical City, where streets that have names are whole miles apart.

"Sixish?" Suzy asked me.

"Well . . ."

"I'll try real hard to squeeze *you* in."

ii

By the Bay we're accustomed to having three or four seasons a day. And San Franciscans have become the world's top quick-change artists: the off-again, on-again jacket . . . the light sweater cached in the briefcase or purse . . .

But it had been years since I'd been in New York. And though the weather had been mild, I knew now it hadn't been sunny at heart. A big storm was coming fast and it would be a dark one.

I could have gone back into Myrtle's, which was getting more packed by the minute. I had gone back in several times. Each time, though, I'd go on to wonder if Suzy had meant this address—which *had* sounded oddly familiar—or if she'd got the digits wrong and meant Veggie Heaven. That made sense. Why Myrtle's? And so I'd go across to look. And then cross back to wait some more.

I stood there for over an hour. Hell, I might have stood there till morning defeating the whisper that said, "You've been had." But . . .

Have you ever *been* to Myrtle's, friend? Have *you* ever tried to resist, primly reminding yourself that, near forty, your salad days must be ahead? The other night, with

Casey, I'd been working and watching. Tonight I was only waiting.

Think what you like, I was hungry and weak. And I scrambled, half-crazed, into Myrtle's. For the glory that is grease.

iii

I had a good seat by the window. And I should have seen the Chevy. I'd spent five years with Pinkertons in my Canadian Years. My degree, 'tis true, had come through the mail, but my P.I. license hadn't. So I am not entirely without the basic skills. The real storm, though, had just arrived and I missed it while watching the weather.

Lightning streaked across the sky, a jagged edge that suited me fine. It had taken Eleanor two trips to clear the table, clucking away at my stuffing. And now I was sitting there, picking my teeth, feeling heavy, contented, and plain out to lunch.

Outside the window the crowd was as thick as the snowflakes that fell through the cold-shattered sky on the formal black topcoats and furs. New Year's Eve. Money in this part of town. Money, too, in Myrtle's. High rollers who were slumming it before champagne and sushi. And me at the window, eyes fixed on that joke: the old self pretending to be thirty-nine . . . and, through some dirty trick of light or curvature of glass, looking more like forty . . .

Cluck. Cluck.

Click. Swish.

Eleanor, in the glass, depositing my sugar pie and carbolic refill.

Something in the Chevy there that seemed to ring a bell. Lightning streaked the sky again. And in the flash a purple streak that vaguely rang another bell.

Sugar blues, I thought.

More pie—

The blues erupted in a flash. In the sky. Across the street.

Suzy waving happily from the long black Chevy. As thunder boomed in Myrtle's. A woman shrieked. Slow bodies crashed, into tables, on the floor. And Hurricane Casey came storming across, with murder in his eyes.

"You FUCK!"

Casey, who had had a few, stopped about six feet away. Paws bunching into fists; unbunching, then, to bunch again. His head looked ready to explode. I took another bite of pie, feeling empty and sick in my soul. It had been about ten years since I'd started Therapy, five nights a week, in the dojo. And suddenly I realized how desperately I needed it, after a few nights away. The sugar high filled up my head with sweet thoughts of the bad bloody end this would be.

"Outside!" Casey screamed.

(Fat Man . . . Pivot . . . Father . . .)

"Please?" I pointed to the seat across, not expecting him to take it. Still . . . "Would you like a piece of—"

"Out. SIDE!!!"

Well, there was just no way, I knew, to get out of this one. It was me and the Fat Man all over again, with Hurricane Casey between us. Ten years of Therapy . . . and the Fat Man was here in the blink of an eye.

I slid out and stood up and heard someone groan. My guess was the snowfall had flattened my insoles and lowered my curls by a good half an inch. While *he* must have padded his shoulders to boot.

Casey came up to me, slow as you please, the big storm rumbling with thoughts of release. He gathered two fistfuls of denim and lovebeads, hoisting me up to my toes.

I couldn't breathe. I couldn't speak. Not even to tell him how wrong this would go. I felt a sharp turning and shook like a doll as he carried me off and stormed out through the door.

"Hang on, honey!" someone called. It sounded a little like Eleanor, but my hearing was not what it had been. And I couldn't think to see.

On the walk people scrambled to safety. Little figures floating with the snowflakes in a ball. Like the one the Fat Man threw that Christmas after throwing Ghost Boy.

Brakes squealing. Tires skidding. A bumpthumpcrash and tinkle as one car stopped a few to watch.

"You . . . smelled . . . my . . . SHIT!"

My guess was that was Casey's voice. But I couldn't see him. I'd never seen a New Year's Eve, never seen a city street, disappear so quickly. It was Christmas, it was Buffalo, and the Fat Man had Ghost Boy three feet off the ground in one of his amazing hands. And he poked with one stout finger, screaming—

"My . . . SHIT . . . you . . . FUCK!"

Hey, it beats divorce work.

I whispered that, a part of it, but the sound that came out was just strangled as he shook me and poked at my heart with each word.

The throw was so close to the Fat Man's that it took my breath away.

I landed—at a rakish angle—on a yellow cab's right door. And fell in a splatter of blood to the street. My guess was that I'd cracked my skull. Or smashed my nose. Or split my lip. There wasn't much difference between them just then. I slumped back against the door. Only the Fat Man could throw me like that.

In the heavy snowfall blurred images of standers-by floated at me.

Whispering: Don't move . . . Stay there . . . Down, pal, down . . .

Frank screaming over the whispers, "I'll tear your fucking heart out, you ugly Frisco fag!"

Oh-oh, now you've done it, Frank. You're the Fat Man now, for sure.

Two shadows helped me to my feet and started to whisk me away. I thought, hey, the other way, prying myself from their fingers.

Suddenly the night felt warm, thick logs crackling on the fire. Gold and green boxes with bows by the tree. I slipped out of the fleece-collared duster. I felt smaller without it and that was the point. I advanced, I advanced to the Fat Man.

"I'm gonna kill you SLOW!" he screamed.

He came at me about forty miles an hour. And if I'd still been standing there, the punch would have taken my head off. I was standing, instead, to the right, a foot back, on the inside of the swing.

The Fat Man blurred into a corkscrew. I think he might have cleared the cab and flown halfway to Brooklyn. Or I could have landed him the way we do in Therapy: grabbing his sleeve, with one hand on his jaw, circling him down to the ground. I whirled, instead, with a two-handed sweep.

The Fat Man hit the cab head-on and dropped in a puddle of lost teeth and blood.

No one knew just what had happened. But my guess is they saw something new in my eyes.

I saw the fire crackling from the edges of my vision. I saw the broken boxes lying crushed beneath the tree. I saw Ghost Boy lying on top of it all, bleeding from his ears and eyes and whooping for breath, his right leg twisted wrong. And I wanted to cry because I was so glad that I'd eaten at Myrtle's and felt so damned mean.

The Fat Man stumbled to his feet. He looked a little wobbly but good, with luck, for one more round. Suzy seemed to think so too. She shook him and kept yelling "Kill him!"

The Fat Man coughed and recolored her hair and Suzy passed out with a shriek. I thought I saw his eyes turn red just before he came at me again.

The kick was a roundhouse, too slow and too high. I could have stopped it in my sleep.

But the Fat Man was all I could think of.

I trapped the ankle with one palm and slipped in for his neck with the other. I pivoted, slamming his face on his knee. Then I whirled him round and round. The circle stopped abruptly with his face on the walk in a thicket of teeth.

I swung myself behind his leg and yanked it till there was no slack.

I heard the whispers around me.

But what did they know of the Fat Man?

What did they know of the fists in your head that grew stronger and younger the older he got . . . and hit even harder the faster you dodged?

What did they care? He was down. He was out. He com-

manded their unthinking pity. He erased my history with
his human sorry eyes. I was him now. He was me.

His treachery enraged me.

He'd taken them in, taken all of them in. All of them
there in their furs and their finest, fresh from their East Side
executive suites.

I gave the foot a little twist and heard the Fat Man
scream. Crackles of bones through his wool argyle socks.

Siren in the distance.

Oh.

No.

No, you don't.

You don't get off this time.

All those years in Canada . . .

Who's got who now? How's it feel?

"NOT THIS TIME!!!" I screamed.

I slammed my boot hard in the small of his back, and
threw my whole body hard at his leg.

The ankle went first. And the snap was a stunner.

Then the hip, with an awful report, like a .44 shot in a
tunnel.

Siren getting closer now.

Vaguely, I came to my senses.

There was no joy in Mudville as I started to slink off . . .
then thought of the Trip . . . and hightailed it away at a
scurrilous clip, boos and catcalls on my heels like tincans
dragging in the night.

II BETSY

When the last cupboard was emptied . . . when not
even the ghost of a Twinkie remained . . . when her Mas-
terCard and *VISA* card had been trashed with her cash
cards and checkbook . . .

Betsy Atkinson slumped at the table. And considered the
enormity of what she was going to do.

Till an hour ago she'd envisioned the gunmetal table covered with linens . . . the silver candelabra filled with tapering ivory candles . . .

a great burger smothered with onions and relish . . .

powerhouse servings of sweet buttered yams . . .

Häagen-Dazs, oh, Häagen-Dazs!

What better way to leave a hell than stuffed with all one's sins?

Then again, one good-bye was cleaner and faster and truer.

Forget the linen tablecloth.

No cover-ups, not this time, girl. Start with the table. Accept it as is: a hobbled ugly piece of junk you bought for thirty dollars. The last money you stole before getting the sack from the helljob that drove you to drink.

Forget the candelabra too.

Start with the fact of the light as it is. That's a two-dollar shade on a sixty-watt bulb. Bright idea. But not enough. The ceiling's still cracked. The walls, peeled to shit. The tile, bubbling and curling away. And the mirror, though warping, refuses to honor your image of a slimmer you. Forget the candles. This is it.

Forget the feast.

There is nothing to mourn.

This room, this life, is garbage. Your life was never poetry. Hell, now it's not even prose. Just a fat, greasy catalog of heartaches and failures and woes.

She upended her purse, still on red alert for some small thing she might have missed: a stick of gum . . . a breath mint . . . a cigarette . . . a crumpled bill . . . a shoplifted mini of gin . . .

But the slim pickings that she'd spilled described a stark circle of hope.

A slender book on fasting.

Purse-sized weight-loss diary.

Two Binacas.

Forty Ex-Lax.

A cracked and faded photograph of herself at twenty.

And the gray Amtrak folder.

Twenty pounds! You're going down! That was the resolution.

Not poetry—no, not for her. That was for the others. That was something others had and others understood.

(Betsy Atkinson!

—Yes, Miss Wilcox?

Did you even read the poem? This is possibly the dumbest report that I've ever seen.

—Oh, no . . .

The "masters" in the poem, child, are painters, not gods. It's right there!

—But I thought . . .

Well, if we're to get you through high school, do another report on a novel. You've no gift for poetry.)

Sixteen years ago and the words still broke her heart. But, all right, then. No poetry. Say, a thin minor romance?

Just ride the rails and don't let go, from here to San Francisco . . . then on to Seattle . . . and all the way back . . . and down to New Orleans! New life!

Twelve days without a cigarette . . . or even the sniff of a cork . . . or a grape!

Suddenly, she shivered, struck by a draft from the window and a chilling neon flash.

Oh God, it was New Year's Eve and Jake's was the merriest bar in the world. Party hats and streamers. *Food.* Ham and turkey, prime roast beef, pickles, shrimp, crabmeat, jellies, prunes, pies to die for: apple, pumpkin, custard, oh!

Mercifully, the sickness came, gorge erupting in revolt. Her bladder and her sphincter blew before she had half-left the table. And she tumbled, shaken and humbled by the stink. Sick in her soul from knowing that the worst was yet to come.

Well, no one said changing was easy.

Happy New Year, everyone.

III ROD

                                  "Aow!"

Aow!"

                           "Chew chew!"

"Aowwwwwwwwwww!"

How many of them were there now? In and out of the doorways they drifted, hooting from the walk below. But where had they come from and how had they heard?

And why, why, couldn't they see that it hadn't been like that at all?

Rod's entrance had been a disaster, of course. But who wouldn't have been paralyzed to suddenly *be there* as Hamlet? Who couldn't understand, in part, how the words could get confused . . . how the Rod Whittaker Voice, a baritone as rich as Bob Goulet's, might squeak:

" 'Uh liddle moah dan kin an' lez dan kah-eeend.' "

He *had* survived that slip, though. The performance *had* gone on. Not brilliantly, all right. But *on.* And *no one* had heard *chew chew*—

"BECAUSE IT WASN'T THERE!"

One tiny slip. One, just one, in south-south-east TriBeCa, off-off-off-Broadway, in New York.

He'd sat by his studio window till dawn, chainsmoking, working it out in his mind:

South-south-east TriBeCa wasn't, properly speaking, New York . . . What were a hundred people in a city of eight million?

He'd drifted then back to his favorite dream: Rod Whittaker . . . Lord Whittaker . . . Hamlet, Lear, Othello! And—

Chew chew! Get your chew chew here!

The first cry had come out of nowhere, from some remote edge of the dream. Lord Whittaker was bowing to thunderous applause, the Old Vic's velvet curtains lined with golden echoes of his voice. When—

Chew chew! Get your chew chew here!

Well now, there it was again, the words nearly lost in the traffic below.

But was there traffic in the Vic?
Chew chew in the morning Sun!
Tires humming . . .
Window . . .
Street . . .
Oh God, it IS New York!
C'mon, folks, get your chew chew here! World's Worst Hamlet Hits New York!
He scrambled to the window . . . to see the newsman whooping.
And at that moment, in that voice—before he took the steps two at a time—he knew that he was ruined.

> Tubby oarrrrrr NODDDDD! Tubby?
> by Crispin Blake III

> *Fasten your seatbelts, O lovers of Shakespeare, and do bring along extra earplugs. A new Hamlet's just hit town—and his performance will move you to tears.*
>
> *You've met Hamlet the Dane. Hamlet the brooder. Hamlet the Mama's Boy/Man of the Sword. Hamlet as Wimpy and Dr. Kildare. Now, if you will or dare, try a schizoid linguist, just come from Oxford by way of the Bronx to avenge the death of his fodder by moidering the Bard's great prose. You know diz guy means biznez the minute he opens his mouth.*
>
> *And you know he'll stop at nothing, not even our own sanity, when he soliloquizes:*
>
> *"Tubby oarrrrrr NODDDDD! Tubby? Dad diz duh quezhchun . . .*
>
> *"Aow! 'diz chew chew salllldddddd flezzzzzh . . ."*

Oh dear God, his life was done.
Rod catwalked now, with his back to the wall. In the corner, on the desk, his ticket to salvation lay in an Amtrak folder: Stan Kowalski! In *Streetcar!* In Oakland . . .
The drunks giggled and whooped on the walk.
But suddenly Rod understood: he could fall no further.

He marched to the window and cried to the day:
"You win for now. But I'll be back. And I'll give you a
Hamlet to die for!"

IV WOLF AND SAM

Wolf pounded the bag, working up a good sweat. The old
gray hair, not quite what she used to be, lashing away at his
glistening pate. Belly bouncing as he danced. Beard dripping from the effort. Getting in shape for the Big One.

That's the ticket. Focus now. Eliminate the walls of books.
There are no books but this one. Eliminate the metal desk,
the gooseneck lamp, the Remington. This one's written on
the rails, the comeback trail in action. Eliminate the index
cards. You've got them all inside you.

Perihelion: the exact time when the comet is closest to
the sun.

Distance from the spaceship Earth: sixty million kilometers.

Speed: 100,000 miles per hour.

Orbit: Does a lazy low-speed turn along the outer region
of earth's solar system in about thirty-seven years, then
gradually accelerates.

Visitations: first in 240 B.C. . . . thirtieth in '85-'86.

Present visibility: Early January with binocs after sunset.
Third week January, visible to naked eye low on the western horizon past sunset. End Feb., before dawn.

Historical: A.D. 66—the Great Fire of Rome . . . 1222—
Genghis Khan slaughters thousands in honor of Halley's
. . . 1607—*Volpone, Macbeth, King Lear* . . . 1759—
Bobbie Burns is born . . . 1910—deaths of Tolstoy, Twain,
and King Eddie . . .

January 1, 1986: midpoint of the Eighties. Midway between Aquarius and the next millennium. The rebirth of
Wolf Cotter, the finest stylist of his time. Sacked, months
ago, by the *Stone.*

(Come on, Wolf. The other Wolfe was doing this shit in the Sixties. It's getting old. Even Tom changes suits.)

(Old hat, am I? Well, we'll just see about that.)

"Oh, perihelion!" Wolf cried.

Never live with a writer, oh never, don't do it, not if you're young and alive and a fox. Rock stars are perverts and actors are vain and jocks wear their brains with their balls in their straps and the less said about cops the better. But even the weakest among them are *men*.

Live with a writer and what do you get? A neurotic paper lion licking its wounds in its lair . . . or *describing* its roar on those legal-sized pads, on sheet after sheet it erases or scraps.

And if you *must* live with a writer, then do yourself a favor. Live with a writer who's very well-hung . . . or one who can just take the money and run.

But, whatever, never, ever, don't even *think* about living with one who is *planning* to write his first book.

Sam, who had real expertise, sat in abject misery, staring at their bags.

A month!

Thirty days on the road, going nowhere at all . . . on the trail of some idiot *comet*.

To hear Wolf tell it—and Lord knows he had—the gods had preordained his getting sacked by *Rolling Stone*. If he hadn't been ruined, he might have missed his Chance in *Rush*'s offer. But he had been; he did not. When they called, suggesting a small piece on Halley's—in Wolf's incomparable style—he stormed through the blizzard, half naked, to scream:

A one-time-only *Special* on a once-in-seventy-five-years *Event?* Three-thousand words on an omen of the world that was to be—an omen containing all worlds that had been? Oh, no! No way! Not unless *Rush* magazine was so petty and so blind . . .

By the time he finished, they begged him for the chance. To send him across country with his Asian paramour . . . explaining the Significance (astrologically, religiously, historically, culturally) . . . noting the mood of the land . . .

and telling it all, in six monthly reports, in Pulitzer prize-winning style. *His* style.

For subsequent expansion into a Nobel-winning book.

A Movie of the Week.

A tale of the Sixties, when he came of age.

A tale of the Eighties, when he would bloom again.

A tale of all times, in between and before.

A tale for the ages to follow.

The story of a comet.

The story of . . . Mankind!

Well, no matter how he puffed it, it still added up to just piddle. Tickets for two on a journey to nowhere, stuck in a cabin the size of their john. Eating the same damned thing over and over for thousands and thousands of miles. West! North! East! South! And on and on and on.

New Year's Eve. But no, not for them. Clubs in better parts of town where Sam's dramatic entrances would turn every head at the bar. Parties in the two neighboring flats blasting into midnight.

Oh.

Wolf would go on for hours, in his boring, embarrassing lair.

Sickened, she stared at their luggage . . . and wished that she could tell him now.

She'd had it to here with his socks on the floor, his scatter-brained dreams and impractical plans. In her life, she'd never met a man with less guile or cunning. Half blustery bear and half blubbery baby.

Well, it wasn't his star that was rising, but hers. For in a month, when they returned, they'd see her picture every-where! Sam on the cover of *Esquire*! Her lithe body slung in a mindblowing split. Ponytail blurred like the crack of a whip. Tawny skin so glossed with sweat that even the arter-ies rippled.

She looked furtively over her shoulder. Slipped the photo out (Still there!) and reread the magic words. By a writer who *knew* how to Write!

Shake it out! (I'm all shook up!)
Miz Hard (Oh, yes!) Bod(Lawd God!)yyyyy!

Button up your seatbelts, bucks: the goddess has arrived!

The dominatrix of desire!

The princess of perfection!

The mistress of muscle!

The lash of the whip!

Samantha Chung (that's Sam to you) is the ferociously feline instructor of the Advanced Aerobics Class at the Midtown Gym. And the relentlessly cheery dispenser of all the physical horror required to give you a body to die for.

Sam is the crest of the wave of desire that seems destined to crash through the Eighties: to be leaner and cleaner and meaner . . .

Yes, yes, good for you! That's the spirit! That's the stuff! "Oh, PER-I-HE-LI-ONNNNNNNNNNNNNNNNNN!" Wolf roared.

And Sam, head in hands, prayed for deliverance.

V SUNDANCE

Newford?

Redman?

You silly old man.

Harry White had been at the Dakota so long he knew all the tenants by name if not face. (All of them except this *one.*) And the names of the ghosts of the tenants before. Even now with the way things had gone in his mind.

It had become a desperate game for New York's oldest doorman: the recollection of their names.

The years had escaped him, along with the rooms. And lately he'd found himself getting confused between the past and present names, questioning whether the faces he saw were on the outside, here and now, or in that mystic inner maze.

But where there were names, there were limits. And, in limits, maybe hope.

"Mornin', Harry!"

A brisk clatter of heels crossed the buffed marble tiles. Pretty blond girl swathed in furs, gone with a wave and a flash of her pearls.

"Happy . . ." he started. But off she went. Her face was gone. Dissolved in the rush of the swift mystic stream of time and lost particulars.

(All's . . . All's high . . . Cats can . . . Sooo old . . .)

That was Mrs. . . . Mrs. . . . Miss . . .

Levin?

Kingsley?

Ono?

Ohhhhhhhhh . . .

You're on an express elevator, going down, going down, with less and less time between stops. And more and more floors that you'll miss on the way to that last stop between landings.

Ding!

The elevator sounded, red arrow switching to green. And just before the doors opened, the express Harry White was on came to a shuddering stop.

It was *him.* Unfailingly, Harry could tell when *he* came. The traffic jam of memories, lined up for miles in his mind, disappeared; and there was no danger, not ever, with *him,* of sticking forever between the lost floors.

"Happy New Year, Harry!"

Sundance, like some movie star, gliding on the tiles. Walls dissolving and high ceiling gone in a sudden uplifting of energy, light. Only the two of them, high in the sky. Sundance in his long black coat. Sundance with his blond mustache setting off those rows of teeth. Sundance with that crazy tan, sailing closer and closer, and—

(All's! . . . all's high! . . .)

"Alzheimer's, Harry. Remember?"

He did. With Sundance he always remembered. He smiled.

"Alzheimer's. I had a cat's—"

"Cat—"

"Scan. A cold table. There were lights."

Sundance beaming as he set his black leather bag on the floor.

Don't go . . . The names . . . I need you. . . .

"You remember, don't you, Harry?"

"Africa . . ." the old man said. "You're gonna go to—"

"Harry. Think."

Sundance touching fingertips to the blue of Harry's temple. Clarity. Such *clarity!* Color slides of Sundance—brilliant!—moving through the dark African night. Closer and closer to—

something he sought . . .

"You came *back* from Africa," the old man said. "Last—summer."

"See? It isn't so hard to remember."

Not, indeed, so hard at all. As if *he* were feeding the memories in. Talking in that Sundance voice of lightly sanded velvet.

"Hey, Harry, what do doctors know? Your memory is fine, just fine. Easy does it. Here we go . . ."

Fingertips on both sides now. Firmness there. A touch of light. Flick of a projector switch. White light, full of promise, hope . . . sparking the smooth irresistible turnings of the reels within, one's life.

1956. New Year's Eve. There had been a terrible snowstorm. And all of the power was off. The Dakota lobby had been lit with candles, and tenants, home from parties, were carried in candlelit settees back up the stairs to their candlelit rooms.

1905. Eleven years old. Racing with Edna—in time, Mrs. White—their long scarves streaming in the wind.

1984. *What's wrong?* Something was starting to go really wrong. Dates dissolving. Faces too. Concentration shot to shit. He still knew the apartment he lived in, but could never remember the number. Or which was the key to the door. Or what he'd been talking about all night long with the new tenant, Sundance. Or whose room they'd been in.

1914. Grand Central. Edna still wearing her honeymoon dress: a white taffeta gown that just reached to her ankles and would flash in his mind in the trenches—when the whole world was going . . . to . . . pieces . . .

1917. Coming to from the strangest and most painful dream, of Edna mending his pieces like socks, to see her, through a maze of tubes, clasping his hand to her cheek . . . reaching out to touch her face . . . and reaching out and reaching still and screaming, "Oh, Jesus where's my arm!"

1939. March 1. A married man, a married man, had there ever been words that could match these? You remembered the quarrels, the out-and-out fights, the perennial dissatisfactions. You remembered the day-to-day hurts to your pride, your failure to *provide* for her. You remembered the sad, patient look in her eyes as she told you, once again: The arm you have is what you've got. The arm you don't, you don't have. What we don't have doesn't bother me. What we have is all we need and all I've ever asked for.

1985. Sometime in the fall or summer. Maybe winter. Or the spring? Edna gone these many years. Fifteen? Twenty? Hard to say. And Dr. Shell (Skell? Snell?) repeating, solemnly: *Cats can . . . Sorry, Harry, but All's high . . .* Sundance, so tanned in the year since he'd come, murmured I'll take Harry home. His finest friend in all the world—but what, for God's sake, was his *name*?

Sundance snapped his fingers on both sides of White's temples. Looking younger and tanner, somehow, than before.

"You see?" he told Harry. "You're gonna be fine."

"San Francisco," Harry croaked.

"You remember why?"

Oh dear.

"Come on, old timer, you know."

"Blood." The old man giggled. "New." Sundance was just such a beautiful boy. Full of the devil. And hell-bent on fun. The women he brought home, at all hours of night! And when they left—those hickeys!

"Harr-yyyyy."

Oh-oh. Boo-boo. A vague recollection of one time before when Sundance spoke his name like that. When Harry, caught up in the memory game, had started to remember something Sundance didn't like.

The doorman slouched, instinctively. Sweating liver polka dots through trembling palm on shiny black. Remember the right things; forget all the rest.

"You mustn't excite yourself, Harry."

"That's right."

"*New blood.* At your age. I'm shocked."

Grab that knee cap. Shake that dome. Look up very slowly, you don't have to talk—

"I know, old timer," Sundance said. "But I can't help you, Harry . . . if you don't help me. *New blood.*"

"*R* . . . ," Harry whispered. "Gonna go for . . . *R* and *R.*"

"Of course I am, no harm in that. New York's too hot—er, cold for me now."

Sundance scooped up his bag without seeming to stoop. A checkered cab pulled up on cue.

"Gotta fly now. You be good."

Gotta *fly*? Sundance fly? Harry struggled with the thought, knowing that somehow it wasn't quite right.

"Just an expression. I'm taking the train."

Harry giggled. "Planes' air . . . too rich for *your* blood!"

"*Ciao.*"

"Bye . . . Sundance."

"Harr-yyyyy. How many times?"

"Mr. . . . Mr. . . . . Austin . . ."

"*Blacke.*"

Sundance winked merrily and glided off.

VI LENNY DIRKS

"Mister? Mister? You okay?"

Stewardess knocking and trying the latch.

He stood before the basin, regarding the face that looked back from the mirror. He tried to see it as *They* would if

They were there and waiting when he stepped off the plane in Chicago. Too close to D.C., still too close to D.C. He was risking it all for a train trip. He should never have left San Francisco.

They'd be looking for Jesus before He got crossed: a righteous boy of twenty-four with brown hair that fell to his shoulders and hosted a trinity facial—strip of fur across the lip, wispy hedge along the jaw, brown fuzzy ball at the ridge of the chin.

Three more knocks. These austere. The voice very much in control. "This is Captain Davis. I'll have to ask you to open the door. Or we'll have to open it for you."

"Just a minute," he managed.

"One minute. That's all."

"In two minutes it will be New Year's." Her voice. "You don't want to miss your champagne, now!"

They'd be looking for Jesus. He still had the hair. But he was a ghost, gone gray from the top down, with weak haunted eyes that crowed, at the corners, of long sleepless nights.

"Thirty seconds," the stewardess chimed. "Time for bubbly bubbly!"

How could *They* see him when he wasn't there? When even the ghost was beginning to fade. His ruined gaunt reflection turned to smoke before his eyes.

"Twenty . . ."

He took out his passport. His thin fingers clicked. He opened the cover and cried in alarm. Before his eyes, the portrait of a Man without a Country.

"Fifteen . . ."

He was losing it. All connections *had* been clipped, despite his hair's salvation. He'd started disappearing the day that he came home. January 17, 1982.

"Ten . . ."

Goddamn you, Raphael Cunningham! Goddamn you! Oh, Goddamn your soul!

"Five . . ."

Fuck my passport!

Fuck the Trip!

"Coming in, sir."

The key turned. The door swung him into a shocked quarter-spin that shot the ghost out in a stream through his mouth.

The captain reeled back, gasping, the vomit a foul dripping mask.

The girl teetered, her own stomach starting to heave. Her eyes grew almost huge with hurt, that New Year's Eve should come to this.

"Oh, Mr. *Dirks!*" she wailed. Then she tossed her cookies all over the captain's fine beard.

VII BRAKOWSKI

Penn Station, always crazy, was bedlam New Year's Day. Guy Brakowski glowered and chewed on his pipe, while the crowds instinctively broke before his bulk.

Damn well better too, he thought.

What did they know of the insult of trailing some stud across country—by *train*? On a case that was already *closed*!

(Listen, Daddy Warbucks. You wanna keep burning your money, all right. But your little girl is gone. She had a nasty secret. It killed her in the end. Forget the lovebites on her neck. I've been on the guy's tail a whole month now. He's clean.)

But Pops was sure his horny bitch was Sweet Sixteen, at twenty-eight, done in by a wolf whom she'd known for a month.

(You dumb poor rich bastard. No one gets terminal AIDS in a month. And nobody dies from a hickey!)

But no-o-o.

Just then the overheads compounded Guy Brakowski's woes:

"Attention, all passengers for the Amtrak *Cardinal* from New York to Chicago. Due to emergency trackwork—"

"Oh, shit."

"—accommodations in a special Amtrak, *Capitol*, which you'll connect with in Washington D.C.—"

"Fuck me."

"—where you will connect—"

"Fuck you!"

"—for on-time connection with the *California Zephyr.*"

Brakowski had started the war cry. Now, from all sides of the station, it rang.

"Passengers *will* watch their language, puh-leeeeze! There are women and children—"

These joined in the cry:

"Fuck my ass, man!"

"Eat my shit!"

"—after ticketing, are directed to Platform 19 . . ."

Coach. From here to D.C. in a—

Whoaaa.

Brakowski saw his man coming, blond hair swinging like a girl's. Movie star handsome. A Hollywood tan. Black leather Armani coat that reached to his boots.

The hackles bristled on Guy's neck. His hemorrhoids started to hum.

He slipped the ridiculous Holmes cap over his fierce bullethead. Time for cover.

He closed his eyes. Counted slowly to ten, disappearing by the beat.

When he opened his eyes he'd become—*Dr. Rice.* The ultimate abstracted genius.

The man can't pick two bags up without dropping his pipe, in a clatter of sparks. He looks confused. He is confused. The logistics of picking his pipe up without dropping one of his bags reduces the man to mere Jell-O. He can't decide. He drops both bags. And when he leans over, his thinking cap falls, just goes on a terrible roll. Then his Burberry spills out his billfold. Oh *dear!* Girls and boys who'd hid from Guy giggle and flock to his side. Bluehaired mummies in wheelchairs burn rubber to assist.

He drifts away on a wave of content. Put Dr. Rice on the top of the train . . . with his beloved meerschaum . . . he'd never know the difference!

Puff!

Dr. Rice is a genius and—

Pufffff! Pufffff!

—the whole world is his blackboard.

Puffffffffffff!

He's never been this deep before. He's lost himself so totally, he thinks maybe he'll be Rice forever and—

Suddenly he knows just how a head-on collision would feel.

Twenty feet away he sees the face he hates most in the world.

Like a guardian demon, Mike Hammer screams in Guy's left ear. And then Rambo screams in the other. And then Brakowski is screaming himself as he spits out the meerschaum and charges him.

"YOUUUUUU!"

VIII DODGE

Arrivals and departures. Twains.

The last arrivals came up on the left: grinning Orientals with backpacks and plaid blankets . . . children waving teddy bears . . . businessmen wed to their lush attachés . . .

And even though the Trip, for me, could not begin till Chicago . . . where I would link up with Peter . . . what can I say, even I felt the rush, the hunger to be on the platform.

Our elbow work grew nervier. Less and less distance between us:

. . . The attractive, but just slightly Rubenesque, blonde, dressed in a lavender sweatsuit. "Betsy" on her workout bag. Wavy hair brushed like Veronica Lake's.

. . . The bearded brute in bearskin, babbling to his Sanyo.

. . . The sleek Asian fox, in her furs and gold chains. Graduate cum laude from the cool school of hard Knox.

. . . The Marlboro Man. The Sundance Kid. Pure rock star charisma packed in a linebacker's frame.

. . . The Actor. There are things one *knows*. The sneakers were a downbeat touch that might have worked without the holes. But I'd seen better shades on lamps. I was wondering if he was better on stage than he was incognito when the bullroar sounded:

"YOUUUUU!"

I turned, thinking "Drake?" to see the Fat Man coming.

He never quit. He never would. No matter how many times I beat him, he just kept on coming. Now with runamuck bags on his shoulders. Cases klunking at his knees. And a ferocious bullethead under the cap that had gone on a roll.

A porter attempted to head off the charge. The Fat Man bowled one aluminum case that cut the man down at the knees. Then he dropped the other case, his stubby fingers twitching.

Twelve feet.

Ten feet.

"GOL-DI-LOCKKKKKKS!"

Well, Sundance was blonder than I was by far.

But—

Six feet.

Four feet.

"Whoaaa!" I cried, pivoting hard to the left.

Sundance mirrored my move and cried—

What? It sounded a little like "Whoops!" But it started so low the floor quivered.

The Fat Man looked as if he'd been slammed in the chest with a Louisville Slugger. He started holding actions that got about down to his waist. His legs, though, had too much momentum. He landed with a smack that gave the old marble a smashing red facial.

Sundance winked and purred, low, "Gets 'em every time."

I watched him walk off. He just glided away, as if nothing special had happened.

Jesus, I thought. That guy *spooks* me.

Then from below I heard the cry from someone who still knew his magic:

"Alllll a-boarrrrrrdddddddd!"

I grabbed my bags and took off on the heels of the other tripsters: plump Betsy . . . the Actor . . . the lithe Asian fox and her gray wolfish man.

THE WALL

Amtrak had improvised a special train of coach cars to get our group to Washington, where a full-service *Capitol* would be ready, waiting. The stopover was minimal. We would make the *Zephyr*. And it isn't till after Chicago that nature starts chewing the scenery.

Still, we'd be deprived of our cabins, if only for two hours. And no one was happy with coach.

Sundance looked like he'd been cheated out of the chance of a lifetime.

The Actor sat still as a street mime collecting a crowd with a freeze.

Graybeard, behind me, kept snarling at his Sanyo: "It was the best of trips, the worst of trips . . . Memo: Disorientation. Contrast the rude change in our routing and that of our plans for the Sixties with the comet's predictable course . . . Memo: Work in the zonked hippie ahead. No doubt he's selling lovebeads or tofu in the Village. . . ."

I drew the line at tofu. But she let him have it first: "Shut up, Wolf, you pompous ass!"

Hell, even Bullethead was a shadow of himself. He'd been the last to come on board, looking pale as a hangnail and vague as a ghost. I wanted to walk up and tell him: *I know what must have happened, Pops. Sundance rubs me the same way. There's something, just something, about him. Acts like he's just looking right through you.*

Well, we all had our problems. And no doubt my own were beginning to show. Give me a closet. A mere stool to sit on. Give me a door I can just close behind me. Give me the sense of—

containment.

And I travel well.

I wilt in the open. My roots circle in. And I begin to feel—
confused.

I began erasing the passengers around me. Pictured myself in my cabin, seeing and feeling the walls.

But tricks are tricks, and facts are facts.

The train rolled on relentlessly. The hours passed in minutes. And we were in Washington before I'd half-started to figure a way of evading the Wall.

Union Station should have done it. We had a little over two hours to kill. And you could spend days there and still not grow tired.

I tried, but the clock was against me. The whole tour took about half an hour. And I found myself sitting at Buck's Country Coffee sipping cappuccino. Trying hard not to smoke the Winstons I'd just bought. I hadn't smoked since Canada. I figured I had a fair chance.

But the Trip had started out all wrong. D.C. was the last place I wanted to be.

I fiddled with the foam of my cooling cappuccino. I fondled the Winstons, which I did not smoke. I eyed the mahogany counter, noting the excellent grain of the wood. I saw myself with Peter, our clipped connection now restored. I fondled the Winstons. Great fun to not smoke.

Then I spun on my stool, thinking, hell, man, all it is is just a wall . . . Come on, Dodge, it's Party Time . . .

The bar across was filling up fast. Wolf had lost no time in setting up shop, his cossack hat beside a jug he'd already half emptied.

Foxy was idly stirring some exotic pink concoction.

Sundance regaled two girls—combined age, twenty-six—with jokes that had them howling.

Betsy streaked by us, a lavender blur, working two pink Heavy Hands.

I saw the Actor reading the morning's New York *Sun.* The red headline screamed: SLAUGHTER IN BRONX ZOO! PYTHON, BATS, AND HYENA EATEN!!! Beneath it,

the subfeature: EXPLOSION RIPS SOHO LOFT! 22
CHARRED CORPSES FOUND!

I wanted to join them. But what was the point?

I was here. The Wall was here. And we'd had this date
from the start.

Constitution Avenue is jam-packed with behemoths,
their stairways topped with solemn statues draped in marble togas. Wisdom of the ages in their stony eyes: Eternal
Vigilance is the Price of Liberty . . . The Taxman Cometh
. . . Curb Your Dog . . . .

The Department of Justice . . . The Court House . . .

Onward, past the IRS, where two vagrants—taxed beyond caring by life—snoozed above an air vent. One of
them soon might be Peter, I thought. If the Trip failed us.
Or if we failed it.

U.S. Customs Service . . .

Department of the Treasury . . .

From 17th to 19th streets, a wall of glaze lay calmly centered in a sprawling park.

Just past the park there was a shack surrounded with
dozens of flags. Inside marines sat under a banner that ran
wall-to-wall: "POW/MIA Since November 11, 1982—24
Hours a Day Vigil at the Wall."

I fondled the Winstons and looked at the shack.

One of the men asked me something.

I asked him what he'd asked me.

"Easy," he said. "You a vet?"

"Yeah," I told him. "I was there."

He gave me that smile, the sad one, and asked me in what
unit.

"Draft dodgers," I said.

"Cocksucker." His eyes were slits.

I started screaming, "Fuck the Wall!"

Union Station. Takeoff time.

Two gray pagodalike portals led to the waiting area, a
high rusted railing around it. The floor was brick, and old at
that, with stained and filthy granite. We sat on wooden
benches from our parents' churches, while janitors milled

about like old-time engineers: baggy pinstriped coveralls, red scarves, floppy caps. Beyond the portals, on one wall, hung a decrepit sign: FABER, COE & GREGG TOBACCO/ CONCESSION/MAG. STAND, EST. 1848.

I began to wonder what time zone we were in.

Then, from behind, high giggles, girls'.

Then a low, seductive purr.

The girls howled.

Sundance *whooped*.

And then we heard that other cry—impassioned, enticing, forlorn:

"Alllll a-boarrrrrddddddddd!"

CABIN FEVER

After we boarded, at five fifty-five, we proceeded to sit in the station. And sit. Bells were rung, walls were banged, and porters ran in circles to pledge we'd be on time.

The group that I'd taken to watching had been scattered the length of the train. Except Foxy and Wolf, three cabins down, who were at it tooth and nail.

("I *hate* trains!"

"Sam—*Sammy*—"

"Oh, shut up, you lazy slob!"

"Why, you airhead!"

"You baldy!"

"You BIMBO!"

"You *senile*—"

"Health nut!"

"Cokehead!"

"Chink slut!"

"Joke!")

I closed my door, drew the ivory shade. And Sam and Wolf were just white noise long before they ran out of steam.

The room's very tininess hugely reassured me. The wall-to-wall sofa was three feet across. Between the couch and toilet the space was eighteen inches.

The predominant colors were burnt orange and gold, with carpeting of orange/black, the warm hues reflected in the mirror on the door. The ceiling was a bit steep for my taste. But it sloped dramatically, and overhead a luggage rack further reduced it to scale.

By the door a waist-high closet skinny-dipped into the

wall. It would hold one pair of slacks, one shirt, one tie—
and, if pressed, one sheet of toilet paper.

Over the gold fold-down seat of the head, a tiny aluminum basin lay nestled into the wall. Above it a mirror hid
three mini-shelves, each about one inch by five.

I reflected on these things and found them to my liking.
And I was reflecting when we pulled out of the station.

The time was seven-twenty. Time to get to work.

I had two bags. I began with the first. From one of two
overhead hooks I hung a small sack for old underwear,
socks. I selected fresh replacements and set these neatly,
right front, on the rack. I kept digging till I found the shampoo and dryer. These I stored in the cabinet, barely, wondering what I was missing. Easy does it. Think now. Shampoo . . . Dryer . . . Yes, a cup! There's no way to fit your
head under the spigot, so you'll need a cup in the morning.

Hairbrush . . . Toothbrush . . . Get the Crest . . .

The Winstons, just to fondle them . . .

When I was done, I stretched, serene. For, in ordering my
small bubble of space I had also organized my own interior
landscape. Everything was in its proper place. Braced by
the logic and insight of a grown, mature adult.

Like this:

————

I had been, from the start, an impossible child. The tin
can tied to the tail of the woes of two good but overwrought
people. The last of six children who should have been five.

I was a midget until I was six, at which time I sprouted an
inch to a dwarf. And then for years I continued to grow, by
hairs and not by inches; until one day, in my teens, I found
I'd attained my full status of Short. By way of compensation,
though, life had given me in surplus certain other—quali-
ties. I learned from square one to attain what I wanted
despite the competition. Through waywardness and willful-
ness, through slyness and plain cunning.

I can't remember exactly when the beatings first began.
Or how bad the first ones were—surely open handed. My
terror of the Fat Man, though, was nothing short of titanic:

Father had bloated to three hundred pounds, stuffed with frustration, overdue bills, and the onset of middle-age crazies. But one day, by accident, after he'd walloped me good, I discovered something: an almost invisible sly, secret smile. Little more to it, really, than an upcurve of the lip. But I had, all four feet of me, a devastating weapon.

Maybe the Fat Man was slurping his soup or noisily chomping a cracker . . . or sitting there, vacantly watching TV, with his bowels rumbling . . . It didn't matter, I'd be there.

He turned to the belt; I would scream till he stopped; then wait until the time was right and really let him have it. He'd smash his knuckles on my skull or give me a shot with his elbow. "Don't look at me like that!" he'd scream. "Like what?" I'd ask him, smiling.

The Fat Man couldn't help himself; I couldn't stop me either. There'd be entire stretches when we'd live together as father and son, and he'd know I adored him, I'd know I was loved. But the dance had begun and it just wouldn't stop.

One Christmas the Fat Man just snapped altogether and let me have it in the face. The punches were brutal, he'd once done some boxing, and boy's blood covered one wall like a man's. The screams of the others just tore at his heart. But then he saw me lying there, smiling at him, smiling. He came at me like a bull, the biggest Fat Man in the world, and you should have heard him roar, then scream as he raised me up over his head. I screamed for salvation. He screamed for relief, and then threw me with all of his force at the wall. I was nine that Christmas.

The Fat Man went to counseling. He watched his drinking, lost some weight. He never laid a hand on me again until he died. But my war with the world had begun.

In the bubble of space that I moved in, the hard weird past made sense to me. Everything, seen in perspective, just *fit*. And, within the bubble, things easily reclaimed their names. No more, no less than what they were.

The Fat Man was Father.

And Ghost Boy was me.

And Therapy was just aikido. A system of pivots, extension, and turns. A way of dealing with the past. The Fat Man had hurt me. Now nobody could. Hell, I could whup three of the damn Sundance Kids. I'd get my black belt the next time around. So what if I'd flunked it four times in three years?

I'd had a minor relapse back in New York City. I'd eaten the food of my childhood. I'd slipped. And, in the fall, I'd met a ghost. But all was well. And fuck the Wall.

I had it all under control.

(You flunk it again, Dodge, you're out on the street. It's like you've got this damned hair in your brain you can't seem to get rid of. Aikido isn't tricks!)

When I looked at my watch, it was quarter to nine. So I fluffed out my curls and set out for some grub.

There were only two seats in the diner. Though ravenous, I passed on both.

Wolf, eyes blazing and pate gleaming, was wielding the mike like an Uzi:

"Memo! The end of the Sixties—when? June something or other when RFK died? Or November—7?, 8?—when Tricky Dick was voted in? When?!"

Heads kept turning everywhere.

Except at the end on the left. Where Sundance leaned against the wall, resplendent in white satin and showing a lot of tanned chest. His left arm draped, real chummy like, over the nearest girl's shoulder, fingers about half an inch from her breast. Her eyes were glazed, her head thrown back, almost as if she were baring her throat. Her friend, across from Sundance, shivered once deliciously.

In the station I'd thought they were both in their teens. But the girl beside Sundance looked years older now. She'd probably started the day she was able to bleed.

My thoughts shamed and sickened me. I tried to go. My eyes refused. I felt my blood start to thicken, snake's head twitching in my jeans. And I wondered how Sundance could lean there like that and talk so softly while Wolf boomed. I wanted to join them and listen.

He turned his eyes straight on me then. He didn't appear

to be breathing. And I was so hungry, I—started to see things. I thought I saw lavender specks in his eyes. And I thought I should really be with them . . . Sundance wanted me there . . . Who was I to refuse . . .

Suddenly there was a crash. And just behind the crash, a blur. Of lavender coming right at me with two Heavy Hands.

"Oof! Oof!" she cried. "Heads up!" I pivoted. Two porters streaked. Betsy never lost a beat. She rounded the corner. She took it full speed. And from the hall came thumps and cries from those who were slower than we'd been.

Sundance fixed me with his eyes. But the spell was broken. And I lickety-split for the lounge car. Fuck him.

The lounge was nearly SRO, with refugees from coach cars stacking cans of Bud and Coke halfway to the ceiling. The smoke was thick as Frisco fog. I slid into the second booth and sagged under the weight of the haze.

Visibility outside wasn't that much better. The night was so black the window glass seemed stained with printer's ink, through which crackled specks of light: cop cars, gas stations, billboards and bars . . .

One's reflection in the glass, little more than a shadow splashed over the ink. While overhead they let you know we were passing Martinsburg . . . but in sixty seconds would swing into Maryland . . . then back to West Virginia, crossing the Potomac twice while the whistle deeply blew, more like a chorus of whistles than one.

And perhaps as the lights crackled, popped . . . as you rocked and rolled into one state, then another . . . the night so black and things so vague . . . those specks of light as quickly lost as other selves you used to be . . .

(What *was* the name of the bar you once haunted in that lost state of your youth?)

perhaps you might have felt a little—

You might not have felt a thing.

For the haze was protective and heavy and sweet. A choice cocoon thickly lined with warm and cozy colors. The earthbrown carpet floated up to panel half the walls. Rows of tables surfaced with splashes of orange and gold.

Smack-center in blue-collar heaven, a table of elderly women, all sporting green Reno visors, staked their lives on liar's dice, clicks topping the clicketywhirrs of the wheels. Grizzled men in baseball caps, plaid shirts, and coveralls made nonstop passes at their beers; and now and then, the passes caught, found grounds to laugh uproariously.

And at a table, on the left, Bullethead glared balefully over the rims of his specs.

My guess is there are moments when, strictly for the hell of it, life turns some to maddened bulls . . . and some to big red flags. And there's no stopping either one.

So Bullethead glared.

And I wiggled my ears.

I'd had ten years of Therapy. Nobody was hurting *me.*

He closed his thick book with a thud . . . clapped his pipe down in a shower of sparks . . . and got up, curling one finger.

I took a slow sip of my soda. Then slid out of the booth with a soft click of beads and moseyed down the aisle.

If anybody noticed us they gave no indication. The state of rage meant no more to them than Maryland or West Virginia. Dice clicked on inside smacked cups. And Buds were ogled like girls on the beach. And songs were sung. And Camels smoked. And monologues were held with ghosts by doomed drunks who studied their pinkies.

Bullethead pretty much took up the aisle. My curls came about to the hook of his nose. My shoulders, squared, stopped at his boobies.

"Asshole." He growled. "I oughta tear you limb from—"

"Peace."

Bullethead gave me a poke in the chest.

Fingerpokes had always been a specialty of mine. But I wanted to know what he *thought* I had done.

"Keep out of my way or you're dead," he went on. "You California dodo. You're a goddamn disgrace to the—Oh-oh . . ."

Bullethead had seen something that took the starch right out of him. I felt a bristling at my back. Still, I was spellbound by the change in his expression.

Those piggy eyes grew huge with hurt and cloudy with

confusion. You could have popped a guppy through the circle of his mouth.

"You swine! Keep away from my sister!" he cried.

I'd been expecting anything, except the operatic slap.

It would have reached me faster if he'd sent it Western Union. There was no danger in it, but . . .

That curious *bristling* behind me!

My left foot swung back sharply as I feinted with a right. His head snapped back instinctively and I pivoted, swinging my hip at his gut, the move whipping my right past his face in an arc that married the swing of his arm. My hand slid right along his sleeve until I had him by the wrist. Not a pause from the start, not a hitch in the flow, and a lurch of the train added brutal momentum as I dropped to my left knee. Projecting and extending him. And adding, at the end, a snap, harder than I had to, harder than I should have. Christ, you could have heard that wrist bone crack clear up in the engine. Bullethead went over me as if he'd been shot from a cannon. Ass over teakettle, half to the roof, and onward, flailing, for three yards . . . before he landed, with a *whooof,* at the feet of Sundance.

Stunned looks from all around us. The car still shaking from the crash. And Buds and Cokes still splashing in those little plastic cups.

Sundance looked around the car, daring any challengers. But the haze just thickened, and you've never seen so many places folks could put their eyes.

Bullethead made it halfway to his butt, then collapsed with a rattle that sounded like death's.

Sundance smiled sardonically. "I'd sure like to meet his sister."

He leaned over, not by much, and grabbed a bunch of both lapels in one enormous hand. Then he dead-lifted Bullethead clean off the floor and set him down light as a ragdoll in the booth where I'd been sitting.

I had no objection. I didn't mind at all.

Sundance slid into the booth just behind, along with his two dead-eyed groupies. He just looked at me and smiled, his eyes reaching out to me.

I focused on a spot of rug a few inches ahead of my

sneakers. That always worked with the Fat Man when the time had come to make tracks. I followed the spot like an old bouncing ball step by step out of the lounge car.

Sundance purred as I passed him, "You're a funny little man."

"Don't push your luck," I muttered, hoping that he hadn't heard me.

Dreading that he had.

WELL, HELLO, CHICAGO!

 I'd stayed up till midnight, sitting by the window, watching the flickering lights and vague shapes through my vague reflection in the blackened glass. Hand poised with a Winston, I did not, would not, smoke . . . and, just beyond that image, the same hand twice reflected from the mirror on the door. The two of me, the three of me, circling, circling on. Through miles of shadowy landscapes. The whistles blew. The wheels rolled on. On we rocked and clicketywhirred, secure in our bubbles as worlds passed us by.

The K mart with the huge red "K" . . . the Nissan sign . . . the First National Bank . . . the Dairy Queen . . . the Amoco . . . the drive-in (oh, lost passion pits!) . . . the church . . . the mausoleum . . . Dad . . .

Here.

Gone.

Rock on.

I slept well, considering. A rattle somewhere in the room, like six tin cans for newlyweds, might have kept me up all night. Brooding on the list of things that were going wrong. But my sleep was dreamless. And at dawn I bounded up, working the compartment before I'd half-opened my eyes.

Done now, and in Trip's regalia, I lifted the shade. And I loved what I saw.

The morning light was misty gray, the vaguest of outlines suggesting themselves: lone houses perched on hills . . .

rolling acres of the void . . . mountains we rolled and clicketyhummed through, sheer cliffs hanging on both sides . . .

I wondered how I'd ever feared the Trip might not succeed. There *were* second chances, there had to be, and this was ours. My chance, and Peter Duchesne's.

For everything was organized and in its proper place.

I remembered that growled

You keep out of my way.

and

You're a goddamn disgrace to the—

What? Human race? Uh-uh. The *profession?* Hmmmm. And don't forget that

Oh-oh . . .

He had to be following Sundance. Somehow he must've heard of me and feared I was muscling in. Well, he could have his Sundance Kid. Offhand, there wasn't anyone I'd rather not be following. I didn't like what I'd seen in those eyes, though I half-wished I knew what I *had* seen. I liked it better when things were arranged, neatly, by me, and controlled.

Seven-ten. Particulars of old barns caught in fogged pinkening light. Peeling paint on loosened boards. Roofs sagging from the strain of hard times and bad weather. While here and there a neighbor, young, strutted fresh red siding, spanking new machinery, the bold sense of fertility. And black/white cows at pasture contentedly fattened themselves for the block. And the light snowfall covered all.

Seven thirty. Crestline. Our Town, U.S.A. Mortgages (just barely) met. Scrubbed kids gotten off to school in ear muffs and handknitted mittens. Home cooking on the tables here. Grace at meals, with all heads bowed.

I followed the telephone wires for miles: level with the windows now and almost within reach, then suddenly swooping away and below as if yanked by their ancient black poles. And when the wheels hit a really rough stretch —and the car began rocking like crazy, luggage bouncing off the rack as high as I did off the seat—Sam shrieked, her high voice bouncing too, and Wolf roared, *"Perihelion!"*

Eight A.M. Lima. Spelling out "Ohio" in dull colors on old

signs: La-Z-Boy . . . Carpetland . . . Febus Motors . . .
Sohio Gas . . . Miles of old factories puffing smoke through
blackened stacks in their desperate race against time. And,
in the smoke, ghost pictograms: the Fat Man shuffling home
from work, twelve more hours toward his gold watch . . .
while Ghost Boy's glued to the TV, dreaming dreams of
Paladin, the hero he will be . . .

Eight forty-five. A major flash.

I hadn't eaten since Myrtle's.

An inviting expanse of creamy cloths and sparkling silver
cutlery. The rush of fresh-brewed coffee. Smiling stewards,
shy on tips, sang of eggs doing flips on the griddle beside
slabs of sizzling bacon.

But I lost my appetite when I looked at the table in back.
Sundance had one leg stretched over the lap of the blond
girl beside him. The girl, with a hickey that covered her
throat, was idly massaging the sole of his foot, while her
friend was slumped over the table.

Sundance appeared to be sleeping, himself.

As I passed him, he drawled "Mornin'," though, without
troubling to open his eyes.

I said, "Christ."

I snagged the last seat in the lounge car, a single in the
back. Across from me, four Amtrak men in royal blue jackets, white shirts, and red ties, set back their watches at eight
fifty-four.

I adjusted my own. Breathed in the haze. Took in the
reactions to my tripster's uniform: the oldest jeans in the
world, paisley patches on the knees . . . the faded, pinstriped, collarless shirt from somebody's granddaddy's
granddad . . . the Sergeant Pepper jacket with gold braids
and epaulets . . .

Eight—no, *seven*—fifty-nine. Fort Wayne, Indiana. Stop
at the station: in such disrepair that you flash back again to
the Forties.

Rock on.

Through miles of dreary marshes, exhausted shades of
green and gray. Drab as your life has become. Almost like

the Fat Man's, though you swore when you left him, a lifetime ago—

Eight forty-five. Warsaw. Just past Winona Lake. Looming in the distance, a plant that feeds on smoke not sun and
blows you back to Buffalo. Where the Fat Man sat you on his
knee and told you how the presses worked: where the rolls
were loaded . . . and where the ink was troughed . . .
and how, when everything fell into place, when every piece
was working, magic happened: *Books were made.*

Ten-ten. Valparaiso. Old tan Rambler by the tracks,
cracked windows patched by the Fat Man with tape. The
wind in your hair as you rode by his side.

Here, gone.

Clicketywhirr.

The wheels rolled on past stacks of ties that seemed to
topple in the wind . . . past junkyards and abandoned
trucks and tracks jammed with Inland Steel cars . . .

The lounge car was starting to empty. My own sense of
abandon grew.

I popped a Winston in my mouth, proceeding not to
smoke it.

To the right, a flash of cerulean blue beyond a snow-white
breakwall. Lake Michigan whispered,

Get ready.

Who was—for that first distant view of the skyline?

The sun lit up.

And so did I, puffing like I'd never stopped.

"Well, hello, Chicago!"

THE WAITING ROOM

"Atten-tion, your attention, please: Paging Mr. Duchesne, Mr. Peter Duchesne, your party is awaiting you in the First Class Lounge . . ."

They'd been paging Duchesne off and on for two hours while I tore through the maze of the station.

North to the odd-numbered platforms, then south. With no way of knowing, till minutes before departure, at which end the train would show. Then east to the old Gothic lobby, where tiles played marbles to see which cracked next and even the pews knew they hadn't a prayer.

While I raced, I reasoned. He was over *there* somewhere each time I was *here.* He had an ear infection—sure!—and couldn't hear the pagings.

I stopped searching around two and checked myself in at the counter. I knew, in my heart, that Duchesne wouldn't show. He'd lost his nerve or his vision had failed.

But I wasn't alone, not completely. Loosely scattered through the lounge were:

Sundance, sprawled out on a black leather sofa, shades giving us all a short break from his eyes . . .

The Actor, pacing the brown speckled carpet with a worn copy of *Hamlet* . . .

Betsy, propped against one wall, looking strained but pleased . . .

Wolf, seated by Sam, all her luggage between . . .

Fine, then, I would trip with them.

I wasn't Peter's keeper.

"Attention: First Class passengers. Your attention, please. Preboarding will begin now from the First Class Lounge

for the *California Zephyr*. Mr. Duchesne, Mr. Peter
Duchesne . . ."

I squared my shoulders. Grabbed my bags. And took my
place in the procession.

The best of other trains are *trains*. You know that the
instant you see the *C.Z.*, a spaceship in comparison: the
blindingly buffed silver engine . . . signature striping of
red, white, and blue streaking down miles of double-decked
cars . . .

For the next two-thousand-four-hundred-and-twenty-six
miles, this Trip is just for you.

The tall bearded Negro, elegantly blazered, takes your
luggage.

Leads you up.

Then down the long hall to your chambers.

You are ready to begin.

At three-ten the whistle blew. Hissing music of the brakes
and a brief shudder of movement. And then a prolonged,
imperceptible slide that slowly, smoothly gathered up
steam as we rolled out of the station.

I'd already started in on getting things under control. The
Deluxe Family Bedroom extended the width of the car,
with full-length windows on each side. A high-backed
queen-sized sofa bed was end-flanked by two facing chairs
that merged into a child's bed. Overhead, two single bunks,
one adult's and one child's, could be dropped with a spring
of a latch. On the door, the full-length mirror reflected
shades of creamy gray and the sofa's intricate orange design. While to the right the broad closet stood about a foot
taller than I.

The real glory of the Deluxe, though, was just to the left of
the mirror. The Family Bedroom below me was identical
except for this: I had the only shower—and private head—
on the car. Hell, the mighty Sundance probably had just a
bedroom.

I was still gloating on this when I heard the footsteps.

I opened the door.

It was Peter Duchesne. Disheveled and chalk-faced and wrathful.

He said, sternly, *"Raphael."*

I knew in an instant what I had done wrong.

I muttered, "Oh-oh."

He said, "Yeah," and all but collapsed in my arms.

REUNION

 And so it began, the Real Trip, after all, just as we rolled out of Chicago. Through Westmont's roly-poly lawns and finely painted ranch homes. And onward to Aurora, the greens getting meaner and golds getting bolder and browns turning almost to ochre in miles of sugar-frosted fields as neatly braided as Bo Derek's hair.

If this sounds idyllic, you must understand: Since we left Chicago I'd had a guilt trip laid on me as long and heavy as the train.

I still plead Not Guilty. In Chicago, when I'd had him paged, the slip was understandable. He *was* still Peter to me . . . the same way I'd always be Raphael to him. Hippie-dippie Raphael C., just back from the Haight, with psyche-delic sunglasses and flowerpussy on my brain. The first real tripster at Buffalo State! And a picture of absolute freedom to that refugee from Central Falls and new hick on the campus: Duchesne with his brush cut and lunch box.

You never know where your influence stops; at least not at the time. In college I met Peter once, that was it. His hair, by that time, half-covered his ears and he was smoking handrolled cigs while doing Van Gogh-style sketches. He asked me in a reverent voice if I'd really been There. And I remember thinking, whoops, this here is one lost puppie. But I stayed for a smoke and, still stoned from the night before, I sipped at my coffee and told him tall tales of flower children in the streets, Lucy streaming in the sky . . .

Scattered flashes from then on, mostly across crowded rooms: his hair to his neck, then his shoulders . . . Vandyke beard and groovy glow . . . old collarless shirts and suspenders . . . I nodded, flashed peace signs, and went my own way.

We were almost strangers, then.

But our destinies were linked. I had become, despite myself, a sort of dashboard Jesus, all the more effective for the fact that I wasn't quite real.

The War brought us together, at least for a spell, in an unusual way.

Peter left for Canada in July, 1968, a month after RFK died. He left with both lips blazing: a crazed lament for Camelot in the college paper. Now, we had all been stricken. But many of us, including myself, had other, more pressing concerns. My grades had come close to rock bottom . . . and I received, certified mail, my 1-A in November.

Onward to Toronto!

Where I added my voice to the furor and passed out flyers on the streets and howled for an end to the War. The War was ruining everything! I argued with such passion that I was christened "Dodge."

One night while I was on the beat I chanced on a familiar face. His hair was halfway to his waist and the beard was a full Jesus beauty. But there was no mistaking my former disciple Duchesne.

He acknowledged the change in my name with a smile. Listened, while he smoked and sketched, to news of the resistance. Finally, he yawned and said the War was just a flimflam. A smoke screen concealing the Death of an Age. For a real American, there could be only one course of action.

My heart sank when I asked what he'd done.

He had renounced his country.

Well, Toronto was larger than Buffalo State. But not nearly as large as New York. So, our paths crossed from time to time in the Yorkville cafes exiles haunted. He went out of his way for these meetings, in fact, and seemed to find them pleasurable in some faintly perverse, obscure way. And it didn't matter if the talks lasted hours or minutes. It seemed enough for him to know that I was up there with him . . . some inner frame of reference to gauge his progress by.

Meanwhile, the War progressed despite our Canadian army.

1970 . . .

'71 . . .

Hup, '2 . . . '3 . . . '4 . . .

The War went on forever. My tenor was shot from the shouting. The occasional flyer would still reach my hands. But more and more my hands were filled with what I could take from the Seventies.

And, more and more, Peter seemed to measure himself by my changes:

the length of my hair—clipped to neck length, with burns . . .

my style of dress—paisley shirts and wide bells . . .

the broad swath I was cutting through Toronto's disco queens . . .

Of all the things we talked about, what I did for a living intrigued Peter most. For a while I wrote ads for Eaton's. Two summers, in Niagara Falls, I worked as a magician. I did a stint for Pinkerton's, an undercover cop. Peter would listen and smile serenely. He sold jewelry on the streets, sang folk songs with an upturned hat, his long hair blowing in the wind.

By the middle Seventies, I might have dodged him easily. Hippie Yorkville was long gone—the old cafes now chic boutiques and high-priced glitzy discos. And Duchesne had split the scene for Eden's last lingering shadows, from which he watched the whole world flock to straighter jobs and bigger bucks. Designer drugs, generic sex. But while I fought for my fair share I came to seek out Peter the same way he'd first sought out me.

"So, where you working, *Dodge*?" he'd ask. "Still got that two bedroom on Jarvis?"

I'd answer almost gleefully, knowing that I was condemned. "No. Got a promotion at Pinkie's and took a small penthouse on Avenue Road."

And Peter would tell me that that must be nice. And I'd love the way he said it. I'd feel almost wantonly sullied.

Hup, '4 . . . '5 . . . '6 . . .

July the Fourth. A grand party at Grossman's, living room

for exiles. I hadn't been there since the old days. But Amnesty was on the way. So the king of the dodgers reclaimed his old crown, storming out of his penthouse in work boots and beads, hell-bent on salvation.

The tables were sky-high with flyers that night, the backroom loaded with cases we'd drained. We smelled the blood of bureaucrats. We raised our glasses and we screamed:

"Two-four-five-six,
Amnesty in Seventy-six!
Beep, beep! Whack, whack!
Grab your socks.
We're going back!"

The room was half-filled with Canadians, most of them laughing and pounding their jugs.

But at a small table, alone, in the back. stroking his long graying beard, the Man without a Country fixed his eyes on me. Then he swiveled his chair to the wall.

We worked around the clock for months. Till the man with the peanuts said, Kids, come on home.

Two weeks later, I sat for three hours at my parents' tombstones. And then I set out for the West like a shot to spend what was left of my youth.

I was down to the small change of it, almost six years later, when the phone rang late one night.

Long distance.

Toronto.

Collect.

I had Peter back by the end of the month via Cunningham's underground railroad. I felt like Father Christmas. No bad blood. No loose ends. All accounts were settled.

Well . . .

The City was gone when he got there. The San Francisco of his dreams. He sank upon arrival, unnoticed and without a sound, while parties by the Bay popped corks, cheered on the Eighties, and roared for the Dows. Even as a ghost, perhaps, he might have found something like peace. But his return had cost him the one thing he had left: his name. Each time I saw him on the streets, I'd wish we'd never met.

So, if any man had reason to think before paging "Duchesne," it was I.

Of course, I could have told him: how everything had been so strange, long before we left New York . . . how The Wall had knocked me cold and one flash had set off another . . .

I took it on the chin instead. I sat there and let Peter tell me how it felt: to fly from the Bay to Chicago, so terribly close to D.C. . . . to hear that first shocking announcement . . . to stop, cold, in his tracks . . . blinded by visions of hundreds of *Them:* FBI, CIA, Immigration, IRS . . .

I listened while the train rolled on, about eighty miles an hour. Through the finest countryside a man could hope to see. Past herds of cattle licking frost from luscious lawny patches. Past blackish, braided acres brilliantly banded with emerald.

"Give me your passport," I told him. "Give me everything you've got. And shut up for a couple of minutes."

I laid out his papers on one of the sofa's broad cushions.

Peter smoked and studied me the same way you watch a magician. He looked gaunter than ever, somehow almost spectral, in earthdaddy jeans and suspenders.

On the adjoining cushion I dealt out my own ID, from the top of the deck, no cards marked.

He shuffled over morosely, swaying with the train.

"Take a real *close* look," I said. "And try to listen for once. You are exactly who these papers say you are. There's the birth certificate, certified. Social Security card. Just like mine. You're in the system, pal. Get hip. You *are* Lenny Dirks."

Peter—Lenny—jabbed with his weed.

"I *can't* work—the IRS!"

"Don't start on that. I've told you—"

"Yeah, you're gonna fix that too."

"I put you on my books, you file your first taxes—"

"No!"

"Then fine," I said. "Whatever." I gathered my papers and slumped by the window, watched him smirk as I lit up.

"That's the thing about you, Dodge. You go the way the wind blows and never think about it."

Clicketywhirrrrr. The wheels rolled on.

"Think what you want to think, Lenny," I said. "Just spare me the suffering artist routine. You haven't drawn a line since when."

Lenny looked as though maybe he'd charge me. Then he looked at his papers, laid out on that cushion, and made an anguished, strangled sound, swiping them all on the floor.

"You haven't got a clue!" he cried. "You can't imagine what it's like. For fifteen years I *played for keeps*! When people asked me what I was—Canadian, American—I told the truth. I said 'Nothing.' Day after day, thousands of times, nothing, nothing, nothing!"

"But you're back now, aren't you?"

Lenny collapsed on the cushion, sharp bony angles going every which way.

"Am I an AMERICAN?"

Well, what could I *say*? I said, "No, you are not. But, Jesus, you were born here, man. What else do you need?"

"That's what I like about you, Dodge. Scam your way to kingdom come. One day in Italian silk, the next as Sergeant Pepper. Now you smoke, now you don't."

I slipped into my blue tripster's jacket, and crossed the room in a couple of strides.

"I don't give a good goddamn if you want to shoot down the toilet. I've had it to here with the guilt. I thought it might be good for you . . . see the country coast to coast. You could have started at the start, you want to feel American. You could've seen your family."

"My family—"

"*You've* got one. But you had to start in Chicago. Okay. I thought you could still get the feeling. And when we arrived, I thought maybe you'd see—"

"The city as it is?" Lenny stood up slowly. The two of us, with me in lifts, were roughly the same height. But he was so calm and his voice was so droll, I'd have needed platforms to touch the nose he looked down. "San Francisco. '86. Where the anthem is 'Hey, I've Got Mine.' And our tour guide for this trip to hell is that chameleon *clown*—"

I hit him so hard my fist knuckled his backbone and drove him a few inches back through the couch. Lenny doubled over, then rolled to his side, whooping for breath while he gave me the eye.

My tenor hit soprano fast.

"Let me tell you something, asshole. The Sixties were shorter than I am. The Sixties were a party? They would have bounced you at the door with your gooey romantical bullshit. The dream you bought was canned and sold by shucksters along with their ginseng shampoo. They sold you the soft-focus version, you jerk. The real Sixties were hardcore. Good dirty dangerous fun.

"That's what *I* miss from the Sixties. That's why I'm wearing the jacket. We're halfway to the Nineties, man. Life's the trip and time's the wheels. And if you don't stay ahead of 'em, we'll be scraping your pieces with spoons."

Lenny managed to sit up, and leaned on the wall. "You've got it . . . figured out."

"I stay ahead of the wheels."

"A guy . . . who pimps for . . . Polaroid."

It had been about three years since I had done divorce work. But what did that matter to Lenny? He'd turned the whole thing all around! And I knew I was going to kill him if I didn't get out of there fast.

"I'm gonna eat," I told him. "You do what you want to do. Just keep your damned stuff on *your side* of the room!"

"I'm getting off the train."

"Hey, you get off, I swear to God, I'll phone Immigration."

"You bastard!"

"Hippie!"

"Copout!"

"Loser!"

Well, it must have been contagious. We were starting to sound just like old Wolf and Sam.

"I'll be back for my stuff later on," I snarled. "I'm sleeping on the goddamned coach."

"*I* am!"

"*I* am!"

"Nazi!"

"VAMPIRE!"

ZEPHYR TALES

I

 "Now, if *I* were a vampire . . ."

The girl in the red leather mini looked up coolly from her book.

Austin Blacke smiled and slid into the booth, as hungry as he'd been in years.

He outstretched one upturned hand, his strong lifeline running forever.

"May I?"

The book was passed. Then something else as he flicked one finger on the pale side of her wrist. Then Blacke leaned back, kicked off his shoes—his feet still troubling him vaguely—and grazed her ankles with his toes.

"Ohhh."

"You all right?" he asked her. Purr.

"I-uh . . . Ha-ha . . . Something weird . . ."

Austin smiled obliquely. He flecked a speck off one white satin cuff and held the book before him.

" 'Salem's Lot. I have a weakness for this one."

"Uh-huh. But if *you* were a vampire."

"Yeah."

Blacke touched her ankles with his own, feeling her pulse through his socks. And then through her eyes as he caught them. Seconds were all that he needed right now. He let her go. Back she slumped, half smiling and wholly perplexed; quickened movements of firm breasts under tight black T, faint pulse throbbing in her throat.

"For me, the real problem is logic."

He stroked one calf with his prehensile toes.

The girl, dazed, murmured, "Uhhh . . . Excuse me, but
. . . what are you do—Oh, *wowwww* . . ."

"Here you have this superior being. And all he does is
sleep all day, then suck blood all night."

"I *know.*"

The girl shivered as Blacke stroked one thigh with his
toes.

Austin said, agreeably, "By the way, if you don't mind my
asking: is your cunt tight and squeaky, or like an airport
hangar?"

"*What . . . ?*" For an instant, she looked horrified, as if
he'd just thrown her a spider. He snaked his toes under her
mini, then shot her a warm, cozy lavender look.

"Be a sweetie, tell me."

The girl leaned over and whispered.

Austin purred. "That's fine with *me.*" Then he leaned
back as if nothing had happened.

"Anyway, where were we . . . Ahh . . . Our genius
fills whole towns with vampires . . . who beget more vampires and—"

"Sir?"

Deep voice at the side of the table. Blacke had been
expecting this and met the steward's eyes.

"Sir, a party of two will be joining you—*Oh.*"

The black steward reeled as if he'd just seen double.
Which, in a sense, he had. Blacke had peopled the two seats
beside them with holographic images of elderly dining
companions.

Blacke clasped his hand warmly, a lavender squeeze.

"We'd all like to order now. If you know what I mean."

The steward did. The waitress came. And promptly left,
as stunned as the steward, with two double orders. For the
blond man, and the tramp brunette, and two spooks who'd
come out of nowhere.

"You must be hungry," the girl said.

Austin sighed. "Oh, I *am.* You don't know the half of it."

II

Brakowski was finally seated at six. Relieved that he hadn't been seated with *them*. Yet wondering why he *hadn't* been. Why those seats were kept open, with a lineup that stretched to the lounge.

Voices still rising in protest were adamantly stonewalled, while Guy, having kept his peace, was led to a table of bluehairs.

"Oh, look! We're coming into Galesburg now!"

"That's Carl Sandburg's own home town."

"Imagine! Carl Sandburg!"

Brakowski slid deep under cover, while with a sliver of one eye he watched the hot moves between Blacke and the girl.

"Ladies," Guy said, "if I may. If you'll look to the left of the station, you'll see a remarkable sight. That old Burlington "464" locomotive—see it there, all in black with silver circles on the front?—now, I know *you're* too young to remember, but that takes me back to the Thirties. The happiest times of my life."

Guy had them now in the palm of his hand, the one he was able to use. He kept the right, now swollen black, discreetly tucked under the table.

"Professor Rice," he told them. "Alexander Rice."

The bluehairs introduced themselves.

Guy smiled and checked off his order, still watching the torrid encounter ahead. The girl a real eyeful, with boobs out to here giving that T some fine stretch at the curves. Blacke sure knew how to pick 'em. You had to hand him that.

". . . your hand?"

Squeaky bluehair on Guy's right staring at his swollen wrist.

"Oh, that. It's nothing. I took a little spill."

"Why, isn't he—"

"My word, he is!"

"You're the poor man—"

"—from the other train!"

"That horrid little creature!"

Had Austin Blacke suddenly stiffened? He couldn't have heard. But Guy raised his voice, not taking any chances.

"I'm a scholar, Lord knows, not a fighter. But, the thought of my sister—with *him*!"

Bluehaired consolations. Guy relented, by degrees. And presently, a few miles from the station, the four of them were best friends. With Rice on automatic.

Guy took this opportunity to reassess the damage.

He had blundered, badly, twice.

But last night, at least, he'd recovered in time.

The cost of the salvage had been his right wrist.

But the price well ensured Rice's cover.

The clown with the curls could still blow it.

But only till tomorrow.

Guy nearly chewed through the tines of his fork, remembering that cable ad he'd seen last year in LAX. Hippie in a denim vest. Long blond curls. Cotton candy goatee.

You know the old expression: you are what you eat. Well, there's no mystery about this fact: What your employees are having for lunch may be eating away at your profits. Call Dodge, that's Dodge Cunningham . . . San Francisco's favorite dick . . . for details on how Intestinal Light can raise your profits through the roof. And don't let the lovebeads fool you. We're tough as nails, shweetheart. Satisfaction guaranteed. Or we eat the bill.

Guy had come close to forgetting the ad—when a clipping arrived from a colleague. In psychedelic colors, posed before a chef's salad and juice, the end of the world as Guy knew it aimed a toy gun with red flag: CALL DODGE!

"Oh, my!"

"My word!"

"Why, look at that!"

Bluehaired observations that the good doctor had bit through his lip.

(Easy, boy.

Tomorrow.

The perfect time.

The perfect place.

A clean shot in the world's longest tunnel.

Then out the window, S.F. Dick!)

Guy dabbed at his lip with a napkin. Then at the tears of joy.

"I'm sorry, ladies. Forgive me. I keep thinking of *him* . . . with my sister."

He caught a blur of movement from the table down the aisle. *Dr. Rice* loaded some corn on his fork, his mind filling with complex equations.

Bluehairs disappearing fast to a mist of chattering.

The whole *car* disappearing—

except for the blur, at the edge of one eye, that stopped at the side of the table.

A long stretch of denim. Black. The waistline halfway to the ceiling, it seemed. Red mini and tan legs behind him, the leather cut off a good foot from her knees.

Rice nibbled at a kernel . . . while Guy erected down below.

He heard from somewhere high above a drawl that was almost a lavender purr.

"I'd *sure* like to meet your sister."

What could Rice do?

He looked up.

Blacke was gone. With a wink. And that cunt in red leather.

Brakowski slumped back in his seat to stop the shivers on his spine. He could not stop what happened next, as his erection roared and raged. And then blew its top altogether.

III

After seven round trips of the *Zephyr*, Betsy was already as familiar as the walls.

(Look, Mom, here she comes again! . . . Whistles . . . Giggles . . . *Work it out!* . . .)

The laughter, in fact, was not wholly unkind. The *California Zephyr* was like a moving party, and she was a part of the floor show. Her life, their hysterical limerick. Conducted by Miss Wilcox.

(There once was a girl who'd be thinner,
But she hadn't a damn poem in her . . .)

This was fine with Betsy, who was disappearing by the pound, on the way to her modest Romance.

(There once was an old maid named Wilcox,
Who liked moving much better than still cocks . . .)

Suddenly she took a left and hit the steps with all she had, Ex-Lax catching up again and in the passing lane. The fourth handle, mercifully, gave. And, before she'd locked the restroom door, the sweatpants were down to her knees.

Yeah, tell me about poetry. You win again, Miss Wilcox.

She studied her tongue, as lime green as the walls.

Heard the devil start to whisper sweetly in her ear: Just one grape . . . or a sesame seed . . . Even your skin is beginning to stink . . . You've been two whole days without

FOOD!

That's right. Betsy slipped her pinkie through the waistband of her sweats. She must have lost six pounds by now—by tomorrow, ten!

Emerging, almost shyly, from the white butter-roll of her jaw was—

a chin!

"I'm shrinking," Betsy almost sang.

Then she started shaking.

"Oh, shit! I want a *cigarette*!"

"I'll give you one, get outta there!"

Laughter from the other side.

Out like a shot then, a blur down the hall, and taking the steps, come on, two at a time.

Huffapuffa . . . Huffapuffa . . . Huffapuffa . . .

WHOOOFFF!

She'd run head-on right into him (thinking even as she crashed that the arms had come to her). That improbably handsome, impossibly tanned, blond *beauty* she thought of as Sundance. Who swept her up under the arms like a toy with a resounding

"WHOOOOOPPP!"

Sundance's eyes were twinkling, though, when he set her
down. He purred, "Nice to meet you . . . sugar."

Betsy raced like a maniac back down the stairs, her bowels turning to jelly.

IV

Beneath the observation deck, in the bowels of the
lounge, were the smoking quarters. Thick Plexi protected
three booths by the bar from the chainsmoking fiends on
wood benches.

Packed in the corner, one slight figure sat inhaling with
the best.

Rod Whittaker as Stan the Man, dressed in a torn T and
don't-fuck-me jeans. Assuming the position, here in the land
of the rough.

Rod took a can-crumbling guzzle of Coors. Then wiped
off the froth with the back of one paw.

Rod's pulse began to pound as bits and pieces, here and
there, moved from his eyes through his body: flick of the ash
with one finger, like that one . . . the cock of his head, like
that geezer's . . . one sneaker propped on his knee, like
that boot . . . the regal leer of hooded eyes—

staring, oh-oh, at him.

A Marlboro Man tipped his Stetson and glared. "Say,
pard, what's your problem?"

Kowalski with a broken nose?

Rod Whittaker decided not and discreetly departed the
lounge car.

At the steps he said "excuse me" to the balding wolfish
man.

And "madam" to the Asian fox.

V

"This is absolutely disgusting," Sam cried as she entered the smoky lounge car. "I can't even breathe down here!"

Wolf hadn't touched her ever in anything like anger. But he grasped her shoulders now and gave them a passionate squeezing.

"I am *working*—understand? I am *on the job.*"

Sam told him a low, slow voice, "You take your goddamn hands off me or I'll cut your balls off."

She looked cute as a button and sexy as sin in her Dior blue jeans and thigh-high red boots. But her heart was samurai and Wolf threw up his hands.

"I'll give you the world, if you'll just give me time."

"Oh, Wolf! Why couldn't you start with a *bedroom*?"

"I *did*!" *Rush* had sprung for a sleeper, roomy enough, with a double sofa bed and two cushy chairs.

"I want to *wash my hair*!"

"You go outside. Down the hall. To one of the four washrooms—"

"NO! And not another word about your stupid comet!"

Wolf jabbed at the air with one finger. "I'm headed for the stars, babe. Either hitch your wagon now—"

Sam started up the stairs and turned.

"Joke loser!"

"Cretin!"

Up a step. Another shot, from another angle. "Oldie!"

"Bratto!"

One more step. "Sadsack writer!"

"*Soulless* whore!"

And then she was gone.

Wolf turned to the astonished crowd, switching on his Sanyo.

"Ladies. Gents. Drink on *Rush.* And if you'd like a chaser, you can be immortalized. Just step right up to the little machine . . . and tell us in your own words what Halley's comet means to *you*!"

VI

Though sunset had been a good hour ago, the view was still magnificent. Nothing in particular to capture her attention—flashes, spaces, shadows of rivers . . .

Particulars weren't what Sam needed, though. Just plenty of good space within and without. She'd lucked into a single seat in the middle of the car, loosely flanked by swivels arranged in broad clusters of four. She stretched her feet out on the footrest that ran the full length of the car. Then leaned back and closed her eyes, letting her long hair flow free to the floor. No comet now. No albatross. And no responsibility for what *he* was or couldn't be.

For, she was *Sam.*

That was all.

Thoroughly modern, material Sam.

Twenty-years-younger-than-Wolf Sam.

Tired-of-the-twistings-their-affair-had-taken Sam.

She brought out the worst in him.

He brought out the beast in her.

He had kindness and talent. Ambition and courage. He loved her. That mattered. And she loved him too. But—

she couldn't remember the last time she'd *laughed.*

It couldn't work. It never had. She guessed she'd known that from the start. But when somebody needed you, it was hard to just let go.

Well I'll tell him tonight or I'll jump from the train. I'm getting off in Frisco. From here to there, I'll screw him blind. I'll be the Chinese geisha girl he's always wanted me to be. I'll rub his neck and coo to him and stroke him and build up his ego. I'll fetch his slippers and walk on his back and whisper all night in his ear. I'll give him everything I've got, everything I haven't got.

But once we get to Frisco . . .

Shit!

Hot tears streaming down her cheeks. Sam did not trouble to stop them. Better now than later when—

"Hi! I'm Pepsi, drink me!"

WHAT?

A high, squeaky voice came from somewhere near one boot.

"Come on! Drink me, drink me!"

Sam looked down to see a sassy cola on the foot rail.

"Do it! Do it! Drink me, please!"

She rubbed her eyes. She might need help. Something was terribly wrong here. Just then she caught a flash of denim from the corner of one eye.

Sergeant Pepper standing there. Curly-haired like Harpo.

"Hi," he said. "You looked so sad . . ." He threw his wizard voice again, "I'm down here, you dummy!" and smiled warmly and walked off under a halo of curls.

Astonishment and wonder.

That funny little man.

Just bought her a Pepsi and vanished. Never even hit on her.

Sam whispered—too late, though, for Harpo to hear— "Thank you. Jeez, I needed that."

Telling Wolf would be easier now.

VII

I sat in the diner and thought about Sam as my salad was brought and we rolled through the night. My reflection on inked Plexi, with that of my bluehaired companions. Who sipped at Bloody Marys and ignored my uniform.

I was thinking of Sam in the lounge car. And how, when I'd seen her there crying like that, I'd been stopped by something I'd lost long ago. The sense of the wide open highway, youth bombing along like a van. Spontaneous. Combustible. Unstoppable. And free. And if I'd forgotten Paladin, the tall thin hero I'd once planned to be, I'd half-forgotten Richard Boone in the last film he made. He'd been bloated, obscenely, befuddled with booze, and flagging his arms like a fool on the screen. The Fat Man had got him. The Fat Man and Time.

I was twenty now, not thirty-nine. I didn't sludge for a living, I played.

I had at my steak (and why not, on a Trip) and grew ecstatic as I chewed.

The Missouri River . . .

It swelled for miles as we clicketywhirred, until it *opened*, on all eights, and seemed half as wide as the sky.

"Roll on, you muddy river, roll!"

The three bluehairs looked at their watches and fumed.

The first said, "Brat!"

The second, "Beast!"

The third gave the fluff on my chin a good tweak.

"You keep *away* from his sister!" she cried.

The Missouri lost its spell. But only for a moment.

As soon as I looked out the window again . . .

VIII

She guessed he was a hypnotist. Or some kind of magician. Whichever, she knew she was under a trance—and an odd sort, since she knew it *was* one. There had been no candles when he'd brought her to the cave. (Imagine a cave on the *Zephyr*—oh wow!) And even if there had been, she hadn't seen him light one. And yet, go figure, here they were with candles burning everywhere. Black ones, fat as horses' cocks, long wicks crackling with lavender sparks.

Horses' cocks. That was a laugh! They couldn't hold a candle to the monstrous thing he waved at her. She figured eighteen inches, with what looked like a hole, not a slit, on the crown. Jeez-laweez! It might split her right up the middle! Which would certainly be a terrific effect but would probably hurt a little. (A lot?) Oh, well. Later on, he'd put her together again. (Wouldn't he?)

She wondered if her mother was baking bread in Monterey, if Dad was still smoking his smelly old pipe.

The man lowered himself to the rock she was chained to, kneeling between the broad M of raised knees.

The rock business confused her still. She seemed to re-member—there *had* been a couch. Burnt orange with a vague Aztec design. But that had been back when the room was a room. What was so weird about rocks in a cave? Hers was a wheel flatly spinning in time to the clinking of her *chains*.

(Jeez, get this guy on Carson's show!)

She really had to work this out. For some reason it still seemed important. If the candles and cave were—

"Illusions," he purred. She'd forgotten his name. Or when he had taken her clothes off. Or his.

"There are no chains," he murmured. "That's where the real magic comes in. Go on. Try it. Raise your arms."

She looked down where he toyed with her vulva with—*that*. Then up at his gray-were-they-lavender eyes. She raised her arms, feeling giddy, as if he'd just told her to walk off a cliff and she had and was standing on air.

"But the fact is," he said, "they feel *heavy*. And what you'd really like most is to *rest*. You'd like to lie back in our warm little *cave*. And *relax* and get on with the *show*."

Auto-auto—something . . . Ha! . . . the man with the tan *was* a hypnotist, then. And a tiny playful spark that had not quite gone under yet made her want to wave her arms. Resist him. And jingle his—

chains.

Oh well . . . There they were again . . . Wrists shack-led so tightly she gasped from the

joy

as he coolly quartered her: two inches . . . four inches . . . six inches . . . eight . . .

She began to writhe and buck, half-mad from his stopping at halftime. He laid one hand upon her mouth. He ignored her ecstasy.

"I wish I could show you the Snake Trick," he said. "I think you might die laughing. Or I'd show you the Face Trick. But then I'd need *yours*. And you have to be careful, you see, on a train. Pace yourself. Spread out the Tricks. You should've seen the other guys. They slept in fucking coffins. Me, I sleep in a bed. I can eat. I can shit. I tell you, I'm amazing!"

The man with the tan took his hand from her mouth and propped himself over her body, silencing her now with his crazycat eyes and heated feral breath.

Soooo fine . . .

"So why don't we try something . . . different tonight? A Trick for party animals."

The man with the tan let her have the full length: rip-snorting, slambanging, furious strokes that lifted her right off the rock when he pulled and slammed her back down with a spinetingling crash. The girl's teeth rattled in her skull. Oh God, it hurt, it felt so good, she just wanted to die in his arms and scream *Yes!*

But when she tried to, his mouth covered hers. And his breath took her breath away. And when she came she would have died to stop the walls from shaking. But the walls cracked and through the cracks fluttered heavenly visions of leathery wings.

"Like it?" he asked her, the man with the tan.

She thought she might be smiling, but she could not imagine why. Or even move her head to nod.

"Mom," she whispered. *"Mommy."*

"Don't worry," he said. "You're not bleeding. Remember that nice little hole on the tip? I clean up as I go. Relaxxxx. Here's the part that works for me."

The man with the tan made his arms—longer, somehow. The stretch arched his spine almost into a U, thrusting him deeper, and then all the way.

He grew quite still.

He did not breathe.

His tan began to glow, though.

Something wrong there.

Down below.

A vague sense of losing things, bits and pieces at the start. The odd memory she wouldn't need anymore. An ounce of blood. Two ounces. Three. A little pride. A little joy. And then a rush of all she was as she started to shiver like crazy.

He's taking me.

He's drinking me.

Oh God, he is!
Down there—
with that!

IX

Lenny and I were stretched out at opposite ends of the sofa. Our earthdaddy socks were just touching. I'd kept on the blue tripster's jacket, less because of the chill in the room than because of the book on Len's lap.

The book had been there when I'd come back to find him about halfway through a thick Baggie of grass.

The book had been there within seconds, I guessed, after I'd stormed out three hours ago.

The time was now nine-twenty. We'd arrived in Osceola, little more than a blip in the black.

The date was January 2, 1986.

The book was *The Summer of Love.*

I knew the book. I remember it well. I was in quite a few of the pictures.

I'd lost my copy long ago and never troubled to look back. (Life's the trip, pal . . . Time's the wheels . . .) But Len was locked forever in a place he'd never been.

After the Trip I would lose him, I swore. I had plans for the Nineties. And good ones.

I took a sip of my Miller's. Then I lit up a Winston, first of my third pack.

He watched. He waited. I began:

"I lied before," I lied again. "This was how it really was back in the Summer of Love. This was still before hiphuggers, jump suits, and bells. Hot pants and Earth Shoes were nowhere in sight. There were no designer jeans or aviator glasses. No one in the world had seen calf-high purple gator boots with two-inch soles and five-inch heels. The world was safe from dashikis and Ultrasuede and mood rings. Woodstock was still just a gleam in life's eyes. And Madison Avenue hadn't a clue yet of the millions to be made: Real lemon polish . . . dead veggies in spaghetti . . . freeze-dried fruits in cereals . . . and organic additives —almonds! macadamias!—in every poison they sold. Rolfing, est, rebirthing were still waiting in the wings . . . And Carlos Castaneda was still warming up with jumping jacks . . .

"For this was where it all began. Once upon a time. In a magical, mythical city. In a mystical Summer of Love."

I feared I was laying it on a bit thick. But when I stopped, Len's eyes just popped. So I lied on with abandon.

"I was home, Len, the second I stepped off the bus. It was noon, in Union Square. And Ken Kesey was there with his old Magic Bus, Merry Pranksters everywhere.

"There were kids wrapped in blankets. And kids wearing flags. And kids dressed as cowboys and injuns and spacemen. Hell's Angels with roses tucked over their ears. Girls in their grandmothers' long sleeky smoothies, with headbands of daisies, and feathers, and flutes. Dogs had posies in their collars. Children wore face paint and danced in the streets, naked and happy. And Free . . ."

I went on in this fashion for over an hour, until the lies exhausted me and I couldn't breathe through the haze.

I made up the large bed. (I'd earned it, I thought.) Then I pulled down the overhead single for Lenny.

I needn't have bothered.

At dawn, when I woke, he was up by the window, still toking, still lost in *The Summer of Love*.

COLORS: ONE

 The Day the World Ended began in sky blue and faded, at midnight, to black: It went to hell in a hurry between. But colorfully, oh colorfully, how colorfully the World Was Lost!

There is no blue in all the world like Colorado blue.

The Day the World Ended began for me around nine as we pulled out of Denver. The windows of the dome car, where I was waiting for breakfast, were glazed on the left in fine doily designs and softly powdered on the right. In the distance, mountains reared like hundreds of Paramount logos.

I sat there swiveling, left to right, taking it in through the glaze and the powder, taking it in, the old U.S. of A.

Beside me an elderly couple went on for a couple of miles about the old station in Denver: how the platform harked back to the Forties, those ancient pillars topped just so with that greening cast-iron pergola . . .

Further down, Betsy, in a rare moment of stillness, shared a singles combo with the brooding Actor.

At the opposite end of the dome car, Wolf had a cluster of four to himself. He hadn't washed what hair he had since Penn Station, or before. It was a foul-looking bird's nest of gray around the dull egg of his skull. I wondered if he'd bathed since Penn. Or slept since Penn. Or gone, since Penn, more than a couple of hours without a beer in his hand. He looked *absurd*. He *was* absurd, weeping and grinding that unlit cigar and shaking his fist at the heavens.

Still . . . The Day the World Ended began in sky blue, with the sense that the flatlands were over for good. The earth itself seemed to be breathing. Breathing in the mystic snow, breathing out tall evergreens shaking white clouds from their branches. The *Zephyr* contentedly clicketywhirred through miles of serenity.

I'd showered, shampooed, and relieved my chin's fluff of just the right eighth of an inch. Fiddled with the basin's knobs till I could turn them both at once and get the temperature just right. Made my bed and bounced a quarter off the folded edge of sheet. Rearranged my shirts and socks, emptied the ashtrays, adjusted the shades. Then put Lenny's droppings in neat little stacks when he finally crashed around eight.

In our car, when the Day the World Ended began, the world was a good place to be in, and blue.

Except for that shocking red mini ahead. The girl might have been pretty if she'd looked less—drained. The only color anywhere, the crimson hickey on her throat.

But the man with the tan had lost interest in her. He was busy chatting up the old bluehair who'd tweaked at my fluff. A few seats down from Sundance, Bullethead was grinning away. So I knew I'd have no further trouble with him.

The *Zephyr* set into a slow lazy S, gathering steam for the Rockies. Through lightly powdered Plexi we saw the front of the train snaking through the first of the twenty-eight tunnels ahead. Car after car disappeared, until ours.

A sudden, seconds-long fade to black. Then—

SLAM! BAM! ROCKIES BLUE!

The mountainside below us now dropping off precipitously. Across from us, and all around, massive striations on towering rocks, with evergreens huddled for warmth in the cracks. And, as we come full circle, the same scene comes at us all over again, from a higher and truer perspective.

Flash! Another tunnel.

Whoaaaaa! Another smashing bolt of blue.

About halfway to heaven.

Tunnels getting closer now. Sometimes just a flash between: the drop, now almost vertigo . . . glass snowball scene, all swirling white and evergreens arched in the wind

. . . ice maiden stripper flashing, by strobe, more and more of her chilling physique . . .

Tunnel number twenty-five. Straight through the heart of the mountain. The train rolling through in almost a straight line, then out to an earpopping view: evergreens, by the thousands, tobogganing straight down the slopes.

Ten thirty. Tunnel twenty-eight.

Silence, mostly, in the car. Except for a gravelly purr:

"Excuse me, my dear, if you don't mind my asking . . ."

Sundance leaned over to whisper the rest. The bluehair clutched her heart. He *whooped*. And I thought, there you have it, it all evens out. Guy laughs like a bloody hyena. Probably can't keep a girl for a week.

Meanwhile, a major announcement: at ten fifty-five we'd be entering the world's longest tunnel, the Moffatt.

"Oh boy!" I shrieked. "I *love* tunnels, don't you?"

Sundance gave me a *curious* look.

But we were rolling through God's country now and if I blushed it got lost in the blue. The long Divide ahead of us was a Great Wall of evergreens. And, on the left, a stretch of plains cried out for Fonda or Stewart or Coop.

Bullethead smiled serenely at me.

He still had ten minutes to live.

And the world was a glorious place.

INTERLUDE:
A SPLASH OF RED

 Brakowski's general outlook on life grew sunnier and sunnier the closer they came to the tunnel. The Moffatt would take some nine minutes to clear and most of the train's lights would fail. Passengers would stay in their rooms, or in the diner or lounge cars.

The trick here was the timing: to get the Dick there a few seconds before they actually *entered* the tunnel. No time to think. No time to act. Get him below by the stacked luggage racks at the door with the latch-open window. Whack the Dick, then slip him through, splash his brains on the tunnel's stone walls.

Guy synchronized his Seiko. Ten forty-nine now. Six minutes to go.

He double-checked his printed note: "The blond man's name is Austin Blacke. Imperative we talk *right now*."

Quick-scanned the scene before him: blond Blacke touching one, then both, of the bluehair's temples. Hmm!

"The time is now ten-fifty. In five minutes, almost exactly . . ."

Time to slip Curly the note on the sly.

But as Guy was passing Blacke's table—

the damndest, weirdest, queerest thing!

He felt a flicker at his wrist. Something like a tingle. But somehow more electric. And the thing of it was, well, whatever it was made Brakowski start to smile. Who could have told him, how could he have guessed, that lavender would feel so *good*? Sparking something in his brain. Urgent sense of mission.

Guy had to have more of it, all he could get. And for that he could only go down to the Source.

His legs seemed to be moving almost on their own. He felt his tingling fingers close, crushing something in his palm as he came to Harpo.

Brakowski smiled serenely and passed. I need more of the sparks, Harp, I'm in a bad way . . . but that's okay, I'm *sailing* now . . .

Hiss of the pneumatic door.

And onward through the coach car. Sleepers, curled under their blankets with no way of knowing. The wildest shade of lavender was

up through one more coach car . . .

Another hiss. . . .

Another kiss. . . .

Halfway through and

down these stairs . . .

to wait here by this luggage rack

for Santa to come

with his lavender bag—

and his now-raging Blacke eyes.

Guy whispered "You!" and that was all before Blacke seized him by the throat and carried him off down the hall to his lair.

"You've been following me."

Blacke slammed him again, then again, on the door, Guy's feet a full foot off the carpet. Guy felt his face turning purple and yearned for the rush of that lavender glow. Now sparks crackled in Blacke's eyes and from the candles on the walls covered with translucent sheeting.

(Oh God . . .)

"You know what the plastic's for?"

Brakowski couldn't think to nod; the slightest move might snap his neck. He managed to blink, though, and hoped that would do.

"Of course you do. You think you do. But think of all you don't know. Doesn't that just
break . . .
you . . .
up!"

Three grand slams in verbal sync, the third nearly cracking Guy's spine. Brakowski blinked and blinked and shat.

Blacke inhaled deeply and with real delight. "Gee, who could've guessed you were mellow as *that*?"

Tears really flowing now. Mike Hammer watching from on high. Guy's wings to be denied him.

"Remember the headlines on New Year's?" Blacke purred.

Offhand, at the moment, Guy couldn't recall.

• So Blacke gave his memory a shaking that popped out Guy's gorged slug-a-tongue one more inch.

Bats . . . He remembered! . . . Something about *bats*!

"Well, of course we *could* do the old Bat Trick," Blacke drawled. His lavender eyes almost twinkled. "But that's old hat . . . A guy like you . . . I sure wish I could show you the Snake Trick!"

Ohhhh.

"You know a full-grown python stretches twenty-seven feet?"

Blacke gave Guy's dome a playful swat. "But even a python would need time for *that*. So I guess that just leaves us . . . the Face Trick."

Well, the Bat Trick sounded horrible. The Snake Trick sounded even worse. Guy could have lived with either, though, and died happy, in disgrace. But—not the Face Trick! Please, not that!

He closed his eyes. He would not look.

He plugged his ears. He must not hear:

sinews squealing, bones popping, whirring sounds of rope or hair, and snaps and clicks and shock reports of razor blades in jungle breath . . .

Look at me!

How could he not?

Helplessly, and with a sort of abject fascination, Guy opened his eyes.

GOD, NOOOOOOOOOOOOOOO!

The hyena giggled. Maniacally. Maniacally. Leaned in almost as if to kiss him.

"I like the chin. The chin's the best!"

Guy heard a revolting crunch before his heart finally gave him a break.

COLORS: TWO

 The Day the World Ended proceeded to pink just as I returned from the diner. The first bright spots glowed on Wolf's cheeks over his great dustball beard. He stretched his legs, had at a Coors, and flicked on the recorder.

"Ah, well, on with the show! What the hell's a broken heart compared to the magic of—Halley's! Of course, nobody's *seen* her yet . . . but what instruments we have agree that she is really out there! So, while we're all sitting here waiting—come on, sugar, flash it!—suppose we examine in detail what all of the fuss is about. In diameter, the old girl is, oh say, five kilometers. She tips the scales, dainty thing, at sixty-five billion tons. Our beauty's heart—her nucleus—consists of cosmic droppings frozen together with water, ammonia, and methane. Nothing to get *too* excited about. But as our beauty approaches the sun—then the magic happens! Solar radiation melts her hard and icy heart. Solar winds expel a stream, celestial and continuous, like confetti thrown after a wedding. Or think of the sun as a hair dryer—yes!—tossing her tresses for millions of miles. Then again—maybe not. Maybe the tail is really like a cosmic chili fart! In the course of this performance, the old bitch will litter the cosmos with hundreds of millions of *tons* of exhaust: prussic acid . . . methyl cyanide . . . carbon monoxide . . . sodium . . . iron . . . copper . . . We're waiting for a *snowball* with a heart of GARBAGE!"

Well, Wolf went on and on. There really was no stopping him . . . or, for that matter, escaping. I couldn't go back to the diner till lunch. And you could still hear him below, in the lounge, where more and more tripsters had headed.

I could have returned to the sleeper, of course. But Lenny would be waiting there with the old *Summer of Love.*

What to do?

Look out the windows, like everyone else, and try to focus on the pink that the whole world was turning to. Look out the window and not at the legs of the girl in the red leather mini. Look out the window and not at the spittle roping down her chin . . . . the glazed expression in her eyes.

Look out the window as Wolf ranted on . . .

and Sundance put his arm around some new girl he'd just met . . .

and the two bluehairs kept shaking the third, who looked stoned.

Look out the window and try to forget Bullethead leaving the car like a ghost.

Look out the window, the world turning pink, this morning, the Day the World Ended for good.

Pass over wood bridges, above frothy rapids, through miles of violent landscapes: mountains shotgunned from the soil, bleeding pink through granite.

Stop a sec at Granby. Pass the shocking pink house on the mountain above the Colorado River's base.

Follow the river that grazes the tracks, then disappears, and circles back, broader now, and charged with pink reflections of the Day.

Rock and roll to pink canyons, Wolf pausing for air as Sundance, the perv of the universe, purrs:

"Excuse me, my dear, if you don't mind my asking . . ."

A sudden squeal.

An astonishing *whoop.*

And then, of course, Wolf's off again as Sundance glides off to his lair with his snatch.

"And, lest we forget her while she is away, she showers mementos for years: meteors and shooting stars. And other nauseous blasts of shit!"

The Day the World Ended was turning to red more quickly than you could imagine.

The color began with the catch of the day, a red snapper

that cried for a split of red wine. I was now regretting both as I dabbed at my strawberry shortcake.

I'd have given anything to go to our cabin and sleep.

I focused on the river. Bathed my eyes in the mud green. Tried to stop it, but could not, from veering dramatically under the tracks as the next announcement came:

"At one forty-five we will enter fabulous Red Canyon."

Light fingers on my shoulders as Lenny passed by to a single. Across from a baby-faced tripster with Navajo beads in her summery hair.

We ricketywhacketyclicketyrocked into the Red Canyon. You think you know what red is? I assure you that you don't —not till it comes at you like blazes with everything it's got:

rose, light red, bright red, bloodred, brick red, scarlet, fire engine—

now a few feet from the side of the car . . . then fifty feet . . . a hundred feet . . . then bodyslamming the *Zephyr* to within an inch of your life.

And then, when you've seen it all, you begin to hear it:

"You work for IBM?" Len shrieked. "You're a fucking ROBOT!!!"

I slipped a tip on my voucher and split, desperate for shuteye.

An hour later, when I woke, we were in Glenwood Canyon, as soothing a sight as I'd seen since New York. Glenwood was a string quartet of muted grays and browns and blues, the rocks baroquely chiseled to almost a quartzlike facade.

The Colorado hit its stride just outside of Glenwood. Stately as a bishop now in a whispering robe of silk rapids. In the distance grand valleys, as green as they come, tumbled and rolled as we clicketywhirred, the telephone wires rising and dipping as if they were mad for the hills.

Onward through Rifle. Gone like a shot.

Cliffs, like cones, sprinkled with jimmies of shale oil deposits.

And then the flat-topped Pearizes, no string quartet, a symphony of autumn golds and oranges.

I hummed as I worked: stacking Lenny's things again

. . . cleaning his toothpaste and hair from the sink . . . thinking how fun it would be to treat Sundance to a little Therapy . . .

I was just getting into some pivots and swirls when I heard them down the hall.

"Come on, Lenny, lighten up."

"You're a slave of the System. You're—"

"Hi, guys." I opened the door, tried to smile. "You want to use the room a while?"

We were pulling away from Grand Junction . . . population of 28,000 . . . at five.

My lungs had grown numb from the haze in the lounge. My thoughts weren't any lighter. More and more doors seemed to be closing . . . or to have been locked all along. Life in Grand Junction or Denver or Rifle—these had never been options and never could be. I felt vaguely alarmed— and I didn't know why. The kids, the car, the dog, the ranch —I'd never even *wanted* them! But the thing of it was, they weren't options at all. Any more than Sam was. Or the Robot who'd fallen for Lenny.

They knew this in Grand Junction. They'd gathered on the platform in K mart clothes, with kids and dogs, to look through the windows and say with their eyes: Your life is not an option here . . . And where *you* live you don't belong . . .

Cornered on the other bench, Sam hiccuped forlornly. Gave me a sad little nod. Turned away.

I wasn't even an option.

We're twins, I thought. Some kind of twins. And for twins it just isn't an option.

I raised my Coors. And smoked away.

And was not surprised at all when the next announcement came:

"In just two more minutes, folks, we'll reach the Ruby Canyon!"

LIGHTS OUT

The Night began in the lounge car. It ended, above, in the dome. It started with a desert and ended with a scream.

But in between there was a glow.

Here is how it happened, then, the Night of the Day the World Ended for keeps.

By eight we'd been clicketywhirring through Utah for more years than I could remember. Miles and miles of barren rocks and boring, useless Utah green.

I'd been drinking for hours and thinking of doors. Of time's lies and filthy tricks. Of how I was thirty-nine, almost as old as the Fat Man was when—

How could he have gone like that, when we were getting close? What in the world had possessed life to pick that particular year? I remembered their trips to Toronto: mother arriving, as always, with home-cooked treats and shirts and socks . . . my father and I at two ends of the couch—with the Fat Man and Ghost Boy between us. I remembered the first time I saw my father winded by a flight of stairs. I remembered thinking, Jesus, hey, that guy is my old man. I remembered that last visit, the day after Carter's election. Victory celebration. My father and I with a buzz on. I remembered almost reaching out to take his hands and tell him, "Dad . . ." Then somehow the Fat Man just got in the way. And I thought, I'll be home in a couple of months and we'll have our talk. For sure. For life's the trip and time's the . . . wheels . . . I remembered the call, around midnight. The thrifty sedan with the gold New York plates had head-on-ed with a black Mack truck on the Queen Elizabeth. Not enough left to spoon into a cup.

"Harp?" Sam, leaning over me, dabbed at my eyes with a kerchief.

Well, I'd been hearing "Harpo," with *my* hair, for years. But never, never, quite like that.

I looked up. She smiled down. I considered smoking her. Instead, I inhaled her perfume and thought: I wish I was your option. I love your boots. I love your hair. Oh—

"FILTHY FLYING SNOWWWWW-BALLLLLL!"

We turned to see Wolf at the base of the stairs.

"WOMMMMMMMM-ANNNNNNN! Get your ass UP-STAIRS!"

"Sam—" I started.

"It's okay. I can handle Wolfy."

I watched them go.

I puffed and chugged.

And, almost manically merry, I watched Lenny appear with the Robot.

Through the great revolving door.

Of the Night of the Day the World Ended for keeps.

"Dodge, we've gotta talk to you!"

"Oh, Mr. Cunningham, please?" The Robot was holding *The Summer of Love.* "Were you really, *really* there?"

Up above, Sundance whooped.

And, God help me, I started to giggle.

Click.
Click.
Click.
Black.

That was how quickly nightfall came.

It was the bewitching hour. Through the inky windows of the *California Zephyr,* in the useless state of Utah, at eight-fifteen on the Night of the Day, twinkling lights in cottage homes made passes at the street lamps. Headlights in the distance sped like pairs of shooting stars. The sky was so black that it glittered. And for a short stretch the Night of the Day just blew away the Rockies and the Colorado blue.

We'd gathered in the dome car like primitives around a

fire. And while none of us knew that tonight was the Night, it was undeniably special. For the first time, Halley's, the bane of Wolf's existence, could really be seen in the heavens. And throughout the dome car tripsters were scrunched at the windows to see.

I know what you're thinking. We'd never thought twice of the comet. Okay. But now that it was here, you see, folks couldn't take their eyes away. This took the starch right out of Wolf. He wasn't booming now. He droned:

"There she is . . . *There* she is . . . flagging her tail like some ginrummy tart. Well, take another look, chumps, behind those ostrich feathers: her tail's as insubstantial as—as hope. As love. As life itself."

"Oh, Wolf," Sam cried. "Can't we talk?"

"You could look a week inside a space twice as big as the *Zephyr*—and not see a single speck!"

"Pipe down," someone muttered.

"What an asshole," another complained.

By and large, however, no one paid him any mind. And within a couple of minutes, I was lost with the rest.

So I lied:

"This was a lifetime before '68 . . . before history cracked and the tragedies came flapping like bats through the fissures: blood in the streets of Chicago and Paris . . . Sirhan playing Santa for Satan . . .

"This was in another world. In a magical, mythical city. Where stamps were a nickel. And acid was legal. And Golden Gate Park had a hill just for us: the slopes were so smooth and so green and so free the oak and eucalyptus trees could hardly stand to watch.

"At twilight you'd trip to the Fillmore to see Jefferson Airplane or Janis. You'd go there in a Magic Bus. They'd give you candy at the door.

"Inside, strobes exploded and light machines flooded the walls with weird seas, while girls from other planets blew dog whistles and capered.

"There was magic everywhere—in the Kool-Aid, on the stage. But what blew you away was the knowing. Before they even named it. That *this* was The Summer of Love . . ."

Click.
Click.
Click.
Black.

At eleven thirty, when we reached Salt Lake City, the Night was blacker than any I'd seen.

Some tripsters had gone for their luggage. Others to stretch in the station a while. Sundance had left, maybe with a new girl—for the one he'd been with looked as dead in her seat as the girl in the red leather mini. Lenny had left with a hard-on and his teary-eyed disciple. And Wolf was in rare form below, for the bar car was no longer serving.

I'd stayed on.

And Sam was there.

For a second I thought, what the hell, so we're twins . . .

But Wolf stormed back.

I slipped below, took the last steps in a tumble. The bar car was empty. That suited me fine. My heart felt as black as the Night of the Day. I stretched out and blew smoke rings and brooded, plotting away for the Nineties.

"Pivot!" I cried happily. "Smile! Kick! Wheeeee!"

"Hey, bud?" The old bartender tossed me a Coors. "Fuck the law. You *need* one."

"Thanks. Wake me up when we're out of the Eighties."

"I hear *that.* I *sure* hear that."

I snapped the ring. The can erupted in a geyser of white foam. I couldn't get enough of it, my fluff muff-diving in the froth.

It was a happy, happy drunk. The smallest things amused me. Smoking, for example, had artistic possibilities I'd never imagined before. I exhaled great clouds of Sams, nude and blowing smoke rings from in between their thighs.

Other things amused me. The station itself was amusingly quaint. And those huge-spoked ancient carts outside amused me to no end. The old locomotive amused me. Same as the train that I'd had as a kid. Jet black with silver rings on front. As if time had circled back in on itself and I was a child of six.

God, it was good to be *happily* drunk!

Bullethead amused me, too, when he finally showed on the platform. All those bags and aluminum cases. Well, he looked so amusing that I really had to laugh! You'd almost have thought for a moment that it wasn't him at all. The Burberry coat looked two sizes too small—it didn't even reach his knees! I'd seen better tans on hides. And Bullethead—ha!—hadn't had one. Oh, Lord God, how I giggled! He looked almost eight inches taller! I couldn't *believe* it! I smoked and I giggled. And when he turned and waved at me, I just cracked up completely. I'd thought I'd seen lavender specks in his eyes!

I watched him glide into the station. I smoked and chugged and giggled, watching him glide off like Sundance.

The bartender slipped one more Coors in my pocket and helped me to the stairs.

"You okay?" he said.

"God, yeah!"

"Wake *me* up when we get to the Nineties!"

"For sure!"

"Cheers, bub."

"Rock on."

I know I rocked, anyway, in my old seat in the dome car, as the comet sailed over Wolf's curses . . .

and the Actor was talking to Betsy . . .

and Lenny came back with the Robot . . .

and Sundance came out of the station, his long hair flying in the wind.

I slapped my knee and giggled, swiveling left to right.

"Dodge?" Lenny asked me.

The Robot said, "Like, wow."

I wanted to tell them. I tried to. But it was *so* amusing—Bullethead with Sundance . . . in the goddamn men's room?

"Life's the trip!" I cried. "Wheee, I'm the wheels!"

"Dodge," Len said. "Snap out of it. Christine's gonna move to the city with me."

Christine said, "Like, we want a place—"

"I know. A small cottage for two in the Haight."

The girl looked stunned. Lenny glared. But it was after midnight now. And, as I've been trying to tell you, there had never been a Night as black.

"I'm sorry, Len," I said. "Christine, I don't know what's wrong with me."

The two of them were holding hands and telling me about their plans at twelve-oh-eight . . . at twelve-oh-nine . . . when

Click.

Click.

Click.

"Blacke." The man with the tan, in his black leather duster, extended his hand to the girl. "Austin Blacke," he told her. "With an *e* for ecstasy."

"Hey!" I swiveled around, a sharp swing of forearm that should have sent him spinning. His arm didn't move. I had hit a brick wall. Christine looked at Lenny. Len looked at me. I looked at my arm in amazement, then up. I shouldn't have. I should have known. I should have remembered those curious *eyes* . . .

steel gray

with flecks of

lav-en-derrrrr . . .

"She'll be coming with me," he told Lenny and me. "If you gents don't have any objections."

Lenny started to bolt.

The eyes started to turn

as the train gave a lurch from the station.

I went with the lurch in a linebacker's charge—five-feet-eight (with insoles) and a hundred and forty-four pounds.

Blacke teetered backward a couple of steps. But before I could get to the good part, he snatched me right up in a dead lift, one hand, as if I had no weight at all.

"Look at me," he purred, real low.

No way. Uh-uh. Not this kid.

He didn't scare me. Nobody scared me. I'd beaten the Fat Man a long time ago. But—

Blacke lifted me higher, about half a foot, until my downcast eyes met his. And how I dug that *lav-en-derrrrr* . . .

Lenny cried something. So did the Christine. But no one was getting *my* lavender glow! I really liked being with Austin like this. He had me so neatly arranged and *controlled*.

He had me there.

He had me then.

With a big *e* for ecstasy.

When suddenly there was a shot. Or something very much like one. And Blacke turned his eyes, and mine followed, to see Wolf slap Sam again and then scream at the window:

"Come on, you piece of GARBAGE! Come on, let's see what you're made of!"

The distraction allowed me an instant to slip through Blacke's lavender squeeze.

I snarled. "Put me *down*, you damned ugly hyena!" and gave him a shot in the ear.

Blacke threw me like a shotput halfway across the room. I bounced off the door and fell hard, with a scream.

He wasn't purring now.

He roared, "Don't you ever—DON'T YOU *EVER* CALL—"

I'd had ten years of Therapy. But all of them were useless now. For the first time in my life, I felt another *mind* whup mine. I just lay and watched him come, an engine of destruction, the flaps of his duster around him like wings. I might have handled the body. But I had no tricks for that mind.

Master . . . I thought. *Master!*

You couldn't have stopped Austin Blacke with a cannon. Let alone a scream like any anyone had ever heard. Rage, pain, terror, grief . . . these would have been music to Austin as he set about breaking my neck.

What saved my neck was that the scream was so different from any we'd heard, even mine. More than fear or grief or pain, this was a scream of *wonder*. The second you heard it you knew you *must* look. Or miss out on something stupendous. Something uniquely compelling, and sad, and awe-inspiring.

Was the scream a woman's? Or was it a man's?

There was no way of knowing. The scream was too pure and too primal to tell.

Besides, by the time Austin dropped me everyone was screaming and staring at the sky. And Blacke the unstoppable, Blacke the relentless, was spinning and screaming and clutching his eyes.

Wolf had called, once too often, for Halley's to show us her stuff. And now the World was Ending in blinding showers of crimson, the *Zephyr* barreling on through the Night.

I could not scream, not loud enough. I whispergagged, "The World—The World—"

To left and right the tripsters started dropping around me like flies. Blacke met my eyes and crumbled hard as my head hit the floor.

The World!

THE SNOWBALL'S
REVENGE

 I've come to speak of Halley's with a great deal of respect. There may be bigger comets out there and there may be faster. But I don't think a one of them could have trashed us as neatly as she did. Another comet would have fucked us up while we were sleeping. Turned us into cinderblocks. Or artichokes. Or Krishnas. With as much emotion as a tidal wave or earthquake.

But Halley's has a certain something all the others lack.

Illustrious Halley's, incomparable Halley's has—a sense of humor.

And she wanted all of us in on her joke before she pulled the punch line. She'd even stopped the *Zephyr* to give us time to take it in.

We straggled onto our butts on the floor, skulls aching, and delirious, as if we had been drugged.

No one seemed overeager to move. It seemed enough for each to know that he or she was there. And so were we. The sky again was thunderless—and though heavily misted, not red now but blue.

"Sparks?" then, from below. Heavy footsteps up the stairs, like a drunk lurching out of an alley.

With the rest I started up—and felt the world start spinning, the footsteps now reverberating redly through my skull.

"Sparks? No way, man—this ain't Sparks!" The old barman from below staggered to one window.

"My God," he cried, "what is this?"

We formed a small circle around him.

The mist was wrong, we could see that. It seemed to stop at the top of the *Zephyr* and drop off a few yards beyond it, as if it had swallowed the train when it stopped. And the mist was swirling, too. Now and then, if you stood there a while, you'd catch glimpses through odd clearings. A tree. A road. The station.

"It *ain't* Sparks!" the barman repeated. "I know Sparks station like my hand."

Ahead, about a hundred yards, there was a station, all right. Flashes of beige with a green shingled roof. On the platform, figures . . . no more than figurines from here.

All this troubled the barman a lot more than us. For the wrongness came at us in flashes that matched our expectations.

The mist was wrong, though. Clearly wrong.

So was the faint pinkish aura below. The windows weren't quite low enough for us to determine the source.

But it was definitely wrong.

The barman, obsessed, muttered "Sparks . . . It can't be . . ."

We looked again. There was nothing to see but a station with some still lifes.

But suddenly our views converged when Sam and Betsy both cried "Here!" and we hurried along to the window.

About thirty yards from the tracks, on a parallel dirt road, a mint condition Packard was really tearing rubber, the driver's white scarf streaming behind him in the dust.

We were under considerable pressure, of course. And this *was* an astonishing sight. Still, there might not have been any fainting—

if only the car had been moving.

It was as still as the train. The racing car was a moment in time, frozen like a frame of film. Which disappeared before our eyes as the mist folded in on itself once again.

All of us, about this time, developed a furious interest in *Sparks.*

So we drifted again toward the barman to have another gander at the freshly painted station. And the frozen figurines.

Blacke looked as pale and shaken as anybody else.

"What's going on, old man?" he snarled. "What is it with the station?"

"Sparks . . . That station ain't been painted since I can't remember when. It's new!"

Blacke looked around the car like some caged, crazed animal. He grabbed his head. He ground his teeth.

Finally, he turned on Wolf, with all the malevolence in him, and shrieked, "What have you done to this train!"

Now, Wolf was a large man. And addled. And clumsy. And, at the moment, as crippled with confusion as the rest. But his face lit up with fear. And he might just have outrun the comet. If our door hadn't been locked.

Wolf raged at the lock till Sam pushed him aside.

She pressed the red handle. Finessed it. Gave it six pokes. Three punches. One scream.

I told them take it easy. This was time for level heads.

I asked the barman, quietly, "EMERGENCY PROCEDURES, POPS!!! HOW DO WE GET OUT OF HERE?"

The old man just looked at the window. "Relax, young fella. This ain't Sparks."

I swung him around and I shook him till I heard his dentures rattle.

He told me that outside the door there was a second, safety, switch. We could break the window. But we didn't have to. Because this *wasn't* Sparks. Besides—

The old man pointed, looney-eyed. "Here they are! Here they come! Don't you worry, they'll get us to Sparks!"

A faint cheer rippled through the car. In the aura-edged mist we could see the first lanterns of the men in Amtrak blue.

They stopped at our car, as at the one before it, to check the glow around the wheels. Confabulate. Evaluate. And mitigate the poundings on sealed windows, and the cries.

"SPARKS?" the old man screamed.

The way they looked and raised their palms, I nearly

screamed out "SPARKS?" myself. But the chief engineer screamed back something or other, pointing at his ears.

Through the glass, we couldn't hear a word, although he was no more than six feet away.

There and then, that was that for any lingering doubts: this fog was mighty peculiar.

My guess is our rescuers would have gone on to the next car. Suddenly, though, the pink glow from beneath began to billow out in puffs. And then expanding clouds. It licked at their ankles and toyed with their knees. And for a couple of seconds you'd never seen a happier or more contented bunch of guys. Six grown men drooling like babies and swinging their lanterns to some mystic beat.

We pounded on the windows—I think even Blacke did— and yelled frantic warnings. But they just stood there drooling, watching the pink fog engulf them.

All six started quivering then like great boilers ready to blow. You should have seen those lanterns shake! We pounded on the windows, screamed.

And watched them blow then, one by one, like a string of cherry bombs.

Or, better yet, imagine six vats of spaghetti sauce—with artichokes and mushrooms and great chunks of meat—going sky high in succession.

We might have colored the windows with chunks of our intestines, if the comet had allowed us time.

That wasn't Halley's style, though, now that she had our attention.

Along with control of the train.

A ferocious crack of thunder rocked the *Zephyr* on its wheels.

And then we started moving, as if we had no wheels at all, as smoothly as if we were riding on air, ten, twenty, thirty, forty, sixty miles an hour, then more, incredibly, relentlessly, while the heavens changed—

like that!

—from blue to black . . . to blue . . . and back . . .

Gather twenty people, the more freaked out the better, in a good-sized room. A few of them have to be screaming, and one should be ripping her hair, like Christine, in huge handfuls out of her skull. Your best friend should be comatose and foaming at the mouth.

Now picture a train that is flying on air, with nothing human at the helm. Not just on the straightaways, but over hills and around hellish curves and through tunnels and over scant bridges.

Now imagine strobelights going everywhere in sync. Day . . . Night . . . Day . . . Night . . . Tick . . . Tick . . . Day . . . Night . . . The sun shoots west . . . The moon scoots east . . . Regular as clockwork.

Now throw in the weather: reverse *varooms* and backward bolts, raindrops backing up off the roof.

Proceed then to the tricky part, the stereoscopic surreal collage:

Horses, planes, and autos, in pop-length flashes, all reversed . . .

Men backing *into* houses like cartoon characters on speed . . .

Houses deconstructing in frenetic blurs . . .

You begin to get the picture.

But don't forget the screams.

Or this: for us, the horror continued for more than seven hours.

Well, the barman was mad.

And Len was a wash, hugging *The Summer of Love* like a raft.

And Christine was already half-balded.

And Blacke had gone into some kind of a trance, he scarcely appeared to be breathing.

And Wolf was so madly repentant you'd think the comet might have stopped.

And Sam had passed out at one window.

And on.

What kept me saner, longer, was the insane compulsion to try to *figure* it. As thoroughly as I'd been figured by Blacke.

I scrambled to a corner seat. Closed my eyes and tried to think. The lighting was doing me, too, though, and soon I'd be flipping my lip. I made my way discreetly, lifting this, snatching that—a scarf, a pin, a shawl, a clasp. Presently the window was pretty nearly covered. And several others were doing the same, raiding the lost for relief from the lights.

I lit a Winston. No one complained. Secondhand smoke was the least of their griefs.

I closed my eyes and considered the facts, carefully, discreetly, not wanting to rile the comet.

Why Sparks?

While I smoked and figured, Pops called out the names of stops that had once been sure things on his map.

"Nine thirty . . . *Reno?*"

I figured and refigured, till suddenly it came to me—and though doomed as the rest, well, I just had to smile.

"Harp?"

Sam took a seat beside me. That heart-shaped face. Those red, bowed lips. Those eyes grown so suddenly steely.

"What's going on?" she said. "You know."

"All I know right now is *Sparks*. Suppose Pops was right and that station was new . . ."

Sam lost it, but just for a second. "You're nuts."

"Look out the window and say that again."

She didn't have to look, she knew. We were going further back with every spin of the wheels.

"The doors," Sam said.

"Pneumatic. They hadn't been invented yet."

"No air-conditioning. No lights."

"No goddamn radio," I said.

Pops chirped, a Halley's windup toy: "Nine forty-five, folks! Now approaching the snow-capped Sierras!"

Sam made a high-pitched keening sound and turned to watch the show.

I gave her chair a sharp tug back. "Keep your wits about you!"

"But how's he know the time? My watch—"

"His watch is busted just like yours. Forget him, Sam. He's out to lunch."

I lit up a Winston, inhaled for my life, and figured and refigured.

The sky flashed blue.

Then black.

And back.

While raindrops whippety-upped off the roof and thunder vanished in reverse. And the *Zephyr* roared on air, on straightaways and over hills and round sharp curves that swung our chairs and nearly launched us from them.

And, still, my mind kept returning to

Sparks.

"I think I know another reason why she picked out Sparks," I said. "The tracks are the originals, from Sparks to San Francisco."

"What are you getting at?"

I tried to smile bravely. "Wolf was in the comet's face from when we left Chicago. But Halley's waited until Sparks. How far back is she planning to take us? At the rate we're moving, there wouldn't have been any tracks here. What if the warp we're in has rules? Then maybe we can *figure* them."

Pops cried, "Nine fifty-seven! Hello, California!"

Involuntarily, I swiveled just as Sam did.

Flash.

Day.

Flash.

Night.

Flash.

Rocks.

Snow.

Flash.

The sun shot west, the moon raced east, a plane flew back out of its wreckage and whizzed twelve hours away in a

Flash!

I turned away, half-blinded, a dim light beginning to flash, though, inside.

What if, just supposing, the looney barman did know the right time? The right time on *his* clock for the stops.

"Ten-twenty—Truckee!"

The sun shot west.

The moon raced east.

And, in between, a tiny flash of a small gingerbread station. A blitz of backward scurriers.

Blue.

Black.

Blue.

And back.

Ten-twenty, though.

At least to Pops.

I tried to persuade him to join us, gently at first, and then strong-arming it. I would have had to kill him, though, to get him away from that window. I turned away from the light show outside, considering how to get through.

Sam, good twin, was wilier. "You're doing fine, Pops, keep it up. You sure we're—on schedule?"

The old man was astonished. "Been doin' this for forty years. That was Truckee, wasn't it?"

"Sure," Sam said. "I saw the sign."

Sam looked at me. I looked at Sam. I hadn't seen any signs. I said, "Sure!"

"Then it's ten-twenty," Pops said.

"Right!"

The sky turned blue.

The sky turned black.

The sun shot west.

The moon flew east.

And now, another nightmare: on parallel tracks just beside us: flash trains rushing in reverse.

I closed my eyes and focused.

"Pops, you reckon we're doing—the usual speed?"

The old man sighed. I was too daft. "We're doin' what we always do. Eighty on the straightaways and thirty on the curves. What else could we be doin'? It's ten-forty—Donner Pass!"

Back in our seats, we attempted to figure—as we held fast to our chairs.

Even if Pops knew the time . . . How fast were we going? How far left to go? Where would we end up—and why?

We were both still figuring when we heard the velvet purr over the screams and the flashes.

"What the hell are you two up to?"

My guess was, if we escaped, Blacke would probably still break my neck. But he was calm enough right now, in an eerie kind of way.

He closed his eyes and tapped one foot, swiveling back and forth.

Finally, he drawled, amused, "Man, isn't it just like a comet?"

"What?"

Blacke shot me an impatient look. "Forget the time, you idiot. Figure by the flashes. Once a second, on the dot. That's thirty days a minute. Sixty months an hour. Midnight, 1986, when we're in Salt Lake City. And, what'd he call out back in Sparks?"

"Nine A.M.," Sam answered.

"That's 1941," Blacke said. "When do we hit Frisco?"

"Four," I told him. "Uh, that's if—"

Just then there was a piercing scream. And Pops laughed hysterically, hanging on for life, as the *Zephyr* rounded a hairpin curve thousands of feet above earth.

"Eleven thirty!" Pops cried. "Jesus, how fast *are* we goin'?"

I swiveled around. It was madness to watch. I looked at Sam. I looked at Blacke.

"Better make that three . . . or two."

Blacke yawned indifferently. "We get there when we get there."

He crossed his legs, calmly nursing one foot, while we swiveled and clutched at our seats. He seemed as unaffected by the laws of gravity as the comet's *Zephyr* was. He closed his eyes. I hated him.

"One year's as good as another," he drawled. "Yeah, any time's just fine with me."

"Well, not to me it isn't—Sam?" I'd just seen something in her eyes, like the spark of a new kind of fear.

She cried, "No!"

I turned in time to see Wolf lurch and start pounding on the glass.

"You fucking bitch!" he screamed. "You whore! 'S that the best that you can do?"

The *Zephyr* took off like a rocket.

In the final stretch there were flashes of quiet heroism: the Actor, of all people, decking Wolf out with a roundhouse . . . Lenny somehow coming to, to comfort the skinhead Christine . . . Pops still calling out the stops, refusing to give up his map . . .

One of the bluehairs stood watch at one window, braving the flashes to look for marquees.

*"Phantom of the Opera—*that's 1925!"

And so it went. And on and on.

The sky turned blue.

Then black.

And back.

Three flashes every second now, as lightning bolted in reverse.

And rain pitted back off the roof to the clouds.

And roads under construction flashed back into dirt, the workmen like scurrying ants.

Onward through Colfax, a flash on the map. Blizzard of bright clapboard stores. Twelve thirty on the barman's clock. And more than halfway to the end of the road.

But if I'd been obsessed with time, it didn't seem important now, not in the way that it had been. Even the flashes, I had to admit, no longer really troubled me. I'd started to enjoy them. The way they strobed the orchestration of the screams and wails.

"One-twenty!" cried the barman, as an entire lumber-yard unloaded in a flash.

Sam called to me.

I answered, "Hmmm?"

She shook me hard and repeated some good advice I'd given.

"Keep your wits about *you*—right?"

"Hmmm," I told her, and turned back.

The sky went blue.

Then black.

And back.

And the times' new locomotives flashed, black lightning, in reverse.

"Two-twelve—Sacramento!"

Gone.

Like youth. Like truth. Like love. Like life. Just like old Wolfy had told us.

The sky turned blue.

The sky turned black.

The Sacramento River flashed scurrying pinpricks of strollers along its dusty banks.

"Come on, get with it! Help me!" Sam started shaking me harder as Pops, whose watch was really *running*, called:

"Two thirty-two, folks—Davis!"

The train, a mere rocket till this time, launched straight into overdrive on an endless straightaway. And there was no timing the flashes now as we raced head-on to whatever it was that the

ingenious comet

had in store for us.

Pops looked like a ghoul at the window, plucking at the last remains of his pathetic map.

"Harp?" Sam cried. "Snap out of it, *please*!"

Blacke chuckled darkly, all stretched out and still, while we swiveled and rocked and held on to our seats.

People were screaming and why shouldn't they, for time was a nightmare, you screamed till it stopped; and when it stopped—why, so did you.

I felt almost giddy about this. Not even my twin could get through my new wall.

But suddenly the sight of Blacke, stretched out so serenely, did. Something snapped inside me. I felt as if I'd been kicked by a mule. I didn't just hate him, I—I couldn't say.

I bolted up. I raised one hand. I grinned like a loon and screamed,

"TRAINS!"

as Pops called, "Three-ten—Suisson!"

I might have cried out "Dow!" or "Love!" or "Jesus
saves!" or "Ivory Soap!" It wasn't the word, but the fact that
I'd stood—a born leader of men with a Plan.

Blacke himself opened one eye for a look. And Pops for
once forgot the time as the waters of the San Pedro Bay
were blitzed with strobelit sailboats.

Now that I had their attention, though . . .

How best to explain—the Plan?

I thought I might soft-shoe around it, to start.

"Remember the spaghetti sauce back in Salt Lake City?"

Well, that didn't exactly have the intended effect. You'd
have thought I'd just pulled out a chainsaw.

"No," I said, "no, listen, wait! That's when the train isn't
moving! When time is stuck and, I don't know, the atmo-
spheric pressure . . ."

It was a tricky business, explaining the Plan, to begin
with. But with the *Zephyr* going about two hundred miles
an hour and the heavens flashing while I flopped like a doll
in the aisle . . .

"But we haven't hit any trains—*don't you see!*"

I needed them to see it. Then I wouldn't have to *say* it
and it wouldn't sound so crazy.

"Three fifty-six—now approaching Richmond!"

Pops sounded almost cheery, pleased that he'd held to his
map till the end.

How could I possibly tell them, how could I find the heart
to say—

"We've all got to jump from the windows!" Len cried,
suddenly cooler and madder than I. "There's a damn good
reason why we haven't hit any trains. It's physics. Simple
physics! As we go backward, so do they! Time travels as fast
as the *Zephyr* as long as we stay on the tracks. But outside
the window . . . If we jump—don't you see—*for a second*
—there'll be a crack we can slip through!"

I could have wept, this made such sense.

Pops chirped, "Four-twenty—S.F. Bay!"

The sky went blueblackblueblackblue as lightning
streaked back through the fog that shrouded the new Alcatraz.

But Austin Blacke had had enough. "You'll be torn to shreds," he snarled.

"Maybe," I told him. "But tell me something, Einstein . . . What if the train *doesn't stop* at the end?"

Suddenly the cool man with the tan looked almost as spooked as the others. As me. And I liked that. I liked that a lot.

I stripped the red safety guard off one window, threw it at him like a snake.

"Friends!" I cried. I shook my fist, Moses to the faithless. "You're headed for the Twilight Zone!"

Lenny added, brilliantly, "We're from the Sixties—trust us!"

I can't begin, even now, to figure out how everything went so totally wrong, all at once.

I saw Len whirl and head back for his seat.

I heard Wolf roar and start the charge of stampeding tripsters. Saw him fall beneath their feet.

I turned to see Blacke backhand Sam, knocking her out of his way.

I heard Pops call out, "Here she comes!"

Then Blacke had me by the throat. Then by the seat of the pants. And then he held me like a ram . . .

snarled, "After you, bub . . ."

and crashed me through two plates of Plexi into the eye of the storm.

Before I even had a chance to scream, "My God, what *are* you?"

FREE FALL

The eye of the storm is a lavender eye.

The eye floats serenely while worlds all around it fly off in tangents like great shooting stars. And time is a blizzard of moments like sparks.

The world of your mother. The world of your father. The world of their mothers and fathers, and theirs. Months shoot by and years shoot by, some once in the present, some once in the past, all time's favorite children now.

From the lavender eye you see spaceships and mummies . . . desktop computers and ancient quill pens . . . crossbows, slingshots, Magnums, stones . . . You see punkers and flappers and cowgirls and spacegirls and concubines to Attila the Hun . . . You see Kennedys dying and Mark Twain reciting and Nixon selling plots of land for hot-dog stands on Mars . . . You see men on the moon . . . You see Vikings on boats . . . You see soldiers in Shermans and nomads on camels and cavemen armed with old dinosaur bones . . . You see Jesus crossed . . . You see Ronald McDonald . . . You see Bogie and Byron and Elvis and Churchill and, yes, even Billy the Kid . . . You see a flapping of something like wings, long and black and leathery, from the receding *Zephyr* . . . You see Vlad the Impaler and Christopher Lee and Stephen King smiling benignly . . . You see your mother on the porch, her first kiss with your father . . .

You see it all from the lavender eye, which closes then to sleep and dream
and float
and fall
through time
after time.

BOOK TWO

SHOCK LANDING

Near midnight, my guess was.

A chiller.

The rain had stopped maybe a mile ago, after I'd walked for five miles or more by the side of the tracks, near the thickets. My first thought on awakening had been to disappear. As if even the raindrops had lavender eyes and might report me to Halley's—

Oh, *all-knowing, heavenly* comet!

But the raindrops just fell through the bush where I hid and soaked me through indifferently. Until I had myself convinced that Halley's was all through with me. There would have been more comfort in this if I'd known which way to turn.

Which way would lead to the desert? Which way into town? I began to reason, to figure, and to calculate. Finally, I flipped a coin. It landed heads. I followed the tracks to the right. The tripster's jacket inside out and over my head like a turban. My hands in my pockets. My eyes on the watch for some trace of the others.

But I walked. And I saw nothing. And I could not start to figure it. I thought: They've gone the other way . . . What if they're right and I'm wrong . . . But when one guess is as good as another, we're better off trusting the coins that we flip.

Rabbits sent me running into the thickets to hide. A coyote's howling sent me back quick as a fox.

I walked and hid. Walked and hid. The whistle of a distant train sent me howling to safety, where I rolled in a puddle, knees to my chest, eyes closed and hands over ears. I wasn't ready, no, not yet, not to be seen—or to see.

I walked some more and hid some more, till presently the darkness fell and I had the cold night to myself. I walked with nothing to guide me except a pale sliver of moon through the rain, and no way of knowing which way the tracks were headed.

I'd walked through the wasteland for hours, despairing of an end to it. But then the drizzle ended and there was some hope in that. And now I saw ahead of me the most welcome sight in the world.

I saw the first embracing mists of the unmistakable fog. A starting gun went off inside me and I started running.

For where there was fog, there was water.

Or there would be spaghetti sauce.

And either one was fine with me—I'd be *somewhere* at least, or be nowhere at all. I couldn't stand another hour of absolute lack of control.

When I hit the fog I screamed and threw my arms out, waiting. But the mist was white and sweet, and I breathed it in, rounding a curve in the tracks to let it engulf me completely.

And so it was that I stood in the fog, under a cool teasing sliver of moon, near the edge of Oakland.

I was cold and wet and lost, but somehow I also felt *grounded* again. I felt protected by the fog, which unveiled the details slowly.

To the left, I heard soft lappings of the icy Bay. In the distance, foghorns. But of San Francisco a man could see nothing that night in that fog.

And that was fine, for now, with me.

To the right, salt flats were crisscrossed with winding streams and pocked with wiry clumpings of grass.

The wind was blowing stronger now and it carried with it the commingled smells of salt and tar and seaweed.

I shivered again, less from the cold than the anticipation. The others—would I find them here? With a little luck, I figured, Wolf had been crushed in the lavender eye. And Austin, with that laugh of his, was probably dumber than dirt: he'd turn left. But what of Lenny? And twin Sam?

Through the misty muddle of distant shapes and lights, isolated details began to focus on my map.

What may have been a trolley car streaming behind it a long row of sparks . . .

Chimneys blazing orange-black from some local iron-works . . .

Ragpickers in tunics, there, working the stinkhills of Oakland's town dump . . .

Here, an abandoned wagon, keeled over on its side, spoke wheels idling in the wind . . .

I stopped beside the wagon. Considered long and carefully. And, in the end, decided to do what I did best: blend in. Pivot. Dodge. Evade. So, I buried the old tripster's jacket . . . my digital watch and my wallet . . . funky leather Love boots . . . paisley patches from my jeans . . . I kept the wet wool socks on. Barefooted might look just a little too strange. Wherever the time was, wool had to be *in*.

I lit the last Winston I'd know in this life, then buried the pack with the lighter.

I proceeded through the mist, considering where I should make my debut.

At the foot of B Street I stood beneath an old-time lamp that looked like a big grasshopper with its supporters and riggings. At last I could distinguish shapes.

Tiny boxlike houses with red roofs of oval slate.

And, just ahead, a sign that was as welcome as the fog: the something-or-other saloon.

Where there were men who were drinking, there were free drinks to be had. Sometimes cash. Always information, if you were subtle and cunning enough.

I saw shades pulled and curtains drawn, on the left, then on the right as I walked along. A dog barked once, then ran away, mewling like a cat.

Which, I thought, was mighty strange.

I was too busy figuring, though, to think about it twice. They had electric streetlights here . . . no TVs . . . but maybe phones . . . no radios . . . but newspapers . . . early 1900's . . . or late 1890's . . .

Nothing that a sly man couldn't get on top of quick.

They'd be like children in my hands. When had I failed, even once in my life, to get on top of the times?

Swinging doors on the saloon.

Heavy smoke beyond the doors and somebody pounding the ivories.

They smoke. They have pianos too.

All right, Dodge.

You're doing fine.

Now step in and knock 'em dead. Just hang loose and play it by ear.

I was struck like the match that spluttered and caught the second I walked in the door.

If you've ever been mugged, then you know what I mean: for you are no longer a *person* when you're at the end of a gun. You are no longer quite *human*. You are a small blaze of perception against a blizzard of details:

the dim lighting in a subway station . . . a pale patch of gum on the floor . . . the lacing on the mugger's shoes . . . a lone hair in the mole on his chin . . . a snatch of graffiti on one of the walls . . . a pigeon ruffling its feathers . . . the mugger's lips pulled back over his teeth and, what's that, a goatee on his chin . . . his baseball cap, no, it's a toque. . . .

You freeze, but it's not out, not yet, that flickering, crazy conviction that if you can, somehow, just take it all in . . .

Then you hear the awful click of something long—no, short—no, green—no, black—no, gold—no—oh-oh . . . And you surrender everything to the absolute darkness and coldness.

Well, Time was the mugger. And it stopped me cold.

I followed the match to the L-shaped tube projecting from the wall. Bracketed onto a short arm of the tube was a frosted-glass flowered shade. The underside of the brass tube had a tiny key-shaped handle. I saw one hand, extending from a starched and studded cuff, turn the key. And then a wedge of blue-edged flame softly filled the globe.

And sent my eyes careening off a dozen other gas lamps. And three glass-and-gas chandeliers.

It was, first, a world of light unlike any I had seen. Soft and dim, crude and raw.

I was burning myself now to take it all in. But Time was a mugger. And it had *some* gun. The blizzard was too cold, too fast.

The sawdust thick as snowfall on the hardwood floor . . . the long table laden with roast beef, turkey, pickles, cheeses, and stacks of brown bread . . . the mahogany bar with its gleaming brass rail . . . the back mirror reflecting tall and frosty steins of beer, walrus mustaches and Smith Brothers beards . . .

My eyes were caught by a flash to the right: brass nailheads glittering on yellow leather soles.

Left: wing collar.

Right: felt hat, shapeless as brown Jell-O.

Left, right, everywhere: voices now, sharper than bits of cut glass:

> "Quaker Sam says . . ."
> "More wind to ya!"
> "Can't get gay with her, you can't!"
> "You bet!"
> "Hooray!"
> "Quaker Sam . . ."
> "Pshaw!"
> "Oh, Lord, ain't that a break!"

Time was too cool for me. Time was too quick. The blizzard was too dark and thick, too woolly and too random. It ended with stretched mugger's lips, as Time cool-cocked the hammer—and I heard the nightmare click of silence all around me.

The faces in the mirror turned.

And the whole world exploded with Fat Men.

Fifteen or twenty, all lined in a row, with beach-ball bellies slung over their belts.

I felt so small.

I felt so lost.

The voices went off all around me like shots:

"Well, lookie here, another one?"
"*Injuns* get you, sonny boy?"
"*Train* wreck? Where's the deucin' train?"
"Robbers?"
"Come to steal—"
"Where you *from*?

Time was quick. But no match now.

Outside, the mist was thicker than some movie dream machine's. I couldn't see. I didn't care. I flew back the same way I'd marched into town. At the foot of B Street, I zig-zagged sharp and hopped a fence and dove underneath a low porch, where I rolled all the way and curled up in a ball and cried myself to sleep in maybe half a minute flat.

Morning. I'd always loved morning. And dawn was the soul of the morning to me. The first glow of rosy light like the opening riff of a muted trombone. Smoothsliding up to the high notes, those glissandos of orange and gold.

Whatever else I'd slept on—including, my guess was, ground glass and old bones—there had been abundant plans for my escape from Oakland.

I'd begin by torturing the owner of the house. A few Therapeutic locks would tell me all I needed: year . . . date . . . rate of exchange . . . lines the ladies fell for . . . and what the hell was going on . . .

I'd have him cook me breakfast then.

We'd eat. We'd chat. He'd understand that the comet, not I, was to blame. I'd use a pillow, so he'd feel no pain. I'd take some clothes and cash and—

"Ohhhhhhhhhhhhh!
Jenny Jingo is a bellllllllllllllle,
And when she sings, oh,
I feeeeeeeeeeeeellllllllllllll
soooooooooo
swelllllllll!"

Footsteps coming down the steps. A rumbling bass voice with them.

                    duuuuu-tiful
"She is my   gal-l-l-l!
                         beauuuuu-tiful

          smiliest
My wiliest
                    beguiliest
                              pal-
                                  l-
                                     l-
                                       ll!"

Muted shuffling in the dust. Pufflike clouds around the
shoes and a flowing cassock. Whistling then, rather cheery
at first; then softer and deliberate, the way one whistles in
the dark, not all that convincingly.

I snaked along on my belly to the side of the porch where
he'd stopped.

A row of hedges blocked my view. Large mulberry bush
in the center. Through scant clearings in the leaves I heard
the whistling fade, then stop, and saw the black shoes lead
black cloth.

"Forgive me, Father," the voice said. "When will I learn?
When will it stop? The devil guys me once again. I begin
this day for You . . . not with prayer . . . not with praise
. . . but with downtown music from the darkness of my
youth. Pshaw! Forgive an old and tired man who is still a
prisoner of the young sinner within him. The flimflammer.
The corker. Forgive me. And forgive us all if . . . If you
sent them, Lord, give us a sign!"

The priest kneeled, clipped at the chin by the house's
baseboard. I glimpsed him through the branches almost
pointillistically: specks of white collar . . . black cassock
. . . gold cross . . .

Surely my deliverance from Oakland was at hand.

He wanted a sign? Well, he'd have one.

If only I could pull it off.

My mentor Wandini, from Houdini's Museum, could have
set that bush on fire with only a snap of his fingers. And

thrown his voice so high you'd swear it had come from a cloud.

The distance—three feet—was no problem. But would even Wandini have known the right words?

My belly rumbled noisily. Low down, like a circus drum.

"Who is it?" the priest whispered. "Is someone there?"

The specks came at me like a wall as he started leaning in, gathering his courage.

Stark terror is faster than cunning. Or sense. I doubt I'll live to give a speech that I would sooner forget.

"Bless you, Father. You have sinned. But the devil has not wholly—guyed you. Pshaw! The Lord loves young—corkers as well as old priests. Verily I say to you that—downtown music suits the Lord. Uh, until eight A.M. or so. And, as a sign of the Lord's love for you . . . He will send a messenger. A very special kind of dude. And now, as a sign of your faith in the Lord . . . you will leave, beneath that—swell mulberry tree—"

"Dear God," the priest cried.

I quick-slithered backward a couple of yards, over the ground glass and bones.

"You're—one of them," I heard him say.

"Oh God!" I shrieked. "Deliver me!"

"It seems . . . the Lord just has, my son. But hurry, there's no time to waste."

ON THE RUN IN BAGHDAD

 The Oakland ferry pulled out of the slip at seven with three merry toots. On the twenty-sixth of March. In the year 1906. The two-decker, flat-bottomed steamer sailed through a veil of mist beneath a cherry blossom sky. The waters were as docile as the minds of sleeping dolphins.

I'd never been a priest before. Even if the great cassock had fit (the old pastor had weighed over two hundred pounds), I would have felt as lost in it as I did in his broad black sombrero. And the rubber galoshes that slopped on my feet.

But, in light of what I'd learned, the disguise agreed with me. We'd only had ten minutes till the pier-bound wagon passed. But the minute the priest started talking, I knew that I'd better be on the first boat. He'd gone on a mile a minute while fetching the cassock and so on. And I was still reeling now, on the *Glencoe*'s upper deck, trying to put it together.

There'd been about a dozen of us in the *Zephyr*'s dome car. And Oakland had been flooded—in about that number —with rather odd arrivals, beginning the first week in March. The priest couldn't say just how many. And no one was sure of the date of the first. But by the third week the whole town had been talking. And those who didn't have a tale knew someone who knew someone who knew someone who did. A tale about some *stranger* just walking up and wondering what time it was . . . what year it was . . . and where on earth he was. They'd showed up, days apart, knocking on doors, walking in bars, begging for money and food.

One claimed that he'd been robbed. One, attacked by Indians! Several had been in a train wreck, but couldn't account for the train. And on and on and on.

I'd been the first out the window. I'd been the last to show. And, in between the two events, the others had made a fine mess of my plans. You didn't just walk in a time warp like that. You went in sly. You went in cool. You played it by ear and were subtle. Hell, just like I'd been, right?

As each stumbled in and blew town, his mind blown, he left a trip wire for the next. And those wires got higher and higher and higher. Clothing was stolen from clotheslines. A gray-bearded man was seen robbing the church's wood donation box. A few days before my arrival, two elderly women walked into a bank—to cash what they called traveler's checks.

Bad . . . Bad . . . Very bad . . . A wonder I hadn't been shot dead on sight. But they had all passed through Oakland. And San Francisco had always been kindly to strangers. The thing to do was catch up quick before they got way out of hand. They needed a teacher. They needed a guide. Someone who knew a few things about time. About keeping ahead of the wheels.

Well, I'd been in worse jams than this one, I guessed. There'd be some way out of it with just a little luck. And a lot of cunning. Besides, there was some consolation: No one had seen, or heard tell of, a stranger remotely resembling friend Blacke.

Way to go, Austin! Dumber than dirt, like I'd thought. Took a left on the tracks and was off in the desert, dying of thirst and not giggling for once.

And so, as the *Glencoe* sailed across the Bay, I was busy figuring while conducting the world's greatest study of shoes. When suddenly two high-gloss wing tips squeaked right up beside me.

"Mornin', Father, how are you?"

"Bless you, my son, bless you." His laces, I noted, were made of brown leather and these I proceeded to study.

"Bang-up weather, Father, eh? Dollar to a paper dime we won't see rain on this one!"

"God's will be done," I told him. Those yellow soles were like thick slabs of down-home creamery butter. I tried to picture them walking away, hoping the image might catch. But nooo.

"Father," he said, "what do you think—I mean, about the *strange*— Say, Claire! C'mere a second, darling. That's the proper caper."

Click click click click click.

"I want you to meet Father—"

"Father?"

The woman, Claire, had a voice like a bell. So clear and so light in its calling that I might have forgotten, if I'd been less cunning, to fix my attention right off on her shoes. I did not forget, though. They had my full attention. Here were shoes to study all the way to San Francisco.

Claire's shoes were exquisite, of supple black leather with buttons of newly cut mother-of-pearl. Crisply wrapped around the toes were bands of scarlet satin.

"Father—Oh, listen, Elmore!"

A tinny jingle from below. Trumpet, bass, and banjo. Music, though, to my poor ears, for I was now forgotten.

Elmore boomed, "Why, that's—"

"*Our* song." Claire sang a couple of measures of "The Ching-a-Ling Dong Fong Song." She stopped and cried, "Oh, Elmore, I want to hear 'The Goo-Goo Man'!" Then added, almost dreamily, "Darling, could we go below and have just one small, teensy *smile*?"

"God, Claire—sorry, Father—it isn't even morning yet."

"But I thought we could . . . share one."

I had no way of knowing exactly what a "smile" was. But, judging from the rush of shoes to the lower deck, my guess was that this was a floating saloon. And Happy Hour started sometime around dawn. I could have used a smile myself. But what I needed most was time . . . to figure and refigure . . . how the others had got there before me . . .

I raised my head an inch or two. Saw:

Elmore's belly straining against a brown plaid worsted suit . . . striped pink shirt stiff as a board . . . French cuffs studded with gold links, set with amber cat's eyes . . .

Claire's large-boned hands on her corseted waist . . . blue calico skirt with a gator-skin belt . . . shirtwaist of pink linen that almost crackled as she breathed . . .

I dropped my eyes. I needed time. Time to adjust to *their* strangeness.

"Go in peace," I managed. "The Lord has no objection to . . . a smile in His name. Go now and . . . more wind to ya!"

Elmore laughed, a cannon's boom.

Merry tinklings of Claire's bell.

Then, happy clickings of her pumps as she followed his wing tips below for a smile.

Close the missile. Clutch the rail. Prepare for San Francisco now. Wade in slowly, by degrees, with your first sight of:

Alcatraz. It isn't the boneyard it was in your day, of crumbling concrete and burned-out wood frames. Today the island has a compact, almost well-designed look. White-stoned, red-roofed buildings nestle crisply on the rocks. Towny streets in T-squared grids. New lighthouse planted in emerald green.

Sea lions sunbathing on jutting rocks as we circle on in toward the harbor.

Ships innumerably nuzzled at the endless line of docks. Mass of riggings blurring into cherry blossom sky. Behemoth hulks—green, black, and gray—straining at their mammoth chains, flanks opened, and cargo, like entrails, spread out in wild disarray. Sailors and stevedores swarming like ants around squealing pulleys and rattling blocks and coughing hoisting-engines.

Skyline calling to you now.

Easy. Easy. Raise your eyes.

See the terraced rows of shambleshanties rising from the waterfront, spreading over, pell-mell, the profusion of hills. Epic confusion of chimneys and roofs dotting the dozens of drops. One-story shacks rivaling two-story neighbors for nods from cocky new 'scrapers below: knee-high, but

horny, tots already spilling their seed in the night for canyons of their kind to come.

Ferryboat pulling now into the slip as shoes begin to shuffle to the gates where we'll debark.

I had the black padre sombrero pulled down halfway to
my ears. And I lowered my knees as I shuffled, sinking more
deeply into the line.

My galoshes flopped, on top, like a great pair of Dumbo
ears. The soles slapped at the glistening boardwalk.

I followed the line through a bank of rear gates into the
Ferry Building, a long stone garage with a low shingled roof.
I forgot about shoes on the spot.

Queues of Fat Men mobbed cashiers with mutton chops
and bushy beards.

Porters in red uniforms loaded luggage on low carts.

Flurries of arrivals rushed the transports at the doors:
carriages and buggies, from graveyards of blurred photographs, now eighty years younger than I was.

The Dumbo ears were flopping as I hurried on my way.
At the back of one carriage, there was a clearing in the
activity's hum. I paused a sec to catch my breath and heard
somebody say:

"Guess what? They just caught two old women. Heard
tell they was really *strange*! Spendin' funny money."

I snatched the first piece of luggage I spied.

Scurried through the first bay door.

And was promptly blown away, along with my flying sombrero.

In my day, we'd call the city Baghdad by the Bay. Suddenly, it was as strange as ancient Baghdad to me.

The world was reborn in a nightmare of sound:

cries and shouts and whistles . . . clanging bells and
whirring glass . . . heavy clipclops of shod hooves . . .
jouncings of the carriage springs . . . wheels wrapped in
iron crashing on cobbles . . . wood groaning . . . chains
rattling . . . leather creaking . . . whips cracking . . .
whinnyings and snortings . . .

The world of sound was then reborn into the world of traffic.

Cable cars still rode the slots, sometimes just seconds between them. But now on pairs of outside tracks there were horse-drawn street cars, too, kerosene lamps flickering in the early morning light. Outside these were passing lanes for:

wagons, chocked with crates and sacks, pulled by tandem teams of drays . . .

two-wheeled hansoms . . .

four-wheeled landaus . . .

gurney cabs . . .

sleek, polished phaetons . . .

and, darting through and around them, honking automobiles, big-wheeled, with pneumatic tires and clubby wooden spokes . . . brass lamps above the rads in front and over sleek curves of their fenders . . .

And then the world was born again into the world of figures.

I saw:

newsboys hawking the early editions . . .

waiters daring traffic with cloth-covered trays . . .

plumbers with their pockets stuffed with wrenches and pliers and sections of pipe . . .

carpenters with wooden tool kits . . .

streetworkers holding long shovels and picks . . .

clerks and shopgirls hurrying on, checking their watches with quick nervous looks . . .

businessmen with boutonnieres . . .

And then the world born again into the world of costumes.

There were:

fur-collared, ankle-length topcoats . . .

bonnets with ribbons tied under the chins . . .

braided black jackets with cloth-covered buttons . . .

head scarfs, capes, and brooch-pinned shawls . . .

shirtwaists tucked into velvet skirts trimmed at the waists with huge lavender bows . . .

weighted canes with thick gold heads . . .

black cutaways and tall silk hats . . .

suede gloves and patent-leather shoes . . .

And then the world was born again into the world of the street.

Market Street, as thick with poles as the harbor was with masts, thousands of pigeons on crossarms and black wires that ran on for miles . . .

corner drugstores with window displays of bright liquids in great jars . . .

stationers' stores with newspapers tacked on bulletin boards on the walk . . .

barber shops with red-white poles, cigar stands in the vestibules . . .

restaurants with oysters by the hundreds in the windows, and pigs and cows of china topping mounds of navy beans . . .

butcher shops with dramatically hung, freshly slaughtered carcasses . . .

cast-iron-framed department stores, their show windows stretching almost to the walk, with waist-high rails of polished brass . . . ribbons and yard goods unfolded from bolts onto supporting stools . . . enormous double doors of brass . . . doormen's boots reflected in glossed entrances of marble tiles . . .

And, blocks ahead, a miraculous sight: the upper tiers of Baghdad's crown. The original Palace Hotel. Fat paunches of bay windows, wrapped around the city block. More imported marble there than in all of Italy. I doubted it had ever looked more sure of itself than this morning.

Soon its flames would torch the sky. The Big One was coming and this was the year.

Suddenly I felt exposed, as a sort of cheat in Time. For I knew something dreadful would happen—but when? I knew the year. So had Halley's, the bitch. But what were the month and the date!

I saw the flames and heard the screams, and knew I had to warn them, but—

(Heard tell they was really *strange!*)

I ran, from fear.

I ran, from grief.

From guilt and confusion and anger, I ran.

I might have run into the Palace, if I hadn't first run out of breath. And dropped the stolen carpetbag. Which opened at my feet.

I took one look and blessed my stars. I took a sharp left on Montgomery, slipped right into an alley, got rid of the cassock as fast as I could, and covered my jeans and striped collarless shirt with a far better disguise.

Wrong again.

The raincoat had belonged to Elmore or one of his well-fattened kin. It hung, in great folds, from my shoulders and collapsed like a great circus tent to the belt, then billowed out in canvas waves to the flaps of the galoshes.

I felt absurd. I was absurd. I stood out like a damn circus clown. I stopped again at Montgomery, beside a cluster of lamps, and waited for the screams to start. The phaetons passed. The landaus passed. The cable cars and horsedrawn carts continued on their journeys. The neatly turned-out figures in their ribboned bonnets and smart cutaways, their hoopskirts and Prince Alberts, passed. Now and then a head might turn, an eyebrow arch. But no one screamed. A child grinned. A baby cooed. A horse whinnied, happily, passing.

I turned and looked around me. And was promptly wonderstruck by my own reflection in the window of a bar. Those Harpo curls, so windtossed they looked like a bad vaudeville wig. The greatcoat and galoshes.

Wait . . .

Could it possibly be—a *new Plan* ?

A wino in a stovepipe stumbled up beside me.

"Pshaw!" he cried.

I cried "Pshaw!"

We cried "Pshaw!" together as I swapped my carpetbag for his battered stovepipe.

There were two ways of blending, they used to tell us at Pinkey's. The middle ground is safer, if a man has time to reach it. But, hard-pressed, a man can blend in at the far extremities, if he has the luck and the nerve.

I had one silver dollar left from the two I'd been given in Oakland. I decided to go all the way. So I hailed a speeding cyclist—and gave him the buck for the horn on his bike. I was broke. But, as a mute, I'd be out of harm's way with the lingo.

I turned to the window, tilting the hat back to show off a little more curl. And cinched the belt tighter, as snug as a corset, to blow out the billows some more.

Harpo, eh? Well, thank *you*, Sam. If life wants a clown, fine with me. Let 'er rip.

I took a breath and capered into the Yellowstone Bar.

God himself had chosen the stage for my debut.

Bas-relief ceiling of satyrs and nymphs. Flickering gas lamps and glass chandeliers. Biblical landscapes with Rubenesque nudes. White-jacketed waiters attending a counter with caviar and clams and shrimps . . . roast beef and lamb and turkey . . . French bread and dark bread, corn bread and muffins . . . chopped olives and cabbage and fruit . . .

I had the waiters' attention right off.

My own was fixed on the Fat Men at the brass-railed mahogany bar.

I stretched my lips back in a Harpo-like grin, gave the horn three mighty honks, and set about, absurdly, the grim business of survival.

STEREOPTICON I

I

(March 25—One day before Dodge's arrival)

He remembered waking from the dream of the lavender eye. He remembered understanding, almost the instant he woke: the others would be scattered, with days between arrivals. Weeks. He remembered his night flight from Oakland, in no particular hurry at first. He remembered the silvery sliver of moon and how, by the time he landed, his hunger had grown ravenous. For blood. Any blood at all. He remembered thinking how curious this was . . . because he'd never needed blood, not in itself, since that African summer of magic, except when the moon had grown full.

Snake Tricks . . . Bat Tricks . . . *Beauty* Tricks . . . were child's play to Austin Blacke.

Who had, somehow, fed ruinously. And now sat, pale and shaken, still trying to figure out what had gone wrong.

The Night has Rules . . .

I won't obey!

Stick to the Classics . . . It starts with the—

"Sir?"

Blacke stirred, painfully. The time had come to feed. On food. They'd been wrong about that. But then, what else was new? The Twelve had been wrong about everything else. There was pleasure, still, in food. There was also energy—primitive and crude, but real to one who knew how to extract it. Despite one limitation, imposed by the Night, in its *passing*.

The waiter set a crisply folded paper down before him. Along with a red velvet menu. He overturned the blue porcelain cup and filled it with dark coffee from a steaming silver pot. He set the pot down on a matching etched tray.

"May I take the gentleman's cap for him, please?"

Blacke removed his bowler, wistfully eyeing the pulse in that throat. He turned his eyes as the sickness started kicking in again.

"The gentleman would like," Blacke said, "for you to come back in five minutes or so." He fixed the white-jacketed youth with a look—

that had no effect whatsoever.

"If the gent don't mind his manners, I'll be back in twenty. This here is the Palace Hotel, Jack."

The boy was gone before Blacke could reply. Just as well. There were no words for the anger he felt. The fear. Or the confusion. His skin had turned paler than Malcolm's. When had his feet ever troubled him so? Since his magical African summer, when he'd commenced his changes, his feet had become riddles he couldn't quite solve. Now and then the arches felt almost entirely numb. From time to time his ankles throbbed, for no apparent reason. And, when he needed not just blood, but a specific type of blood, the soles of his feet were on fire. Like now!

Easy . . . Easy does it now . . . Perhaps they were barometers . . . indicating what was required to *level* the blood he'd so drastically changed . . . The thing to do was love the feet, heed their strident messages . . .

Blacke fingered the menu, still working things out. The feeding had been disastrous, yes, and his strength had never been lower. But the room had not been bare of riches that he *could* digest. He had five hundred dollars in greenbacks and gold coins. He was well dressed as a man of the day: custom double-breasted suit, with broad shoulders and silk-faced lapels . . . striped double-pleated shirt of muslin and pure linen . . . one-pound-silver watch fobbed in the black-braided vest . . . knee-length black embroidered hose . . . and walking shoes (a size too large, for which he was thankful—

Feet . . .)

THE YEAR WAS WELL BEFORE HIS TIME. BUT THE ROOM
HE WAS IN WAS ALREADY BEGINNING TO FEEL—*familiar* to
him. Fine lace curtains on the door. Rich sterling and cut
leaded crystal atop white linens edged with silver lace.
Straight-backed chairs upholstered in ribboned felt of royal
blue that matched the floor-to-ceiling drapes. Four great
crystal chandeliers with dozens of porcelain gas jets. Memories bled from Harry White and the bluehair on the train
flickered, vaguely, in his blood. In time, with proper feeding, the memories would crystallize into a feel for this time.
Old blood was tired blood, but theirs would serve him well.

Blacke opened the menu, fingers trembling with anticipation.

LUNCH ONE

Appetizer	*Fruits de Mer of Lobsters, Shrimp, and Scallops*
	Brandy or Table Wine
Course One:	*Consomme Royal, Pheasant Stuffed with Prunes and Chestnuts, Oysters Casino*
	Cognac
Course Two:	*Fillet of Beef Wellington, Salad, Camembert and Brie*
	Table Wine
Course Three:	*Brandied Liver Pâté, Duck à la Ravennaise, Shallots, Beef Marrow*
	Brandy
Dessert:	*Iced Sherbet*
	Champagne
	Cigar

He thought he might die, in the state he was in, *passing*
just a single course.

But if he did not feed—and *soon* . . .

He turned the page. Began willing his eyes to see himself
passing

LUNCH TWO

when his attention drifted to the folded half of headline:

ND DEAD IN ROOM!

Blacke opened the paper to read it in full:

BAY MILLIONAIRE FOUND DEAD IN ROOM!

He saw his victim's photo, within an oval frame, beside a crude sketch of the corpse. Beneath, stacked subheads screamed:

FAMED KLONDIKER DIES SUNDAY
AFTER CUTTING OWN THROAT
IN PALACE HOTEL

HACKED, GASHED, AND SLASHED THROAT WITH
RAZOR
BUT POLICE FOUND LITTLE BLOOD

IS SAID TO HAVE BEEN PUTTING AWAY
TWO AND THREE BOTTLES
OF WHISKEY DAILY FOR SOME TIME

LONG YEARS IN THE ICE AND SNOW,
AND INSUFFICIENT DIET,
BROUGHT ON RHEUMATIC SEIZURES

Blacke whispered, "I've been poisoned!"
By a healthy-looking, filthy-rich, diseased, rheumatic drunk!
He heard the waiter's quiet "Sir?"
Austin looked up in alarm.
His own blood, customized, was eighty years from theirs!
And he lacked both time and strength to find the humans from the train.
"What's your poison?" the boy asked.
Blacke responded instantly with a scream-torn *passing* of quarts of red and black.

II

(March 21—Five days before Dodge's arrival)

The Montgomery Block was the only real rival had by the Palace Hotel. The Montgomery Block was four floors high and occupied a city block. Its stone walls, as thick as the Palace's, were set on giant redwood logs sunk deep into the ground. The Montgomery Block was earthquake proof. The Montgomery Block was fireproof. The Montgomery Block habitués did all the shaking and blazing.

Mark Twain had taken rooms here. Ambrose Bierce. Jack London. Frank Harris. Oscar Wilde. In the basement steam room, *Tom Sawyer* had been sweated out . . . *The Devil's Dictionary* . . . *The Call of the Wild* . . . *The Picture of Dorian Gray* . . .

The sureness of his karma came close to humbling Wolf: He would become immortal thirty years before his birth.

He'd nearly blown it yesterday. Yes, Oakland had been a real nightmare. But he was in the city now. And the silver he'd snatched seemed a fair enough price for the beatings he'd once had from nuns.

Still, his first steps would have to be careful and sly. And it was these he plotted in the rear of Papa Coppa's, the Bohemian café.

Cartoon black cats topped the walls, with calligraphic names underneath them: Aristotle, Goethe, Dante, Rabelais, Verlaine, Kant . . . The walls themselves were covered with drawings in charcoal and chalk: Fat waiter with cartoon balloon under pasta-laden tray—"Paste Makes Waist." Devil with a giant wand. Rubenesque nymphs with a banner—"Oh, Love, Dead, and All Your Adjectives Still in You!"

Dead . . . No, Sam couldn't be dead . . . She was here and in good time he'd find her . . . But first . . . *Joke loser*? . . . *Bum*? . . . Let her stew for a while . . .

Fame was a serious business.

The waiter came over to refill Wolf's mug with more fresh-roasted mocha. All you could drink for a nickel. Turkish Trophies cigarettes—line drawing of a sultan with two bare-breasted beauties—lethally potent and ten for a dime.

He could get used to these prices. The Sunday paper, a nickel. Wealth of ammunition here for his initial foray against the citadel.

The Sunday S. F. *Chronicle* was a rather startling cross between the later *Chronicle*, the *National Enquirer*, and *The New York Times*. The front page was decidedly *Times*-like in its crisp alignment of columns. But stiff photographic portraits in hand-drawn oval frames were joined everywhere, at the hip, with lurid tabloid sketches. And, of course, the stacked subheads would take some getting used to.

WILD WEST TACTICS CATCH A BURGLAR

POLICE SHOOT UP AN EMPTY HOUSE TILL ONE COMES OUT

HE IS A SMALL BOHEMIAN BUT HE'S THE MAN SAYS CAPTAIN HAYES

The news itself was a mystery, and something he'd better steer clear of for now, knowing nothing at all of the times:

PLAIN WARNING FOR GERMAN EMPEROR

BRITAIN WILL SUPPORT THE FRENCH PLANS FOR MOROCCO

DARK CLOUDS ARE SEEN BY EDITORS GLOOMY OUTLOOK FOR THE COMING YEARS SUSPICIONS ALL POINT TO GERMAN EMPEROR

GOULD AND HARRIMAN LOCK HORNS OVER OAKLAND TERMINAL

GREATEST RAILROAD WAR IN STATE'S HISTORY HAS NOW FAIRLY BEGUN

Then again, the city desk had real possibilities.

In a complaint for divorce filed yesterday, Mrs. Louise A. Covey complains of the alleged fascination by her hus-

band, Wesley J. Covey, of the fair sex. According to her allegations, he claims to have a wink of the eye that is irresistible to women. . . .

Wolf chortled, lit up a fresh Turkish, and flipped to the editorials.

Chad Williamson, Crime Lord, has a moral intelligence scarcely higher than that of a trained chimp; look at the low, cunning light in the small, rapacious, vulturelike eyes; look at that low, dull-comprehending brow; the small sensual mouth; the soft puffy fingers with the weak thumbs, indicating how he seeks ever his own comfort before others!

The society page—*Lady Yarbro?*

There is not as yet that excess of social excitement which was prophesied for the New Year, and the Season still goes very limpingly. . . .

The ads—dear God, the Stone Age!

Find a child with dimples and chubby arms and legs and you will find a healthy child. Find one with drawn face and poor, thin body—and you will see one that needs Wilhemena Relling's Emulsion!

Wolf was still considering the endless possibilities when he heard four shots and screams. He raced to the window to see a tall man raise his pistol calmly. And put a fifth shot cleanly through a fallen woman's eye.

He took off like a shot to the scene of the crime.

III

(March 15—Eleven days before Dodge's arrival)

Oh, Wolf! Where are you, Wolfie? Help!

Sam was in hell. This was certainly hell. And she had been condemned for sins that she could not imagine. She did not know the year or date, but knew the time was wrong, for her . . . inescapably, basically wrong. She'd known this the instant she'd stopped at the dump heap, thinking, ah, Chinese, they'll help. She'd known it was wrong from the looks in their eyes. She'd tried to run, a foolish girl who'd got unstuck in time. But she'd already walked for miles. The chase had been a short one. And she remembered nothing after the tea they had forced her to drink. Nothing until her arrival, hog-tied and delirious, and dressed in a blue cotton tunic,

in hell.

Hell was a packed room, the size of a warehouse, over-hung with an opium haze. Hell had about a hundred chairs for smoking and chattering ghouls in thigh-length baggy tunics . . . wooden shoes and coolie hats. Hell had a platform the width of the room, manned by evil-looking thugs with long queues wound tightly on top of their skulls. Hell had crates marked "dishware" lined at the edge of the platform. And in each crate, from the mainland of China, were girls as young as twelve. And eight.

Hell reserved these delicacies, though, for after the opening bids. In which grown women of fifteen and up were marched to the platform and stripped.

The girl behind Sam spoke some English and tried to explain the importance of not ending in a "cow yard." The girl was sixteen and about four-foot-nine, long hair pulled back in a chignon. Her name was Hay Ming Lee. She had an almost horsey face, but seven gold teeth she was proud of—which might earn her a place in a "crib." The rope-binding on her feet, which forced her to walk on her toes, might even lead to a "parlor." The girl told Sam to be "Ah Toy." Oh yes, Ah Toy was a *good* name for Sam!

"Ah Toy very popular. Keep you out of cow yard good."

Hay Ming Lee worried that Sam's teeth were white. And that Sam, at twenty-nine, was—very sorry, body maybe not be good.

"So pretty name important, hey? You be Ah Toy and be safe."

Sam smiled bitterly.

From the bodies she'd seen on the platform—pint-sized, bony China dolls—her own was the least of her worries.

One of the thugs on the platform barked some order in Chinese with a flourish of his axe. And the old ragpimp from Oakland echoed the cry to his girls: Sam, Hay Ming, and two girls as ugly as any she'd seen.

Come on, girl, think. If you're in hell . . . try to stay clear of the cow yards, at least. Whatever a cow yard may be.

Hay Ming Lee nudged Sam, who headed the line.

"Him Lim Poon Lee. Head Boo How Doy tongs. Very bad. You chop-chop—Oh!"

The ragpimp screamed at Sam again and Hay Ming Lee pushed her and moaned a high prayer.

Sam fixed her eyes on the behemoth wielding the axe on the stage.

Lim Poon Lee, eh? Boo How Doy. Oh, you're a badass, you are. Well, you're not putting me in a cow yard, you pig.

She was shaking, but she never lowered her eyes. She ignored the ragpimp's cries. And Hay Ming Lee's desperate urgings. And the slappings of the axe head on that massive thigh.

I've got the best damn body in all of San Francisco. And if I'm gonna be a whore . . .

She took the stairs in slow motion, knowing this moment would not come again. Her place in hell depended on her unfailing courage now.

"Ah Toy—please!" Hay Ming wailed.

Sam took the last step with defiant finesse. And posed, at the top, with her hands on her hips.

"No, Ah Toy!" Hay Ming Lee cried. "You go to Yellow River!"

Lim Poon Lee smiled. The sight would have stopped a mad bull in its tracks. He had six teeth in front, all gold and filed to razor tips. He was swinging the axe in a slow, lazy arc, beckoning with his free hand.

"Ah Toy! Must kneel-bow to him!"

Sam saw herself floating, headless and humbled, along the Yellow River. But in her life she'd never bowed. And now, instinct told her, was no time to start. Hell, Harp, wherever he was, was probably knocking them dead. Keep your wits!

She strutted across like a dancer. She felt the light breeze from the swing of the axe. The stinging heat of the tong's eyes.

She stopped three feet away from him, just out of reach of the axe. Her heart began to fail her when the axe froze at the peak of its swing, poised for a murderous chop. There was no time. The time was now. Sam gave the tong a sassy wink and slipped the blue tunic over her head.

And that was when all hell broke loose in the hell that she was in.

The head tong was stunned by her body. The muscles, under gaslights, rippling in a sheen of sweat. Breasts, as firm as cantaloupes, their stiffened tips as hard as nails. The belly, rippled like a washboard. Tight thighs, as muscular as any arm in the room.

Lim Poon bellowed, charging.

"Ahhhhh Toyyyyy!" Hay Ming Lee screamed. But Sam needed no further persuasion. Her knees buckled on their own. She hit the platform hard and knelt, head back and waiting for the axe.

From the corner of one eye she caught a blur of movement as Lim Poon Lee snapped his right clog in a roundhouse that lifted her clear off the floor. Stunned, she saw lavender eyes as she fell and imagined herself, for a moment, centered and floating serenely. Abruptly and explosively, the image was broadsided. The floor came at her, hard and fast, and laid her out winded and down for the count.

"Ahhhhh (ahhhhh) (ahhhhh) (ahhhhh)

"Toyyyyy (toyyyyy) (toyyyyy) (toyyyyy)!"

Four hysterical, horsey Hay Mings flagging their eight arms at her. More gold teeth than Sam could count.

It's okay. Sam tried to smile; knew she'd managed better; coughed. *There are worse things than a cow yard. Like this.*

Seven Lim Poon—Poon Lim?—Lees advancing with thunderous slappings of clogs. *Chew through rocks with those gold teeth. Points of them sharper than needles. What's he weigh, three hundred pounds? Three hundred pounds times seven. Oh.* A ton of Ping Poon Loon Lim Lees kneeling now, a new slant in their hooded eyes. Spreading her legs like a wishbone, not stopping till the hipbones popped. Then raising her up by the ankles.

"Ahhhhh Toyyyyy!"

Her snatch half a foot from his gold-needled jaws.

"Ha (ha) (ha) (ha)

"Yung (yung) (yung) (yung)

"Chi (chi) (chi) (chi)!"

called the four of the Hay Mings.

Sam turned her head. She could not look. But maybe one of the four Hay Ming Lees could, if not save her, explain.

But they were smiling, all of them, all four of the looney Hay Mings.

"Good (good) (good) (good)

"Luck (luck) (luck) (luck)!

"Taste (taste) (taste) (taste)

"Test!"

Sam screamed. She heard something wild, like the snort of a boar.

And then Lim Poon's tongue went to work.

IV

(March 12—Fourteen days before Dodge's arrival)

"Ladies! Gentle Ladies! May I have your attention, please?"

The tall man stepped onto the platform on Market. Flourish of tails and a tip of his hat.

"That is, if you *care* about fashion . . ."

And Betsy, who'd thought about nothing but food since escaping Oakland, stopped.

"Ladies. Gentle Ladies. Even the managers of our various departments are fairly reveling in the charms of our new Dove Gray Pony Suits. And when such staid persons find aught to enthuse over, there must indeed be a jauntiness that no one can gainsay. We must insist that you see them—right now!"

To her left, she heard a startled cry. She turned to the display glass—to see its mannequin moving.

"It's a person!" someone cried.

"Why, devil take the hindmost!"

The model strolled on lustrous oak, illumined by electric globes.

"Ladies, gentle ladies, our Dove Grays, as you can readily see, are of incomparable beauty. Nor must you overlook"—dramatic pause, one finger raised—"the delightful . . . Alice Blue!"

A second model joined the first. The crowd was struck dumb by the sight.

Betsy turned, struck dumb herself with hunger and fear and confusion. A dollar in her pocket. One of the two she had begged in the bar before the hard questions began. (Train wreck, eh? That's kinda *strange*. We ain't heard nothin' about it . . . That's a mighty *strange* outfit you're wearin' there, ma'am . . . How's about you tellin' us exactly where you're from . . .)

She figured she'd walk till her legs just gave out. Then stuff herself on all a dollar could buy and—

"Sister? Pardon, Sister?"

Ruddy-cheeked girl in a shirtwaist, madras with dainty lace ruffles. Smiling at her, sweet sixteen.

My God, I forgot—I'm a nun!

Betsy nearly jumped out of the habit she'd snatched from the clothesline outside the chapel. She'd run there to pray . . . but old habits died hard. Her fingers were always ready with a quick solution. And terror was faster than faith.

"What's that?—I mean, bless you," she answered.

"Your cheekbones, Sister—and your chin! How did you make your face so thin?"

Betsy wheeled to the window, on fire with hope. Her eyes did not betray her. The plump, buxom models in Blue and Gray Ponies weighed easily twenty-five pounds more than she. Their waists were roped to will-o'-the-wisps that six men, likely, had to tie. She saw her face framed in its oval of black—clear-eyed from her fasting—her cheekbones almost chiseled.

She did not stay to answer.

She made her way around the crowd, paused at the liveried doorman to ask:

"Bless you, my son, could you possibly tell me—where your *largest* handbags are?"

She was ushered through the doors of solid oak and gleaming brass. She lost it again, for a moment, within, beneath the dome of leaded glass, its rainbow thrown by the sun's light upon the marble tiles. Fleets of wire baskets swung from cables overhead as clerks yanked on pulls to send cash to the tellers who sent them back receipts.

A dollar in her pocket. The road ahead was perilous. But what if her watch had been wrong all along—and here, now, was the time of her life? Not poetry. Oh no, not she. But why not an *epic* Romance?

Come on, hands, don't fail me now!

Near sundown and her fingers had not failed her yet. They had grown so nimble she had, in fact, to restrain them. They could no longer distinguish what was essential from what was not. And now and then she'd have to pry them from a French fan, for example, or a chic ostrich boa. Nor could she really trust her eyes, which had grown obsessed with price tags.

Cotton hose . . . 4 prs./1.00
French handmade drawers . . . 3.95
Matching chemise . . . 1.95
Brocaded silk-taffeta shirtwaist . . . 5.00
Black leather traveling case, with cut glass bottles, ebony-backed brushes, and shell combs . . . 4.00
Calfskin shoes with dip toes and high heels . . . 2.97
Initialed hankie . . . 5¢
Black cotton walking skirt . . . 1.95

But the walrus-grained handbag (98¢) was already more than half full. And the boutonniered floormen, though dumber than cows, watched, now and then, from a distance.

"Those kerchiefs," she said to a salesgirl. "Are they cotton, child?"

"Oh, no, Sister. Silk. Would you like to see one? Here."

Betsy took it. Clucked her tongue. "Mother Superior would never approve. Perhaps something a bit more—severe."

The salesgirl turned for the instant required for the handbag to snatch up two silks.

"Good day, Sister," said the next salesgirl. "We don't often see—I mean . . ."

Betsy, caressing the walking skirt, blushed. "Good Heavens, not for me," she said. "It's for my sister's birthday. But . . ."

"Would you care to try one on? I mean, that is, if you . . ."

"Bless you. Perhaps I might try—two or three, to be sure?"

7:00 P.M. Market Street. Clusters of street lamps, beginning at Powell, dimly illumined the gauntlet ahead. Nighthawks, in bowlers and derbies, smoked cigars around the lamps and whistled at the ladies while horse-drawn buggies clipclopped by and street cars jingled to their mates.

Her fate to be decided—not in minutes, but in steps.

She slipped her shawl into her handbag as two corseted beauties in hoopskirts strolled, arm in arm, through the gauntlet ahead.

Her own first steps were gingerly. But gradually the whistling stopped. And the cock of the walk banter faded. And cigars dropped from mouth after mouth.

She had Time on her side and she went with the flow. The commodious sway of uncorseted breasts under the taffeta shirtwaist. Subtle lines of hips and thighs—so full to her, so lean to them—rippling under the snug cotton skirt. One amber wave brushing one emerald eye. She'd found herself. She knew just who she was.

The nighthawks whispered like small boys.

"She ain't wearin' one!"

"She is!"

"She ain't!"

"Must be—she ain't got no waist!"

Betsy dropped her kerchief.

She heard the commotion behind her and waited for the hawks to fly.

Whatever happened, happened.

She'd been in heaven at least once.

V

(March 10—Sixteen days before Dodge's arrival)

Rod's performance in Oakland had been a disgrace, but only in his own eyes. He'd been the first to play the bar. And, though the figure he'd cut had been strange, he had been ahead of the rumors. He'd left the bar with safe passage, a belly filled with beef and beer, and one pocket with coins. His terror had been genuine, crazed butterflies with razored teeth slashing in his belly. His grief—an epic sense of loss—had splashed in buckets from his eyes. *(They got me, boys—outside of town—not a penny to my name . . .)*

But now, safe for the moment, the Actor had taken command.

He ignored the props for now—the streetcars and hansoms and landaus. He dismissed the costumes—the cutaways and sack suits.

The Actor focused, rather, on the essential details, the tiny subtle differences that made these people what they were. The way women relaxed, for example: sitting stiffer than boards, but with overskirts turned.

His trained ear took in their talk like a script: *Savvy? . . . Fiddlesticks . . . By jingo . . . Let's go fetch some hen fruit, eh? . . . Don't be so free with your china. . . .*

Gestures and inflections . . .

Timber, tone, and pitch . . .

Rod brooded on these things and watched, a thin man
from the future in a blue cheviot shirt, neatly knotted white
silk scarf, and a new pair of Levi's (thicker by half than the
ones of his day and studded with real copper rivets).

He sat on the edge of the fountain till dusk, analyzing,
synthesizing,

(Face it, Rod, you're stalling!)

smoking and inhaling more *atmosphere* with every puff

(For God's sake, Rod, it's getting dark!)

and wondering at the turn of luck

(It's getting cold, you're gonna freeze!)

that had landed him here—to what end?

If he could just

(You're gonna starve!)

survive a little longer.

(You've only got two dollars left!)

The darkness and cold were compelling. But so were his
fears for the future. He might have sat there well into the
night. If an old wino, stretched out on a bench, hadn't
sneezed twice, rapid-fire, in his sleep.

"Ah-*CHOO*! Ah-*CHOO*!"

And Rod bolted up to his feet, as if shot.

Chew Chew, eh? You *think* so?

The wino sighed and turned onto his side, under thick
layers of news.

The Actor marched over, cold fire in his eyes, snatching
the theater section.

I'll give you Chew Chew, you son of a bitch. . . .

Rod lit a Turkish Trophy and kicked back on the rim of
the fountain.

Hmmm . . . Special from *The New York Times* . . . Review of Wilde's *Salome* . . .

> *. . . sensual, licentious, abhorrent!*

So . . . Shaw opening on Broadway with *Cashel Byron's
Profession* . . . Cohan's newest coming up . . . I could do
that . . . Sure I could . . . But gotta start right here and

now . . . Make it here . . . Then take New York . . .
Come on, fingers . . .
Flipflipflip.

NOW AT THE CALIFORNIA!

*A brand new and bubbly Burlesque! See Glorinne and
the Radium Girls! Peter Miller, Prince of German
Clowns! George T. Davis, California's Favorite Baritone!
Bragg and Ashton's Eccentric and Comic Delights! And
. . . a Bevy of Jolly Girls who can Sing and Dance!*

NOW AT THE ALCAZAR!

*'A Stranger in a Strange Land'! The enormously funny
farce with the Three Live Indians!*

NOW AT THE GRAND OPERA HOUSE!

*Last Performance! Nance O'Neil, America's Greatest Tra-
gedienne in The Jewess! Tomorrow—See Nance Conquer
Lady Macbeth!*

Shakespeare . . . They have Shakespeare here . . .
Chew Chew, eh? . . . We'll just see about that . . .
First I've gotta eat, though . . .
How?
Come on, fingers . . . Come on, eyes . . . Come on, it's
here, I know it is . . . Come on, come out, I know you're
Here!

LAST NOTICE: AUDITIONS!.

*The Majestic Theater will hold auditions for its new Bur-
lesque Review on March 10, 1906, at 7:00 P.M. Seeking
Comely Girls! Comedians! Acrobats! Magicians! Actors!
Etc. !!!*

The bed for the night was forgotten.
Rod took off for the stage with a vengeance.

VI

(March 1—The first arrival)

Lenny knelt at the wagon across from the dump heap and smoothed more dirt over the things he had stashed under the furthermost wheel.

He stuck the book—his bible—in the waistband of his jeans, under the collarless shirt and the vest.

He felt strangely calm and protected. Though he still heard the screams from the dome car, twelve bodies sucked through the window. And he still saw the train disappearing, from the lavender eye, in a red scream of fog.

The first shall be last and the last shall be first . . .

He studied the lights of the town through the mist.

One time was as good as another to Dodge. Wherever they were, Dodge would just blend right in.

But what if Time for once, just once, was on Lenny's side? What if . . .

He set off, with a Chaplinesque click of his heels, humming "Sergeant Pepper's . . ."

HONKEY AND PATCH

 I'll give those Fat Men credit. They must have been as stunned by me as I was by them. But they were true San Franciscans. After battling a bit with their eyeballs, they turned around, just as cool as can be, put their elbows on the bar, puffed at their Havanas, and chattered away as if I wasn't there.

It was good to know at least one thing had remained unchanged. In this wicked, most sinful of cities, the only unforgivable sin was acting like a tourist.

So I cocked the stovepipe back and sidled on up to the bar, where I grinned like a loon at the barman. Enjoying the part. I'd be free of it soon. I was a serious man.

"Good day to you," he said.

I honked.

"What's your pleasure?"

Two more honks.

"One Raniers comin' up." He slapped a cold one on the bar. "That'll be a jit, gent."

Well, I didn't need to know what a jit was to know I didn't have one.

I gave the horn another honk and reached for the tall, frosty stein.

The barman beat me to it. "Don't give me none of that," he said. "I don't make the prices."

I wiggled my ears.

"That'll still be a jit."

I honked to the right, I honked to the left—
and knew that I had found my mark.

A dapper old man, in his sixties, with a Mark Twain mustache and a patch on one eye. On the bar before him, beside a large snifter of brandy, was spread an inviting assortment of coins, one of which might be a jit.

I wiggled my ears.

He regarded me slyly.

I extended my leg.

He gave it a shake.

I reached over and picked up a small silver coin.

The old man smiled. And then *clicked*

a pearl-handled derringer he placed between my eyes.

"Careful, sonny. Careful. I comes from the old San Francisco."

There was no doubt in my mind that he'd shoot.

But there was no doubt either: I'd die without that beer.

And I had Harpo's angel sitting on my shoulder.

I rolled the coin over and under my fingers . . . palmed it . . . pulled it from my ear . . . and then my nose and mouth. I changed it into a Havana (which I'd just palmed from the bar) and lit it from the fat cigar he clenched between his teeth. Then I took his right leg and I gave it a shake.

The old man didn't bat an eye.

"Crazy as a bedbug. But, by deuce, you ain't no pinkieboy!" He clicked the hammer back in place and pocketed the derringer. "What'd you say your name was?"

I responded with two honks, the first one long and plaintive, the second short and snappy. I'd always liked Franklin and Peter.

But to the old man it was perfectly clear. "Honkey, is it? There you go. Tell you what, kid. Call me Patch—and don't be so free with my china."

Free with my china . . . I took that right in. I'd learn the lingo in no time.

Patch had a little magic trick of his own he showed me. His arm disappeared to the elbow inside my right coat pocket, and reappeared with the coin that I'd snatched.

The coin was pure gold and substantially sized, a Liberty bust on the front, The value read ten dollars. He slapped it on the bar.

"This here, you see's, an eagle, Honk. Men gets attached to their eagles. Forget about your shinplasters—greenbacks, yellowbacks—paper dough's for pinkieboys. Pete, put that damned warm beer away and set Honkey up with a cold one."

The barman returned with a freshly drawn brew and a fistful of silver and smaller gold coins. My eyes were burning to take it all in: half-eagle . . . quarter-eagle . . . silver dollars . . . quarters . . . dimes . . .

"Honk," Patch said, delightedly, "I ain't never seen a fella look at money quite like you!"

I gave the horn three random honks, two short and one long in the middle, wondering what I'd just said.

Patch slapped the half-eagle before me and cried, "Well, why didn't you say you was busted? Let's eat!"

Patch took a bone china plate from a pile, and a fork and knife swathed in linen.

One of the waiters—about Patch's height, but forty or fifty pounds stouter—wagged an admonishing finger. "I be watchin' you there, Masdah Patch. You eats like a man or I fessin' you *strange*."

Patch loaded on a block of cheese, seven slices of dark bread, a thigh and breast of turkey, four thick slices of roast beef, three hardboiled eggs, twelve olives, and a slice of apple pie.

The waiter fixed his eyes on me. Damned if I'd be strange. Blend in! I stuffed my pockets with two loaves of bread and left with two bone plates so packed a wishbone more might have cracked them.

Patch watched me eat. His eyes were sad.

"I'll never see eighty at this rate," he said.

He nibbled at some turkey breast. Fiddled with his beef and eggs, then morosely unfolded a clipping that he'd slipped out of his vest.

"Doc says I'll be dead in a couple of years if I don't gets some calories."

I turned the clipping upside down and read it that way as well as I could. I'd learned the trick at Pinkerton's, but never had much luck with it. All I could swing was the little boxed chart:

CALORIES FOR SURVIVAL

Type of Work	Calories Needed
Moderate	3,500
Active	4,000
Severe	5,700

I didn't like the looks of that. So I began to play with it and read from different angles. Till I caught a flash that nearly knocked me off my feet: two elderly women, caught acting *strangely* yesterday, were being held on Alcatraz, pending further questioning. Must've been the two old girls I'd heard of at the ferry. Patch took the paper from my hands.

"Don't worry, Honk. Keep eatin' like that and you're gonna live till the Eighties!"

I reached for the schooner. I needed a drink. One swig and I reeled like a beanbottom doll.

Patch chuckled and stroked his mustache. "Yeah, three or four of those and you'll tear up the town enough to make the old cows laugh. Had to give it up, myself. Still got the germs inside it. And germs digest the calories, see. So now they age and steam the rest. They sterilize and lagerize. They freshen 'em. They filter 'em. Scarcely fit for pinkieboys!"

I flexed a small muscle under my coat, took a giant bite of beef, honked, and raised my schooner, one pinkie stretched out like a flag.

"Death to the pinkieboys!" Patch cried. "Hooray!"

One Fat Man after another, along the mahogany bar, raised his glass and echoed.

And before I knew it, now that I was one of them, the drinks began to fly. And two Fat Men on my right were wondering where I was from.

My use of the horn was still at, you might say, the experimental stage. So, I answered with a honk to see where that might get me. It didn't get me very far. The two Fat Men scratched at their derbies.

The first said, "Nevada?"

The second said, "Maine?"

Patch threw his arm over my shoulder and winked.

"Boys, if you asks the right questions," he said, "talkin' to Honkey's as easy as pie. Watch this, you lugs, and you'll learn somethin'. Kid, two honks for no and one for yes."

I wiggled my ears and I shook Patch's leg. I'd be out of my clown suit in no time.

"Calm down," he said. "Relax, you dunce. I just want to show 'em you're right in the head. Now . . . You come from west of—Chicago?"

Two honks.

"So . . . You come from east of Chicago then?"

Honk.

"Uh, west of New York City?"

I rolled my eyes and gave two honks.

"East of New York City?"

I rolled my eyes and wiggled my ears and gave him two more honks.

"South of New York City?"

I rolled my eyes and wiggled my ears and then squiggled my nose along with them. Two honks.

"North—Say, wait a minute! You *come* from New York City!"

HONK!

"Well, by the deuce, don't that beat all!"

"Why, strike me straight!" one Fat Man cried.

"Let's smash the sauce!" cried another.

"Sure, sure, that's the word!" Patch was so excited he pushed his plate aside. "Come on, Honk, drink up," he said, "no time for the blue devils now. Let's have a cheer for Quaker Sam—best streetcorner preacherman the damn town's ever seen!

Now, I didn't know Quaker Sam from shinola, but the name sounded vaguely familiar. I remembered it, maybe, from Oakland. And anything that sounded even only half-way strange here was grounds for celebration.

There were more toasts to Quaker Sam than you could shake my leg at. And I was on my second stein of pinkieboy-killing Raniers . . . when I decided the great Quaker Sam deserved a proper toast. I raised a shot glass with a honk.

Patch gave me such an affectionate look I felt almost like

a lost son. "That's the proper caper, Honk! Bottoms up to Quaker Sam!"

I raised the shot like a trooper. The rye was nearly as dark as the beer, but extraordinarily sweet. For a couple of seconds I felt warm all over, pleased with my general progress, and sly. Then I started to feel dizzy, and then woozy, and then queasy. I saw three Patches spinning like a set of juggler's balls.

And then I collapsed in his arms.

BLUE BLAZER I

What I'm about to give to you is at once a recipe that even a child can make . . . and a miracle that you can't hope to perform.

Place one tablespoon of honey in a sterling silver mug.
Now stir in water, not quite boiling, to the halfway mark.
Fill another silver mug with an equal dose of scotch.
Set a match to the whiskey . . . and add it to the honey. The whiskey, not the match.
Now, very slowly, pour from one mug to the other until the flames die down.

The drink was the fabled Blue Blazer. You can make one if you like. But don't ever think you can *drink* one. For that you'd need *their* silver . . . *their* Scotch . . . *their* honey . . . *their* minds . . .
But if we can't walk through the front door, perhaps we can slip in the back.
Like this:

I was dying when I woke about six hours later.
The entire world had turned a sickly shade of lime. Green Fat Men in green derbies puffed enormous green Havanas and stroked their green Smith Brothers beards. The room had settled over with a thick green haze of smoke through which words came like bubbles in a cauldron of pea soup. Someone wanted to call a green doctor. Another, a green mortician. Another was trying to ask me if I had green next

of kin. Then Patch appeared, like a mildewy statue, with a green mug that was steaming green mist.

"I knows what Honk needs," he said.

He slipped his green fingers behind my green head, raised it gently to the mug.

"Just a sip, kid. Easy now."

The first drops dribbled through closed lips I had no strength to open. Patch waited, knowing just how it would go.

The droplets settled on my tongue. Tastebuds came to in a three-alarm choir. I began to salivate. Then to swallow greedily.

What Patch had brought me was the sky in a giant silver mug. A Colorado blue so deep it made the sky in Denver look washed out in comparison.

I wanted more; I needed more; I wasn't kidding when I reached.

Patch still had some iron, though, left in his arm.

Two sips were what he allowed me until I was able to sit. Then a third. He checked my eyes. He checked my pulse. I walked a straight line. Then did two figure eights, honking and jabbing at the mug.

"Hooray for Honkey!" someone cried.

"More wind to Honk!" cried another.

"He's cured!"

Patch stroked his eyepatch lightly, then announced his judicious decision.

It appeared that I had an imbalance between my germs and calories. And—since I was no pinkieboy, as anyone could see—for some unfathomable reason the germs from neither rye nor beer were able to live in my blood. My body had been stricken low by who-knew-how-many calories running around undigested. What I clearly needed was a drink containing germs my blood would be able to use. And what had just been proven was: That drink was the Blue Blazer.

I threw my legs around Patch's waist and honked ecstatically, wiggling my ears, while he teetered and struggled for balance.

"For God's sake, set him up with one before he breaks my deucin' back!"

I know what you're thinking. You'd call it a hair of the dog. You'd be wrong. I'd been poisoned; I'd been cured; no —more: I'd been fully restored. What I could never have guessed was that the cure would prove equally toxic. And even if you'd warned me, I'd have honked and turned away. For I'd sipped at the sky from real silver.

How could the sky turn against me?

I'd learn.

All I knew *then* was that something had changed—dramatically, essentially. As if my center, somehow, had been rooted in the earth. There was no Dodge watching Dodge watching Dodge, on the outside looking in, three steps ahead of the Fat Man and two steps ahead of the clock. There were no plans. No strategies. I was *here*. And this was *It*.

I hoped the others would lie low. I hoped the two bluehairs would zipper their lips until I was able to save them. I would. But—how could I think of the others just now . . . when I'd finally found it?

The Sweet Spot in Time.

Patch and I were clipclopping along in a phaeton through Chinatown. The aroma of the leather seats was as potent and entrancing as the smoke from his cigar. Through the circular window in back, the moonlight, filtered through the fog, threw his image in silvery relief. He smoked and watched me thoughtfully.

We in turn were watched by throngs of men in felt hats and blue tunics.

We made our way through the warren of hell-red buildings with window frames enameled blue, vermillion, and lime. The facades were honeycombed with wrought-iron balconies, some crammed with flower pots and gaily colored lanterns, some sporting streamers and windchimes. Street-level windows were filled with brocades and carvings of ivory, jade, rose crystal. From the higher windows half-dressed whores called out their rates. ("Two-bittee lookee! Flo-bittee feelee! Six-bittee dooee!") I heard a gong, a pipe and lute thundering, trilling and strumming. And the light mist was redolent with the varied fragrances: incense and exotic herbs . . . sandalwood and opium . . . roast pork and sausages . . . freshly skinned fish . . .

Patch smoked and stroked his patch and sighed. "You can almost feel it here. Now and then, when the wind is just right, and the fog ain't too light or too thick . . . The way them whores with their long ruby nails look out them windows and sing for a poke . . . Sayyy, wait a minute . . . There . . ."

I craned my head to see where he was pointing. Saw a small man, from the back, in an enormous derby. Chinamen flocking around as he roared, "BIG ONE! BIG ONE COMING!" And then he was lost as we clipclopped along.

Patch cursed softly. "Missed him again. Ol' Quaker Sam covers the town like cement, and there's just no tellin' where he's gonna show. Only caught him once myself. But damn, Honk, he whips up a storm."

At the edge of Chinatown, Patch told me to close my eyes. His own eye was twinkling in the misted silvery light.

"There's nothin' here but banks," he said, "and deucin' Painted Ladies. You wants to see the Real San Francisco— ah, well, what's left of it—there's only one place to begin."

I rode, by and large, as instructed: the left eye was closed, the right open a slit. The area was *toney* here, with rows of Painted Ladies—the pinkieboys' gingerbread homes.

I thought I knew where we were headed, but was in no hurry to get there. As magical as Chinatown, to me, was the fog-swept procession of Prince Alberts and top hats and bonnets and capes along the gas-lit cobbled streets.

"Almost there, Honk. Almost there."

But he was wrong. We *were* there and it kept getting better and better. Time had brought me here and now to put some Romance in my sly, cunning soul. How could I ever have thought that one time was as good as another?

Darkness now. Just a few scattered lights. My body was lost in the leather as we ascended a vertical hill. I heard the driver crack his whip. Then heard the horse's labored breathing as the slope began to soar.

At the top, Patch called out to the driver, who stopped. The horse had no objection.

"All right, Honkey, open 'em!"

Patch slipped out of one door and stood waiting for me.

I took my place beside him to catch my first glimpse of the Barbary Coast. From where we stood I could see little more than an amazing denseness of masts and sails in the harbor, and matchbox shacks along the wharf. I could hear little more than ghost echoes below. But my senses were so finely tuned I felt as if we were already there.

"You feels it, don't you, Honk?" Patch cried. "You feels it, just like me!"

I honked.

Patch half-dragged me into the buggy. The driver cracked the whip again before the door had closed and we began our swift descent into the soul of Baghdad.

FADE TO BACK

Fisherman's Wharf—with its tourists and trinkets —was a hundred yards out and years under the Bay. But I was no stranger to strangeness by now. So I adjusted my map as we cruised through the crowds along the shifted waterfront, which now began around Broadway.

The Coast's population, Patch taught me, was roughly 40,000, as densely packed as Chinatown. Men lived in wood shanties and jerry-built huts all along the waterfront and over the steep slopes of Telegraph Hill. Hundreds more lived in rooms above bars, of which there were some four thousand. Half of these were "cellar joints," unfurnished except for a ramshackle bar, a "stage" for several can-can girls, and makeshift chairs for the worst of the drunks. Then there were the "wino caves," some without windows, some without doors, the bars themselves consisting of planks on wooden horses. The remaining bars, dismissed by Patch, were pinkieboy-style saloons, a few of them sporting real Tiffany lamps.

Patch snorted whenever he passed one. His cigar was fragrant in the cesspool of the air: a heady rush of piss and gas, beer, whiskey, garlic, chili, vomit, sperm, and fresh-spilled blood.

Of the last there could not be a shortage, despite the pairs of water cops: steely-eyed under their tall blue felt caps, and swinging their lead-weighted clubs. Thugs prowled the wharf in drunken packs, watched by beefy bouncers with sawed-off pool cues and oak bats. Some stood in alleys, barely concealing the clubs and conches in their hands.

I kept a safe distance, which amused Patch to no end. He

seemed to be looking for something. Or waiting for something to happen. One place looked as bad as another to me: The Dew Drop Inn . . . the Cock o' the Walk . . . the Billy Goat . . . the Mountain Dive. But he just walked and stroked his patch and puffed and repeated, "Not here. Not tonight."

Finally, the old man stopped at Pacific and Sullivan's Alley. He raised one finger in the air as if he were testing the breeze. "Honk," he said, "hold on there. I feels the hairs on the back o' me neck—"

Just then there was an explosion of glass as a body flew out the window of a bar across the street. The victim straggled to his knees, teetered there a moment, then crashed face down in a still-steaming mound of glass-sprinkled horseshit.

Cheers from the passersby. And a great roar of approval from the Hell's Kitchen Saloon. A chair came through the window next. Followed by a table. And then a Pretty Waitress Girl, bleeding through her ears and mouth.

Patch tugged at my sleeve. "C'mon, Honk! This is it!"

Well, I'd had the Blue Blazer some hours ago and the buzz was beginning to blur at the rim.

But Patch kept tugging—"C'mon, bother you! We're gonna live sixty the minute tonight!"—and so we stepped over the bodies and in.

Friends, if you think you've seen Fat Men, you're wrong. I'd thought I'd seen Fat Men. But I had been wrong.

The real ones were here, a good hundred or so, a great wall of blubber that buried the bar. I saw gorged bellies shaking with laughter under torn and filthy shirts, thunder thighs covered in canvas and denim, enough to have tented an army. Their arms looked like great sides of beef. Their beards were Fat. Their eyes were Fat. Their jeering, cheering mouths were Fat.

And the Fattest of them all, his dirt shirt streaked with blood, was presently bashing the brains out of the second Fattest. Secondo lay there like a corpse, Primo squatting on his chest. Over and over the oak bat was swung.

Thump! Thump! Whack! Whack!

"That's the proper caper!" Patch nearly tore my sleeve off. "Come on, deuce him, bash his pate!"

But Primo had grown bored with that. He rolled his Fat eyes gleefully and tossed the bat aside.

"I will chew you down to a *dwarf*!" he roared.

He leaned over then and chewed off Secondo's left ear. He shook it like a terrier, blood still splashing from the ear, while Secondo writhed, screaming, beneath him. Finally, he spat it out and lurched up to his feet. He proceeded to the bar, thinking the cheers were for him.

They were not.

Secondo was already up with the bat. He delivered a skull-crushing roundhouse that dropped Primo to his knees and sent blood gouting from both ears.

Patch screamed his approval.

The Fat Men gestured with thumbs down.

But Secondo lurched over to pick up the ear. Then wiped it off on one now-scarlet sleeve, teetering up to the bar.

"What the deuce," Patch murmured.

The Fat Men gave Secondo berth, but seemed to be as stunned as Patch.

Secondo said to the barman, "I believe I'll be havin' some pepper."

He was obliged with a shaker, with which he proceeded to pepper the ear.

Secondo told the barman next, "I believe I'll be havin' some salt."

Secondo continued to season the ear. He blew off a few extra crystals. Added one jigger of pepper. Then took the ear over to Primo, holding it out like some dainty hors d'oeuvre.

"Now," Secondo said sweetly, "I do believe you'll be eatin' me ear."

Primo looked from the ear to the bat, measuring his chances. I guess he saw what I saw: that the next swing would knock his head out of the park. Still, if a man had to do what a man had to do, at least he could do it in style.

He turned the ear a quarter and chewed off the lobe. He nibbled at it thoughtfully, then set into the ear like a steak.

You could have heard him chew for blocks. When he finished, he belched and stood up, cool and slow.

"Y'know," he said, "I'll tell ye . . . Coulda used a jig more pepper, but it really weren't half bad."

Secondo gawked at Primo.

Primo answered with a wink.

And then they exploded with laughter, slapping their knees, thunderstomping their feet, and clapping each other's great shoulders.

Secondo boomed, "Lemme buy ye a rum!"

"Rum an' gum!" Primo roared.

I looked over at Patch, whose complexion had turned an off-shade of ivory. It grew even paler as the two men clunked their schooners.

Before you knew it, Hell's Kitchen Saloon was fraternity row. A piano started up. Pretty Waitress Girls jumped in the laps of the drunks, diapers underneath their skirts so they could stay at the tables. Three more ascended the stage in black stockings, garters, and frilly white drawers.

The old man looked around the room.

I barely heard what he mumbled. But it sounded like, "Me heart is broke." And those words would have matched his expression as he shuffled to the bar.

The barman looked like Mr. Clean, with a face half as scarred as the bar.

Patch clamored for attention.

The barman looked over, then went back to cleaning, or adding more dirt to, a glass.

"C'mon," Patch cried, "get a move on, you lug!"

Clean rubbed the glass on one dirty sleeve of his striped pirate's jersey.

I gave a tug at Patch's sleeve.

"You feels it, don't you, Honkey?"

Honk!

"Oh, aye, the deucin' town is dead. Ten years ago—I'm tellin' you, ten!—you could come to the Coast and see *Frisco*! Look at 'em—just look at 'em! Mollycoddlers! Milksops!" Patch smashed his fist on the top of the bar. "Give us two Blazers, you damned pinkieboy!"

I was a foot away from Patch and I could scarcely hear him. But he had said the magic word. Suddenly the music stopped. Around the bar the Fat Men turned, one after another. And Clean started whapping an ice-smashing bat on his palm with a murderous look.

I had to do something and do something fast.

I stretched my left leg out to Primo. He took it, with a goofy smile. And I thought I was doing fine—till he swept my right leg from beneath me. I fell with a crash on my shoulders, with both of my legs in his grasp.

Oh-oh, I thought. The airplane spin. I was preparing for takeoff when he said something that turned my blood cold.

"So, yer a *strange one*, are ye?"

Secondo added, "Aye, yer *strange*. Put *you* on the Rock with them women! Passin' their damn funny money an' askin' where their train went. Pshaw!"

I heard Patch, behind me, cry, "Aaa, he's no stranger than you are, you lug. And you're gonna look strange with a hole in your—EEEEEEEEE!"

I turned to see the derringer slipping from his fingers as Clean wrung and twisted his wrist. Then Clean raised the bat and smashed a second elbow out of Patch's arm. Patch dropped to his knees with an agonized scream as Primo started to spin me.

When Primo let go of my ankles, I had, I thought, some good ideas—for shifting my center, adjusting my angle. But the Wall was the Wall was the Wall, after all. I'd only thought I'd escaped in D.C.

I heard the Fat Men roar and howl as I lay there whooping, like Ghost Boy, for breath.

"C'mon, Honk," Patch screamed, "bash their pates! For the love of Jesus, kid, show 'em you ain't *strange*!"

My head was spinning. But I stood.

My knees were spinning. But I honked.

I saw the Fat Men coming, spinning, each like a blade on a millsaw.

It would have been over in seconds.

But Patch, inspired, roared, "Ahoy! Give the man a Blazer! Go on and honor his dying request—or are y'all just pinkieboys?"

Well, you'll never see a more stunned group of Fat Men. Not if you travel to Baghdad yourself. The front line exchanged looks with the men at the bar. Who shrugged at the men by the window. Who raised their palms to the men at the wall.

Nobody liked the suggestion. But since Patch had put it that way . . .

A Blazer was mixed in a couple of mugs, one wood and one silver. The rye might have been used for tanning a hide. For when the brew was lit the flames shot halfway to the ceiling. But Clean poured the Blazer from schooner to mug, then back to the schooner, then back to the mug, and so on, until he was holding the silver, which started belching black cumulus clouds.

Clean winked and said, "Here ye *are*, dearie!"

Patch staggered my way with the mug.

"It's a Blazer, Honk," he whispered.

I wasn't so sure about that. The mug, inside, was green as a statue; the brew was black as a virgin nun's soul.

"It's a *Blazer*, damn you."

I raised the mug. What it was smelled like something that should have been flushed.

"Drink it. It's a *Blazer*. If you're *strange*, kid, you'll die on the Rock."

Now that I thought about it . . . How could I have been so mistaken?

I placed the mug to my lips—

"Come *on*, kid!"

—and what I took in was a bolt of the sky that rocketed through me and lit up my eyes. It was bluer than blue. It was richer than rich. It was warm as a kiss from the President's mom.

"You done it, kid! You done it!"

I honked and started to roll up my sleeves.

The Fat Men looked at one another.

They'd waited long enough.

They charged.

I was ready for them.

I'll hand it to the Fat Men.

Only six came at me. Which may have been something resembling fair play.

But I had eighty years on them and I was as high as a kite on that sky. Even as they came at me, I saw them shrinking down to size. The Fat Man was dead. No, he'd never been born. I was my father's father's dad, free of him now and forever.

I felt lighter than air.

I felt faster than light.

Aikido, still years in the future, was—*strange*; I couldn't fight them that way. But *slapstick* was forever.

Primo came first, with his club overhead. I met him halfway. I dodged under his arm. I spun and as he swung the club, I extended the arc with my fingers, brought the club down and around and in back, the move smashing his face to his knee. Primo screamed. I continued to turn, yanking up until his shoulder popped. I shuffled in and with a honk, I rolled him at Secondo, who sprawled right into a bonk from the horn. I dodged and whirled into the third and the fourth. The room was filled with roars and grunts and cries as bodies flew and bones were smashed and skulls were bonked with the bell of the horn.

When the six lay at my feet, I wiggled my ears and I honked for some more.

There was a moment's silence.

Then the room erupted in roars and hoots of laughter.

"Hooray for Honkey!" Patch cried out. "That's the proper caper!"

"Drinks on the house!" roared the barman, friend Clean. "Rum an' gum! Deucin' Blazers! Haw haw, what a lark!"

I had come to the Coast an invisible mute, secure in the extremities. Soon I'd be invincible. My allies included, for starters, a hundred of the roughest wharf rats anywhere in town. Within weeks, they would be in the thousands. There wasn't a chance of *my* seeing the Rock while I searched— well, in time—for the others.

I was going to *find* Sam and Lenny. I'd *get* the bluehairs off the Rock. Of course I would. I knew I would. I was a serious, serious man, who'd once had dreams of Paladin.

Still . . . Still . . . Just for now . . .

I stretched out, with my feet on the table, the stovepipe on my lap, and surveyed my kingdom, while puffing a Havana.

From time to time one of my subjects would wave. Or come over to drop a gold coin in the hat.

Patch—whose arm had been reset, in spectacular fashion, by Clean—stroked the dirt sling he was wearing. Then he toyed with the edge of his patch.

"San Francisco," he said dreamily. "San *Fran*-cisco, Honk! I ain't seen nothin' like that since the early Eighties. Quaker Sam's right, kid, we gotta *get back*."

A hundred wharf rats turned, as one, and raised their glasses solemnly.

"To Quaker Sam!" they roared. "Let's hear it for the Big One!"

I raised my own mug with a—

HONNNNNKKKKK!

"Hey, Honkey, you all right, kid? You looks like you just seen a ghost." Patch followed my eyes to the window. Too late.

The pale apparition I'd seen had moved on.

The red-eyed, ashen, haunted face.

Of my old buddy, Austin Blacke.

LA ISLA DE LOS ALCATRACES

Men had had plans for the Rock since men came. And those of the men on the ferry the twenty-seventh of March meant as little as any before.

The twelve-acre island to which they would come was only the tip of a mountain, once the tallest in a valley lost with the end of an Age, one melted by Time and the sun.

The Cosatoan Indians arrived first, in *tule* canoes, ten thousand years ago. They gathered eggs from the seabirds who flocked here by the thousands. They made plans to prosper, to build and live long. The Rock, swept clean by the tides and harsh winds, impassively watched them depart. Each looking over his shoulder.

Men came and left. Men came and left. Men came with hunger in their eyes and left looking over their shoulders.

A Spanish frigate strayed one day through the Golden Gate. The captain entered the date in his log. August 8, 1771. The Old World had discovered the New World again.

They did not stay there very long. Just long enough to name it:

La Isla de los Alcatraces.

The island of the pelicans.

The Mexicans came. They had good plans. They left, looking over their shoulders at *La Isla de los Alcatraces.*

The Americans came. The Americans left for richer spoils across the Bay.

Across the iced waters that lapped at the Rock, cannons roared and humans screamed and lives—to the Rock, short as fireflies'—nourished the soil with crimson.

The Mexicans died; the Americans stayed; California had been born. The Rock went on with the business of perfecting its marriage with Time. Fluidly and lovingly. Soundlessly and smoothly.

Until the day—until which day the rock had known nothing of months, even years—the clock began to *tick*.

On the twenty-fourth of January 1848, an itinerant construction boss picked up a sunstruck fleck of gold from the millrace of a sawmill in the Sierra Nevada foothills.

By year's end, eight hundred ships had sailed from ports on the East Coast, all bound for San Francisco—with a thousand more in tow, from Australia, Asia, Europe . . .

Within five years, the miners' town was the principal port on the coast.

Such a prize needed protection.

They began with dynamite. Halfway up, a wide plateau was blown into the slopes for cannons weighing twenty tons apiece. A road was carved out of the sandstone from the only approachable landing. The road was then blocked by a guardhouse. The guardhouse was fronted with an oak door studded with cannon-proof iron. The door was then blocked by a medieval moat, crossed only by a drawbridge.

Atop the island, the drawbridge was watched from the defensive barracks—three stories high and nine feet thick.

The cannons continued arriving.

The soldiers' fingers were itching to fire.

The Rock turned the dirty work over to Time.

The hoped-for war never came to the Rock.

The men built and waited, drilled and waited, as War after War passed them by.

The Civil War.

The Philippine War.

The Spanish-American War.

By 1901 not one cannon remained.

The Rock might have told them before they'd begun.

On the day this particular ferry pulled in, the Rock showed little evidence of ten thousand years of failed plans. One might have thought it had been, at last, tamed. Its surface was sprinkled with red-roofed, stone buildings and well-tended emerald gardens. Alcatraz had its own hospital now. Bowling alley. Bakery. And once again the men were blasting and building with passion.

For fifty years, while they'd been courting War after War that ignored them, the men had been timidly flirting with a sort of Sister Plan.

Their first advances were modest enough: small shacklike cells over the guardhouse for military prisoners.

Before the men knew it, the small cells were filled. The men began to wonder . . .

Inch by inch, they shifted over to whisper their hopes in the Sister Plan's ear.

To the men's astonishment, they met with no resistance.

Emboldened, the men built a complex of cells around the original guardhouse. They filled these with civilian scum: arsonists, rapists, mass killers.

The Sister Plan moaned with excitement.

Political prisoners were thrown into cells.

And a spanking new stockade now housed twelve seditious Indians. Along with two elderly women whose crimes had not yet been determined. But whose confessions, it was said, were growing stranger and *stranger.* Surely more cells would be needed.

And soon.

The Rock let them come. It let their clocks keep ticking as they planned and hoped.

Men were mere moments and all moments passed.

The Rock dreamed of the old days, when changes were measured in hundreds of thousands of years.

"Got the time, mate?"

One soldier asked the prisoner this as the ferry pulled into the slip.

The others laughed. Except for the sergeant, still eyeing

the prisoner's watch. The watch had a sort of expandable band. And was, apparently, worn on the wrist, as Lincoln's crazy Mary was said to have worn hers. The watch read "Rolex" on the face, and had tiny windows in which appeared the month and date. The numerals were Arabic. The lettering was—very *strange*. Everything about the watch filled the sergeant with wonder and fear.

He slipped the watch back in his pocket. He turned his hard eyes to the prisoner—the ashen-faced, bald-headed man on the bench—and hated the man with his soul. There was something, just something, about him . . .

"What's your name?" he snarled.

The prisoner moaned. "I—told you."

The sergeant leaned over and cuffed the man's ear.

The prisoner groaned fearfully, closing his eyes.

"Bra-kowski . . . Guy . . . Brakowski . . ."

BLOOD BANK

 Blacke dreamed he was in Africa, the heat as thick as tsetses. Congos thumped out impassioned tattoos while Twelve Beauties sat on their haunches at the edge of the lavender mist.

What tricks he was going to show them tonight!

The Bat Trick!

The Snake Trick!

"The Face Trick! That's what you've come to see, isn't it, oink?"

They looked at each other with low, cunning eyes. As if they'd caught wind of a wildebeest, a gazelle, or a succulent pig.

Well, Blacke almost laughed at the last thought. For—by the Night, this was odder than hell—for a second there he could have sworn he had oinked.

"My beautiful children," he told them. "Sit down and listen carefully. You're on the right track, but you're still stopping short. It isn't the blood, but the essence of blood. What you want's not the face, but the soul of the face. Then you throw in a little Blacke magic and—oink!"

The Beauties stirred and chuckled, lowed.

Well, they were only children. His speech had been too technical. What he had to do was *show* them.

Alacazam Shlazam—

"OINK OINK!"

Like this—

"OINK OINK!"

Like THIS—

"OINK OINNNNNKKKKK!"

The Beauties stirred and rustled. Stretched and licked

their carnassial shears. And began to circle him, their faces changing as they walked. Soft whirring sounds in the lavender mist, music of vanishing face hairs. Snaps and pops of jaws and chins; cheekbones, brows, and noses.

"OINNNNNKKKKK!"

Blacke pawed his wiry snout hairs, stared with disgust at his pink belly's spots . . . then with horror at the Beauties —whose faces were the Twelve's:

"The Night has Rules," they chanted. "The Night has Rules we must obey!"

An illusion, certainly. All right—a great one. But no more than that. The Night had tricked him, while he slept, into thinking he'd changed to a pig. Into thinking these *hyenas*—

"OINNNNNKKKKK!"

Malcolm grunted.

Mad Ingmar howled.

Then the giggling began as all Twelve of them charged.

Malcolm came straight as an arrow for the puckered delight hidden under Blacke's tail. And Mad Ingmar went for the hairsack of goodies as Romaine tore into Blacke's throat . . .

Austin awoke with a violent start in the hospital built on the island that year. He might have screamed if his throat hadn't been on fire. But he had enough left of his senses to know it wouldn't have mattered a bit if he had.

If the sunlight didn't kill him, or the hunger, or the thirst, he would die from the sheer state of shock he was in.

One of his hands had been shackled to the cast-iron harpstyle headboard.

With his free hand he explored the face he was going to die with.

The face of a pig:

Guy Brakowski.

Blacke felt the presence of the Twelve as keenly as if they were here.

Who has the last laugh now? they asked.

The Night has Rules we must obey.

"Fuck the Night," Blacke whispered.

He lay back to wait for the end.

His plan for the Rock had been Blacker than any the Rock
had yet seen. To Face-Trick his way to the island and learn
where the old women were kept. The two whose blood type
was A. B. Bat Trick his way, after feeding, back across the
Bay. Then alternate his feedings—now from that time, then
from this, now and then a short trip to the zoo—until he had
leveled his blood. It should have worked. It would have
worked. But the Face Trick had cost him; he had no
strength left.

Through the day, men came to check on him. To taunt
him and gawk at his old battered mug. To offer him water
. . . and, now and then, throw a little on his face and watch
the steam rise up from it. As if he were burning alive.

Not even the doctor would touch him.

"What's the use?" he asked the guards. "The man's already dead."

"You got that right," whispered Blacke.

"Eh?" The doctor turned.

Blacke smiled weakly at him, eyeing the pulse in his
throat.

"Flick my Bic," he answered as he closed his eyes again.

The doctor checked in before leaving on the last boat to
the city.

"I'll be back tomorrow. It'll be a deucin' pleasure to drop
you in your grave."

At the door he looked over his shoulder. "By the way," he
told Blacke, "you may be getting some company. One of
your *strange* little friends appears to be running a fever."

At seven, when the new patient arrived—one of the elderly bluehairs—she heard the rattling in his throat.

Too bad. She remembered him fondly. Lonely, gentle Dr.
Rice, so savagely beaten that night on the train.

It broke her heart to see him, shackled like an animal.

Emily cried out in protest. The cry went up an octave as she was shackled to *her* bed, across from Dr. Rice's.

"Now, see here, you animals! I won't be treated like this! Give that man some water and let me go this instant! I want to make a phone call—this is 1986! I'll put you on the Late Night News! I'll have your jobs! I'll sue! I'll—"

Emily stopped, her heart, not strong, weakened by the men's threatening looks.

"She wants us to give him some water," one said. "Miss *California Zephyr*."

"Miss Polly Ester," said the next, touching the hem of her dress.

"Miss Late Night News."

"Miss Radio."

"Miss Master Card."

Emily listened helplessly, unable to explain herself or reason with these creatures. Her friends had warned her this was a strange town.

She wept like a schoolgirl and suffered their taunts until the supply was exhausted.

The first soldier lit a Havana. He puffed at it thoughtfully and studied the porcelain jug by her bed.

"Don't you worry, Missy. We'll give your friend another drink." He winked, raising the jug overhead. "But as me mother would say—ladies first!"

The men did not stop laughing till they were out the door, the last splash still sizzling on Dr. Rice's skin. Almost as if the moonlight were hotter than the sun. He shuddered, once, then was totally still.

And Emily sank back, exhausted.

"Life is one long process of getting tired, my dear."

Father had said that to her on her fifteenth birthday, six months after Mother died and nine months before he went broke.

She would never get a present she cared less to receive. Or one she had more trouble losing than that heavy sigh of wisdom, uttered on a Kansas porch, one hot night a lifetime ago.

She'd buried her father the following year. And, in time,

she parted with two husbands, one daughter, three sons, and one breast. But Emily had sworn to keep her father's truer legacy: the gold hearty words she'd heard all through her youth:

There is always tomorrow. And, till then, today.

Even in her dreams she'd kept two steps ahead of the other, dark gift.

So it surprised her, how clearly she heard, as she floated along the long river in her white communion dress:

Life is one long process of getting tired, my dear.

She awakened instantly. She rubbed her eyes. She tried to think over the strong, measured breathing of the sleeping Dr. Rice.

Lie down, Emily . . . Close your eyes . . . Sleep . . .

Father, she thought. It *was* Father! But where?

Close your eyes and come to me . . .

Daddy!

Through the barred windows, she saw the veranda, with its low white wooden fence, a sycamore towering above it . . . and, through the branches, flashes of Painted Ladies for the guards.

Daddy might be on the porch, thinking that he was in Kansas . . .

So tired . . .

Close your eyes, child . . . I command you . . .

But she knew his voice couldn't have come from the porch. She'd never felt closer to Daddy than this. He was here, surely, standing just across the—

Oh.

Dr. Rice, looking tanned and well-rested, sat up very slowly. His lips were set in a curious smile that struck her as neither quite happy nor sad. He spoke, somehow, without moving his lips. His lavender purr overwhelmed her.

Daddy's feeling better now. But Daddy's still feeling so terribly tired. And Daddy's hungry, Emily. Close your eyes and FEED me . . .

She closed her eyes, with no thought of resisting. She heard the chain clink as she folded her hands.

Again she was sailing, as she'd never sailed, on her barge

through the lavender mist. And time was a river that went on forever, life a mere drop in a wave.

Life was good, very good.

But death was so much better.

She heard a sudden, astonishing *snap*—brittle and cold and metallic. She couldn't have asked for a clearer sign of her liberation.

She opened her eyes. For she wanted to see the world she had known wave good-bye from the shore.

She was sailing, all right.

Across the aisle.

In her bed.

To the smiling figure of the unchained Dr. Rice.

BAT TRICK

The station was used maybe six nights a year, when the tides rose too high for the Cliff House's boat. Tonight the sea was calm enough and there was little danger of the stationmaster showing in his leather-visored cap.

The station would have been perfect. The brick wall around it was bordered with shells. And on the lawn six rowboats bloomed with fuchsias and geraniums. The station was very romantic. It even had a cot.

But it was also in earshot of the old Presidio. And echoes from the barracks rippled through the mist: whistlings of men as they polished their boots . . . a lone bugler sounding taps . . .

Here, in the boathouse, they could be alone.

Here, they felt inviolate.

He had dreamed of this night since he met her. Now that the moment was here, though, he wrung his derby on his lap. The shack was too humble. He should have brought candles. The bedding looked shabby and made him feel cheap.

"Johnny," she said, "look at me."

She stood before him, his girl, spotlit by the moon.

"Don't you want me, Johnny?"

"Sure . . . It's just that—Well . . . I, see . . ."

How could he tell her that he was brand new?

"It's all right," she told him. "I know what to do."

"You *do*?"

"Oh yes, I've done it lots of times!"

"I see," was all he managed.

"Sure." She winked. "It's lots of fun. You put your fingers

in my ears and whisper 'Tinkle tinkle.' *That's* how you make babies."

Something astonishing happened: fear was lost in wonder. The red desire melted into something that he'd never known. He relaxed. He felt *affection* for a girl and hungered to express it.

He whispered her name. It was Lucy.

She raised one finger to her lips. "That's an end of talking, before I get scareder than you are."

Slowly and exquisitely, Lucy slipped out of her black patent pumps. The rustle of her overskirt merged with the soft laps of waves in the night. Her shirtwaist, starched to a rattling stiffness, sighed as she undid the ribbon that swathed her slender throat. Around her waist, in place of a belt, she wore the latest word: the collar of a Saint Bernard. This, too, she unfastened and dropped at her feet.

She stood before him, trig and trim and crisp as a crack yacht. Emanating from her, a barely perceptible odor, as subtle as her perfume, but infinitely wilder, sailed across the distance and half-knocked him off the bench.

For a moment she just stood there. Not a single pin was loose. Not a seam out of alignment. Till the tide swept the last of her shyness away.

Her hair, a rich buttercup yellow, fell in a tumble of waves to her waist. She began to sway, deliciously. The moves were so subtle, and yet so erotic, he wanted to capsize and drown in her musk.

She took her time, for they had time, and this was the first time, the best time of all.

She came at him in sections and layers.

She unbuttoned her shirtwaist, removed it; unclasped and stepped out of her full, pleated skirt; untied the strings of her petticoat, then dropped it with a sigh.

Her breasts swelled over her corset, so tightly tied he saw outlines of ribs. The straitjacket was fastened to straps between her thighs. The sight inflamed him painfully.

But he shared her relief as she undid the laces and eased the corset down her legs. The silk undershift stuck to her body in the patterns of the stays. She breathed once, ecstatically, then raised the shift over her head.

With a slip of one hand and a flip of one foot she lost her lacy underwear. And stood before him, naked except for the embroidered stockings with thick bands around the thighs. These last restraints she left in place, as if she could stand no more freedom than this.

He was twenty. She was eighteen. And they still had six minutes to live.

He stood, already ready—

and cried out in astonishment.

"Johnny?" she asked him. "What is it? What's—"

"Shhh. Stand over there," he said. "Out of the light."

He walked to the window facing the Bay as if he were walking on glass.

He looked more puzzled than frightened. But suddenly the boathouse seemed very cold and much too dark. The girl slipped her cloak from the hook on the door. She wrapped herself in it and shivered, while he stood at the window straining to see.

"Johnny?" she called.

He ignored her. He leaned forward, pressing his face to the glass.

"My God," he said, "what *is* that?"

She caught a flash of something over his shoulder, out under the moon, hovering over the Bay. Two tiny points of lavender that somehow appeared to be moving.

Then, as quickly, they were gone.

"Fog's thickening," Johnny said.

Indeed it was.

So was the cold. She pulled the cloak snugly about her, her teeth clicking as she approached him.

"Come on, get dressed. Let's go," he said.

"What was it?"

"I don't know. I thought it looked like it was—flying."

"Flying?" she cried. Then she giggled. He looked just like a little boy, standing like that at the window with his face against the glass.

You nearly forgot the bull jut of his jaw . . . those powerful shoulders and swaggering hips . . .

"Oh," she whispered. "Johnny . . ."

"There—look, there!"

It hovered a moment . . . weaved left and then right . . . then seemed to charge forward before it was lost.

"It's a bat, you silly."

"I guess." He just stood at the window, his face to the glass.

"That's all it was, just a bat."

"That's the word."

The girl laid her hand on his shoulder. Traced her nails in a light path down his arm. She tried to swallow, her throat thick as fog. The cloak fell from her shoulders.

He turned to her. She took his hand and placed it on her sex. His jaw dropped and his breath came out in short astonished puffs, like hers. He did not move, she could not breathe until he covered her mouth with his mouth, kissing her and breathing in, breathing out, and then his hand began to move.

"Oh Johnny," she moaned, "what you do to me . . ."

He picked her up and carried her to the bedding he'd set in the corner. She sat, her arms around her knees, and watched him come at her one piece at a time: the jacket . . . the collar . . . the shirt studs . . . the cuffs . . .

And then, after the red flannel longjohns, the prize.

"Oh Johnny," she said. "Fancy *that*."

"Do you?"

"I'm scared of it . . . I'm mad for it . . ."

On her back now, knees high and spread, arms stretched up to meet him.

Johnny gave her a look that was thoughtful and sad. "I surely do wish I could use it," he said. He raised his hands to his ears, with a wink. "But . . . I want to give you a baby."

He was still wiggling his fingers when the window glass exploded and the shack started filling with lavender fog.

STEREOPTICON II

 "Ah Toy?"

Sam, beginning to take to the name, pressed one cheek to the bars of her window. Saw Hay Ming's fingers waving happily and proudly.

Their "work stations" were side by side, on the prestigious second floor of the Municipal Crib House. They were at once more visible than the whores above them and safe from the hands on the street. Hay Ming giggled, announcing her seventh *lookee* of the night.

"It's so funny-funny, hey? White boys thinkee Chinese girls all got parts go easty-west, not northy-south like white girls, hey?"

Sam nodded miserably, choking back the tears.

"Ah Toy, no cry!" Hay Ming called. She reached her tiny fingers.

Sam reached back but her heart wasn't in it.

The distance between them could never be breached.

For Hay Ming the Municipal Crib House was a Good Address. As many as three hundred whores would ply their trade in cow yards, in cubes the size of closets. The noise and stink were ferocious. The cow-yard girl's quota: a hundred per night. The roughest, foulest men in town.

Oh, even the lowliest crib house was better than a cow yard, hey. Though the whores worked in groups—up to six in each crib—there were a few amenities. In front there were chairs for the whores on display or those who were resting their privates . . . and behind embroidered drapes, mats for the whores on their backs. The crib quota was still high at eighty. But on a good night, white boys came to beg them for a *lookee*.

And, ah, the Municipal Crib House . . . Just close your eyes, relax your mind—and you might be in a parlor. Almost.

The three-story house was partitioned into ninety stations, one whore assigned to each. The eight-by-ten cribs were kept spotlessly clean. And they were, in comparison, luxuriously furnished: a cushioned easy chair in front, beside a shrine with Buddha . . . a single brass or iron bed . . . a washstand . . . a coal-oil stove with a kettle for tea . . . a flask of carbolic for douching . . . clean towels . . .

Above each bed, in a nest of hand-painted roses, was printed each whore's name.

The walls were a source of endless pride and pleasure to Hay Ming. Because of Lim Poon's obsession with Sam's, apparently, singular taste, their walls had been freshly painted, hell red. And they were covered with keepsakes: postcards . . . ragtime music scores . . . gaily colored sketches . . .

Of all their good fortunes, though, none could compare with the reduction in quotas: only sixty tricks a night. For this, Hay Ming Lee was so grateful that she often turned eighty or ninety.

"Oh-oh, gotta go," she said. "Lookee-feelee-doee sure!"

Across the street, a window sported jugs of brilliant liquids filled with sea horses and toads. Nearby, a public letter writer worked at a small cane table while men around him played mah-jongg or drifted in thick clouds of smoke.

There were no women on these streets, except a few vegetable peddlers. Nine out of ten Chinese women were whores. The rest were seen on one occasion every seven years, the Festival of the Good Lady.

Sam drifted out of the bars, on a sweet opium high. This special blessing from Lim Poon she did not share with Hay Ming. She drifted back through the lavender eye to the sweet spots of time in her life.

It was getting easier by the day for Sam to float. She'd weighed in at zero-fat and had lost at least ten pounds. She tried to force herself to eat . . . but opium was sweeter. What the body fed on first was what it needed least; muscles, here, were useless. She was a whore with three holes to pump sperm in. And, night after night, sixty Chinamen pumped with their eyes closed anyway. Besides, the smaller "Ah Toy" grew, the happier Lim Poon became. And a happy Lim Poon was an opium high, if not the front cover of *Esquire.*

Still, there was a riddle she could not seem to fathom. It had been so easy, being Asian in the Eighties. The very color of her skin had set powerful fantasies off in white minds. The tawny beauty of her skin had whispered of submissiveness; her finely chiseled body had promised exquisite control. The combination, to white men, had been irresistible. Now even her skin had betrayed her. It had been her ticket once; now it was the mark of a whore.

She remembered her last night, and first night, with Wolf and the handful of good nights between. He'd needed her . . . believed in her . . .

She remembered the lovers before Wolf: the jocks . . . the studs . . . the rich boys . . . the rockers . . .

She remembered Harpo, on the train . . . the only man she'd ever met who made her laugh and walked away . . . and never asked a thing . . .

She remembered wondering what it was like . . . back in the Summer of Love . . .

She remembered the first time she saw Wolf—

and then she really saw him, through the bars, on the sidewalk below.

She called his name.

And then she felt the fat hand on her shoulder.

Lim Poon had returned with more postcards and dope, his fat tongue snaking through his teeth.

II

March 22, the day after the shooting that should have made his fortune, Wolf decided to jump from the bridge. He was halfway through Chinatown when he thought he heard somebody—Sam?—call his name.

Sam in Chinatown—that was a laugh. She'd be where the money was, or be knocking them dead in some gym. Still, it *had* sounded like Sammy. . . .

When he looked, though, he saw nothing but an ocean of blue tunics . . . coming at him, and at him, in waves.

And screaming at him as they came, just like the other voices—his mother, his father, the nuns of St. Mary, Shakespeare, Shaw, and Piltdown man:

You are an absolute failure!

He wanted to cover his ears. He could not. Both hands were holding the paper. He needed to hold it to read it. He needed to read it to scream it while tearing it to shreds.

JEALOUSY MOTIVE OF A GRIM TRAGEDY!

"Isn't *that* a beautiful headline? How's *this* for a dramatic lead?

> *As the dinner-hour crowds streamed past the Montgomery Block at six o'clock last evening, they were startled by revolver shots that turned a sordid story of love, lust, and jealousy into grimmest tragedy. Many of the hungry hundreds . . .*

"That's great!" Wolf shrieked. "Alliterate!" He tossed the shreds like pieces of his own heart to the winds. "The horrified, hurrying, halted, hounded hundreds—"

> *saw William S. Walbridge murder his former wife, Mrs. Belle Robins, wound two passersby, and then blow his brains out before the law's hand could be laid upon him.*

He threw the paper to his feet. And he covered his ears as he charged through the crowds.

"I was there! I had it! The story was mine and they scooped me! The sons of bitches, they stole it! Oh Jesus, I'm not going anywhere!"

He'd been going places, one hour after the shooting, when he landed at Newspaper Corner.

The *Call* and the *Examiner* stood on opposite corners of Third, the *Chronicle* across the street where Kearney met with Market.

He'd been shaking with fear and excitement, the scribbled story in his hands. He stood there like a schoolboy trying to pick his first dance at a prom, his sights settling on the *Call*, the tallest of the three.

Be bold, my heart, he thought. Be bold!

In any age, the man of style, if he had the gall and the chutzpah, would break away from the herd.

The way to fight a comet was to pull out *all* the stops. Don't follow these idiots, lead them!

He rushed in with a mighty roar, the world's first New Journalist.

MORTAL STAKES BY MOONLIGHT!
An Exclusive by Wolf Cotter

Quiet night in San Francisco.
Almost too quiet to die.
I am seated in the Montgomery Block . . . sipping mocha coffee . . . and inhaling Turkish Trophies along with some dark thoughts of time's filthy tricks when—
BAM!
EEEEEE!

BAMBAM!
EEEEEE!

BAM!
EEEEEEEEEEEEEEEEE!
—the screams and explosions began . . .

Twenty minutes—and three pages—later he'd found himself on the street . . . a gold eagle in his pocket as payment for their theft . . . and his ears still echoing with the men's giggles and whoops.

Wolf's breath came now in anguished heaves as he tackled the steep rise of Powell. His legs had grown nearly too heavy to lift. He could not raise his hand to wipe the sweat that poured from his brow.

Since Chinatown, though, he'd been feeling the rise of a curious lightness within. The sense of understanding.

Art was a mine field, and pure luck and timing determined who crossed without losing their legs. Before, he'd been ten years too late; sixty years too soon now. Luck and timing. Nothing more.

He rounded the crest of the hill, his lungs on fire, his legs pure lead.

He saw the Bay before him, glorious in twilight, its surface rippling serenely. He saw the lights, heard the laughter, from the Coast below.

Oh, it was a wonderful evening to die.

He took a breath and held it, his heart hammering as he turned—

Oh, dear God! Oh no, not this!

Wolf collapsed to his knees, flopping his arms like a grounded seagull.

Where the Bridge should have been there was—nothing but fog-swept, moonlit water.

He would have screamed, but he hadn't the wind.

He would have wept, but he hadn't the heart.

Time's fool again, as always.

Then—

something peculiar happened.

He felt a presence behind him.

Then something warm, and very strong, gripping his glistening pate. It felt like a hand, except hands did not glow. And his whole mind felt filled with a lavender rush.

He felt his attention shift, as if his gaze were directed, to *La Isla de los Alcatraces.*

The lighthouse twinkled at him, innocently, vaguely.

He could not begin to say why the sight of the island relaxed him.

But the island did, relax him.

The feeling began at the roots of his hair. Then it washed over his body in waves.

He repeated the words like a mantra:

"The Rock . . . The Rock . . . The Rock . . ."

"That's right," the voice behind him purred. "You see it now as I do. A warm and happy place. But most of its rooms are still empty. Think how lonely our dear friends must feel. I want them all to feel happy and warm. A man of your talents could help me. You do want to help me."

"Yes . . ."

"I'm sorry?"

"Yes . . . master."

"Good. Good, that *pleases* me. Money, fame, it's all yours. Your name will live forever, Wolf, if you do what I tell you."

"Yes . . . master."

"Very good. We'll work just fine together. Now, there'll be a lot to remember. But first there are two things you're gonna forget. I want you to forget about that ballbuster Chink bitch of yours. She belongs to me."

"Sam . . ."

"I'm sorry?"

"*Sammy!*" Wolf felt something *squeezing* his mind. God, the pain!

"I'm *sorry*?"

"Who was . . . I forget . . ."

"Good. Good, that pleases me. And, while you're at it, forget about me. You never met me. I do not exist."

"Yes . . . master. Who?"

"Good. You're more fun than a barrel of monkeys. I know just where we'll have you stay. A place you will not want to leave. Now, pay real close attention. Here's the poop on Alcatraz and what you're gonna do next week. After we get started, babe, every day is April Fool's."

III

From the Buena Vista Tavern, the view of the Bay was the finest in town. Tonight, though, all eyes were fixed on the tragic figure reeling at the bar.

Just four hours earlier, halfway through his best-ever "To be . . ." Rod had been hissed off the stage. He'd been too stunned to leave at first, scurrying back like a crab to the wings. Life hadn't wasted any time letting him know where he stood. So he sat, downcast and uniquely afflicted, trying not to notice the others' knowing looks.

Two ordinary-looking men in flat-brim derbies and checked coats strutted past them to the stage.

They took their places behind the curtain and alternately barked:

"McGillicutty *and*—"
  "McGillicutty *and*—"
"We're readddddy—
  "We're readddddy!"
"—when *you* are!"
  "You *are*!"

The iron curtain rose, a steady roll of thunder. When it had risen completely, the twin McGillicuttys winked over their shoulders at Rod and began.

They took two shuffling steps to the right.

Then two shuffling steps to the left.

They shuffled backward a couple of steps.

Then shuffled quickly forward. And then, without a hitch, did three pirouettes in perfect synchronization.

The first McGillicutty tipped his derby seven times in lightning-quick succession.

The second matched him move for move.

Their voices rose high and away above the screams of laughter.

"As *I* was going down the street yesterday—"

"Ah! As *you* were going down the street—all right!"

"I *say*, I saw a *girl* at a window—"

"*You* saw a *girl* at a window!"

"—and this *girl*, she was a *corker*!"

"Ah! As *you* were going down the street yesterday, *you*

saw a *girl* at a window, and this *girl*, she was a *corker*! All right!"

"All right!"

"Go on!"

They did. They went on for four more minutes, each mimicking at every turn the other's expression and gesture.

They slapped their knees.

They tipped their caps.

They shuffled left and shuffled right and did more crazy pirouettes.

Rod did not stay for the acrobats . . . the zitherist . . . the yodelers . . . the Esmerelda Sisters and their Four Flower Girls . . .

He stood out on Market and howled at the moon.

They were different in their souls.

And there was no way to reach them.

What would become of him?

How could he live?

Now, in the Buena Vista, the sickness of his body matched the sickness of his soul. On the bar before him stood six beer bottles, nine scotch glasses, and three brandy snifters.

"Well," someone concluded, " 'least we know this one ain't *strange*. He drinks like a real San Franciscan."

The men watched respectfully, placing bets in their quietest voices on which drink they sent would do him in. San Francisco had always been that kind of town.

Rod saw a man with three heads and six hands handing him three more Raniers.

He reached for the one in the middle, hoping that this one would kill him. He raised the bottle to his lips—and then the floor began to move. A lowdown earthy rumble swelled into a series of powerful shakes. Across the room, a table tipped and glasses toppled to the floor. The mirror cracked behind the bar. Around him, men cried:

"Eeeeeee-hahhhhh!"

"Here she comes!"

"Let 'er rip!"

"Quaker Sam was right—it's here!"

The quake lasted all of six seconds.

But even as it settled, the knowledge rocked him in his soul.

This was the year of the Big One.

Suddenly the wall of time between his world and theirs collapsed.

The words just *came.* He could no more have stopped them than he could stop breathing. The voice that spoke hardly seemed to be his.

To be, or not to be, that is the question:
Whether 'tis nobler in the mind to suffer
The slings and arrows of outrageous fortune,
Or to take arms against a sea of troubles
And by opposing end them. . . .

Soft clicks of glasses on the bar.

Long puffs of fat Havanas.

In the Buena Vista Tavern, there was not another sound.

Rod felt a wrenching in his throat, the words twisting the cords, reshaping the voice. He surrendered, going, gone.

To die: to sleep.
No more; and by a sleep to say we end
The heart-ache and the thousand natural shocks
That flesh is heir to . . .

No need to think. No need to scheme or struggle for the high notes. The words were linked and they unwound. He felt his throat relax and cool, as if a stream were bathing the cords they'd torn and twisted. The words now seductive and hopeful, serene.

'tis a consummation
Devoutly to be wish'd. To die: to sleep.
To sleep? perchance to dream. . . .

The silence now was absolute. Men leaned on their elbows, slackjawed and dewy-eyed, as ashes grew on their cigars. A mere puff might have ended the magic.

When the speech was ended, Rod came to, as if from a

trance. Men wept and stared forlornly at *La Isla de los Alcatraces.* Their lives would never be the same.

Rod waited for lightning to strike him, the earth to open at his feet. The voice that had used him had come from the gods. And now that they'd used him completely—

He felt a hand on his shoulder.

Surely it belonged to Zeus.

He looked over his shoulder, ready to go, grateful for his moment.

What he saw was a small portly man with blue eyes about the same size as his derby. He pressed a card in Rod's left hand: *David Francis Kelley, Stage Director, the Alhambra Theatre.*

His lips quivered like hummingbird wings.

"My God," he said, "who *are* you?"

Rod straightened an inch or two taller.

"I am," he said, "Lord Whittaker."

IV

Earlier, a miracle continued in the library, where Harriet had worked twelve years.

Hopeless Harriet.

Spinster Sally.

Mustache Mary.

Skinny Minnie.

She knew what they called her. The whispers now across the aisles were the same she'd once heard in the schoolyard.

But Harriet had known something for longer than she could remember:

One tended one's garden and trusted to time.

One planted, carefully, beautiful thoughts.

Until the inner garden bloomed. And one day someone Special came.

Someone as special as you were.

He looked—and saw, not a mole or a mustache, but the

roses in your eyes. Saw Plato, perhaps, in the purse of your lips. Heard Shelley and Keats in your laugh.

Such was love!

Harriet's miracle maker sat in the corner, as always, surrounded by tall stacks of papers and books. A small man whose graying hair had been cropped almost clean to his skull. His beard, just a spike from his chin.

They whispered about him as they did of her.

Quaker Sam, they called him. He'd arrived out of nowhere the first week in March, breathing hellfire and damnation. And warning the town of the Big One that surely had to come.

And his was the name she would whisper, alone, at night when the gas lamp was flickering.

She saw him looking up at her with that Quaker twinkle.

He didn't need to ask her twice.

She rushed in her sensible shoes to his side.

"Harriet, I do believe that we have found another."

We!

He tapped his quill pen on the notepad he'd filled.

"Sit down, my child. You'd better. I'm feeling faint with excitement myself."

Harriet sat, palms on her knees to control their shaking.

"Ready-made clothing, Harriet. We overlooked that entirely. Ready-made clothing—I feel like a dunce!"

Harriet's dress, just bought for tonight, had come off an Emporium sale rack. She touched the collar nervously, shifting forward in her seat.

"You say—ready-made, Sam?"

Sam's pencil tapped at the circles and charts, his whisper getting snappier.

"It all began with the War Between the States. The sudden demand for *tens of thousands* of uniforms at once. The only solution, of course, at the time had been to work with *averages*. If a man's waist, for example, measured forty inches, and his sleeve length thirty-four, then, on the average, his shoulders must be such and such."

"Why, yes," Harriet said solemnly.

"No, no, that's not the problem. Pshaw! Average and

ready-made are fine for soldiers, in a war. Perhaps it rein-
forces the regimented frame of mind."

"I *see*," she said emphatically.

"Yes, yes, 1860, that's all well and good. No trouble with
the Sixties. The Civil War—"

"The what, Sam?" She'd never heard the term before.

Quaker Sam cleared his throat, looking, for the life of
him, as if he'd made a mortal slip. Why, if you didn't know
the man, you'd have thought that he almost looked scared.

"The War Between the States, my child, that—made the
South more *civil*!"

"Ah."

Sam's relief was so extreme that Harriet wanted to hug
him. The Civil War, indeed. Good Lord, what a wonderfully
strange thing to call it!

"The War brought us together. It made us stronger. If
ready-made for soldiers was the price we had to pay . . ."

Quaker Sam stroked the gray spike of his beard. Then
tapped a circle he had drawn, as if he were stabbing it. The
circle had four numbers.

"1880, Harriet . . . The more closely we look, the more
closely we see: 1880 is the year the whole world began
going wrong. In 1880 a demon named Daniel Edward Ryan
—and may his name forever be accursed on your tongue!—
Dan -iel *Ed*- ward *Ry*- an published his tribute to Satan. And
do you know what he called it?"

"No!"

Harriet couldn't imagine. But Sam's voice was swelling
and her heart began to quiver in lovestruck admiration.

*"Human Proportions in Growth: Being the Complete
Measurements of the Human Body for Every Age and Size!"*

"Oh nooo!"

"Oh yesss! Within *ten* years ready-wear profits increased
by one billion dollars a year!"

"My word!"

Sam waved an imperial hand. "It's all here. In these books
you've brought me. Now ninety percent of the clothing we
buy is purchased ready to wear."

"My *soul*!"

"So, what does the government do?"

"I don't *know!*"

"Form a National Bureau of Standards! The high priests of measurement at their shrine to Quantity. Now they've got us thinking we're *sizes,* not people!"

"OHHHH!"

Well, Sam was really wound up now and everyone knew what was coming. He pounded a fist on the table. He took a deep breath, enough air for them all—

but stopped short before he began.

"Wait a minute. Wait a *minute . . .*"

Sam's fingers flipped through the notepad.

"Harriet!" he whispered.

"Yes!"

"We may be on to something here . . ."

"Tell me, Sam, oh tell me, please!"

"1883!"

"Oh, Sam!"

"Another tribute to Satan? Is this what I see? *The Contents of Children's Minds* by *Mis*-ter *G. Stan*-ley *Hall?*"

"We are *lost!*"

"Not yet, my child! We'll fight them here and everywhere. At every turn we'll stop them!"

"Yes!"

"Get it for me, Harriet. Bring me Hall's tribute to Satan. Bring everything you have on childhood psychology before and after '83."

Harriet flew from the table with a wild, ecstatic chirp.

She was halfway across the room when Quaker Sam began.

He roared, "There's a Big Quake coming! Friends, friends, hear me please—we've got to get back to the Eighties! That's when the whole world began going wrong!"

V

"Ooooo!" Betsy'd said to him. "You got a *bar*. I can't *tell* you how *many* men have-n't. But perhaps we'd better clar-i-fy what you *mean* by a *drink* at your bar." She hadn't done Mae West in years. But she figured she had it down just about right.

"I assure you, madam, I mean nothing irregular."

"Good. 'Cause I'm the kinda *girl*, you see, who likes her reg-u-lar-i-ty. Now, *who* you got be-hind the bar?"

"Why, Jake Muldoon. He's tended bar—"

"I'll bet he *has*. And I'll bet *yours* is gettin' mighty ten-der. Take care of your *bar*. It at-tracts me. If you *know* what I *mean*. And I *think* that you *do*. What you *need's* a good bar-ten-dress, Clark."

"Bartendress? A wo . . . A wo . . ."

"I *knew* you wanted to woo-woo the minute you *came* with my ker-chief."

That had been a week ago.

Now a new star had risen in the city's Cocktail Route. The star was called the Richelieu. But the real star was a woman unlike any woman the men in the Richelieu had met.

The night she dropped her kerchief, the Richelieu's ten-grand mahogany bar had only been half paid for. In the week since Clark had "rushed" her, the rest of the bar had been paid for, along with the Tiffany lamps.

There was scarcely room to stand these days when she was working the bar. The men lined up like children, smok-ing and ogling Mae.

Watching her hands fly as she made their drinks.

Watching her sweep back that thick amber wave.

Watching the natural curves of her hips as she moved from one end of the bar to the next.

And, devil take the hindmost, the things the woman said!

No, not exactly. It was the *way* she said things.

"Say-y-y-y . . . 's that a *gun* in your pock-et, or you just *glad* to *see* me?"

Well, nobody, not even Clark, knew exactly *what* she

meant. But it all sounded just so suggestive and innocent at once . . . so inviting and yet nonchalant. You'd have felt like a cad if you figured it out.

"Come *on* up and *see* me some *time,*" she might purr.

What could you do, you just swaggered and winked. And watched her sashay to the next guy, who, feeling emboldened, might reach. And then she'd stand back with her hands on her hips, daring yet denying.

"You're ska-tin' on thin *ice,* my *duck.*" Little jiggle of her head. "The best *kind* to *skate* on . . . if you *know* what I *mean* and I *don't* think you *do* . . . 'cause your *blades* ain't *long* and point-y."

If she had sat at a table, a hundred men would have followed there and hung around her to listen.

But behind the bar the woman was a sorceress.

She'd needed coaching on some of the drinks: she'd never heard of Pisco Punch or even a Blue Blazer. But she'd never needed telling twice. And the odd drink she mixed queerly —Manhattans, for example, without the jigger of bitters— seemed to taste even better that way. She remembered men's names. She remembered their drinks. She seemed to know instinctively just what to say to each. Especially when they got *that look* and set into the town's latest game.

(*Come on, Mae, who's president?*

—Well, the name es-capes me now . . . but you just turn the *lights* off an' I'd know him any-where.)

Clark watched her. And he wanted her.

He'd never met a woman so outrageously—*herself.*

Why did she persist, though, in calling him Clark—when he'd told her his real name was Billy?

Betsy tapped the ash from her cheroot and surveyed her kingdom.

Heaven got better and better, she thought.

One hundred men, hale and hearty, beefy and well-padded. No anemic androgyns. No sipping carrots through a straw with gym beaus or gym bimbos. No obsessive joggers with aggressive ribs and hangdog eyes.

A chance to be the woman she'd always wanted to be.

"Say, *Pete*, your glass is emp-ty. Loosen *up* your in-hi-bish-uns!"

Men, here, real men. Like the stars from the films of the Thirties. Garfield. Cooper. Bogart.

Gable . . .

Clark watching every move she made. Those ears jutting out from his neat, slicked-back hair. About five-ten, one-eighty, he moved with the grace of a boxer. Except when he was around her.

It had been longer than she could recall since any man had looked at her with open, unbridled desire. That had been pounds and years before the last squalid room she'd departed. And there were no men to remember, till now, who'd stood back, respectfully. As if she were worth the wait. Sex had been quickies between drinks at Jake's, about as pleasant as scratching an itch. And remembered just as long. She'd let them do anything to her, if they'd make up a few lines of verse.

> (Roses are red, violets are blue,
> I'd like to go down on you . . .)

She wondered how long it would take Clark . . . to *screw* up his cour-age and *take* her to her room above the bar.

Not too much longer, she figured.

Things were going perfectly. If the others were here, she hoped they'd found happiness to equal hers.

Prose, shmose. Verse, shmerse.

Miss Wilcox was an idiot: life was a cabaret.

How could anything really go wrong?

VI

It was wrong to take candy from strangers. Even if Mommy was very near by, looking in the Emporium windows. It was wrong to talk to strangers, too, except for "Good morning" or "Good afternoon." It was important to be nice—yet at the same time sensible.

The girl was six. She knew these things. She had no trouble remembering that they were no longer in Kansas. But on weekends, when they came downtown, she did find it hard to remember why the difference should not delight her.

Each day was an amusement park, filled with new thrills and astonishing sights.

The merry crimson cable cars, trundling up and trundling down, and clanging their bells as they passed her . . .

The phaetons and hansoms and landaus . . .

The magic auto-mobiles: Pope Toledos and Detroit Electrics . . .

The Palace Hotel—where one day she would live!—towering high and majestic . . .

And oh, the people who passed by, each more fashionably dressed than the last . . .

And

oh . . .

Who was that now coming toward her, smiling, a half-block down Market. She'd never seen a smile like that, or a pair of more beautiful eyes. The tawny-skinned man, in his Prince Albert coat, his long blond hair streaming behind him. The tall man with the thick mustache, a gold brick set on chocolate. She knew he must have candy, the way he just floated straight at her.

And

oh . . .

Here he was now. Lavender, pure lavender, glowing in his eyes.

He didn't have any candy. But that was all right with the girl. He made her feel warm all over instead. He winked at her. She liked that, too, and wished that her mommy would join them. And soon.

But when the man spoke, she forgot about Mommy. She'd never heard a voice like that: softer than velvet, yet sandpaper gruff.

The man with the eyes said, "Excuse me, my dear, if you don't mind my asking . . ."

He leaned over to whisper the rest in her ear.

Blacke was half a block away before the girl began to scream.

She would remember nothing, nothing in particular. But from her screams he knew she knew: something special had been lost. And the wound was as deep and as bloody as if he'd plucked out her heart. He'd used nothing more than his fingers. She'd felt the Blacke touch of his mind through their tips. And she'd known that she must fuck her father.

Her terror had been sweet and strong.

There were so many ways to feed.

All of them delicious.

TREMORS

I woke up the following morning, the twenty-seventh of March, in a nicely furnished room. The last thing I remembered after sighting Austin Blacke was Patch leading a choral rendition of "The Goo Goo Man" in rounds. I did not recall feeling queasy or drunk. And I remembered nothing of the trip from the Coast to my chambers. I felt a little light-headed; otherwise, alert, at ease.

Austin was no threat to me. I wasn't scared of Blacke, not me. He'd been white as a corpse. Hell, he'd looked like a fool. Big, bad Austin Blacke. Another sawdust Caesar.

Well, this would be a busy day. I wasn't a dummy like Austin. And neither were Lenny or Sam. We'd all be lying low, real low, getting the lay of the land . . . hoping to link with what others there were . . . before the bluehairs on the Rock started to sing like canaries.

I slipped my feet over the edge of the bed. Heave-hoed a foot and a half to the floor. *Pittapat* of the flop-eared galoshes. *Flopawhoosh* of the billowing Harp-coat. I rotated my neck. Circled my arms. The most natural thing in the world.

Being here.

The carpeting was thick and lush, with bunches of red and blue roses in yellow baskets on white ground.

The wallpaper, no less lush, stopped a yard short of the ceiling, white plaster bridging the two. Endless Asians, on all walls, assisted their almond-eyed ladies into long junks on a lake . . . while, nearby, storks sat under palms, planning their nine-month deliveries. Here and there, a few were buried underneath framed pictures: hypertense fox terriers and kiss-me-quick little girls.

The brass single bed that I'd slept on lay under a wealth of white netting. Beside the bed stood a black walnut dresser with porcelain knobs and a white marble top.

In the corner, an oak rocker passed the time of day with a small table covered with tasseled green felt.

The morning sun, filtered through starched lacy curtains, threw the whole scene into mystic relief.

My attention drifted to the gleaming yellow oak of the rolltop desk. On its green-felt blotter, beneath high stacks of upper drawers, were:

two bottles of Daly's Best bookkeeping ink . . .

two round cardboard boxes with pen nibs and wooden holders . . .

a penwiper, stained red and black . . .

and an oval photograph of a pretty but stern-looking woman and a much younger Patch . . .

"That was Caroline, me wife."

Patch stood at the door in red flannels, an unlit cigar in his hand.

He gave me a look. The look lasted a second. Then he turned and started off.

"C'mon, let's get some calories!"

I snatched my horn from the nightstand and followed Patch down the hall.

The way was long and narrow, passing three rooms on each side before it opened at the end into a spacious parlor.

Last on the left was the one room I needed most to use.

The walls here were painted, not papered, death gray. The wood tub was the size of a coffin, lined with, apparently, sheet lead. Beside the tub, a boxlike apparatus squatted, a small petal at its base.

"So," Patch said. "A wise guy. You think I can't have a lead bathtub and drink to Quaker Sam?"

I remembered, vaguely, last night's toasts to Quaker Sam and the earthquake. Something about the Eighties, about getting back to the Eighties.

But what did tubs or toilets—?

I honked the horn.

I had to go.

"So. You're thinking tubs weren't lined with lead till after 1890! You're thinkin' I can't use the tub and raise a cheer to Quaker Sam?"

I shook my head, horrified.

"Well, I'll let you in on a secret," he cried. "Wood tubs was lined with aluminum thirty years ago!"

I agreed!

But Patch went on relentlessly. "Made one of 'em a day, they did, in the manufactories for deucin' Pullman cars! We had 'em in the Eighties—an' I'll damn well drink to the Eighties, like Sam!"

I was looking at the buttons on his flannel underwear. Surely flannel underwear had been around forever. Even in the Eighties. They were fine with me.

"Oh, I know what you're thinkin', boy. You're a sly one, you are. You're thinkin' the crapper came later."

I lowered my eyes to his slippers. I sent him vibes of approval.

But just then Patch surprised me. "You're right," he said. "But it weren't my idea, Caroline wanted the crapper. So, let's just shake and forget about it and you go do your business. What the hell, eh, a crap's just a crap."

Patch extended his right leg.

I gave him my left.

I watched him walk off to the kitchen.

I know what you're thinking: The old man was mad as a hatter and the sensible thing was to go.

But go *where?*

I was worse off than a baby. A kid slips up, he screams all night till you beg for his forgiveness.

My first slip would be my last.

Or I'd be stuck in my clown suit for good. And I was a serious man.

About half of the day's calories were waiting in the kitchen.

Room center, on the clean brick floor, a round table laid

with gold oilcloth swayed beneath its load: flapjacks, ham, steak, toast, scrambled eggs, and apple pie. And a copy of the *Call* with the scoop on calories. The old man had circled what I guessed was our objective: 4,000 calories daily.

Patch looked over from the oil stove, where he'd been making coffee. The stove was the size of the rolltop, with nickel-plated castings and a zinc spatter shield. Around the shield hung a flashing array of copper and porcelain-lined pots and pans.

By the door two gas lamps hissed and threw off their flickering light.

I had to watch my step with Patch. But I figured he might still be harmless enough . . . if I could just figure out the Quaker Sam connection.

The Big One and the Eighties.

So I gave the horn a honk while giving the table a shake. It seemed clear enough to me. But then I'd never been good at charades.

The old man roared with laughter. "You's scared about the Big One, eh? Oh Lord, ain't that a scream?"

After filling two porcelain mugs from the pot, Patch kicked back and lit his Havana. He waved the cigar like a wand at the feast.

"Go on, now, get your calories. I'm savin' mine for later. An' don't give me none of your horn. Let me set you straight on earthquakes, Honk."

Clearly my role had its limits. I could no more steer a talk with Patch than navigate Niagara with only the horn in my hand.

Then again, if I went with the flow, I might make my way from one day to the next. And, in time draw up some respectable charts from what I was able to gather. Get out of the clown suit and blend in just fine, with nary a fear of the Rock.

I'd set out to learn one thing. Instead, I would learn quite another. Still, my ignorance was total. And San Francisco with its quakes was not a bad place to begin.

Patch began:

From 1850 to 1906 there'd been 465 "tremblers," most of them not worth a hoot.

The last killer quake had been in 1868. San Francisco had spit in its eye.

And you didn't survive nearly five hundred quakes without learning a good thing or two. Homes were constructed of redwood and cedar, the better to withstand the shock. And the walls of most stone buildings—take the Palace or the Monkey Block—wouldn't budge if the earth split wide open.

The city had six hundred firemen. And millions of gallons of water were stored beneath the streets, with additional conduits to reservoirs in Alameda and San Mateo.

As Patch went on, my certainty grew:

The Quake couldn't possibly be in the spring.

And summer sounded wrong, all wrong.

Early fall? Possibly.

But mid-fall . . . Say, November . . . Yes, that suited my purposes fine.

A man might make it rich here . . . of course after finding the others . . . if he blended and played a sly hand.

And those were my specialties: blending and playing sly hands.

We set off around noon in a hansom, Patch puffing away as he lectured and me honking away on the horn.

We rode the Line on Market. The five-block stretch where respectable girls strolled and dropped their kerchiefs; where droves of dapper "mashers" whistled under street lamps or from inside the open cigar shops.

We stopped before the Palace. Whole forests of rich, golden oak, felled just for the floors. The lobby, paved with silver dollars . . . to give one the feel of real money. Toilets with genuine Chippendale seats. Gold cuspidors on rugs so thick they cut them once a week.

Van Ness was a hundred and fifty feet wide, without a used car lot in sight. Thirty blocks of Baghdad's best cathedrals and Victorians.

No alternative lifestyles on Polk Street. Ladies promenaded, discreetly gloved and veiled, or chatted with butchers and grocers, while men in passing cable cars tipped their derbies and puffed their cigars.

We saw the "nabobs" on Nob Hill boarding their new Pope Toledos and Fords. The men, in tails and top hats; the ladies, in furs and silk opera cloaks.

They came from the Flood House, at Mason, through the $50,000 bronze fence.

They came from the Stanford, at Powell, across the circular hallway with its zodiac signs set in onyx and gold on the marble tiles.

They came from the Mark Hopkins House, which had more turrets than towers. More towers than steeples. More steeples than gables. More gables than gargoyles and pigeons combined. The master bedroom, it was said, would have shamed a doge: walls of ebony, fifty feet high, and inlaid with diamonds and sapphires.

Patch showed me Mechanics' Pavilion, whose main attraction these days was "mixed" roller skating. The pinkieboys came in their tuxes and suits, their bowlers and their derbies. They paid their twenty-cents fee at the door. Then strapped on their skates and took off like damn fools after pinkieshopgirls.

Beat North Beach was warehouses.

Chic Russian Hill was shanty town.

The Tenderloin was *toney*, the Wall Street of whores.

Patch only stopped talking to light a cigar. When he stopped, I waited for Niagara to start up again. My fortune —my salvation—depended on learning the tiniest things.

The lighting, for example. I had to learn to see it from Patch's point of view. See it as a man of the time. When I looked, I saw the magic of kerosene lanterns and gas lamps. But Patch's gaze was focused on new 'lectric street lamps with their "hideous" bluish-white light. They weren't strange to me, of course. But a few years before, the lights hadn't been there. And soon, he was certain, the quieter and warmer glows would be things of the past.

To blend, I had to learn to see not just what was there— but what hadn't been there, what had just newly arrived.

Newspapers were changing too. Nearly ten percent of

the ads now showed drawings of the products. This infuriated Patch, although he wasn't certain why. If he wanted to see it, he'd buy it, he said.

The three-hundred-and-thirty-pound William H. Taft was a "fine figure of a man." And the daily consumption of seven-course meals was a tribute to Health and Success, though the fair sex had their problems with burst bladders, collapsed lungs, and overtaxed hearts.

Dr. Lyon's Perfect Tooth Powder still "cleaned and beautified teeth," as it had for some twenty-five years. And Patch saw no serious challenge from the upstart Colgate.

John Philip Sousa had begun complaining about "the menace of mechanical music." For the infernal Edison had sold his first gramophone in 1897. And now you couldn't take two steps without hearing one play for a nickel in some pinkieboy saloon. But Patch knew the gramophone was just a passing fad: wasn't the beauty of music in hearing a song fresh each time?

Typewriters were changing fast. Now they were starting to make them with upper and lower case letters on a single keyboard. Well, the typewriter had been around since 1868 . . . so, Patch concluded, it wasn't the end of the world. Then again, Mark Twain had turned in the first typewritten manuscript in 1885. Could *Huckleberry Finn* be good—if it wasn't *written*?

Patch sighed. Sometimes he felt certain that Quaker Sam was right: that the world had been good 'till the Eighties, and then . . .

Quaker Sam . . .
Quaker Sam . . .
Patch couldn't go an hour without mentioning Sam's name; about the same frequency he worried for the horses. Regular as clockwork, one hour into a ride, he'd decide: The horses must be tired now, we ought to change cabs, give the ponies a break. And, while we were at it, parked as we were in front of another saloon, why not raise a glass or two.

To, of course, old Quaker Sam.

At one, when we made our first pit stop, heads turned as they had in the Yellowstone Bar. This was pretty much what

I'd expected. But I hadn't expected the nods or the smiles, or the rippling whisper of "Honkey. . . ." Or the men coming up to drop coins in my hat as I sat there being filled by Patch with facts and still more calories.

"Kid," Patch said, "you're gonna be rich. By the way, long as we're on the subject, why don't you set up some drinks for the house, let 'em know you're all right in the head."

So I did. I honked the horn and I wiggled my ears and Patch took my leg and he shook it and roared, "That's the proper caper! Drinks on Honk! To Quaker Sam!"

"To Quaker Sam!" a chorus roared.

"Down with the gramophone!" one cried.

"Down with the kinetoscope!" cried the man beside him.

We left at two and stopped at three to give the next set of horses a break. And fine-tune my germs and calories.

Heads turned again when we entered. But this time the men didn't whisper. It was:

"Hey—it's them, boys, it's Honkey and Patch!"

"Sure, sure, that's the word!"

"Shake a leg, Honk!"

"C'mon, do the ears!"

"Down with *Huckleberry Finn!*"

We arrived at the Cliff House at seven, our reputations before us again. And Quaker Sam starting to gel in my mind: He was one of the end-of-the-worlders you'd always find in Baghdad. Neither Patch nor anyone gave two hoots about the Quake. But Sam's predictions had a twist: something to do with the Eighties . . . when the town had still been good and Real . . .

We took a table by a window, tipping our hats to our fans on the way. Below, the surf crashed on huge, jagged rocks, on which seals perched and flopped and barked.

From a room adjoining the bar, I heard the suave clicks of billiard balls.

Along the bar, under the Tiffany lamps, one "fine figure of a man" after another raised his glass and gave a cheer. To Honkey, and Patch, and, of course, Quaker Sam.

Two tables down, three nabobs shared about ten thousand calories with a voluptuous whore. A "fine figure of a woman," blond, a black evening wrap over the shoulders of her long gold dress. A fist-sized ruby brooch closed the gown at its high neck. And crested on top of her high-piled hair was a saucy little velvet hat with two great ostrich feathers. Under the hat, on the sides, she'd tied a couple of live butterflies, which fluttered, as captive as I was.

"Hello-o-o-o, Honkey!" She blew me a kiss. "(Oh, he's not *strange*—he's beautiful.) Tell us, now, who's president?"

Well, I knew the answer to that one, of course. It was Wilson. Woodrow. So I gave the horn two honks.

The woman squealed, delighted. "See? Two honks for *Teddy*. Roosevelt!"

The men roared with laughter.

"Come on, Honkey, do the ears!"

I gave it all I had.

I was beginning to feel right at home here. This was the Real San Francisco, for me. The velvet seats. The gas lamps. Yes, oh, down with electricity. The seals and surf. The top hats and tails. A woman who dressed like a woman and knew how to talk to a man. No 1980's lip. Not here. Some of the questions were tricky. But, hell, if they liked you, they helped you along.

"You like it, does you, Honk?" Patch growled.

I honked and gurgled like a tot.

I gave my hat to the waiter. He brought it back jingling with silver and gold.

Patch just smiled sardonically, stroking the edge of his patch while he smoked.

He waited a moment. Then slipped out his watch, a one-pound silver railroad man's.

"Well, I'll be," he said. "It's eight. Time for some serious drinkin'. But it's okay with *me*. If you's happy here in the Cliff House . . . Hell, there's some *gorgeous* pinkieboys. And the Sutro Baths, why, they's just down the road!"

I was up on my feet before Patch was.

He chuckled darkly, grabbing my sleeve. "And don't bend over to fix your galoshes, kid, until we's out the door."

We reached the Coast just a bit after nine.

Primo and Secondo and a hundred and fifty Fat Men

were there, wondering where we had been. And raising cheers to Quaker Sam . . . To the good old Eighties. And to the capture and arrest of four more strange loonies in town . . . lookin' *strange* . . . actin' *strange* . . . wearin' *strange* jackets and dresses and shoes . . .

Seven Pretty Waitress Girls set into a can-can especially for us, flashing their fishnets and diapers.

Things were bad. And getting worse. But I'd found my niche and I had a good plan.

I was going to be a rich man.

A rich and a protected man.

And pity poor Blacke when I saw him again.

Me and my army of Fat Men.

I wasn't scared of Blacke.

Not me.

Which of us was master now?

THE BLUE BLAZER II

Yeah, the Blazer began with the Sweet Spot. And not even Patch's carpings could spoil the magic for me.

He still bitched about the diapers. A cheap illusion of the past. On the old Coast, whores wore diapers because they were chained to their tables. Now, bold as daylight, some walked in back to change. Pshaw!

But, ah, the Pretty Waitress Girls were still the P.W.G.'s. They cuddled me. They tickled Patch. They tweaked my horn and stroked his sling. And now and then Patch would give me a look: *Well, it ain't the Real Frisco . . . But it's close enough.*

He still fumed about the brawl. My style had shown promise, but it had been too—playful. In the old days fights were serious, life-and-death wars between monsters of men. You'd see the sawdust sopped with brains, chewed or hacked-off fingers, eyeballs plump as grapes.

But when Primo clapped his shoulders, and Secondo roared, "Why, you's all right!" I saw the look again in Patch's eyes: *The town do have its moments.*

He, too, was a celebrity and fame was as pleasant as smashing the sauce.

San Francisco had never been Realer than this.

Until around midnight.

When Patch eyed his watch.

And said, "Why don't I have *me* a Blazer?"

We were seated in a corner, away from the hullabaloo.

We had the same table that we'd had last night when I saw Blacke in the window. Blacke wasn't in the window now. Austin Blacke was possibly the furthest thing from my mind. I had three hundred Fat Men in my pocket in bars across town. What were Austin Blacke and his lavender eyes to me? One honk and I'd have *his* damn ass on the Rock.

I was thinking about 1880 and how beautiful it must have been . . . before things began going wrong. I couldn't say for certain when I felt this in my blood.

Not with the old man's first Blazer. Not quite, although his eyes lit up and he flopped his sling like a rooster.

Then raised his glass to Quaker Sam.

I thought it best not to honk. I did not.

Patch took a puff of his cigar.

I did not wiggle my ears. I leaned in.

"He's got the right idea," Patch said, " 'bout gettin' back to the Eighties."

I cupped my hands around the mug.

Patch didn't disappoint me. " 'Course Quaker Sam's reasons are all wrong as rain. If there's a Big One comin', we ain't gonna stop it by gettin' rid of telly-phones. Or goin' back—like Sam would if he could—to build some City on a Hill. Hell, the whole reason the city was better was 'cause, well, it had a *soul* back then. An' there weren't no city in the world had a wickeder soul than the old San Fran. Things was simpler then. An' that was nice. But things was so much badder too. An' that was even better. Ah, I misses 'em, Honk, the old Eighties. Hell, if *I* could go back, I'd go back in a blink—an' I wouldn't change a thing."

There was nothing like the Blazer for putting a mystery in place. If I never learned the *who* of Sam, at least I knew the *what* of Patch's obsession with him. This was grounds for celebration.

And Clean set us up with two Blues in a wink.

With his second Blazer, Patch grew as mellow as marmalade skies. But words were still his medium. And a sly man like myself could still resist the magic, cling to the illusion that *this* was San Francisco: Primo and Secondo and the Pretty Waitress Girls . . . the sense—the scent—of danger and hormones on the rip . . .

He began with deft acts of erasure.

There was no damned 'lectricity then. . . .

There were no auto-mobiles roaring up and down the streets. . . .

There were no women in bars after dark—not since the magic ordinance of 1875. . . .

The newspapers weren't cluttered with photographs and pictures and deucin' trick typography. No, in the Eighties, when Patch had been young, all ads were printed in agate type: a businesslike appearance . . . emphasis on what was said . . . product, price, and quality . . . not loyalty to "brands" . . .

"UNEEDA Biscuit?" Patch screamed. "I *don't* need a deucin' biscuit! I want a biscuit, I'll buy one!"

There were no phones to speak of. Oh, the first had been displayed, back in 1876, at the Philly Centennial Expo. And two years later, don't you know, you had one in the White House. But all it was, was just a toy. Useless and ridiculous. Now there were *two and a half million* phones in homes across the country! And what were they used for? To listen to twaddle from someone you'd seen just last month! Someone who lived just a few miles away! In the Eighties, you wanted to see someone, you sent 'em a message by carriage. There'd been something, somehow, romantic in that. And on and on and on Patch went.

I listened. I was spellbound. But I still had one eye on the men at the bar . . . the cigar smoke and the striped dirt-shirts . . . the sawdust and gas lamps . . . the can can on stage . . .

My San Francisco . . . the Real San Francisco . . . This was the Sweet Spot and I was secure. . . . I was going to be a rich man. . . .

So it wasn't the second drink either, when the poison began to kick in.

I believe it was his third.

When the words weren't words but splashes of sepia in the live photos he flashed.

And we were *in* the Eighties, when *sparks* and *sports* and caped *big-spenders* drove in hired hansoms, steam coming from their ears, new gold eagles jingling. Through the misty night we rode to the corner of Powell and O'Farrell. To Joanna Peyton Cooke's Sporting House for Gentlemen. Liv-

eried Negro doormen whisked us from our cabs ("Yas *suh!*")
into the elegant parlor where the finest whores in Baghdad
basked in the warm glow of Tiffany lamps. The whores,
veiled, wore glitter gowns that had cost them as much as
our hansoms. Their corsets had been tied so tight one finger
could circle two waists. So many decisions. But all of them
right. Each tart was like a universe you couldn't begin to
explore. So you chose. You were led with your whore up a
circular staircase, carpeted so lushly it swallowed your legs
to the knees. At the top, the steward bowed and waved you
ahead to your room. The satin drapes were rich bloodred.
The light of the gas lamps, golder than gold. The damask
tablecloth was set for an intimate dinner for two. Your room
gave off a heady scent of sin and body powder, good Havana
leaf, red lobster, and champagne. The steward filled your
glasses and the champagne bubbled in a way that made you
ache for release. He withdrew politely. He shut the door
behind him. The room was yours. The night was yours. And
so, for this night, was your whore. She smiled and lit your
cigar, tracing her long ruby nails on the shaft, the tip exploding into flames.

Oh, magic! Oh, Baghdad!

Oh, heaven . . .
Patch had drawn my bath for me and I could feel the
steam rising clear across the parlor, where I must have
blacked out around dawn while he talked. The clock on the
wall said ten-thirty. I'd scarcely shut my eyes and yet, again,
I felt rested and calm and alert. My tolerance for the Blazer
approached, it seemed, infinity.

Patch scurried in and out, in his nightcap and mauve
carpet slippers. He disappeared with my galoshes, which he
insisted on airing. He reappeared with a clean towel, a pair
of new red flannels, an impeccably ironed white collarless
shirt, gray checkered pants, and white wool socks. He set
the pile at my feet, then stepped to draw the fringed purple
drapes, flooding the room abruptly with light.

"C'mon! C'mon! Get up!" he cried. "The day's wastin'
away, we got work!"

I stretched on the brocaded settee. Wiggled my toes,

their first fresh air in days. Thought how good the bath would feel and honked three times excitedly.

"C'mon," Patch growled. "Get a move on, you lug. Your feet's startin' to stink like an old cow-yard whore's."

Patch adjusted a vase filled with cattails on the marble mantelpiece. Fluffed the purple pillow on one wood-and-black-leather rocker. Snatched a piece of dust from the blooming-lilacs carpeting. Ran a "roller-sweeper" over the offending spot. And scurried out of the room.

I bounded up from the sofa. Unbuckled the Harp-coat and breathed in the steam. Stretched for the ceiling. Then breathed in. And tugged at the tightening waist of the jeans that I still wore underneath. Those calories were catching up. Four thousand a day? God, I had to cut down!

I was still fooling with the waist when Patch came back in with a big cotton sack.

"Here, this is for your laun—Sayyy . . . Where'd you get them denim pants? Ain't never seen a pair like—"

HONK!

I scrunched up the Harp-coat. My eyes had gone mad, but I still had some use of my ears. I wiggled them and stretched my lips and cartwheeled out of Patch's reach with a *flopawhoosh*.

"For God's sake, I ain't gonna touch 'em!" he cried. "I just wants to see 'em with them buttons on the front."

Patch had me cornered in back of one chair. I readied the bell of the horn for his skull. He feinted right, then lurched left. But his balance was off, with that arm in a sling. I sprang off the seat, bounded over the back, snatching the sack as I landed. I zigzagged, crazy legs, for the pile of duds on the settee. Saw Patch coming, hard and fast, and led him through a figure eight that left him sprawled on the cushions.

I slammed the bathroom door shut and gave the lock a twist. I braced my back against the door, propped my feet against the wall.

Nothing for nearly a minute.

Then Patch exploded in laughter. "Haw! Just like me deucin' weddin' night!"

My breathing started to level when he padded on into the

kitchen. I heard the jangle of a pot, the soft clink of porcelain mugs. Patch whistling while he worked.

The thick steam from the tub slicked away the cold sweat. I breathed deeply again, getting it down in my lungs.

There.

There, that was better.

Got careless for a moment.

But I was safe.

Protected.

I was still invisible. Secure in the extremities. They couldn't catch me if I couldn't talk. Just make sure no details do the talking for you, kid. Let the bluehairs sing away!

I slipped out of the Harp-coat. I set it beside the pile I'd taken from Patch. I stripped off the collarless dirt-shirt—with the giveaway tags still in place:

MACY*S
65% COTTON/35% POLYESTER
15/32

I undid two buttons more of the denims that nearly undid me. I slipped the jeans in the sack with the shirt, noting more tags that had passed me:

GUESS?
WAIST 30

The minute they were laundered—

But, oh, the steam was sweet and thick. The Sweet Spot hadn't failed me yet. I'd figure a way out of this one. There was a way. There had to be. No one was putting my ass on the Rock. A clever man, a sly man—

The door behind me rocked and shook. Patch pounding away like the end of the world.

"Open the damned deucin' door or I'll shoot!"

Well, Baghdad had been good to me. But I saw no sense in prolonging the scene, so I slipped off the lock and stood back, my hands up.

The knob turned slowly. Inch by inch, the door opened till it was ajar by a foot. Enough room for the old man to slip in his pearl-handled derringer. And tell me that the jig was up. He'd known all along I was stranger than strange.

Instead, he slipped in an etched silver tray. Laid out in a neat row were: a coffee mug, a fat cigar, a hand-painted china ashtray shaped like a tomato, a brass match container . . . and a crisply folded paper.

"Same thing I said to Caroline: Open the damned deucin' door or I'll shoot! Haw haw. Well, here's your paper, dearie. And a nice Havana. And stay in the tub till the see-gar is smoked. Or, by God, I *will* shoot."

Honk.

"I'm gonna fetch us some hen fruit, then cook us up some calories. You's gettin' 4,000 a day!"

Patch shut the door. I stood there in shock, coffee splashing from the mug into the china ashtray. I heard a faint rustle of something—Patch, my guess was, slipping into his coat. Then footsteps moving down the hall. A click, soft squeal of hinges, then the close of the hall door, and the receding echoes of his footsteps down the landing.

Peace.

I set the tray beside the tub and tested the water with one filthy toe. The bath could have boiled a tarbaby clean.

I stepped right in and slid down off the back, down till the water line enflamed my throat. I held fast till I was boiled good and proper through and through. Then I sat up slowly. Leaned my head against the wall. And breathed in more steam, deep-massaging my lungs.

I had a sip of coffee.

Ah.

I reached for the Havana. Then struck a wood match on the brass holder's base. Hot crackle of Havana leaf. And, heaven, the smoke—tart yet rich—in the mist.

You didn't take showers in Baghdad. You soaked. And while you soaked, you mused and smoked. And had a thoughtful gander, maybe, at the morning's headlines.

Yes, what *was* the news on my third day, the twenty-eighth of March?

I tapped the ash from my cigar. Opened the paper a quarter to read:

SITUATION IN CHINA GRAVE
MISSIONARIES SLAIN BY CHINESE MOBS
BATTLESHIP OHIO PREPARES FOR EMERGENCY

I thought about that as I puffed, long and hard.

WAR CLOUDS AGAIN GROW DARK
EUROPE IS IN FEAR OF A GREAT CONFLICT
CRISIS BETWEEN TURKEY & BULGARIA
POSSIBLE STARTING POINT OF
CONFLAGRATION

Eight more years, right? Eight more years . . .

FRANCE WILL NOT YIELD TO KAISER!

Shit . . . But eight more years, I'm sure of it . . .
Ah, here's a good one, topping off the centerfold:

CARUSO EARNS RECORD SUM IN NEW YORK
FAMED TENOR RECEIVES OVER $100,000
FOR SEASON
SCHEDULED TO SING AT GRAND OPERA HOUSE

Hmmm. Puff. How about that. Wonder what he looks like.
I unfolded the paper the rest of the way, still feeling
warm and protected. World War I still a few years away and
the Big One not due till—November . . . Still time to
make my fortune . . . get out of the clown suit . . . find
Lenny and Sam . . . Be nice if Sam knew what a serious
guy I really was underneath. . . .

Caruso glaring on the right. More hair on his lip than the
top of my head.

Puff.

Puff.

Oh—

oh . . .

Something dark had caught my eye a few columns over.
Just a flash, I'd been too quick.

I carefully folded the paper, till it was just me and Caruso.

His eyes as baleful as Tyson's would be. Need an axe to part that hair.

But—always the perversity . . . I had to know what I was missing.

I flipped the paper over.

Slapped it down.

Sank a foot in the tub.

The sketch didn't do him justice. His face was much squarer and rawer than that. But there was no denying: It was Bullethead.

And his eyes were blazing, almost like Austin Blacke's. That lavender, that laugh.

(WHOOOOOPPPPP!)

The stacked headlines screamed:

FIRST MAN ESCAPES FROM ALCATRAZ
ONE OF TWO ELDERLY STRANGE PRISONERS
DEAD
POLICE CAUTION SAN FRANCISCANS
HE IS STRANGE & DANGEROUS

Dear Jesus, what was *happening* there?

The picture had Brakowski's name.

It had to be Brakowski.

But it couldn't be Brakowski.

How?

And what the hell had the old woman died of?

And—no one, but no one, escaped from the Rock.

Something was terribly wrong here. In some way beyond my figuring.

Patch was whipping up hen fruit and flapping some jacks when I finally showed in the kitchen. He looked over and roared at the sight: Honkey in baggy red flannels, towel-dried curls like rat tails.

"Haw haw! Kid, you look like a drowned—Sayyy . . . Honkey, you's white as a—Whoaaa!"

I collapsed in a chair, my chin stuck to my chest, and slopped the sopped news on the table. Dead of unknown causes—apparently exhaustion—was one of the six special prisoners now detained on Alcatraz. . . . The five remaining prisoners would be questioned soon by authorities from Washington. . . . Meanwhile, authorities urged extreme caution, while assuring San Franciscans that "Brakowski" was certainly dead in the Bay. . . .

Washington . . . Oh, Jesus Christ . . . They think we're fucking spies. . . .

"Honk! Hey, kid! C'mon, shake a leg!"

Patch did a small jig by the table as the hen fruit sizzled in the pan.

He extended his right leg.

I gave him my left. But, I tell you, my heart wasn't in it. *Brakowski*, I thought. But he *couldn't* be here. I'd seen him leave in Salt Lake! Five of them now—and, goddamn them, they'd talk!

"Say, Honk—watch this!"

Patch wiggled his ears. Rubberduckied his lips.

I smiled wanly at him, detaching my chin half an inch from my chest.

"That's the proper caper! Hey . . ." Patch swung the paper around, facing him. "You wasn't readin' upside down. No wonder you got the blue devils. Why, I'll be a monkey's uncle! Ain't that that Dago—"

Patch never saw Brakowski. The singer's photo enflamed him. He flipped the paper over . . . saw the operatic headlines . . . and pounded his fist on the table.

"CA-ROOO-SO! Oh, mother o' Jesus, no! Not at the Grand Opry! Squeakyboy! Lily lungs! Oh, I hates 'im, he sings like a girl! I-EEEEEEE!"

Patch hit a high C that Caruso might have sold his soul for. I followed his glance to the stove. The black cloud hanging over us was thickening from puffs of smoke that rose from copper skillets.

"This is war!" Patch bellowed. "Goddamn it, they's ruinin' our town—not even the Grand Opry's safe!"

Well, the war required calories. More calories than ever. Patch threw the old skillets right into the trash, as if Caruso's influence might have bled into the copper. The way he cracked eggs, the shells might have been skulls. He slapped slabs of ham, half as thick as my wrists, into another skillet. He shoveled batter, like mortar, into the base of a third. Then he whacked a loaf of bread into three-inch bricks.

It was awesome to watch him.

I feared for our hearts.

But I needn't have worried for Patch's.

When the table was set for an army, he poured us some coffee. Then lit his cigar.

"Dig in," he said. "You needs your strength. I'm savin' mine for later."

I almost never saw him eat. But he watched me like a hawk. Was I strange? Hell, no, I *ate*.

My education continued.

Grant Avenue was DuPont Street.

The Embarcadero, East Street.

As late as the Eighties, ninety percent of the Negroes still lived in the South. Not a city in the country had more than five thousand blacks. Now, God save, even in Baghdad, wherever you looked you saw *niggers* dressed like pinkieboys . . . or dressed as doormen and sayin' "Yassuh" but *thinkin'* "Call me Mister" . . . Pshaw!

Hell, in the Eighties, only one in four Americans lived in deucin' cities. In 1890, one in three. Now, one of every two.

I took it in. I took all of it in.

The old man showed me Woolworth's and nearly chewed through his Havana. The first five-and-ten-cent store had appeared back in '79. A harmless curiosity. Folks damn near laughed their heads off; they still believed in Quality. By the middle Eighties, there were six or seven, though. And today they were clear across the country. Folks were ushered in like sheep, and once in they were gone. Because their thinking had been changed. They had nickels and dimes in their pockets—and there were the goods for a nickel or dime.

Which was good. Because the cost of living had been rising through the roof. Forty cents for a gallon of cider or a deucin' dozen eggs . . . Twelve cents for a half pound of raisins . . . A quarter for three pounds of figs . . .

I took it in. I took all of it in.

And whatever happened to books you could read? *The Jumping Frog* . . . *Tom Sawyer* . . . Hell, old Hermie's whale book . . . Those were stories a man could relate to. Real life. Why, today you went into a book store, you were puttin' your mind in your hands. Some pinkieboy clerk tried to sell you a tale about Chicago meatpackers or some idiot dentist on Polk Street. Pshaw!

And on and on and on.

Niagara thundered that morning. I held on for life as Patch just let 'er rip. But it was hard to concentrate.

I kept trying, but couldn't forget: the sack of laundry on my lap that might still undo me . . . the evil-eyed sketch of Brakowski . . . the need to keep telling myself: You whupped his ass once, you can do it again . . . You had ten years of Therapy—and you're spooked by a *sketched* pair of eyes? . . . For a second they looked just like Austin's? . . . You're building an army of Fat Men . . . Come on, Dodge, relax, all's well. . . .

At the foot of Chinatown, Patch whistled to the driver. The hansom clattered to a stop. Across the walk, through a thicket of tunics, stood a chow mein box-sized shop. The chicken scratches on its shingle were all Greek to me. But white canvas sacks like the one on my lap were stacked against the window like sandbags at a breakwall.

End of story.

Here and now. Despite all the pep talks and pivots, I'd found no way around this scene.

Patch slipped out of his side of the hansom.

I stepped out and shut my door. The click, to me, was the thunderous slam of a steel door on Alcatraz.

Patch waited for me on the walk.

My galoshes knew the drill. Left, right, left, right, to the left. Right, get it done. Undone by a handful of details. The slyest man in town, undone, by a couple of tags he'd forgotten.

I accepted this. I had no plan.

And so, my feet surprised me. Left, right, left, right, to the right, though, not the left. Away from Patch's startled cry and the sing-a-ling shouts from the tunics. Right into the path of a phaeton, which veered with roared oaths and high whinnies. Left, right, left, right. A milk wagon just missed me—but not the Ford that plowed into the cart, horses squealing, drivers screaming, glass and splinters raining down. Left, right, left—whoaaa! Garbage wagon passed so close one horse's hooves brushed my galoshes. I spun once like a top. Then stopped on a dime. Saw horses rearing. Cart buckling. And the load of garbage starting to fly. I cart-wheeled into a cyclist. He swung into a hydrant, sailed over the bars and through a plate-glass window. I landed neatly, and not far from Patch. But something broke within me. I'd had it made here, and it was all lost. It had all turned to shit overnight. Fuck the Rock! I honked. I nearly broke the horn. I swung the sack back like a ball on a chain and hurled it at the shit-mobile. It zeroed in right on top of the load.

Come on, I thought. *Put* my ass on the Rock.

"Oh, Honk," Patch murmured. *"Honkey!"*

When I looked, I saw tears in his eyes.

"God love you, kid. God bless your soul. Aw, that's just like we did in the Sixties!"

Patch threw our driver an eagle. The horses looked exhausted. He took my arm, he was happy as Christmas, and there were toasts to be made.

More wind to ya!
To Quaker Sam!
Here's to it, and to it, and to it again! And if you e'er get to it and don't do it, may you n'er get to it or do it again!

There was nothing like the Blazer.

One swallow, and the Sweet Spot settled back into itself and took root.

Another, and the Sweet Spot stirred, alive and warm and growing.

Another, and the Sweet Spot bloomed.

By the second pit stop, and my third Blue Blazer, the fragrance was so powerful I felt I was breathing in colors.

The Blazer looked after the Sweet Spot. It weeded out anxiety, doubt, and the sense of malaise.

It arranged the facts like seeds in neatly tended rows.

Somehow—and the *how* didn't matter, it said—back in Salt Lake City, Brakowski got back on the train. Or I'd been drunk and seeing things. It had been Blacke all along.

But, either way, Brakowski surviving a swim from the Rock? No way. It had never been, could not be, done. Not even Clint had arranged it.

That left five on the Rock: tripped up, perhaps, by the tag on a shirt . . . or a gold Rolex watch . . . or a few careless words . . .

Alcatraz . . . Alcatraz . . . Of course we'd go to Alcatraz till they knew what to make of us. My guess was we'd be Chinese. Or Germans. Or Hungarians. Spies blown in on the new winds of war.

National security . . . No stories in the papers yet. No more than occasional slips:

HE IS STRANGE. . . .

Slips and rumors, that grew in the telling: *lookin' strange . . . actin' strange . . . didn't know the damndest things . . .*

Five on the Rock. And they'd sing. That was bad.

But there were more of us walking the streets—and three of us, at the least, were slyer than the rest. Lenny must have learned something in our twenty years. And Sam—what of Sam—hadn't Sam been my twin?

The thing to do was *blend;* be sly!

The Blazer had it all worked out.

The Blazer whispered in my ear:

You *are* your father's father now. . . .

You never went to Canada. . . .

You never ran. . . .

You have beaten the Wall. . . .

You are safe in the Sweet Spot, protected and loved. . . .

Forget Blacke. . . . A trick of the light on the train . . . There was nothing to his eyes . . . He never crushed you with his mind . . . Never threw you through two windows as if flicking some lint from his sleeve . . .

(WHOOOOOPPPPP!)

Forget Blacke . . . He got lucky . . .

Forget Blacke . . .

Surrender to Baghdad. . . .

By the time we arrived on the Barbary Coast, I was high as a weather balloon. And the forecast was clear skies and sunny for life.

Primo and Secondo roared the second we walked in the door. And before you knew it, there were Fat Men lined up at the door.

I honked and capered and wiggled my ears.

Jumped from the bar to a high chandelier, where I swung, from one arm and one foot.

Full of myself again. Feeling no pain.

I would have stayed there forever, a king.

But hark! I heard Patch calling.

I turned to see Clean set us up with two Blues.

Saw Patch light a cigar, cup the flame in his palms.

And felt the Sweet Spot drifting to the fire like a moth.

THROUGH A CRACK
IN CHINATOWN

1880. Chinatown. The time: two o'clock in the morning. All's well. I'd go three more days in the clown suit—well, make that a week. Sam would need a guy with some money. For now, 1880 was a good Sweet Spot to be. Twenty-six years from the Rock. And from Blacke. Who'd never really scared me.

Dupont Street was Really Dupont Street.

And Chinatown was Chinatown.

The cribs were Cribs, the whores were Whores, you could smell 'em a mile away, they was Wild.

Hell, even the fog had been Fog in those days. It was the breath of Chinatown: sinuous and rhythmic, hypnotic and palpably thick. Wind chimes tingling in it, singing of sin and corruption. Padded footsteps of Real Tongs, swinging Real Machetes, murder in their slanty eyes.

The Chinese Whores were the wickedest whores a whore-minded man could desire. When you'd been had by a Real Chinese Whore, you couldn't piss for three whole days or walk straight for almost a week. It wasn't like it was today, their privates just like white girls'. No, in the Eighties —and I had Patch's word on this—their privates truly ran east-west.

Somehow we had slipped through a crack in the fog. And the streets we were walking were those streets, not these. There were no elders, half dead over mah-jongg, watching like stunned cattle as the New World passed them by. I saw broad-shouldered tongs with Real Fire in their eyes. And the breath of Chinatown was raw with sperm and opium.

I followed the Sweet Spot. And it followed Patch. I might never get back if I lost him.

But why should I want to, it asked me, the Sweet Spot, now that I'd Really Arrived.

Of the world before the crack, or my self, almost nothing remained. Not a follicle stirred with the memory of the IRS, the IRA, Americans in Exile. Not one cell remembered Coit Tower or the *Zephyr* or Joe Pulitzer or—

"Harrrrrrrrr—

"poooooooooo!"

The sound came from behind, miles behind, through the crack. It might have been faint as a windchime, but it shook me like thunder.

I pivoted. My stomach turned, the whole world out of joint.

"Harrrrrrrrr—

"poooooooooo!"

I should have turned away right then. Behind me lay protection, peace. I wished I'd never met her, or felt that click, or called her twin, or learned how I'd forgotten her.

Sam!

I started looking, crazy-eyed, from one window to the next . . . when suddenly the peach fuzz bristled on my chin.

Something . . .

What, though?

Something . . .

Wrong!

Across the street, a tall, well-heeled stranger came to a long-legged stop. He hitched one boot against a post and tipped his cap, staring boldly.

What it was, I couldn't say. But there was *something* about him.

He wore his Prince Albert as if he were Albert; his derby, a solid gold crown. His dark mustache was as thick as Caruso's. And the starched white of his shirt front stood in blinding relief to his tan.

His eyes were uniquely compelling, though at first glance

I'd thought they were—wrong for his face. Now I saw how wrong I'd been. They made me think of

lavenderrrr . . .

I began to feel tingly all over.

I thought he might have candy or . . .

"Hey, Honk!" Patch cried. "What is it?"

I was going to tell him, and goddamn the horn.

Something was funny, no, something was

BAD!

I was missing something. Some small, essential detail that was beyond my figuring. And everywhere I looked, men's eyes were beginning to spook me. Like Austin's.

I took hold of Patch's sleeve, tugging him my way to see.

But the man with the tan wasn't there when we looked.

A trick of lighting through the crack. The fog playing tag with my nerve ends.

Sam's voice had been windchimes, or laughter, no more.

We were back in the Eighties in no time at all. Blocks away and so far gone I just *knew* that there couldn't be screams from behind.

They were whistles or pigeons or windchimes.

STEREOPTICON III

I

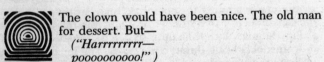 The clown would have been nice. The old man for dessert. But—

("Harrrrrrrrr— pooooooooooo!")

—By the Night! He'd caught her scent three blocks away and *she* sounded done to perfection, while Harp still needed seasoning. A little more fear and despair.

Well, Harp's scent was as peculiar as the costume that he wore and he'd always be easy to find. All of the bonbons would be Blacke's, in time.

Blacke took the stairs to the floor she was on, on the heels of a heavy-necked tong. Though his right foot still troubled him slightly, he thought he might do anything with just a bit more leveling, fine tuning of his blood.

To that end, now, *dim sum.* Then a quick flight to Alcatraz. Before the boys from Washington came to ruin his plans for the Rock. They'd find five "special" prisoners there . . . but would leave with more questions than answers. Just the way he wanted it.

It was the twenty-eighth of March. Four more days was not so long to wait for his favorite day. But it felt like it used to feel, when he was a boy, before Christmas.

His whole life, as a man, had been little but sorrow. Well, at least after death one could play.

II

Sam had taken to dreaming of Harpo and guessed that she'd been dreaming now. Waking dreams . . . sleeping dreams . . . where did the boundary lie?

In hell, perhaps, there was none. Night and day, again and again, one was crushed by the thundering hooves.

Of Might Have Been.

And Shouldn't Have.

And Once Upon a Time.

But now and then, when the pain was the worst, and the weight was too heavy to bear, if she relaxed she could see Harp. A ray of light and purity. Lost innocence, come home a king. He'd never asked a thing of her. Just come and gone, and remained in her mind.

She heard a grunt outside her door. Then a click and the slow creak of hinges.

She dreamed of Harpo, herself on his lap, high on a hill in the Summer of Love.

Then she turned to her forty-ninth trick of the night, not dreaming she'd never see fifty.

She drew the curtain behind them, leaning over to blow out the candle. He placed his hand over hers, twice its size, stopping her.

For an instant her heart quickened.

But then he took his hand from hers and slipped the straps of her slight shift. It fell with a sigh to her feet. He stepped back, boldly admiring the view, unlike the other white boys. The smile he gave her was boyish enough, but those gray eyes of his had some mileage. Sam wasn't sure that she liked them one bit.

Until he *touched* her with them.

Here, there, oh, and there.

She felt now how wrong she had been.

The gray was the color, perhaps, of dry ice, but it warmed her in her soul. And in the lone candle's flickering light small flecks of lavender blew her away.

"Sam," he said.

He knew her name.

And he had brought her candy.

"Tell you what I'll do, Sam. I'm gonna get you out of here. If you'll do me one favor."

Sam wondered how he knew her name; how he could possibly help her, and why. But she'd never heard a voice like that. Well, Once Upon a Train—no, Time. It purred just like a kitten. And, like his eyes, it touched her. Here, there, oh, especially there.

"You know what you need," he purred.

He wasn't like the other men, who told her what they wanted. He thought of *her* and filled her heart with womanly needs and desires. He cherished her, for what she was. And nothing she felt could surprise him.

She grew bold, emblazened. "Will you still give me candy. . . . Can I crawl over there on my knees?"

"Of course, I will. Of course you can. You are such a goose. Come here."

She dreamed she heard a honking sound. Saw Harpo waving frantically. She couldn't help but giggle. Sorry, Harp, but there are times when a girl needs a . . . real man.

"That's it, honey. *On your knees.*"

Sam stopped before him, panting, pawing at the floor.

"Can you bark like a dog for me, Sammy?"

"Oh, sure! But . . . Daddy doesn't like that."

"*Sammy.* Don't you know it's Party Time?"

"Arf arf."

"Say what?"

"Arf arf!"

"What's that?"

"Tee hee! Arf *arf!* Whoof *whoof!* Arf *arf!*"

She heard him chuckle lowly. Oh, it was *such* fun pleasing him! She yapped and shook her head and pawed until he started giggling.

"That's a good dog, Sammy. Now, I've brought you something I just know you're gonna like."

She saw his hands go to his buckle. Her eyes caught a great shadow of movement a few inches under his belt. The shadow rippled like a wave across the whole front of his trousers. Improbable. Impossible. But this was doggie heaven, right?

He dropped his trousers to his knees. The length of him, unfettered, snaked in a ferocious arc, then dropped and bounced, stiffened, bounced, and bounced, inching toward her lips.

(Harpo slapped her. "Keep your wits!")

Sam felt a tightening in her throat. He'd promised her candy, but he'd brought her pain. She whimpered; growled; snapped fearfully.

He stopped her with one finger. A hot shower of lavender sparks.

There was no way to stop the tears. Her Master's voice condemned her soul.

"I ask you one small favor."

"Please . . ."

"I didn't hear the magic words."

"Master, please."

"I'm sorry?"

"Master, please . . . I'm begging you."

"Ah."

He palmed the base of his member, supporting it and waving it, fanning the flush on her cheeks. A thin stream of saliva trickled from one corner of her mouth. His phallus jerked, then bounced and quivered, now almost audibly humming. It did not stretch, it seemed to spring another full inch till it reached her. She'd never seen anything like it. That eerie and curious hole on the tip, the crown half as large as her fist, the shaft so thick and boldly veined and slowly turning

lavenderrrr . . .

"Now," he told her, "please me."

Sam wanted nothing more from life. She flicked at the hole, felt it quiver and grow, wide enough for her tongue, which it captured, sucking it in through the shaft. The suction tugged, hard, at the root. Then, slowly, it released her tongue.

Flood of juices everywhere.

"*Please* me," he commanded. He clenched his fingers in

her hair and pulled, slipping through till her jaw popped. She was going to drown in the juices and—

Harpo!

"*Please* me!" he insisted.

His member like a ramrod now, battering her gullet. There was no way, another inch, Oh God, no—

Harpoooo!

"*Please* me!"

His fingertips pressing the sides of her skull, branding the message in lavender sparks.

"Relaxxxx, you cunt. And *please* me."

She felt her throat begin to give. And give. And just keep giving. Until she thought she felt the crown nestling between her lungs.

She could not breathe. She dared not move.

"*That* pleases me," he told her. "That's the hard part. To get in position. Now . . ."

Sam raised her eyes pathetically. If he could see how hard she'd tried, how she lived to please him. She caught a glimpse of wolfish white teeth, looking remarkably pointy, as he tightened his grip in her hair.

"You know a full-grown python stretches *twenty-seven feet*?"

Oh, no.

"Oh, *yeah*. It's time. The Snake Trick."

He slipped himself out, inch by inch, till the crown perched at the tip of her gullet. Far and away, from the pendulous balls, she saw a ripple of shimmering scales. Then, before she could think, he slammed back all the way, slipping out, slamming home, growing and filling her more with each thrust.

She felt her teeth exploding, the monstrous growth pounding the roots through her gums.

Her jaw broke once.

Then twice.

Again.

Her last conscious thought was of Harpo.

Then it became unspeakable.

III

She was teaching the boys a few limericks when a flash in the mirror sent her flying.

Betsy crashed through the doors to the kitchen with two sparkling steins she'd just smudged. In the weeks that she had been in town, things were going to hell in a hurry. And avoiding the man she'd just seen in the mirror was taking all of her wits.

"Ez-ra! U-ri-ah! You're *at* it a-again—if you *know* what I *mean*— an' I think that you *do* 'cause you ain't here to *wear* these damned glass-es!"

She saw the back door swinging and knew they'd seen her coming. The two blacks, though well in their sixties, were fast as young bucks when Miz Mae had her mood. As she'd had for three nights running now, and always around ten.

No time to find an apron. She plunged her arms up to the elbows, ruining her gown as she dunked the two steins.

From the serving window she watched the heavyset man cruise the bar. He was wearing his usual black braided suit, gold watch chain through one button hole. Stroking his walrus and asking:

Had anyone seen any *strangers* tonight? Anybody strangely dressed, or talkin' or actin' unusual-like

It nearly made her laugh to think that the earthquake had been her worst worry. She yearned for the serenity of knowing disaster was sure months ahead. September. Or October. Now in every moment lurked the deadly potential for ruin.

She looked furtively out through the window.

Just as the inspector looked in.

(Oh, God. Who's the mayor here? What school did I go to? And where did I live?)

She heard the doors swing open.

But—

"Mae, dear?"

—it was Clark's voice.

He stood in the doorway, astonished again. "Darling, we have *niggers*. Why do you insist—"

Think!

Mae shook the glasses at him, the fine spray Niagran.

"Don't call *me* dear, you con-temp-ti-ble *cur*. You put your *arm* a-round my *waist*!"

A look of horror crossed Clark's face, his rugged features shrinking into a mask of shame. Tonight he had taken her skating, progressing at long last from grazings of her pinkie . . . to, just barely, circling her belt.

"Mae," he cried, "you mustn't think that I'm some common masher! I beg you—I assure you—"

She saw the cop grilling a couple of drunks.

"You as-sure me one more *time*, I'm gonna pull your *schnozz*."

"My—word!"

"Your *word* ain't good for noth-in'! *Hell*, how you gonna two-time me if you can't even half-time?"

"Mae—"

"You know damn *well* what I'm talk-in' a-bout—you put your *arm* around my *waist* . . . and then don't *do* noth-in' a-bout it!"

"For God's sake, I—respect you!"

Flash of the inspector nodding toward the window.

Betsy reached inside the sink. Came out with a jug half the size of a keg.

"You *dunce*, if you re-spect-ed me, you'd come up an' *see* me some time like I *asked*!"

Clark turned a little to the side. Not exactly cowering. But savvy enough about glass in '06.

"But, Mae, dear, you can't be suggesting—"

(Come on!)

"I ain't sug-gest-in' noth-in'!"

"But I'm supposed to *rush* you first!"

She cocked the jug over her shoulder.

Footsteps coming closer now. The inspector's spit-shined boots.

"You *rush* me any slow-er, I'm gonna *die* an old *maid*! Now, come on or I'll *bean* ya!"

Clark took a couple of hesitant steps.

"Do you mean what—I hope you mean?"

She met him easily more than halfway.

"I mean what I *say* I mean. Now will you *kiss* me, you lum-mox?"

He did.

And the kissing was good in '06.

And it was even better when the swing doors opened . . . and the inspector cleared his throat . . . and Clark looked over his shoulder to roar:

"Get out of here, you idiot, or you'll never get pie-eyed again in my bar!"

IV

Quaker Sam watched her run off for more books. Lately she'd taken to wearing high heels. If the effect intended was what he feared it must be, she should have grown a beard instead, to go with her mustache. Her ankles wobbled absurdly. The rise of the heels threw her skirt up an inch to flash two sticklike calves, so hairy they might have been covered with bugs.

But his time was drawing short. It might be days. It might be weeks. But he could feel the tremors . . . the rumbles . . . and the shakes . . .

He wished to God he could remember.

He could see the earth's maws swallow carriages, people, and houses.

Taste the smoke of the towering flames.

The town could not be saved, he knew. There were no words to warn them with that they would choose to hear.

But what of *his* salvation? If he could only show them the errors of Time's ways . . .

And so he worked. And so he slaved. Though the price might be high, even Harriet's love.

1880, Sam thought . . . 1880, that's the word . . . Cable cars, typewriters . . . Wait a minute . . . Hey, what's this . . .

His small eyes, sharpened, settled on a detail he had

missed. And, in a flash, he understood how this, too, might be used.

He heard the clattering rush of her heels, as if his fever had drawn hers.

"Sam," she cried, "what is it, de—er, I mean, of course, what *is* it?"

"It's *1881,* old girl. It's *dry-plate photography.*It's *improved, convenient* cameras that only weigh eight pounds. So *Mis* -ter *Al-* fred *Stieg-* litz can carry his red bellow hellbox around, with his dry plates in a box, *capturing the moment.* Mothers doing their laundry. Kids playing ball."

"I see," she said. "I think. Uh, yes . . ." Then, to Sam's astonishment, Harriet's eyes filled with tears. "Sometimes," she said, "I can't . . . keep up. And Sam, it breaks my heart. But I'm trying to, Sam, oh, I am."

Sam gave her hand a nervous squeeze. He still needed her help and her books.

"I know you are," he told her. "And I know you do. You *see.*"

"I do?" she said.

"You most certainly do. You just don't know you do, you see."

"I see."

"You *do.* And now I'll prove to you you do. Dry plate photography. *Mis-* ter *Al-* fred *Stieg-* litz. *Capturing the moment.* Photographs are different now. They take 'em anytime at all. They're changing how we see ourselves!"

"They are," she whispered. "Yes, you're right."

"Now we're starting to pose for the camera, see, just like we're not posing at all!"

Sam pried his fingers from her clasp, thinking, as her eyes lit up, that the price might be too high.

"They *are.*" She almost hissed this. "They're making us act—"

"Naturally."

"OHHHHHHHHHH!"

V

From outside his door, in the newsroom, he heard the mad clatter of typewriter keys. The callow voices of young cubs shouting through brass speaking tubes in the wall. ("Hey, send some coffee up here, eh?") Five or six more of them queued at the phone, the one phone allowed in the newsroom. They looked prepared to wait some time; it was still a lark for most to hold the earpiece to one ear, adjusting the mouthpiece to height, then crackle to, be crackled at, and call it all reporting.

The *Chronicle* was said to have one phone for each reporter. And a few of the boys here had stars in their eyes, already planning, no doubt, to move on.

Let 'em, Frank McGuane thought. As long as he was editor at the S.F. *Call,* he'd decide which changes, in what number, were allowed.

The publisher wanted a daily? All right. But it would be a daily with the stamp of Frank McGuane. Let Joe Pulitzer smuggle reporters into Bedlam for the news! Let Bill Hearst "report" a war by going out and starting one! The S.F. *Call* had Frank McGuane stamped on every paragraph.

Just a few years ago in the newsroom you heard soft scratchings of men's pens. The quiet voices of seasoned reporters searching for something like truth as they *worked.* Now they *played* at working, raucous as hyenas.

Frank McGuane lit his Havana, puffing at the rich man's smoke while *they* chainsmoked their Trophies.

He gave the typed note he'd received one last look.

March 27, 1906
Dear Sir:
As your Publisher, it is with a heavy heart that, at this time, we readdress a point of ongoing concern. Last month, at our meeting, Sir, you assured us the *Call*'s circulation, dwindling now these past months since . . .

Frank took a long and thoughtful puff, chewing the end like a bit.

He drew a fresh penful of ink from the well . . . squared

his elbows . . . drew in close . . . and, with a swift spurt of the pen, he began:

March 28, 1906
Dear Sir:
As your Editor, it is with an angry heart . . .

He laid the pen on the wiper, blotting what he'd written, as if setting a seal of approval.

There, he thought. *There.* Like *that. That* is how *I* write. Take this!

He was filling the pen, now with acid, not ink, when he heard a fierce commotion.

"See here! You can't come in here!"

"Stop!"

"He don't want to *see* you!"

Then a roar, unstoppable in its rage and power.

The crash of someone falling hard.

And footsteps pounding to his door.

McGuane set his Havana down. He looked up with a patient look that promptly turned to horror.

"You!" he sputtered.

"Mornin', Frank."

The bearded madman smiled, slamming the door shut behind him. A thick wad of notepaper jutted from one pocket. His eyes were wild. What hair he had made a foul-looking nest on his skull. He looked as if he had slept in that suit. And he was doing something with his hands that Frank had never seen before: snapping his left fingers, snapping his right, then slapping one fist with his palm. Snapsnap-*slap*! Snapsnap*slap*! Like a *stooge*!

McGuane said nothing. He leaned back, inching open his top drawer.

"Oh, you won't be needin' that, Frank. But hell, just put it on the desk if it makes you comfy."

The madman, Wolf, walked over, sat down as if he owned the chair, and hitched his feet up on the desk.

Frank smelled the liquor on Wolf's breath and set the pearl-handled Colt on the desk.

"Oh, that's a big one, Frank." The madman seemed delighted.

"I promise you, I'll use it, sir."

"You won't have to. I will."

"What?"

The crazed would-be reporter took out a cheap-looking watch. He leaned over, grunting, and tossed the thing beside the Colt.

"Clock me," he said—and then, damn him, he winked!

McGuane stared at the watch; the words didn't compute; but, vaguely, something else had.

"Yeah, Frank. You got that right. Forgot to tell you last time: you see . . . I'm kinda *strange.*"

"My God!"

McGuane fumbled with the gun, but his hands were too crazy and it weighed a ton and suddenly the bearded one roared out with laughter.

"Frank, forget the gun, Frank. *Clock* me . . . that means *time* me. Jeez, don't you guys know anything?"

"What—do you want? I've got money!"

"I know. And you'll give me lots of it. But first, you're gonna *clock* me. I want ten minutes of your time. Your circulation's down, Frank. They say you're gonna get the sack. They say the S.F. *Chronicle*'s the only real paper in town."

"Pshaw!"

The editor pounded his fist on the desk, a few gaskets ready to blow. The Colt thunked and rattled, the barrel swinging his way. The madman's watch bounced up, then dropped, the spring-latched cover popping.

"Me," the madman purred, "I say the *Call* 'll kick its ass. Your circulation's gonna soar. And all over this damned country publishers are gonna whisper 'McGuane' with respect."

"McGuane . . ."

"That is, if you just *clock* me, Frank. And when the ten minutes are up"—he leaned in and snatched the Colt, barrel to one temple—"you just say the word, Frank, if you ain't convinced. And I'll pull the trigger myself."

"Convinced, you say? Convinced of what?"

The madman set the pistol down, regarding it with real affection. From his pocket he removed his notes and slapped them down beside it. The pages were filled with foul scribblings.

"Convinced we've got a story here that'll rock this old town to the ground. We're gonna call this *Monster Time.* You're gonna start it this Sunday, the first. Gotta be the first, Frank. And you're gonna run it just the way I write it. It'll make us famous and it'll make us rich. Ready . . . Set . . . Read me, Frank. Here's the poop on Alcatraz . . ."

VI

"Lord Whittaker?"

"Yesh."

"Lord *Whit*-taker!"

"Yesh!"

"Lord Whittaker, PLEASE!"

"I'm TRYING!"

Rod felt himself dying all over again in the Buena Vista, so drunk that he could scarcely speak. But trying so hard to remember, not with his mind, but his soul: that lost spark.

A small man, saucer-eyed, tugging at his sleeve. David Something. Francis David. "El" sound in there somewhere. Wait. Francis Delby. David's Deli.

"For God's sake, your lordship, pull yourself together!"

"Yesh . . ."

"Remember, just try to remember! We've come back here to *help* you *remember!*"

"Yesh!"

"The play's the thing."

"Yesh, that'sh it. The play . . ."

A few more nights till his debut. Which theater, though? Which planet? Rod set the shot glass down beside five others in a row. A seventh was already waiting. But just then the barman set a hot toddy before him.

"You had one of these around now, your lordy. And you put it down right quick."

Rod groaned. "I did?"

The small man—Shelley?—screamed, "C'mon, for God's sake, drink, *drink*!"

The toddy was a scorcher. But the play, oh God, *what* play, would go on without him, his understudy waiting, a hyena, in the wings. Rod's last rehearsal, a hoot and a half. Like all of the others before it. Weeks of them and each a bust. He had lost whatever it was he had found, after sobering up the next morning.

Things were getting *stranger* in the city by the day. It really was essential . . .

" 'To be or not to be . . .' " he cried.

"We're ruined," said—Kelley Welley?

Rod agreed. And collapsed to his knees.

"I remember *that*." A ruddy-faced boozer a few feet away stroked his whiskers thoughtfully. "His lordy went down like a sack, then got up . . ."

"Get up!" The small man shook Rod's arm. "Get up, goddamn it, on your feet!"

Rod stumbled up, doubled over, crashing his chin on the bar.

Whiskers thought about this. "Hmm. I don't remember *that* . . . But I remember distinctly . . . His lordy was lookin' exceptionally—shaky."

Rod bolted upright, in his mind a lone candle flickering. *(Shaky?)*

"I believe his lordy had . . ." Whiskers paused, "a Manhattan."

"Yesh . . . No . . ." Rod said.

"Naw," said another, "a Margarita. I bought it meself."

"Yesh . . . No . . ."

"A hot sling!" To the left of him.

"Yesh . . . No . . ."

"Mountain Riesling!" To the right.

"Yesh . . . No . . ." Rod murmured. "Quake . . ."

"What's that?" The small man, his nemesis, cried. "You remember, don't you?"

" 'To *be* . . .' "

"No!"

" 'To BE . . .' "

"No!"

Rod looked over his shoulder and out at the Rock.

(He ain't strange, not this one. . . .)

"He looked out," said Whiskers. "I remember it distinctly."

"Think," the small man whispered. David Francis Kelley. "You remember—you *remember*!"

"Six . . ." Rod said. "Six—seconds . . ."

"What?"

"There was an earthquake, you asshole!"

"My Lord!"

"You want your Hamlet?" Rod cried.

"Yesh!"

"Then make the fucking earth move—now!"

Kelley began it. It spread through the room: boots stomping . . . fists pounding . . . glasses rattling . . . mirror cracking . . .

(Oh, there's a Big One comin' . . . Come on, baby, come to Rod . . .)

He saw two water cops stop at the window, frozen by the spectacle. Over their shoulders, and out on the Bay, just right of the moon's silver shimmering track, the lighthouse twinkled in the mist.

(The Rock . . . Oh, yes . . . Alcatraz . . . That's where Hamlet comes from . . . Hamlet's done time on the Rock . . .)

" 'To be or not to be . . .' " he began.

Whispers of "Lord Whittaker!"

Then a silence deep as death.

The Voice was back.

And Rocking in Rod's very soul.

And now he knew just how to tap it.

THE
BLUE BLAZER III

 By all accounts, I had it made. I couldn't blink without making more cash. And I'd finally figured the date of the Quake: New Year's Eve had a ring of Destiny I liked.

But Baghdad was turning to bedlam right quick. In Thursday's news there were more flashes that I couldn't miss though I read upside down. Folks were complaining about feeling—*tired* . . . Bones had been found near the Cliff House—parts of skulls and some patches of hair . . . Police speculated that a pack of wild dogs . . . The search was on for a boy and a girl who'd been reported missing . . . as well as several others reported in the past two days . . .

The police were everywhere, fierce in their brass-buttoned blues and tall caps.

They flashed Brakowski's picture everywhere they went.

They even flashed the thing at me. I'd point east-west with both my hands, then north-south with my feet. And Patch would tell them, as only Patch could, "Leave him alone, he was dropped on his head! Whyn't you catch some criminals and leave the poor idiot be?"

And that would be enough to start a chorus at the bar:

"Shake a leg, Honk!"

"Do the lips!"

"Wiggle 'em, Honk, g'on, wiggle the ears!"

"Sure, sure, that's the word!"

My education continued.

I listened, learned. We rode, and stopped. We toasted the horses and rode off again. Yes, there was danger, certainly, but only outside of the Sweet Spot. And that was never sweeter than when, work done, we returned to our table and Clean set us up with two Blazers and the old man's eyes lit up . . . and he began erasing things . . . then taking me back to the Eighties, our home . . . a lifetime before the whole world went all wrong and things began getting confused . . .

Friday, the 30th, there were three fat screaming headlines:

SLAUGHTER AT THE S.F. ZOO!
BATS, PYTHON & HYENA EATEN!

and:

5 SPECIAL PRISONERS
FOUND COMATOSE ON ALCATRAZ!

and:

POLICE STILL BAFFLED BY MURDER
OF CHINATOWN WHORE AH TOY

The headlines enraged me. Every time I took two steps toward making my fortune in Baghdad, the papers set me back four more.

A Chinese whore . . . Chinatown, that was all, just Chinatown . . . What kind of name was that—Ah Toy?

Who cared about the animals? A hyena, for Christ's sake!

And the prisoners—goddamn it to hell, they should've kept their damn butts off the Rock!

What was I, their keeper?

Patch took me back to the Cliff House that night, thinking the pinkieboys might cheer me up. I watched a pair of boys in blue flashing their sketch of Brakowski. Asking the question heard all over town:

Had anyone seen any *strangers* tonight?

Patch gave me his left leg.

I gave him my right, glowering at his shot glass. Why *couldn't* he have a Blue Blazer before we got to the Coast? I'd ordered mine. Why couldn't we start tripping sooner?

He winked and switched the glass with my mug. Then winked again and switched them back. We'd just found a brand-new game!

"I sure would love *me* a Blazer," Patch said. "But I believe I'll save mine till I've had me calories."

That black patch had never looked eviler.

Patch switched the glasses again.

Switched them back.

"I *sure* would love one sip," he said.

He switched the glasses.

Switched them back.

"But I ain't a young sport like you, kid. Hell, I takes one sip before the Coast . . ."

Under the table my hands shook away. I wanted to *get back* right now. I needed Patch to take me.

Patch switched the glasses.

Switched them back.

"Caroline would just spin in her grave."

Another switch.

He raised the mug, passed it a couple of times at his lips, like a brandy snifter.

"Funny thing about Blazers," Patch said. "When the fog is nice and thick. . . . and the gas lamps they're a hissin' . . ."

Patch set the mug down dreamily.

But he didn't switch just yet.

"Well . . . It's just an hour or two . . ."

My teeth had started chattering. I wanted to rip out his throat.

"Say, Honk . . ." Patch's good eye opened wide, innocent, sadistic. He raised the rim of the mug to his lips. "You don't suppose . . . I mean—one sip?"

I banged the bell of the horn on the table. Patch's shot glass flew.

He inhaled the Blazer's steam.

"You sure you won't tell Caroline?"

HONK!

The cramps began, an iron fist squeezing my insides to pulp. I doubled over, tried to scream. He had to take me back—I'd die! And he needed a Blazer to get in the mood! Just then Patch relented.

"Well, I guess *one sip*," he allowed. "One eensy-teensy *little* sip . . ."

The scream had almost reached my lips.

"Just one," he said. "Just one!"

He did. He just sort of tipped the mug to let a few drops pass his lips.

But then, thank God, his eyes lit up.

And, bottoms up, he *drank* the Blazer, life force running down his chin.

"To Quaker Sam," he roared.

And then, the magic words, the Blazer words:

"Ah, I misses 'em, Honk . . . The old Eighties . . ."

It was easy after that. Candy from a baby.

Saturday, at 10:00 A.M., we took the steps two at a time out the house. Straight out the front door and into a hansom before it was able to stop. Patch screeched at the driver to *hit* it. And when we'd hit it a couple of blocks, he wailed that we were dying, stop, just stop the goddamn horses, *stop.*

The nearest saloon was a half block away. By the time we got there, there wasn't enough breath between us for one. We needed both hands just to steady our mugs and, even so, half our Blues were over our chins and the table. But we'd made it, that we had.

So, it was cheers to Quaker Sam.

And drinks on Patch for the boys at the bar.

And ears and lips from Honkey.

And then, oh then,

it

happened.

With his second Blazer, the old man's eyes lit up again.
He lit a Havana and sat there and glowed with love and
peace and gratitude.

"Things was simpler then, in the Eighties," he said. "And
that was good, yeah, that was good. And things was a lot
badder too. And, yeah, that was better. . . . But"—Patch
made an empty gesture with the palm of his right hand—
"oh, Honk! I can't forget. I tries, but I keeps—seein' you
. . . throwin' that sack to the wind! Just like in the Old Days
when the town was wild and young. I wants to go back—to
the Sixties!"

Oh, yes.

The *Sixties* . . .

Len had been right all along, I was wrong. The Sixties
were safer and Sweeter by far. Come on with us, all, to the
Sixties, for real:

The Coast is long gone when we get there. And, from the
heights, freed at last of all our pathetic illusions, we *see*:

Time and again, we had been deceived in thinking we
knew San Francisco. This is It, here and now. We've come
back all the way to the Source. Nothing but nothing can
touch us. All is illusion, but this.

No one has heard of the Barbary Coast. In the Sixties, it's
still Sydney Town, the wickedest, bloodiest place in the
world.

In Sydney Town there are two murders a night, one
dozen robberies, two dozen brawls.

The Sydney Ducks—Australian cons—would have the
Tongs of the Eighties for lunch. No one lurks in alleys here.
They prowl the wharf like packs of wolves with wagon
spokes and barlow knives. The water cops don't fool with
clubs, they walk in groups of four or six, swinging swords
with three-foot blades.

There's only one woman for every four men. But nine out
of ten of 'em's Real as they get. In the Fandango Palace "the
tiddies put your eyeballs out on stems." The Hoochie-
Coochie Girls wear red slippers, black stockings, rosebud
garters, and mini-crimson jackets—with nothing underneath them . . . except their stained Real diapers. And the

shows they put on stage would make Caligula blush. Across town, Adah Menken is stopping men's hearts every night, crossing the stage in her flesh-colored tights on the back of a fiery stallion.

Soon the lighting will change—gas first, then 'lectric—but here, now, the lighting is as lighting should be: crude and raw. In the Sixties, when the world is Real, you see, from on top any hill, a vast blackness *pricked* with lights. You see the city in a way men to come will be blind to. And in your dive in Sydney Town, though the tip of a knife is a short scream away, you *see* San Francisco in the candles' gentle flickerings and the coal-oil lamps' modest glow.

And you are alive, for the booze is *alive,* men know how to Drink in the Sixties: Mountain Dew . . . Leadmine whiskey . . . Red Eye . . . Forty Rod . . .

You see Mark Twain!

You see Bret Harte!

But mostly what you see are Men who still look like the miners they were. There's a healthy scruffiness, an air of wealth made from the earth. You see slouched hats rakishly cocked over manly tangles of hair . . . heavy boots caked with mud, some still thickly greased or tarred . . . red wool shirts redolent of manly work and play . . . Levi's jeans, I mean Real Ones, bought back in '50 from young Strauss himself . . .

You see men throwing used clothes in the trash. There's only thirty-thousand Chinks in all of California. And in San Francisco they're charging two bucks for twelve items to wash. So it's cheaper to send your shirts off to Canton, though the round trip takes six months . . . and just scrap your smelly old flannels and socks.

Nothing can touch you here. No one can reach you. Because the town is new, brand new.

I felt the poison spreading.

I had to get on top of things. Get out of the clown suit and get out of town. Take Sammy along. I had money, enough. And . . . I was a serious man.

But there could be no turning back, unless—

Unthinkable!

—I turned back now.

"C'mon, Honkey! Do the ears!"

"Sure, sure, that's the word!"

"Shake a leg, Honk!"

"Toot the horn!"

I heard the voices at the bar. Echoes from Time's prop room, where the lifted screens were stored. I saw the ghosts of shadows from illusions I had lost: Fat Men from the year '06 waving and clunking their schooners . . . shades of Pretty Waitress Girls blowing me kisses . . . gas lamps flickering in the window as if they were there—they were not: Only candles and one or two coal-oil lamps . . . here in the Sweet Spot, the Sixties . . .

"Anyone seen any *strangers* tonight?"

Water cops, mere shadows, too, attempted to slip through the crack. They could not.

(SLAUGHTER AT THE S.F. ZOO!)

(HE IS STRANGE AND DANGEROUS!)

Headlines came like snowflakes, all melting on my bubble's wall.

(5 PRISONERS COMATOSE ON ROCK!)

They could not reach me, for they were not Real. Nothing was Real after this, here and now. Oh, the Sixties were the

(CHINESE WHORE!)

warmest and truest and best

(CHINESE WHORE!)

and sweetest times of all.

(CHINESE!)

And

(HYENA, BATS & PYTHON EATEN!)

no one was taking *my*

lavender

glow.

"Ah, Honkey," Patch said, "in the Sixties—"

"Shut up."

The words were no more than a whisper. Patch couldn't have possibly heard them. The voice was the voice of a ghost.

"Honk?" he said. "By Jesus, kid—you's cured—you's tryna talk!"

(CHINESE!)

In my throat, a molten lump. But what deliverance could there be? To speak was to lose it, the Sweet Spot.

I set the horn down, then the mug, gripping the edge of the table. My throat would burn before I'd speak. I'd die before I screamed.

(CHINESE!)

"C'mon, kid." Patch leaned over, purple veins bulging all over his snout. "C'mon, I tells you, you can talk!"

"Sh . . . Sh . . . *Sh* . . ."

(CHINESE!)

"C'mon, Honk—it's a miracle! Say it, sing it, whisper it, an' I'll buy you a *hundred* Blue Blazers!"

"SH . . ."

Oak table shaking in my hands. Trachea ready to blow. I will not. Will not betray the Sweet Spot.

"C'mon, Honk!" boomed Secondo.

Then Primo, "Haw, more wind to Honk!"

Fat Men slipping through the crack to watch the Patch and Honkey Show.

"Shut up, you lugs," Patch told them. "Can't you see he's tryna talk?"

"Aw, he can't talk, hell, he's dumber than rain. Uh, no offense there, Honkey."

"*SH . . . !*"

The lump was the size of a golf ball, hot as a Frisco filly frying your eyes in a fern bar.

No!

"Say, Honk's lookin' kinda—strange." Primo said that. Or Secondo. Or one of the others who'd slipped through the crack and had started to circle around us.

Patch's lips were just inches from mine. His breath, a fetid stew of smoke and rum and Blazers.

"C'mon, kid, you can do it. You just takes a breath and moves your lips and thinks in the back o' your mind, 'I can talk.' C'mon, Honkey, *talk* to me, I *needs* someone to talk to. Please!"

"*SHU . . . !*"

"Yeah, yeah, that's the word! C'mon, we'll have a high old

time, we'll talk and talk and talk all night and laugh until the
cows come home and—"

The veins on his schnoz looked half ready to gout. The
stench of his soul passed from his mouth through mine.

I turned my head. I couldn't breathe. I took a breath
(AH TOY!)

and swooned, catching our reflections in the window behind Patch.

(A toy . . .)

So, I thought. Time had tricked us again. Even here, even
now, even *we* were shadows on another screen. *We* were
the reflections thrown by the Real Thing in the glass.

A drunken old man, scarcely able to stand.

And a fool with gold curls and a bicycle horn.

"C'mon, Honk, talk to me, talk to me, talk!"

"Shake a leg, Honk!"

"Do the ears!"

I snatched my mug, there was no way to stop, though this
cost me the Sweet Spot forever. The mug sailed through the
window glass and shards the size of tables fell to shatter on
the walk and floor.

The lump scorched through my trachea and flew, like a
shot, out my throat.

"SHUT UP!"

Patch looked at me in horror, speechless for once in his
life.

The Fat Men started murmuring.

"Why, strike me straight."

"Don't that beat all."

"I'm tellin' yez, this *is*, it's *strange*!"

"Shut up, you fucking idiots." My voice was like some
fresh-freed thing that could not be denied. "I'm not your
thing. I'm not your *clown*. I got a NAME, a HISTORY!"

In a lone, gigantic shard still quivering in the window
frame, I saw two water cops coming my way.

I turned on them and let 'er rip. "Eat shit and die, you—
PINKIEBOYS!"

They were reaching for their clubs when I bounded up
over the table and out, the shard dropping behind like a
guillotine blade.

Chinatown. I'd been walking for hours, trying to find it, the crack we'd slipped through. I might as well have been circling the block, for they all looked the same to me. On corner after corner I found old men playing mah-jongg, blue tunics drifting in thick clouds of smoke. In window after window I saw the same displays: jars with brilliant liquids filled with sea horses and toads and snakes . . . carcasses of duck and ox . . . Everywhere I stopped I saw the post where *he* had stopped, hitching his boot up to rub at his foot . . . that handsome, square-jawed, well-dressed,

(TANNED)

stranger, who just stared at me, while from a window high above—

Which one?

That one?

That one?

Where!

—her voice had pleaded:

"Harrrrrrr-

pooooooo!"

But I was as lost as I'd ever been lost. The Chinatown I stumbled through was a feverish, lunatic nightmare. I'd never had, or not had, a Blazer but with Patch. I felt as if I'd been ripped from the womb and thrown naked and screaming into a maze, each turn taking me further within.

I whispered, "Sam."

I croaked it, "Sam."

I heard, vaguely, the voices around me.

"Chingaling sing wiggle, Honk!"

"Chow hoy hey pong shakee, Honk"

"Doee ah toy oh boy horn!"

Then, near the center of the maze:

"Sammy! Hing ting Sammy!"

"Chow boy hoo toy lookee Quakee!"

"Quakee Quakee ding ling boy!"

"Mokka heya long dong Quakee!"

Then, at the very center, a heartfelt roar that topped them all:

"Oh, there's a Big One comin', gonna level this town to the ground!"

I caught a quick glimpse of a small, sticklike figure in bowler and raggedy jacket, before the crowd thickened around him.

And I heard myself honking the horn like a fool as I rushed off to follow them.

ALMOST HOME

Patch was stumbling home through Chinatown when he saw Quaker Sam with the Chinks on his heels.

He took a right on Jackson, away from the fire and brimstone, his own world already in ashes.

He still hurt in places he hadn't known he had, but wished the two water cops hadn't been there to stop the frenzied mob.

Honk's strange!

Ye knew it!

He took our damn dough!

Fists then. And more fists. Boots. Patch screaming, *He ain't strange!*

"Aww, kid, you could talk all along!" Patch tongued at a loosened tooth; felt it give; spat it out; and wished he could cough up a few busted ribs. "You's one of 'em. Whyn't you tell me, you lug?"

He leaned against a street lamp, shoulders racked with mournful heaves. What had *possessed* Honk when they'd gone so far? How could he have lost it, just thrown it away, and forever, his beautiful mask? The town going to hell in a hurry, and Honkey there to ease the pain with a few merry toots of his horn.

He'd come back, he had to. If he was *strange,* what of it then? They had it right in Oakland: San Francisco had always been strange, from the start. And that was the best thing about it.

"Oh, Jesus, we was almost home. . . ."

When Honk came back, 'course he couldn't be *Honkey*— Wait a second . . .

Not so fast . . .

Why couldn't the two of them, when they's alone, carry on just like they used to? Pshaw! At night, in the flat, Honk could bring out the horn—

Patch scarcely heard the *clops* of hooves till the hansom had pulled up beside him. He heard a horn inside the cab and rushed to the door, crying, "Honkey!" without even troubling to look.

When he was feet from the cab, the handle turned and the door swung open.

Oh.

The dark, well-dressed stranger leaned against the other door, legs crossed and hands on one knee. The rim of his bowler enshadowed his face except for the ponderous outline of his black mustache and, when he spoke, a flash of white against the chocolate of his skin.

"Come in," he said. Not a request. A raspy purr of a statement of fact.

Patch swallowed once. And then again. "I thought you was me—Well . . ."

"Come *in.*"

"If it's all the same to you . . . I'll walk," Patch answered, stepping in.

He started to reach for the door. But no need. The door clicked shut all by itself as he sailed across the black buttery seat. He had a crazed impression that the cab was the size of a field and as the driver cracked the whip and the hansom bolted, that he was falling back and down, even as he sailed across. It lasted forever, yet no time at all. He felt his body slam, back first, against a towering wall. Long arms, inhumanly wrong, wrapping his. Hot breath panting at his throat. Sandpaper caress of a tongue, oh my God, Patch fumbling for his derringer, when—through the tongue that licked and stroked and seemed to stretch around his throat —came a new shower of lavender sparks.

And then the words: "It's monster time."

Patch slumped back, exhausted, yet unaccountably thrilled.

To hear the snaps and pops and squeals . . .

To see the hands bristling with hair thick as hides . . .

To feel the sudden stillness, the two of them, intertwined, at the top of an endless abyss . . .

To smell—

Oh God, it stinks in here! Sweet Jesus, I hates lavender!

He buckled once, ferociously. The arms that pinned him coiled like snakes.

He heard a low chuckle behind him. And he hated it more than he feared it.

"Lemme go, you—pinkieboy!"

A loud, manic giggle.

"You crazy, damned—*hyena*!"

A growl. An angry bark.

And then
one hundred knives
at the back of his neck
went for his throat as he screamed,
"HONNNNNNNNNNNNN-
"KEYYYYYYYYYYYY!"

BOOK OF
REVELATIONS

"Friends," he cried, "I beg you! Hear me!"

A crowd of a hundred, and growing, had gathered at Quaker Sam's feet. I'd elbowed my way through the throngs to the front, without a thought of Alcatraz.

I watched Sam climb up on the base of a street lamp, holding the pole for support. With his free hand, he jabbed at the air with one finger, or wiggled his bowler like Jolson.

"Oh, there's a Big One comin', gonna level this town to the ground! I've told you before and I'll tell you again: We've got to get back to the Eighties—get back and get it right this time, stop the times from goin' wrong!"

Well, it was like a carnival. Or like a spaced-out concert, where everybody knew the words, but only knew them more or less—and in no particular order. So, you had people crying out, to the left and to the right:

"Down with *Huckleberry Finn*!"

"Down with child psychology!"

"Down with lager!"

"Down with phones!"

Hell, even the Chinamen got in the act. You could've heard them singalinging halfway to L.A.:

"Hing ting hoo boy Eighty, Sam!"

"How now long dong shakee bakee, Colgate, hey boy, gramophone!"

Sam's voice began to fail him as he croaked his thankless pleas.

He begged them to ban the Sears catalog, the first of which had appeared back in '86 and which had spread, like a plague, from a hundred to six hundred pages—now read by three million sinners! They called it the Big Book. They'd started to keep it on nightstands, where once the Good Book had been kept. They taught their kids to practice math by filling out the orders. And children learned their ABC's by reading Sears' hokum ads: "The Best in the World! Lasts *forever*— or your money back!"

Sam damned the incalculable damage done by Satan's own *cash registers*. Oh, not the originals, patented way back in '79. Hell, '79 was a very good year. No, Sam was screaming about *'84* . . . when they started adding bells! Now you had your NCR with sales across the world. Salesmen screaming as they sold 'em, "NCR—It pays!" And bells, bells, bells, bells, ringing up the sales . . . and more bells *classifying* sales by department and type of transaction. Bells jingling when they rang your bill, bells clanging when they took your cash.

"Get back!" Sam screamed. "Get back! Get back—to where we once belonged!"

Sam's arguments against the bells grew so inspired and impassioned, I wished I could have followed them. But my eyes were so thoroughly boggled I was no longer listening.

Quaker Sam . . . We'd met at last. . . .

Me and the mad Lenny Dirks.

BOOK THREE

THE CLASS OF '67

 "What took you so long?" Lenny asked me.

He slipped the chimney from a gas lamp, turned the key, and lit the wick. He shook the match out in one vigorous move, wasting no more on the shake than on the smile he gave me.

I'd followed Lenny from the Coast, shedding bits and pieces of Harp along the way: the stovepipe here . . . the greatcoat there . . . galoshes in an alley . . . horn . . . They might have been looking for Honkey, after that scene in the Hangdog Saloon. As if I'd needed an excuse for trashing the clown suit forever. I'd been careful also to keep as much distance between us as I could swing without losing the way. Just in case some cop thought I still looked like a clown.

But Lenny wasn't asking why it took so long to get there. And I had no answer to give him. I should have known. I should have guessed.

I closed the door behind me, barefoot now and shivering.

"Jesus . . . You were *Quaker Sam.* . . ."

Lenny chuckled, the equivalent of screeches of laughter from anyone else. He tossed his bowler, Bond-style, across the room to a coatrack; it stuck. He rubbed the stubble on his skull; stroked the spiked beard on his chin.

"Harpo. That was *good,* Dodge."

I didn't have to nod. My head was shaking with the rest of me.

Len slipped out of Sam's faded cord jacket and kicked off his high-button shoes. He wore the same denims he'd worn on the train, and had worn all through Canada. Real ones. Levi's classics. The same collarless shirt. The same braces —

slipped off of his shoulders, as always, when he felt really relaxed. And he was.

He'd cut his hair.

He'd changed his beard.

But he'd remained, even as Sam, somehow quintessentially *himself.*

A direct continuum from 1960 to 1906.

There are no words to tell the joy of shared blood and shared history after the week I'd just had. But . . . the fact is, I also felt cheated. I'd been the one in the clown suit, while he had been *Len* all along.

I'd been cold since I scrapped the galoshes and coat. Now the chill cut to the bone. Lenny brought me a wool army blanket. Then led me to a cushioned chair.

"I'm gonna make us some coffee. Here, have a cigarette, warm you up a little." In a humidor beside the chair he'd stashed a dozen hand-rolleds. He stuck one between my lips, then flicked a match with the nail of his thumb. "I really dig the matches here. Be back in a couple of minutes."

A sliding door hung with chenille portieres set the kitchenette off from the main room. There wasn't much to be set off. You could've put the kitchen floor inside a Barbie-Doll house. But Lenny moved so smoothly within I guessed he could have lived in there, slept on the stove, and been happy.

The sitting room, my guess was, was like the dozen others in which he'd holed up in Toronto. Only now, it was new and not some mausoleum.

Clean white matting on the floor. Gray paper, spotted with pink and green flowers, fresh laid upon the walls. The walnut headboard of Sam's bed, blooming with hand-painted violets, matching the bureau beside it. Work table with spiral legs by the window draped with green and gold. Stacks, feet high, of news clippings and books. Two filing cabinets of rich yellow oak, so stuffed the drawer handles looked ready to blow. Just left of the entrance, the closet, sporting a gleaming new lock. Beside the closet, a washstand with two clean white towels on its rack. Communal bathroom down the hall.

So, this was where the job got done. Maintaining the continuum. Lenny being Lenny, regardless of the time.

"Hey, Dodge!" Lenny cried. "Take a look—check it out!" I looked over. He was beaming, wood coffee-grinder in one hand. "I got this in a thrift store, man. Hand carved. They've got thrift stores!"

I chattered "Wow" and turned away to swipe another cigarette. And I was still sitting there, puffing away, when Lenny came in with the coffee.

He set my mug beside my feet.

Then stood back, grinning impishly.

"All right," I told him, "I give up."

"You're kidding me."

"I'm *buffaloed.*"

"You really haven't figured it?"

"I haven't got a clue."

"Jesus, this is wonderful. Never thought I'd see you stumped."

"I'm gonna count to three."

"All right!" Len sat down, kitty-cornered to me, on a brocaded settee. "The way I've got it figured—"

"One."

"Okay, okay. The comet's cycle is seventy-five years. And the comet brought us here."

"Two." I set my mug down, fingers beginning to twitch.

Len shifted back the same number of inches that I'd shifted forward.

"The comet's last appearance was in 1835, the year Mark Twain was born—"

"Three!" I was up, about halfway, when I saw where this was headed. "Nawww . . ."

"We're going back! In 1910!"

They didn't have smelling salts back in '06. But Lenny had revived me with a coolly watered towel and second-hand smoke from a joint.

I sat up, little bluebirds flying all around my head. I took the jay, inhaling half, and passed the roach to Lenny. And then I continued to sit there as he unfolded the saga of the birth of Quaker Sam.

Len had *understood* one thing the instant he woke from the lavender eye. We'd come unstuck from one time, and had been restuck in another, by a force that was greater than Halley's. And possibly benign.

He had just seen the *Zephyr disappear* in a whirling crimson fog, with how many others still on it.

Why us? Len had wondered. Why this particular time, place?

As he'd stood by the wagon near Oakland, squared off before the mystic lights, it had come to Lenny: *Time.*

Time had spared only those who took the leap of faith.

A leap of faith. A test of faith. What did we believe in?

A leap through Time. A game of Time: each of our arrivals spaced for a series of personal tests?

He'd been last all his life. Now he was the first. But why?

Within minutes of entering Oakland, ascertaining the year and the date, Lenny knew: This was the year of the Big One. With no way of learning the date.

1906 . . . Why 1906? Unless the Quake was the key to the game . . . What if the one thing Len could not divine had been divinely provided? The comet and the earthquake—they had to be connected! And had to be connected in a way he was able to use.

At the time, he'd been able to figure no more. Except that he'd never survive for a week, let alone till the comet's return, not as a man of the day. He had no gift for blending. Even in his own day, he'd been a man of the past.

Yes, the *past* . . .

On the ferry, he'd started to see "Sam" : the severely cropped hair . . . the short spike of a beard . . . the faded, patched corduroy jacket . . . A harmless eccentric who lived in the past, dreaming of days Len could master . . .

Which past, though? And to what end?

The Quake and the comet . . .

The Quake and the comet . . .

The connection, and the answer, nearly caused Len to jump overboard from pure joy.

Lenny knew a disaster was coming, but was powerless to

stop it. Even if he'd known the date, how could he tell it without seeming strange? But *Sam,* yes, Quaker Sam, there was a man with a vision! Sam would tell men, far and wide, that the Big One was coming unless they *got back.*

They would not hear.

The Quake would come.

But *after* the Quake, with the city in ruins, men would sit at his knees as he told them: of the Good Times . . . the Real Times . . . the—Eighties . . .

"But *why*?" I cried. "My God—what *for*?"

Lenny looked at me, stunned by my daftness. "I already told you."

"You're going back."

"We're going back. You're not gonna *stay* here?"

"Fine. We're going back. In 1910."

"To '86. By Halley's."

"Right. So, first you're gonna spend four *years* taking *them* back to the Eighties?"

Lenny clapped. "And you're gonna *help* me!"

"WHY?"

"Because," he answered slowly, " '86, when we get back, will be in the Sixties."

It's an hour later now and I'm feeling better, much. Lenny's crazed logistics are starting to make sense to me. This may have something to do with the joint, one more from the great stash that Lenny has brought.

The whole setting is very serene and relaxed. Len has changed to a comfy pair of high-grade flannel pj's. The gray top has a splendid military collar, jumbo faux-pearl buttons, and silk military braids. I'm in a spare flannel nightshirt with pink/white barbershop striping. And, though he has no candy, Lenny has given me cocoa. It's sweet. I enjoy the cocoa and grass. He looks like Sergeant Pepper.

"Values," Lenny tells me. "Time's just a big game of values. And the Sixties were only the Sixties because of the values they held. Once I understood that, the whole game came clear to me. The year we returned to was out of our hands. The way to set the clock back then . . . was to turn men's *minds* back now."

I sip at my cocoa and smile as Lenny lights me up a cigarette. He's started pacing as he speaks. He looks like a Patton of Time. Stoned, I sense that he cannot be stopped.

An army of objections stands before him, muskets raised: Any single one of us might be *undoing* whatever Sam did . . . A hundred million trillion things made the Sixties what they were . . . Lenny blows them all away with his Looney-Tunes passion and hope.

He paces and repeats his plan, examining his strategy in detail for the slightest flaw. There are none that I can see. I know I'm in good hands. We're going back to the Sweet Spot for keeps. I see him floating as he paces, no longer a Patton . . . a Caesar of Time!

At the start, he'd tried to focus on a particular year. But libraries weren't what they'd be in our day—his resources had been limited. And Progress, Quaker Sam-style, had been spread clear through the Eighties.

Gradually, though, he'd realized: He didn't feel any more certain of when the Real Sixties began than of the date of the Big One. He was forty-one years old and had to play it right. Too far back and he would land in the exhaust of the Fifties. Not far enough, in the Seventies. The only way to play the game: by the Law of Averages.

So Quaker Sam dated his demons over the course of a decade: '82 . . . '86 . . . '88 . . . '89 . . .

How could we lose?

The Law *had* to be it!

We'd arrive, in '86, in '65 . . . or '66 . . . to the heart of the heart of the Sixties.

It's wonderful!

It's brilliant!

Len's plan is a mad work of art.

Until I begin to come down from the grass and he no longer looks like a Caesar of Time.

I whisper, What about Sammy? What of the five who are still on the Rock? What of Brakowski—who can't be Brakowski . . . and Blacke, who doesn't scare me, but . . . He scares me . . . Yeah . . . But *why?*

Len bristles off to the kitchen, returning a few seconds later with another jumbo joint.

I'm still whispering, as he lights it, that something's happened to me: I've started seeing Blacke's eyes everywhere I look . . . in the news . . . in Chinatown. . . .

Lenny gives me the quietest look in the world. He takes an heroic toke, smiling grimly when I pass.

"What's your problem, Dodge?" he says.

I start to softshoe around it, whispering this and whispering that—about Austin's eyes on the *Zephyr* . . . how inhumanly knowing and wrong they had felt . . .

"What's your problem?" he repeats.

"The Wall," I tell him, growing agitated. "It's the Wall."

Lenny's blowing smoke rings now, the same as I blew on the *Zephyr*. And I remember sitting there, smoke-doodling visions of Sam. . . .

Come on, Dodge, what's your problem . . .

"I'm a coward," I tell Lenny. "I knew it at the Wall. All those years in Canada . . . I never gave a good goddamn. I didn't want my ass shot off. And there wasn't any more to it than that. Hell, I've been running all my life. I only thought I was fighting."

Lenny tokes, serenely. "I told you that on the *Zephyr*."

And this time I take the jay, for Lenny's inside of the Sweet Spot I've lost. I want to be there with him.

"Dodge," he says, and it sounds like he's singing, "that's eighty years in the future."

(You are your father's father now . . .
You never went to Canada . . .)

"Man, we're *creating* our futures today."

(You've beaten the Fat Man . . .
You've beaten the Wall . . .
And Ghost Boy has never been born . . .)

"Dodge, for God's sake, look around. Tell me—where's the Wall?"

"It's . . . everywhere," I tell him.

And then it happens:

I explode.

Top and bottom, both at once.

Shitrocketed out of my chair.

The Blazers coming out of me . . . The Blazers and the calories and forty-odd years of evasion.

I'm lying on the settee now. And Lenny's flat smells like a cow yard, despite the candles and incense and the window he's propped all the way. I've been rolled like a rug in three blankets. They help. But Len's keeping a gingerly distance, with a weather eye on me, as he completes his rounds.

At the dresser he stops, kneeling, to pass his hand under the edge of the rug. His hand emerges with a key—a three-inch length of gleaming brass.

One eye half-closes in a wink.

"I'm gonna show you something, Dodge. Man, this is the ultimate cure!"

"Lenny . . ." I croak. "The Big One . . ."

"Eh?"

He's floating to the closet now, with no time for small talk. But, still, I've got to know.

"The Quake, man . . . *When*?" I ask.

"Oh, *that*. Jesus, how the hell should I know? June, July . . . Fuck it, it's two months away!"

"We've got to *do*—something."

"What? You got a thing for Alcatraz?"

And that's the end of that for now. Napoleon is at the door. He holds the key before him.

"Close your eyes," Len tells me.

Click of the key in the lock. A light twist. The doorknob turns. The hinges squeak, very softly, and just for effect.

"Not yet," Lenny tells me.

Soft clink of glass. A muted hiss. Scratchpop of another match mastered by Len's thumbnail. And, through closed lids, I see the change in the room's soft lighting. The glow ahead, still more inviting.

"One more second," Lenny calls.

A light thud, scarcely audible, yet freighted with tension and impact. Two quick snaps. A sense, no more, of movement. Then something faintly like a hum.

"Ready . . . Set . . . Open 'em!"

Open 'em and see Len smiling, there by the door, a guitar in his hands. See the wall of the closet he's shrined floor to ceiling with pix from *The Summer of Love*.

Whisper, "Oh my God . . . You're *mad* . . ."

Then hear Lenny laugh, laugh, knowing that he's got you now, still laughing as he starts to sing:

"It was twenty years ago today . . ."

Try to stop the Song of Songs from breaking free, great flight of birds, from the sands of your cynical heart.

Sergeant Pepper taught us all to play . . .

Try to stop the lies you still, still can't keep from loving.

"Let them take us down . . ." I whisper, drifting to the photos. ". . . to a magical, mythical city . . . in that mystical Summer of Love . . ."

MONSTER TIME

If I was to go with Lenny—and the Sixties had never looked better to me—I had some immediate business.

We put Sergeant Pepper away around four and spent the next couple of hours getting rid of Harpo's ghost.

Lenny shaved and barbered me. He had a high old time cropping my curls to my skull. Put a spike on my chin and we might have been twins.

I soaked for an hour in the tub down the hall, planning what I'd say to Patch. And by the time Len's neighbors started stirring in their rooms, I was ready to get on with it.

I left around six. I wore Lenny's felt slippers and the flannels and plaid pants I'd borrowed from Patch. I had the streets pretty much to myself.

There were no cries of "You! Hold fast!"

Or:

"Shake a leg, Honk!"

"Do the ears!"

San Francisco Sunday. Dawn. Sinners straggling homeward, planning, vaguely, to repent . . . but earnestly trying to time it: To the end of the line, the last Saturday night that they can hope to survive.

Even in the Eighties, mine, I'd always thought this hour was uniquely San Francisco's.

This morning it seemed even more so.

The walk was not a long one. Lenny's second-floor flat was on Mason near Geary; my destination was Sutter and Polk. But, again and again, I was stopped by the loss of the Sweet Spot I'd found here for just a few days. Now I looked at the gas lamps . . . and I saw antiques. I looked at the phaetons and hansoms and landaus . . . and saw museum pieces.

Still, there was a lurid fascination in all this. And so I stopped. And so I smoked, blowing rings at the mist that lay over the streets like the haze in some waterfront bar.

I stopped and smoked.

Smoked and watched.

Watched and forestalled, just a few minutes longer, the unavoidable moment of truth.

I owed the old man that much.

I stopped and smoked, smoked and watched, and had still made my way up to Sutter before I heard the cries.

The cries were faint and they came from the left; they seemed to be scattered for blocks along Polk. I had a passing flash of that first cry on the *Zephyr* . . . the night Halley's rained down its sparks. These had that same uniqueness.

A light wind, nearly as faint as the cries, started to rustle the instant I turned. And I found myself faced with an unsettling sight. A block away, on Polk Street, men drifted in stoned trances, eyes plastered to the News. As they walked, they dropped, pell-mell, other sections to the street. These rustlestirred about their knees, while high above, like dreamparty streamers, sections dropped from windows danced and floated to the ground.

The cries were like sleepwalkers' ramblings, vague and thick as Baghdad's fog.

I had the same sinking feeling I'd had nights ago in Chinatown . . . when through the crack I heard her cry. The same sense that there might be time . . . if I just . . . turned my back.

It was April Fool's. Of course. There'd been some wonderful, wonderful joke.

But I found myself drifting, lost in the fog, to the dreamy procession on Polk Street. At the corner I froze, looking up, my eyes fixed on his window.

I saw myself knocking . . . Patch opening the door . . . and looking at me sadly as he shot me through the eye.

(You's strange!)

I caught a sudden flash of brass in the old man's window. Then the blue that it was buttoned to wholly filled the frame. A block-jawed mug with a walrus and two curious, curious eyes was looking out, straight at me, from underneath a tall felt hat.

I saw one of his hands move as if it were swimming through a fog as thick as mine. In the hand, something gleamed, as blinding as the buttons.

Then the whistle sounded.

And, in the distance, from a newsstand, shriller than the whistle's blast:

"Monster time! It's here! C'mon, c'mon and get it, monster time!"

There was a seconds'-silence. Milling zombies, shockstopped, turned, one by one, and faced me. Faced me and then looked at me. Looked, still stunned and dreamy-eyed, and then with horror, all at once, as if they were looking at—

"Honkey . . ."

It started as a murmur, thin, almost gelatinous. Then, terribly, it thickened into a low, menacing growl:

Honkey . . ."

It seemed as solid as a wall, while all the fog in Baghdad had gathered at my feet. Dear God. I could not move. I could not breathe.

The men dropped their papers, which capered and swirled. They looked at one another. They looked back at me. And then they started chanting:

"Honkey! Honkey! Honkey!"

Another whistle blasted. Then, thunderings of feet down stairs. The front door exploded. And a half-dozen flashes of brass-buttoned blue came through it hard as hand grenades.

"THAT'S HIM!"

"HONKEY!"

"GET HIM!"

Friends, I've got news for you.

It really is astonishing, given the right impetus, how fast a forty-year-old clown can run.

I HEARD
THE NEWS TODAY . . .

 Lenny bolted the door as I dropped to my knees, huffapuffing and wheezing for air. Not a drawer in the dresser of life right-side-up. And just when I'd got everything back into place.

"Len . . ." I started. "Mob . . . nuts . . ."

"Shut up," he said. His voice was low; calmer than I'd ever heard it.

"Paper . . . zombies . . ." I said. "Cops . . ."

Len marched to the window. He pulled the shade briskly and whipped shut the drapes.

"Something . . . *bad* . . ."

"I said, shut *up.*" Lenny started pacing, one hand clenched behind his back, the other stroking the spike on his chin. He never took his eyes from me. He paced very slowly.

"Lenny . . . something awful . . ." Better. Up to two words between gasps.

Lenny walked over. He stood right before me. I looked up and guessed he was seven feet high.

"Dodge." He almost whispered this. "Did anyone follow you here?"

"No . . . I ran . . . too fast for 'em . . . Caught a . . . phaeton. Switched then . . . hansom . . ."

"Are you absolutely positive?"

"Yeah . . . doubled back by . . . cable car . . ."

"I swear to God . . ." Lenny started.

There was no need to finish it. If I'd ever thought I'd
known Len, I'd been wrong.

He pulled up his suspenders. Gave them a concerted
snap. Then hooked his thumbs in, thoughtfully.

"You seen the morning paper?"

I shook my head. "I heard . . . oh God . . ."

Lenny helped me to my feet. I braced myself on his
shoulder. That helped. But my knees still buckled. And I
began to shiver. For the folded paper's headline screamed,
upside down, in crimson:

ǃƎMIT ЯƎTƧNOM

"Oh-oh," I said.

And Len said, "Yeah. Now you'd better sit down. It gets
worse, a lot worse. Let's start off with the best of the worst."

World War II heads were a ways down the pike, but the
letters, though thinner, were three inches high. And they
had the intended effect. The entire front page had been
printed in red. And I came to my senses as quickly as if I'd
been splashed with a bucket of blood.

Beneath the headline, in triple-sized type:

> The San Francisco Call *begins a series of weekly col-
> umns about the group on Alcatraz, referred to by some as
> the strange ones. Learn the shocking truth about:*
> *—Their real identity.*
> *—The world that they have come from.*
> *—The terrifying threats they pose to all of mankind if
> released.*
> *The truth will amaze you!*
> *The truth will confound you!*
> *The truth will frighten you out of your wits!*
> *Monster Time has just arrived.*
> *Without further ado, then:*
>   *HEEEEEEEEEERE'S WOLFY!*
> *(Please turn page for story.)*

"You maniac," I muttered. "Jesus, Wolf . . . what have you done?"

"Don't even guess," Lenny said. "It's worse than your worst nightmare. Smoke?"

Len pointed at the humidor.

I shook my head. "I'll take this straight."

I turned the page, folded it over and read.

Monster Time!
by Wolf Cotter

Gather round me, children, for you're about to hear as weird a tale as any tale your ears have ever heard.

You've heard about the five "special prisoners" on Alcatraz.

Curious *rumors!*

Incredible *rumors!*

Dark and surpassingly strrrrraaaaannnnnge *rumors!*

No one's confirming.

No one's denying.

No one's saying anything.

Why?

Because, friends, the rumors, each strrrrraaaaannnnnger *than the last, are true.*

They have come, as They claim, from the future.

They have come from 1986.

They have come from another dimension . . . a Twilight Zone of time and space . . .

There are more of the Zonies among you. They are walking the streets as you read this.

Trust me, children. Trust me.

Why?

Because, you see—

I'M ONE OF THEM!

"Oh! Oh! Oh, God!" I cried.

Lenny chuckled bleakly. "Wait till you get to the bad part."

I shot him an edgily woebegone look.

"Believe me, you'll know when you get there."

Wolf began the story proper with a revisionist twist. He portrayed, and brilliantly, his heroic quest: to stop a whole trainload of sinners from heaping abuse on poor Halley's.

Who in Baghdad was so heartless not to weep to learn: how, hour after hour, Wolf alone had warned us . . . how he'd prayed to the comet for mercy . . . how he'd been beaten, almost to death, while attempting to stop us from leaving?

I felt my own eyes moistening.

"I'd say you're almost there," Len said.

Our long, slow, and disparate treks along the tracks to Oakland were Wolfed into a thunderous, alien march. And only man could stop us: a small man from the future . . . a *strange* man, but a noble man . . . You guessed it—Your Reporter!

I turned the page.

Len said, "Now."

I quick-lit a cigarette.

In weeks to come Your Reporter would tell them of the Future. He would tell them of the First World War. The Second. The threat of the Third. He would tell them of street gangs and organized crime. He would tell them of millionaire niggers and Chinks. Of men and women who married . . . but not to women and men.

Well, it got worse and worse and worse.

Orwell might have sold his soul for some of the effects.

Still, I was still sitting.

Till the bottom of the page.

Where Wolf signed off with his best shot:

The Future is here—and it isn't your friend.
I have much to tell you, children.
But worst things first.
And worst of all:
The Zonies "sleeping" on the Rock are part of a subspe-cies infested with a virus so potent and so evil their kisses are more deadly than a bullet to the brain.

The disease they carry kills. Next week I will tell you how. Next week I will tell you, in horrifying detail, the progressive symptoms of this ravaging disease.

This week, let the sickness be given its name.
The Zonies' kiss of death is:
> *AIDS!*
Look closely at your neighbors, friends.
Look closely all around you.
How well do you know the man . . . standing right beside you?

I threw the paper to the floor and started stomping on it.
"Maniac! Asshole! There's gonna be blood in the streets!"
"Dodge—"
"Riots! Fucking martial law!"
"Dodge—"
"Vigilantes! Lynchings!"
"Raphael."
I looked up to see Len dangling something like a broadside. The print was facing his way. But from the way he dangled it, I knew that this was serious.
"Pull yourself together, Dodge. That was the good news. This is the bad."
I started toward him.
"Uh-uh. Sit."
"Gimme that." I reached for it.
"I'm not kidding. Have a seat."
I slunk back and slumped on the cushion and snarled, "Now let me have that paper."
"Dodge . . . uh . . . before I do . . ."
"You fucking give it to me now!"
I snatched the paper from his hand. Took one look and lost my mind. And started kicking and screaming "No!"
Next thing I knew, I was down on the floor, Lenny holding a pillow down over my face while I flooded its casing with tears.

"You okay?" he asked me.
I nodded and stared at the flyer.
"Let me get you something. Hey."
I shook my head and muttered "Patch" and continued to stare at the flyer, inserted in the morning's *Call*.
"You knew him?" Len said.

I said "Yeah . . ." and could not take my eyes from the flyer.

The headline screeched:

ZONIE KILLER AT LARGE!

On the left, beneath it, Patch glared within a hand-drawn frame.

On the right, that rugged face I had seen in Chinatown. The sketch was crude, the mustache wrong. But they'd got the eyes just right. The eyes were hypnotic and blazing. They still spooked me as badly as Austin's.

Looming in between the two was San Francisco's favorite clown: a cartoon sketch of Honkey, fangs dripping blood from Patch's throat.

My eyes kept returning to the cabbie's statement.

"It was Honkey, all right," said Paul Wilson, hansom driver. "But you'd never've guessed it to look at him first. Dressed up just like a gent, he was. Had a big trick black mustache, and he'd colored his face half as black as a nigger's. Taller, too, wearin' stilts. But it was Honkey, on my soul. 'Cause I heard him honk, bejeez. Next thing I knew, Patch was callin' his name. And as Patch was screamin', I heard Honkey laughin', like nothin' that ever has laughed on this earth."

Lenny whispered, "Who, Dodge?"

"What."

"Who? Who the hell could have done it?"

"Not who, Lenny. *What.*"

I let the flyer flutter.

What . . .

"Whatever it is," I said slowly, "this may be lots worse than we think."

Lenny shrugged. "Maybe," he said. "Then again, maybe not." He had another section of the paper he'd been saving. He took this from beside his chair, crossed his legs, and tossed it. He watched me snatch it and folded his hands, swinging his leg, smiling tightly. "Maybe in a few more weeks we'll be the least of their worries."

I thought what the hell and unfolded the thing. Caruso glaring, big as life, and bound for the Grand Opera on April 17.

Wait . . .

"Dodge," Lenny cried. "Don't you get it?"

"Caruso . . ."

"Man, it's April, Dodge. The Big One. It's only a couple of weeks." Lenny leaned forward, still swinging his leg. "Don't you remember the stories . . . how he ran from his room, in his shirttails, screaming he'd never come back? He'd been up late when it hit. Partying and carrying on. So, it's after midnight sometime. Maybe two. Maybe three."

I glared back at his picture as if I might beat the truth out with my eyes. *Did* I remember? And, if I did, *what*?

"Later," I said. I was looking at Lenny. Looking hard at Lenny now. "Maybe four. Or five."

Lenny said, excitedly, "Yeah! Yeah, I think you're right!"

I crossed my leg like Lenny, folding my hands on my lap. "Come on, let me have it."

"What?" Lenny's leg stopped swinging.

For some reason mine did not. "I think you think you know the date."

Lenny's leg started swinging again. "No—I mean, I can't be sure."

My own leg stopped. I said, quietly, *"When?"*

"Well . . . I can't get it out of my mind. Not since I saw the picture there. It seems right. It has that ring. It goes off, and it keeps going off. April twenty-fourth. The morning after Caruso's last show."

"You're . . . really *sure* about this."

Lenny looked at me, then he looked at his shoe.

"I feel it," he said. "I *remember*."

"The twenty-fourth," I muttered.

Len looked up. "I'm sure of it!"

My eyes drifted down from his eyes to his shoe.

For a crazed second, I feared he was lying. Jesus, I *was* getting paranoid.

Len's leg started swinging then.

And so did mine.

"Can you *see* it?" he asked.

"I said, "Yeah . . . *Yeah* . . . Now get me a pencil and paper. And a towel to mop up the blood."

"What?"

"I can't walk around like this. You're gonna break my nose."

"I can't do it!" Lenny whimpered.

He was standing by the door, as if he might bolt any second.

"Sure you can," I told him. I penciled in some more things I'd be needing, then scratched at my chin where the peachfuzz had been. I looked the list over. It was a long list and would keep Lenny hopping. "There," I said, "that'll do it for now."

"Dodge, I can't—come on, Dodge . . ."

"Len." I started folding the list, very neatly. "If you don't do exactly what I have asked you to do, I am going to walk to that window . . . open it wide . . . and scream, 'Zonie!' "

"All right, all right!" Len flagged his arms. "I'll do the list. I'll get it all. But, Dodge, please, you know me . . ."

"Mmm."

"I haven't got it in me!"

"Shhh. Shhh. Sure you do." I had the long list folded now to my satisfaction. I retrieved the flyer and treated myself to a punishing look. Then I swallowed the lump I still had in my throat and took five steps to Lenny. I slipped the list into his pocket. Patted it down. Gave one brace a good snap. "Yeah, you've got it in you."

I gave the brace another snap. This one brought a little color to the Crisco of his cheeks. I waved the flyer at him, then plastered the sheet to his mug with my palm.

Lenny slapped it away and cried, "Hey, cut it out!"

"Cut it out?" I said. "Like wow." Then I gave him a shove. "You're a killer. Come on." Another shove. This rocked him. His lips started to quiver, his fingers to clench. "Let 'em all burn, take the heat off of us. Kids sizzling on the griddle like weenies at a roast—"

"Shut up!"

I threw both hands into the next shove. Then stepped right in, our eyes inches apart.

"You hypocrite," I growled at him. "You fleabag hippie sack of shit. Sammy's dead. An old man's dead. Five people just like you and me are rotting on the Rock. Fuck yourself up the ass with the Sixties. I may be dead in a couple of weeks. But I'm checking out like a man, not a clown. I'm gonna get me a monster. Come on!" I slapped him. "Do it!" I slapped him again, then I backhanded it.

He was shaking, as if in a seizure.

But, still, he couldn't do it. So I played the joker I had up my sleeve.

"Look at me." I smiled at Len. "I'm *your* monster, you dumb fuck. I set you up for Canada. You went because of me. I left you high and dry up there when the man with the peanuts said we could come home. Oh, we had a high old time screwing the dregs of the Sixties. But all things pass. And so did they. And I got to thinking, hey, the Man without a Country . . . He might be good for a laugh. So I brought you home to watch—"

"Shut up! Or I'll—I'll—I'll—"

Well, Len was almost ready now. One has a feel about these things.

"Naw," I said, "you won't do squat. You never have. You never will. Hell, I hope you land in the Sixties. A middle-aged goof who'll die slapping his meat."

Len knee'd me square between the legs. It took the heart right out of me. Then I felt my balls explode. I teetered backward a couple of steps, reeled there a second, and dropped to my knees, breathing, it seemed, through my scrotum, the air tearing through me like shrapnel.

"You want it?" Lenny asked.

Ha-ugggghhhh!

"You want it, well, you got it." He was rolling his sleeve as he came.

Ha-ugggghhhh!

He made a fist with one hand, grabbing the nap of my hair with the left. He raised the fist high and it shook in the sky.

"I've been wanting to do this for twenty-one years!"

Ha-ughhhhhh! Ha-ugggggghhhh!

"Go on, have it, here's your nose!"

It wasn't a fist but a planet that hit me.

I saw stars and satellites. And then a red, galactic splash that sickened and delighted me.

I heard Lenny crying, "Dodge!"

But I was dead, the man I'd been, before I hit the ground.

STEREOPTICON IV

 The Rock might have told them of Time and men's plans.

But men were mere moments.

And all moments passed.

The Rock dreamed its dreams of the lappings of waves over hundreds of millions of years.

I

The new *Hamlet* debuted at the Majestic that night.

Rod waited calmly in the wings while David Francis Kelley stood beside him, match in hand, and asked yet again, "Now, your lordship?"

Rod shook his head. Just a few seconds more.

Slowly, he opened the valve in his mind, timing the pressure's release.

Alcatraz—oh, Jesus, no!

Zonies—oh, you madman, Wolf!

Harpo here—a killer!

Strrrrrrraaaaaaannnnnnnge!

Rod closed his eyes and swung the wheel, opening the valve all the way. All of his fears, pressure-cooked into one: the Big One was coming—the Big One!

But it was still in his mind.

So he gave a snap of his fingers.

And instantly twenty men, lined up behind the stage, began breaking their backs as they rocked it.

Yes . . . Now . . . There it was . . . The heart and soul of Hamlet in the ground on which he stood . . .

Lightning flashing in his eyes, Lord Whittaker thundered on stage.

II

"Three hundred," Wolf said. "In advance."

Frank McGuane sputtered, "That's—robbery!"

"I know. Ain't life grand."

"We had an agreement, you blackmailing—"

"Four."

Wolf leaned over, slipping his hand inside the editor's jacket. His hand came out with a Havana.

"You cad! You unconscionable scoundrel! You—"

"Cur . . ." Wolf passed the Havana under his nose and struck a wood match on the sole of one boot. He fired the Havana, musing while he puffed. "You know . . . where I come from . . . cursing . . . Well, it ain't the same . . . cocksucker, we call a man . . . mother-fu—"

"How dare you!"

"See? . . . All it does is get a man . . . all fired up . . . and ready to blow . . ." Wolf puffed away contentedly. "But *cur* . . . That's got a *mellow* sound . . . Something a man can . . . relate to. Pshaw!"

Enraged, McGuane let Wolf have it. The Look. Hardened reporters fell speechless before it. Women's hearts just turned to mush.

"This conversation is over," he growled. "Not another penny. You'll honor your agreement or, my word, I'll turn you—"

"Five!" Wolf cried. "And that's my final offer."

"What?" McGuane slumped back, wiping his brow with his sleeve.

"That's five hundred buckaroos for each and every column. Cold cash. In advance. Or"—Wolf leaned over the table, not smiling at all—"I just mosie along to the *Chronicle*. Pay me, Frank. Or kiss my ass."

"Five hundred dollars . . ."

"Sold! Frank, Frank, don't look so glum. Jesus, look around you!"

A wave of epic grandeur. McGuane followed the generous path it inscribed from their table in back through the dimly lit bar. Drunks stood in clusters, transfixed by the News, their slurs, like soggy wires, stretching on for miles until short-circuiting into hot flashes of sparks . . . buzzings of *Zonies* and *strange ones* . . .

McGuane nodded. "Wednesday night."

"Attaboy, Frank," Wolf said. "And one more eensy-teensy thing . . . One of your hotshot reporters may have spotted me in the Montgomery Block. From here on, it's off-limits. And you make sure all their damn mouths stay shut. It's gonna heat up around here, and real fast. Oh yeah, I'll be needing ID."

"Eye *what*?"

III

"Oh, Billy," she said.

And he said to her, *"What . . ."*

Betsy stretched like a cat, the move tugging the sheet over the rise of her nipples, lightly fanning the fine amber fire below. The memories of his kisses and his amazed caresses ("Lord . . . Your body . . . It's so—new") like some exceedingly rare vintage wine.

He reveled like a child in the subtle flaring of her hips.

She couldn't get enough of him. He overwhelmed her again and again, with not just his size but his general way. There was nothing self-conscious about him. No "How'm I doin'?" Eighties-style gymnastics or scoring of 0's. No "I'll do better next time." There were limits to the things he knew. But none to what he'd been willing to learn. There was a rugged what-the-hellness to his loving that she craved.

Tonight, though, he seemed so abstracted: now gazing at the ceiling . . . now at the *Call* on the nightstand . . .

(Come on, you can handle him!)

She slid her hand beneath the sheet. Raked her nails, in a feathery flurry, through the thick mat of hair on his chest. And down to his belly, solid but ample, her last finger grazing the head of his cock.

He squirmed, started to say something, stopped. She cupped her palm beneath his balls, needing him, kneading them.

"Oh, Billy," she said. "Darling Billy . . . we're gonna be so happy . . ."

He said nothing. He stared at the ceiling and writhed as her fingers encircled a third of the shaft, and slyly started pumping.

"Billy," she crooned. "Billy, Billy . . . we're gonna get a house somewhere . . . I'll be the best damned woman—"

"Stop!"

His hand over hers, through the sheet. His eyes wrong.

"You're calling me—Billy."

"But—that's your name."

"You always call me Clark!" he cried. "And you're not talkin' like you do!"

(Oh-oh.

Oh, God.

He thinks—

No way!)

"Oh, *Clark,* I know your *name,* you lug, I'm—talk-in' to our little *friend.* If you *know* what I *mean,* an' I *think* that you *do,* 'cause it's feel-in' ex-cep-tion'ly friend-ly."

Clark groaned, lying back . . . but still trying hard to consider. "But, Mae, your voice—it sounded strange . . ."

"Well, if you real-ly gotta *know,* Clark, I's—relax-in' my *throat* for a little sur-prise."

She released his cock for the second it took to whip the sheet off the bed. Then she had it, and had him, hot-pistoning while stunning him with a downfall of quickflutter kisses. From his throat to his nipples; around them and over;

down to his navel, flickfucked with her tongue; and, still pumping and milking him out of his mind, she snaked her tongue down to love's deep hand-to-mouth.

His whole body shuddered. "Mae . . . where did you say . . . you were—Oh, God!"

Betsy proceeded to blow him away, relentlessly, exquisitely.

And when she had finished, no questions were asked.

Would there be more tomorrow?

Fine.

She would answer them all with her magic.

She'd come too far for Miss Wilcox to win, scribbling an F on her life.

For now, she nestled in Clark's arms, certain of the only things she needed to be sure of.

Together they'd prosper.

Live long.

And grow fat.

IV

Overnight Len had acquired two major liabilities. With Dodge and Wolf in the game with the clock, who *knew* where Lenny might end up? The variables may well have grown too complex for Quaker Sam.

Still . . .

What else could he do?

What else could he have done?

Later that night he stood, shrouded in mist, at the top of Polk's drop to the Bay. He adjusted the kerosene lamp on his bike.

Dear God, I beg you, hear my prayer . . . Don't let Dodge know, Lord . . . Oh, don't let him guess . . . I need the Quake, just give me that . . .

Lenny straddled the seat, his right foot on the pedal, and tipped his hat to the crowd, kicking off.

"Eeeee-hahhhhh, Sammy!"

"Let 'er rip!"

He hit the hill with all he had, and had all he could do, in a couple of seconds, just keeping his feet on the pedals, and his ass on the seat and not over the bar.

He had to go faster and farther than Dodge . . . He had to work longer and slier than Wolf . . . He had to cover the town like cement, complete a foundation that time could not shake. . . .

As he plunged through the traffic on Polk Street, he screamed:

"CELLULOSE—AVOID IT! CELLULOSE IS '89! STICK WITH REAL SILK! BIG ONE! BIG ONE COMIN' SOON!"

V

The comical man on the bike sped away. And they watched him, smiling.

Blond, for now, and wholly Blacke, Austin cradled her head on his shoulder and thought how nicely things were going. Weeks ago, he'd nearly died for want of a droplet of blood from his times. Now that his blood was leveled, they just popped up left and right, the travelers from the train. The thing to do was save them. They were not essential now. But when his sweet tooth acted up, nothing was quite like a bonbon.

Alcatraz, though—that was best! How to explain its distinctive appeal? Or account for the fact that, on the Rock, somehow a man just tasted *better*?

The girl, whom he'd met seven minutes ago, brushed her lips against his sleeve, enflamed with a light, night-chilled lavender glow.

Blacke pointed over the steep drop of Polk . . . over it and through the mist . . . to the lighthouse twinkling on the vaguely outlined Rock.

"Isn't it lovely?" he asked her.

She hooked his leg between her thighs, which she began to scissor, unconsciously, obscenely.

"By the way, if you don't mind my asking . . ." Blacke leaned over to whisper the rest in her ear.

She giggled.

So did he as she snaked her hand under the flap of his coat, recoiling in alarm.

Austin hushed her with his eyes.

And led her eyes to Alcatraz.

"I call that my happy place. When I'm feeling down or tired . . . You know what I think? Everyone should come to San Fran when they die."

He raised his fingers from her temple, just a fraction, just enough for her shoulders to heave and the tears to begin.

"Good . . . good . . . That *pleases* me. Come on, I know a little place not far from the Presidio. Little cabin built for two." Lavender sparks from his fingertips passed through her temple's blue traceried skin. "You wanna see a Snake Trick?"

"Yessss."

"I'm sorry?"

"Master."

"That's my girl."

SNIPPETS AND CONNECTIONS

 Lenny played the Invisible Man all that week, except for his scattered deliveries. As if his life depended on not knowing what I was up to. I wasn't all that sure myself. I had until Sunday to figure it out, and then Lenny was throwing my ass on the street. By midweek the flat was a war zone.

The battle began with a tenderloin steak and ended with a Wall.

Like this:

For two days I did little but vomit and shit . . . and lie swaddled in blankets, a steak on my nose to reduce the swelling. Time and again I passed out, coming to from more feverish visions of hell. Then I'd stumble down the hall and heave and shit with my head on my knees.

When I was done, for an hour or so, I'd stumble back and lock the door. And then the shakes would start again. I'd add another blanket . . . flip the steak . . . hear it sizzle from the blizzard of my thoughts.

Withdrawal . . . You're in super shock . . . not from this and not from that . . . Pure, absolute withdrawal . . . from everything you've ever known . . . from o.j. to Blazers . . . from MTV to gramophones . . . from Cadillacs to hansom cabs . . . from joints to Turkish Trophies . . . from Therapy to Harpo . . .

Shocccccckkkkk!

There is no world but in this room . . . and only you are
in it . . . for the first time in thirty-nine years, you haven't
a thing to distract you . . . There are no evasions here . . .

And then came the red spiders and pythons and bats . . .
the death's heads of Harpo, the Fat Man, and Blacke . . .
Sammy, bleeding everywhere, screaming at me, screaming:
Start!

I began around three with a corkboard, one of the three
Len had fetched me. I slid it along the carpeting, pausing
for breath every couple of steps. Then I went back for the
hammer, returning again for some tacks.

I rested for a nightmare. Puked and shat for half an hour.
Then proudly, and all by myself, I raised the corkboard to
the wall, propping the base on my knee—hammered the
nail of my thumb good and square, driving the tack through
the wall.

I continued in this fashion until all three were hung. Then
I added two more blankets, threw out the old steak and
slapped on a new, and treated myself to more spiders and
snakes.

Tuesday, the sicknesses were fewer. But intense? My
whole system seemed torn between keeping the poisons
inside me and getting them out. My voidings were holo-
causts that left me more dead than alive . . . and led to
astonished cries from those who followed my trips down the
hall.

The nightmares, too, grew worse, much worse. Today's
were scream-of-conscious, heebie-jeebie horror shows that
had me waking on the floor, chewing the steak to stop
screaming.

In between, though, there were flashes of powerful lucid-
ity: names . . . words . . . impressions . . . scenes . . .

The flashes came at random, as scattered as those in my
dreams:

Austin Blacke . . .
Brakowski . . .
Women on the train . . .

The flashes mystified me with their sheer *physicality*.

They began in the brain and went off in my gut, a baffling sense of—correctness.

I wanted to control them, prearrange them, get them pat, the way the old Dodge had arranged things.

I could not even begin to begin.

And so, time and again, I betrayed them. And lay back and closed my eyes and felt them fading as I drifted into the next nightmare.

Blacke was coming at me fast, his black leather duster around him like wings. I let him come at me. I just lay there and watched, for the man was an absolute master and—

"Harp?"

Sam's voice, a sigh of silk.

Well, there was no decision between Sam and Austin Blacke. I turned. And found myself back in my sleeper in a dream within the dream, clicketywhirring and rocking away. I was amazed and delighted to see what Sammy had done to the room. She'd changed it somehow to a cave, with hundreds of candles all over the walls, black candles thick as horses' cocks. The rock we were on was a trip and a half. And so were the clicketychinks of her chains. Sam knew how to please a man—I mean, *really please* him. There's nothing like a girl in chains, at least on special occasions. Her head lay on a poster-sized, red headline from the *Post*. And as we rocked, and her head turned, the letters appeared to come at me in waves:

SLAUGHTER IN BRONX ZOO!
BATS, PYTHON & HYENA EATEN!

"Harp," she whispered. "For God's sake, wake up. Keep your wits about you, please!"

"Please . . ." I repeated. "This *pleases* me . . . Yes . . ."

I rolled over between Sammy's legs, more to me now than yesterday, and growing by the inch, the foot.

"Sam," I said. "Jesus Christ, what a dream . . . I feel great . . . I'm a king . . . This'll kill you!"

"Kid, kid, over here!"

Oh, no.

No fair.

The old dream-within-the-dream-within.

I looked over my shoulder. Patch lit his cigar at our table in back of Hell's Kitchen Saloon.

Beside him sat a figure from a half-remembered photograph: a thin man, tanned, with golden curls . . . and, under his T-shirt, two powerful arms . . . my father, a year before marriage . . .

"Dad," I said.

And he said, "Son."

And there *she* was, standing beside me. My sloe-eyed unchained mercurial twin.

"Sam."

"Raphael."

Raphael . . .

"Come on," Patch growled, "get up. School's out."

"I don't know where to start. Sam—"

"Use your head," she whispered.

"I just can't seem to figure this!"

"Use your heart," the thin man urged.

And Patch roared, "You idiot! Use it *all* or we're all deuced and here and gone for nothin'! The game is Time. The whole man wins. And all fractions just get torn to pieces."

"Build it," said my father, the thin man I'd forgotten.

"Build it," Sam said. "Build our Wall."

Patch winked, setting down his Havana. He paused a second, for effect, then lifted his patch like a flap. Glowing on the pupil, in a pale shade of lavender, were the two words: *Austin Blacke.*

"Now get up, kid. It's monster time!"

There was no more transition than there had been between my dream's turnings. My eyes opened. That was it. I felt quiet and calm and alert.

At the desk I scratched the words on a scrap that I tacked to the Wall:

AUSTIN BLACKE

Now, I had had plans for the corkboards. And for the newspapers Lenny had brought; plus the boxes containing my latest disguise. I was a monster hunter on the trail of what killed Patch . . . but certain that slyness and cunning could win . . . if I could figure enough of the facts and arrange them on the boards in neatly ordered rows—

But suddenly my thinking had been sharply rearranged.

Suddenly, I, Dodge, was being asked—no, compelled—to listen, not to reason . . . to feel the truth, not figure it . . .

And it was exhausting and scary as hell.

The words sat there for hours, bold and black as the name. They mocked me. They tormented me. They defied my continuing efforts to outfox them or outfigure them. The harder I figured, the softer they purred. And then twinkled like Austin's amazing gray

EYES

How many eyes had I seen in my life? Had any eyes ever spooked me like Blacke's? A woman's eyes might break your heart. A man's might turn your spine to mush. But Blacke's eyes were something else . . . Gray . . . No . . . not quite . . . Gray with specks of

LAVENDER

When these were tacked beneath the first, they mocked me as relentlessly. *What do you know,* I could hear Austin purr. *You're a frightened little nothing who couldn't outwit his own shadow. You're a loser. A clown. Come on, Harp, where's the horn?*

I dozed and woke, dozed and woke, without a second's relief.

Where was the next brick?

Contained in the last.

Quit figuring and feel it . . .

What?

I faced the Wall and shook my fist. "You're in there, I know it. You're in there!"

Nothing . . . Nothing . . . And more nothing still . . .

I slept and woke, while Blacke purred right along.

What's the matter, Harpo? Can'ty findy big bad Blackey? Clowny-wowny wantum clue?

Blacke's chuckle bounced all around in my brain, mellow, mad, and menacing. The sound seemed to feed off the echoes themselves, until my head head was splitting from the

GIGGLES

and the

WHOOPS

I scratched the words on two more scraps at twice the speed of write, then slapped them both hard on the Wall.

But Austin was still giggling when I lay back, exhausted, to sleep.

Late Wednesday, April 4, I began to eat. A little more than half a peach and some bottled water. I had all I could do to hold even that down.

I needed strength, though.

More than that.

If I was in shock, and in total withdrawal, I needed a *link* to my sense of myself. A direct connection.

I returned, by the ounce, to Intestinal Light.

There was a rhythm to the Wall. And it was this that drove me. The rhythm was stronger than I was. It was stronger than fear. It was stronger than loss. It was stronger than guilt or exhaustion.

At the start, the rhythm was torturous and labored, as heavy as my steps had been toward the Wall in Washington. Each beat was a beating that dropped me, half-senseless, until the next pounding came.

But, beat by beat, the Wall just grew.

The rhythm grew lighter and gathered in speed. And

took me along with it, body and mind. I'd be pacing the carpet, and blind to the Wall, crazywalking to the beat, when—

whap-a-dap dap-a-dap dick-a-dick
DING!

—a nifty set of rimshots would erupt into a cymbal clash that dissolved in a shimmering word in my mind. Or a phrase or a feeling. A scene.

And I'd scribble it down—man, the pen would be tapping!—and slap the scrap down on the Wall.

I took to napping at Len's desk, in the soft gold-green glow of the small student lamp. I would doze for an hour, sometimes up to two. Then I'd feel my eyes open . . . my back start to straighten . . . the next words in the air like the crash at the end of a long and spectacular drum roll.

The Wall had a rhythm I couldn't resist. Faster and lighter and righter it grew. And I was in the grip of it. It rocked me. It shook me. It moved me.

I had an apple Thursday around dawn when I awoke. And two pints of bottled water.

And then cravings began to go off a series of rimshots and drum rolls.

The pen could not move fast enough:

1 dozen apples
1 dozen bananas
2 pounds of grapes
1 pineapple—large
6 oranges
6 tomatoes
2 heads lettuce
1 bunch of carrots
1/2 pound of radishes
3 onions
sprouts
1 head of celery
1/2 pound of walnuts

1/2 pound of cashews
brown bread

At nine, I heard the soft click of Len's key.

The door opened wide enough for the three dailies to slip through. Then there was a crinkling sound—the list that I'd tacked to the door.

"This is *it*," Lenny said.

I answered him, as softly, "Yeah."

"You're out of here on *Sunday*. Sunday morning, *dawn*."

"Yeah."

"I want you *out* of my life."

"I'm gone."

"My fucking feet are killing me."

Len shut the door, just this side of a slam. His receding footsteps were somewhere between a stormy shuffle and a limp. As if he'd been pounding the pavement too long and each foot was protesting the other.

I started to turn to the Wall. Then I whirled and found myself pacing in sync with the beat.

Shuffle-limp. Shuffle-limp. Shuffle-limp-limp-shuffle—

FEET

I thought I heard Blacke giggling.

Harrrppp . . .

But I didn't care, I was on a hot roll, and I shuffle-limp-limp-shuffle-limped to the Wall, where I hammered it home, as I cried, "You're in here, you bastard, I *feel* you!"

Thursday. April 5. Midnight. Just two days to go. Then out on the street on the trail of a monster . . . with nothing to save me except what I knew.

What do you know? Austin chuckled. *Come on, Harpo, honk for me.*

I stood before it, barely, with a carrot that I was too tired to chew. And the maddening sense that I knew . . . but knew what?

You don't know a thing, Blacke purred. *You'll be my clown . . . forever . . .*

ONE TIME'S AS GOOD AS ANOTHER TO ME

I slapped the scrap upon the Wall.

And suddenly the rhythm stopped.

For the first time in days, I knew something a little like silence and peace.

I stopped, a small man with a carrot, half of my face a vague purplish-green, and let the Wall come at me.

As a whole.

Then piece by piece.

Condensed, the first board looked a little like this:

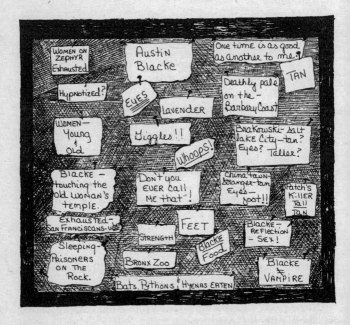

Friday morning. Crack of dawn. I was attacking a two-pound fruit salad and gazing a little forlornly at the three stacks of the news since March 1. One pile for the *Chronicle,* one for the *Herald,* and another for the *Call.*

Just then I heard the newsboy's cry outside the window on Mason.

"Five *Zonies* dead on Alcatraz! Get your early morning *Call!*"

I hadn't opened the shade once all week. But there was no stopping the rhythm.

I sent the shade rattling up on a roll. Then up with the window, V'd fingers in lips, and out with a shattering whistle.

"Boy! A dollar for a paper! Quick!"

The boy kept a gingerly distance.

I kept the door on the chain.

He was a short but stout Chinese, chipmunk-cheeked and slanty-eyed, with a shrewd, tight little smile. He was both twelve and a hundred, I guessed.

He tugged at his cap. Flipped the coin in his palm.

"Buck for a paper, hey? That's kinda *strange.*"

"I had a bad fall, son. I can't get about."

He squinted at the eye I showed. The left eye was off-color still.

"National Guard, hey, they marchin' the street."

"Are they?" I purred. "Send them up. By all means. Maybe one of them'll run an errand for an eagle."

"Gwan! They got better things— Hey, wait a minute, mister!"

"I need a book from the library, kid."

"Book, hey? What kinda book?"

I told him.

He said "Hey" and smiled. "I dunno . . . that's a *strange* book . . ."

I flipped him the first gold half-eagle.

"Now, go on," I growled. "Get a move on, you lug, or I'll call the damned Guard myself."

The second board was begun like the first: with a lone and mocking scrap:

5 ZONIE SLEEPERS DEAD ON ROCK!
AUTHORITIES HOPE AUTOPSIES EXPLAIN
THE MYSTERY OF 'AIDS'

I'd gone as far as I could go with only my instincts and
memories of Blacke. What I needed to do was examine
Austin from a fresh perspective. Follow the news from the
first day of March, Lenny's arrival in Oakland . . . Stop
thinking that I'd *figured* Blacke . . . Read all three dailies
from front to back . . . Get a feel for the town before Austin arrived and see where that might lead me . . .

I read for hours. Everything. Even the want ads and
comics. But the news was just news, at least halfway
through March: war, murder, madness, marriage . . . not
a thing that had the hairs bristling on my neck.

I took a break to stretch my legs and make another salad. I
was halfway through it when the boy came back around
ten.

He'd been thinking on the way. He wanted an eagle on
top of the half. I was a cripple, after all, and this certainly
looked like a mighty—*strange* book.

I smiled grimly through the crack. "Wait here a second.
Don't go 'way." I hobbled to the window, where I sent the
shade rattling and whipped up the frame. "There's two
coppers down the street, you scheming, treacherous
Zonie!"

"Mister—wait a minute—hey!" The boy rattled the chain
as he wiggled the book.

I hobbled over, leering, groaning once for show.

"Hey, we make a deal," he said.

"No deal," I said. I snatched the book and slapped the
gold coin into his palm.

He shuffled back, just out of reach.

"I take book back, hey, you gimme 'nother silver."

I said, "You're a heartless thief."

This wasn't worth an answer.

I said, "Come back tomorrow. What's your name?"

He told me, "Chan."

I shut the door. I stilled my heart. I waited till I heard his
footsteps skip down the landing and out. I examined the

book. It had lots of nice pictures of lions and cheetahs and panthers and monkeys . . .

and pythons and bats and hyenas.

I dropped the book off on Len's spiral-legged desk.

I finished my salad and chewed and reflected and tried hard to clear out my mind. Forget about Blacke. You don't know him, not yet. He's in here somewhere, in the news. Just let him show himself.

I hooked my feet under the sofa and did situps in five sets of twenty. Then propped my feet over one armrest and did pushups with claps in between. Four fast sets.

I rotated my neck and I shook loose my arms, getting the feel of my body again.

I pivoted once. Then I tried it again. And the two led into a third, then a fourth.

I heard Austin giggle. *What's the matter, Harpo? Getting scared? Honk for me.*

I snatched up the scissors and had at the news.

Nothing through March twenty-first, just two short weeks ago.

Or on the twenty-second.

Pages and pages of nothing but news and odd obit-sized blurbs of "new" prisoners.

The twenty-third.

The twenty-fourth.

Day after day of it, blanks and more blanks.

The twenty-fifth.

The twenty-sixth.

The—

twenty-seventh—

Bingo . . .

Millionaire Klondiker found dead in room . . .

The day before my own arrival . . .

Throat hacked and slashed with a razor . . .

Suicide . . .

Odd way to go . . .

LITTLE BLOOD

I circled that.
Then:

RHEUMATIC

And then:

ALCOHOLIC

I slapped the story on the Wall.

From here on, day by day, the news came to seem less and less like white noise. The Wall began to rock again. The rhythm gathered momentum. And the clips of my scissors were swept in the rush: Brakowski/not Brakowski escaping from the Rock . . . the bluehair dying in her sleep . . . missing people . . . complaints of exhaustion . . . odd bones and patches of hair on the beach . . .

Eight A.M. Saturday. Chan had just gone off to fetch me my cards, the ones Lenny ordered on Monday.

I watched him go, through the sliver of space between the shade and the window. The street seemed less busy. But all appeared well, except for a couple of brass-buttoned blues having words with two Guardsmen on Mason.

A milkwagon clippetyclopped past a phaeton parked beside a diner. When the milkwagon passed, I saw one of the Guardsmen call something or other to Chan. The boy looked over his shoulder, but not up toward me. The Guard asked him something. Chan shook his head. The other Guard asked something else. Chan shook his head again. One of the coppers said something and laughed. And Chan laughed and pointed north toward the San Francisco Bay. He made a motion with his hands, a voluptuous curve, as if drawing a whore, and walked off, whistling, on his way.

I paced the room for a couple of minutes, praying my luck would hold out.

I looked at my face in the small oval mirror over the boxes I soon would unpack.

I whispered, "Jesus . . . That's some nose . . ."
Then I leaned over to pick up the book.
And to learn what I could about pythons and bats.
Pythons and bats and hyenas.

BLACKEBOARD JUNGLE

 Saturday. Midnight. And what do you know?
    Pythons and bats and hyenas. The same animals eaten in two different zoos. And that ain't no coincidence.

Let's try again. Who, or what, precisely is this Austin Blacke?
    The point is, Blacke's *nothing* precisely. He's part man, he has to be. He eats. He fucks. He likes the sun. He has a reflection, admires the view.

So, he isn't a vampire. He can't be.
    Correction. He isn't, and can't be, a vampire as such. But he is, and must be, a vampire in part.

Run that by me once again.
    The women on the train. One after another, all through the *Zephyr*, looking more dead than alive.

Sounds to me like a case of whopping penis envy.
    Oh, sex is at the heart of it. But not like any sex we know. They didn't look happily fucked, they looked dead. And not just the young but the old. If they'd been sporting puncture marks instead of hickeys on their necks, you'd have reached for a cross and screamed "Vampire!"

If.

Grant me that *if* for a second. Let's say you were a vampire . . .

Moi?

For the sake of argument.

How long would you last . . . if all it took to spot you were a couple of marks on a series of throats . . . or the fact that you had no reflection?

What if you'd devised a whole new bag of tricks?

What if.

Look at the Wall and remember. Remember the first time you looked in Blacke's eyes. You didn't feel spooked—you felt mastered. Remember that curious *lavender* glow? Remember the bluehair—one touch of her temple! Remember the hickeys—he can use just his lips!

All right. Calm down. Suppose we allow for a second your ifs. So the vampire part of this creature—

"One time's as good as another to me."

—survives on blood—

And energy?

—that he extracts with a new bag of tricks. For the sake of camouflage.

And for the sake of tricks.

I'm lost.

All right. You're immortal, with a little luck and cunning. But you got bored with sucking blood and playing by the Rules. What fun is immortality if you're not unique? You teach yourself some great new tricks. But, the fact is, you're *still* just a vampire. One day, like any other day, in your vast eternity, something clicks inside you.

You've learned to feed off *energy*, which is the essence of blood. What if you got to the heart of it, though? What if you digested the soul?

The soul?

What else is form but the shape of the soul?

If you could digest the soul, let's say, of certain animals, you'd have their form within you. And that might be really useful.

You started off with a vampire bat . . . a natural choice for a vampire. And it certainly gave you some mileage. But the fact was, you were *still* a vampire. So you began to shop around for new ways to diversify. And to prove your mastery.

There were lions and panthers and cheetahs to choose from . . . eagles, apes, rhinos . . . You examined them all. And you found them all wanting . . . until you met the hyenas.

They were fast. You liked that. Up to sixty-five miles an hour.

You related to their cunning, their ferocity, their strength.

They hunted by night . . . the best time for you, too.

But most of all what you loved was their sheer *voracity.* Here was a total feeding machine, able to not just devour but digest: blood, skin, bone, marrow, brains, feces—

faces?

What!

Hey, what's a face, but skin and bones—that is, if you're *just* a hyena.

But, as you watch them, once again you begin to wonder. What if you could step things up? Not just the face, but the soul of the face.

Good God, man, you can't be suggesting—

Brakowski/not Brakowski. The rockjawed dude in Chinatown.

I'm telling you, they got to me the way only Austin Blacke could.

You can't prove a word of this!

Do I really need to? You tell *me* how "Brakowski"— who

must've been dead on the *Zephyr*—got his ass off the Rock.
No one's found a body. No one's found a boat. Blacke flew.

*All right, just for the hell of it . . . Say Blacke actually flies
like a bat. In hyena form, he eats the works, including the
soul of the face. Scraps are all he leaves behind. And he
could look like almost anyone!*

True. But that *almost* of yours is almost as large as my *ifs*.

Think of Brakowski a second, first on the train platform,
then in the news. I was drunk in Salt Lake City. But he
didn't look right to me then, not at all. That coat of his.
Christ, the sleeves came to his elbows. And even the face—
it was his, and yet not. I thought he looked tanned—and yet
how could he be? We see what we expect to see. But look at
his picture now, there on the Wall. Brakowski. Not Brakowski. At least not exactly Brakowski. The eyes! The first time I
saw them, I knew they were *wrong*. I didn't believe my own
eyes, but I knew.

Blacke captures the soul of the face. But not all of the
particulars.

He either can't, or just can't be bothered, to change his
height or his eyes or his tan.

Aha! But in the Call, *Brakowski is described as pale.*

That's even more interesting than you may think, though
not in the way you imagine.

Two days before my arrival, we capture our first hint of
Blacke in the news. A suicide. With little blood, though he's
hacked his throat to ribbons. My first night in town I see
Blacke on the Coast, and he looks like death warmed over.

That must have been his first feeding. A rheumatic and
arthritic drunk, whose blood was eighty years from
Blacke's. So there he is. He needs a fix, blood from his time.
He hears or reads of the bluehairs—captured the day I
arrived—on the Rock. Instant private blood bank.

The thing is, that first time Austin didn't fly. My guess is
that his strength was too low to make it and learn where the
women were kept. Abracadabra. The Face Trick. He turns
himself in as Brakowski, so no one is looking for blond Austin Blacke.

He was pale when he went there, but not when he left.

Slow down just a second. I'm not nearly as brilliant as you. Blacke in his weakened condition grows pale. At full strength he has a remarkable tan. What do you intend to do —drive a stake through the heart of each man with a tan?

Oh, finding Blacke is child's play . . . compared to what to do with him.

I don't like the sound of that.

There's no reason why you should. Since Blacke is a big bag of fractions and tricks—and is only in *part* like a vampire—I doubt a stake would do the trick. Or garlic. Or a crucifix.

So, he isn't just unfindable—

He's findable. He's beatable. The only question's how.

And the best place to start, for my money, is with his plans for Alcatraz. Who knows, the Rock may tell us why he settled on the python, the third "victim" in those zoos.

I have a snaking—er, sneaking—suspicion that you may already know.

Hey, what do I know? Here I am in 1906. But think: The Rock, in the beginning, is like a private blood bank. Blacke puts the last five prisoners in a sort of sleeping trance. That way there aren't any questions and he can feed when he needs to. Let's say he alternates feedings until he's leveled his blood—one of them and one of us. He begins to recover his powers.

It's only after "Brakowski's" escape that we read of disappearances. The first odd complaints of exhaustion. The zoo. Bones and patches of hair on the beach.

But now all the original prisoners are dead.

That's right. The original prisoners. All five in one fell swoop. And when did Austin wipe them out, cutting off his private stock? Right after Wolf starts screaming that they've all got AIDS. Coincidence? I wonder. My guess is . . . Alcatraz might just soon be hopping.

Really. Just a minute. Why? If Blacke is at full power—

I don't think he *needs* the Rock. Not the way he used to. Somehow I think the Rock appeals to the hyena in him.

So far, you've still accounted for only two out of three.

Pythons.

Yeah, that stumped me. Once again, Blacke seemed to have everything he needed. For all practical purposes, he'd become immortal . . . undetectable . . . unique.

Well, a python was pretty impressive, but not the most practical thing. According to this little book, some grow close to thirty feet. And they can swallow objects, whole, four times their own diameter. But their teeth are useless for biting. What they use the teeth for is to hook and hold the victim's head while they coil around the torso—

Enough!

—and start flooding slimy liquid all about the skull—

No more!

Well, you begin to see the point. If the python were only a python, as such, the limitations would outweigh the gains. Digestion takes time. Way too much time for Blacke. He could hardly walk around with a fully outlined torso showing through his shirt.

Checkmate.

That's what I thought. As a python, he could have just crushed a man, sure. And, in crushing him, fed off his force.

But Blacke could do that with just one of his arms.

No, he didn't *need* a python, not in any conceivable way. But then I got to thinking . . . about lions and choices we make.

If you even try to tell me that he is also part lion . . .

Oh no, no, no, no, God no. That's the last thing on earth that he *could* be! No, he hasn't got it in him.

Can you imagine the king of the jungle stooping to feces and scraps?

Hyenas are basically scavengers. They hunt when they

have to, the book says. But they *prefer* to steal. It's easier—
and it's more fun. And lions are the animals they like to steal
from best. They've got a weird relationship, lions and hyenas. Hyenas almost seem to hunger for the king's approval.
Sometimes they'll follow prides of lions—just to watch them
from afar. Hyenas like to "hang" with them. When they
can, they sleep nearby.

How do lions repay this attention? Contempt.

And the hyenas, they keep coming back.

Which tells us zilch—

Which tells us all, just maybe, about the goddamn python.

I dress as Harpo—oh, just a disguise—and show myself off
as the clown I've become.

And Blacke? And, for God's sake, the python?

Blacke chooses a hyena, so he *thinks*, for the reasons
above. Now, I don't mean to gross you out—

That hasn't stopped you so far.

—but, as you can see in these pictures, you can't tell a
female from a male hyena. Not unless you're up real close.
See there? The females have clitorises so big they scrape the
ground.

Good God!

They even have sham scrotums: two sacks, filled with
fibrous tissues, that look like a great pair of balls. These
ladyboss hyenas are like lions to the males. When they want
sex, they want it. They'll follow a male, snap at him and
bark, until he's fucked out and can't stand on his feet. When
they're not in the mood, they'll snap right at his dick. Half
the time, when the female is ready, the male is so flustered
he can't find the hole!

*Are you out of your mind, man? You can't be—oh, no. You
are NOT suggesting—*

I tell you, personality is where this bastard's at.

He doesn't transform to a python to feed. He exaggerates

the part of him that once gave him the most grief. Pussy-whipped. That's our boy.

Wait a minute . . . Wait a minute . . . "Don't you ever call me that" ?
  Bang on, wizard. On the nose. The only time I got to Blacke was when I called him what he is. I was dead in his hands, on the *Zephyr,* till I called him hyena. He freaked.

I don't care what you call him, friend. Or how you analyze him.
  Ah, that's the part that scares me too. A hyena *is* still a hyena. And, frankly, they're vicious as hell. Says here that strychnine gets 'em good—but if Austin is just *part* hyena . . .

Then how—
  Well, if I knew I'd tell you.
  But, you know, I just can't quite forget . . . Austin's feet.

SAY WHAT?
  He has trouble with his feet.
  Whoops, it's late. Back to work!

What are you doing? That bottle—it's hair dye!
  Yes, it is, isn't it. And this is a bottle of glue.
  Let's just say I've still got a few tricks up my sleeve.

Hey, we're in this together—wait!
  Sorry, head, you've ruled too long.
  Here I am. Whee, here I go!

BALLAD OF THE MAN IN BLACK

The Man in Black arrived in town
   That Sunday morning at seven.
His hair was jet and his clothing was pitch.
   He towered at near five-eleven.

His nose was hooked, his look was lean,
   His mustache was a cruel little line.
With a twitch of his lip, he strode into the mist
   And he seemed to have death on his mind.

The Man in Black walked tall and straight
   Through the thick anguished crowds with their *Calls*.
He had an expression that couldn't be missed:
   It wasn't with *strangeness* he'd kill.

He never spoke, he never stopped,
   Till he came to the Palace Hotel.
With brisk clicks of his heels he emerged from the mist.
   No need to ring the bell.

The deskman said the rooms were gone.
   Till he looked in the Man in Black's eyes.
Then he looked hard at the card he'd been slipped
   And he offered a suite. That was wise.

They showed him the Indian carpets.
  They showed him the oak parquet floors.
The Man in Black couldn't have seemed less impressed.
  He spat in a gold cuspidor.

His suite was the size of a stable,
  With a deep sunken bath and a phone.
They showed him the fireplace, the rich marble bust
  Of a king who had loved here and gone.

They showed him his bed, it was big
  As a yacht, with sail-sized linen sheets.
He told them to go and he meant it. He hissed,
  "None of this, to me, means shit

"If I fail, boys, to clean up your town."
  And from the way he said it,
So fiercely determined and yet so lost,
  They knew his fate was wedded

To whatever demons he stalked.
  They looked each other in the eye
And walked discreetly down the hall, then placed
  Bets on how soon he would die.

The Man in Black dropped his satchel
  To the carpet of Indian pile.
Of all Baghdad's riches, the Palace was best.
  And so he wept like a child.

"I'd mastered the arts of evasion.
  "My powers were often sublime.
"Now my heart flies as straight as an arrow at last,
  "But I'm crushed by the sadness of Time.

"There's no forgetting what we know.
  "And I guess there is nowhere to turn.
"I just wish I could look at a woman with lust . . .
  "And not end up thinking of worms."

The Man in Black looked all around,
    Then lay back in despair on the bed.
Insubstantial as a ghost, what he'd come to miss
    The most was the lost love of the dead.

"The ancient dead, the freshly dead,
    "All had their times and places.
"They walked the earth as lost as us . . . but the least
    "Of them died with real faces."

The Man in Black began to drift
    Through a stream of his eviler crimes,
And was surprised to find how slyly the worst
    Had been done against Time.

Life's pleasures, in the end, were few.
    Its miseries, though, were amazing.
A man checked in naked and checked out with just
    The prayer that he die with his face on.

At dawn he woke. The fog was thick.
    But his blue eyes were shockingly clear.
The dead did not judge us by what we had lost.
    They judged what we did with our fear.

The Man in Black slipped on his Stetson.
    He tugged his boots over his shins.
"I fear my final hour may be coming fast.
    "By God, it is time to begin.

"The streets I love must now run red.
    "Am I doomed? Am I damned? All the same
"To me, unless the dead have blessed my quest.
    "Ready . . . Set . . . It's monster time."

STEREOPTICON V

While the Man in Black was dreaming
  Through the long dark night of his soul,
So were the others, who all turned and tossed,
  Kissing the dice they must roll.

The dice clicketyclick, bank, stop,
  Teeter, drop, and cry "Surprise!"
One sees seven. One eleven. One sees all was lost
  At birth . . . and weeps, softly, "Snake eyes."

I

Betsy stirs, snuggling in, draping her arm over . . .
space. There is a space beside her now, where, hours ago,
Clark had been. His pillow is warm, though. She gathers it
in, inhaling his rugged male scent. And, with a turning of
her dream, she feels his muscles fleshing from the feathery
embrace.

No soldiers shouting on the street. No questions or quick
nervous looks in Clark's eyes. No whispers or desperate
jokes in the bar *(Havin' a BEER tonight, Harry? I dunno,
that's kinda strrrrraaaaannnnnge . . . Well, you're a fine
one to be talkin'! I hear tell them Zonies all write with their
left hands like you . . . Gwan, I'm no stranger than Mae is
—Hey, Mae, where'd you say you were from? Haw!)* No
steely-eyed Inspector, stroking his walrus and asking, again,
Anyone actin' unusual-like?

There is another turning. She can scarcely believe her good luck. They are in New York City. 1986. Clark stares, like a child, at the whores in their shortshorts and minis . . . winos crashed in alleyways . . . taxicabs and buses . . .

Betsy gives his hand a warm, protective squeeze. They're close. She feels her nostrils start to flare.

Suddenly, she sees it in the jumble of blinking marquees.

AZS

The lights are flavored strawberry.

And chocolate.

And piña colada.

"Azs?" Clark wonders. "Mae, dear . . ."

"Run!"

Yes, they're off, and how they run. Until the marquee spells out in full: absolute heaven on earth.

"Häagen-Dazs," she whispers. She murmurs it and says it loud, caressing the sounds with her tongue.

"Oh God . . . Oh God . . . It's Häagen Dazs . . . Milk shakes, Billy . . . Ice cream floats . . ."

"What's *hah gen doz*?" he asks her. His voice sounds unaccountably stern, and somewhat oddly positioned. As if he were not quite beside her, but above her, a few feet away.

"Carrot cake . . . Banana splits . . ."

"What's *hah gen doz*!" He snaps this and gives her shoulder a rattling shake with the hand she was sure she'd been holding.

Oh.

And where did New York City go?

And this isn't Clark . . . it's a pillow . . . and—

"*Hah gen doz!*" He shakes her hard.

Betsy opens her eyes very slowly, already dreading the worst.

Sees him dressed and crazy-eyed beside her on the bed.

"Oh, *Clark-* y, I musta been *dream-* in' . . ." She tries.

"What's *hah gen doz*!"

She dares not move. She knows that, at best, there is one way to play this.

"Listen. Just one minute. *Please.*"

"What's *carrot cake*!"

"I'll tell—"

"YOU BITCH!"

Clark unfolds the front page of the *Call* he's just bought:

MONSTER TIME!
THE KISS OF DEATH!
IS YOUR TEENAGE DAUGHTER A ZONIE?

"Oh, Clark," she whispers. "Billy . . . Please . . ."

He refolds the paper slowly, with almost hysterical calmness. "Catch AIDS from 'bodily fluids,' it says here. Catch it from a goddamn *kiss*," he says. And his lips begin to stretch in a smile that half-looks like Harpo's. Except his cheeks are streaked with tears.

She hears a rustling sound, of something hard against leather.

But still she knows she must not move.

Not even when she sees his fingers clenched around the handle. The glint of the long, wicked barrel as it homes between her eyes.

"YOU AIN'T GIVIN' ME NO AIDS! "

The hammer's click is thunderous.

She sees his finger start to squeeze.

"You were worth it," Betsy says.

And then she shuts her eyes.

II

Lord Whittaker, as Hamlet, has succeeded in making the role so his own that at his first appearance, when the stage begins to quake . . .

. . . a Hamlet with the elegance of an Oxford don, and a surprising toughness that seems almost born of the streets.

The reviews have been unanimous.

Nightly, the theater's packed.

Rod sleeps in a small rented room blocks away, dreaming, at night, of those hours on stage. Of genius triumphant, once rightly placed in time.

But tonight was not like other nights. And he is back, it is no dream, waiting in the wings.

The crowd tonight seems edgy. He hears them shifting in their seats. Their faces are lost in the footlamps' warm glow, but he can feel their furtive looks. Exactly *what* is bothering them?

Kelley taps his shoulder.

Rod nods, the signal to begin.

And, as the stage begins to shake, he feels his genius at his feet.

Just before he speaks, though, something astonishing happens. Through the auditorium, beginning in the back, there is an airy *ripple*. Very quick. Very cold. It feels like the breath of a ghost. The footlamps, for an instant, threaten to extinguish. And Rod's eyes appear to deceive him. He seems to see, in the very last row, two tiny specks of lavender boring through his soul.

He shivers once in nausea.

Then again, in ecstasy.

The footlamps swell; the glow is lost.

But when he speaks in a lavender glow, he knows that tonight is perfection.

Suddenly the dream is done. Over the memory the curtain falls. And he awakens in his room, slick with sweat and shivering.

Those eyes!

III

Wolf's chambers, in his dreams, are more renowned than Bierce's were. Jack London often comes to call for pointers on his style. And Mark Twain has taken to sending him wires, begging to collaborate.

In his dreams, as in tonight's, anything seems possible.

If he can survive the town's madness. And find a subject, any subject, worthy of his *style*.

Papa Coppa's, in his dreams, is packed with his admirers.

Wolf enters boldly, as himself. There's no need to skulk in the shadows. No need to finger his ID. No need to worry about the reporter who spotted him here that one night. No need for spylike assignations every Wednesday with McGuane.

No, not tonight. Never in his dreams.

A murmur spreads throughout the room, swelling into a round of applause.

Wolf waves and puffs his Havana, the smoke as sweet as an opium high. He is led to his favorite table, beneath the black cats on the wall, the banners filled with illustrious names: Dante . . . Plato . . . Shakespeare . . .

The waiter arrives with his coffee. And it is the top of the pot.

The thick crowd begins to queue, each holding something for signing.

Pure style. They understand this. In his dreams, they know. *Monster Time* is really an exercise in style, no more.

How can he be responsible for the uses to which it is put?

In his dreams, they realize: It is the books he means to write that he must be judged by. Not by his sketches. Not by his life.

He believes this, in his dreams. And now and then he can

almost imagine a face he's forgotten but feels should be here. Sharing his hour of triumph.

(I don't know any—I forget . . .)

So why, then, suddenly, does he bolt up straight tonight, cold and alone in his soul?

He shuts his eyes. He starts to drift back to the Sweet Spot he craves.

When outside the window the hawking cries begin:

"Monster Time! Monster Time! Come and get it, *Monster Time!"*

IV

Lenny is so close to *being* there his dream nearly tears him to pieces.

He is on Dodge's Hill in the mythical city. The green slopes are running with tangerine dreams. And girls in psychedelic Ts mirror roses in marmalade eyes. The air is rich with incense, grass, hashish, and musk.

But tonight, in his dream, there's a sudden, astonishing turning.

Lucy begins to descend from the sky. She is shockingly naked, sticklike and furry. Her black pointy hat is as sharp as her beak.

Sam! she cackles. *Quaker Sam!*

Her wet and hairy shadow spreads until it has covered his world. He cannot move. He cannot breathe. He cannot see.

Oh, God! Oh, no!

Harriet's knees grip the sides of his skull as she writhes in the saddle, her beard glued to his.

He awakens, with a gasp, into a far greater nightmare: Harriet, in her pink nightdress, stretched out beside him on . . . her couch.

"Sam, love, it's all right, I'm here."

He sees with shocking clarity the bristly fuzz of her mustache . . . a hair stuck like a barb in a mole . . . Then she throws her arms around him and begins to kiss his nose, his eyes.

He should have slept in the park, on the street.

Or, better yet, shown Dodge the door.

What lunacy persuaded him that Harriet's place would be safer?

Each night she's been leaving the door to her room open an inch or two wider. Her signals growing bolder with the approach of tonight, his last night before Dodge is out of his flat.

Her lips are just inches from his now. Her warm breath's as inviting as swamp gas. Her pelvis shifts and inches in until it is lined up with his, bone for bone. His penis stiffens in horror.

Harriet coos to him, "Oh, Quaker Sam. I've come to feel so—close to you."

Lenny kisses her, tight-lipped, to stifle his scream. And croaks, "Darling . . . in the Eighties . . . folks waited . . ."

"Yes? *Yes*?"

". . . uh . . . until they were—"

"MARRIED?"

"Uhhhh . . ."

V

Austin sleeps on satin sheets in the Mark Hopkins Hotel.

He sleeps in the buff, with his penis outstretched. Now and then it stiffens slightly, quivers, caresses the sides of his knees.

He prefers the windows open on even the chilliest nights. The cold's fine.

As a rule, when things are well—and things are going *beautifully*—he does not dream in images. Austin dreams in colors.

It has been thirty years since he's *slept* with a woman. And if he ever writes a book, it will be a book about that: the eternal pleasure of having his way with all women, without having them stink up his bed . . . or pollute the colorful landscapes of dreams with their idiotic fantasies . . . of Babies and True Love and Men who are Men . . .

Austin sleeps in color, and lavender—that is the best.

Lavender is safe and warm. The color of forever.

Sometimes the dream screen is flooded with red, slowly and exquisitely. For then he is remembering a feeding he has known and loved.

There are other colors too.

He sleeps, serenely, enjoying them all.

That is, all the colors but black. When something is troubling Austin, or he senses that danger is near, the edges of the screen begin to darken, then turn black.

The screen tonight is featuring the finest shade of lavender that Blacke has ever known.

Until the edges start to go.

And Austin sits up wondering:

Where . . . Where did Harpo go?

THE TALKING BUSH
REVISITED

Father Duffy, the elderly pastor of St. Mary's Church in Oakland, found what peace he could find in his garden.

The horror did not live here yet. But, in passing, it had left its shadow, spreading like a stain. Each Mass was a burnt offering to let the horror remain over there. San Francisco had always been strange, from the start.

Father Duffy paced the garden, head bowed and fingers laced behind his tent-sized cassock.

Low seventies, at midday, with a mere whisper of breeze. At the very edge of town, when the sun was right like this, with hours to go until drink loosened tongues, even a priest could believe: the Lord's will had been done . . .

Father Duffy stopped in back, beside the rectory window. Saw his housekeeper shaking her broom at the cat. Stole back to light a cigarette, not one of the six she allowed him each day. Stood facing the mulberry bush as he smoked.

"Had they not souls, Lord?" he wondered. The forbidden cigarette tasted uncommonly sweet. It was a filthy habit. The finest filthy habit he ever hoped to have.

Now then . . .

The *strange ones* had had bodies. Not even a Jesuit could contest the fact.

"If they had bodies, they were men. If they were men, they had souls." The priest inhaled, holding this point in his lungs. He blew out a smoke ring, remembering the small man with the golden curls.

(Oh, God, he'd said, *deliver me!)*

"Lord," he cried, "I touched him! He was as frightened as I was. A man."

The faint breeze seemed to shiver. Blossoms trembled. Branches shook. Dust swirled in thin clouds as if huddling for warmth.

On his deathbed, years later, he'd try to recall: how he could have felt the presence at his back so keenly.

As if in a dream, the priest turned. A dark angel, all in black, from his spit-polished boots to his Stetson, slowly emerged from the dust.

The priest was struck at once by the intensity of those blue eyes, and their extraordinary sadness.

In another face, those eyes might have belied the hard features below: the cruel hook of the nose . . . the black mustache, as sharp and as thin as a blade . . . the grim, unyielding line of mouth . . . It was the face of a killer. But somehow it belonged with the eyes.

The stranger nodded. He said, "Father," closing the distance between them.

"My son," the priest said carefully.

"Look at me, Father, and tell me. Is a man a man . . . regardless of his color?"

"Yes . . . Yes, my son, of course he is."

"Regardless of his age?"

"Why, yes."

"Regardless of his politics?"

"Yes . . . But I must say the Democrats—"

"Regardless of his *time*?"

Father Duffy blinked, once. As if blinded and struck from his horse.

He said, "Yes."

If the stranger was smiling, it wasn't a smile like any the priest had yet seen. He said, "Do you believe . . . in monsters?"

"What?"

"Can there be such things as monsters?"

"My son, I don't know what—"

"You know."

"Well, of course, the Scriptures tell us—"

"Don't quote me the Bible, man—look in your heart!"

The priest did, and answered, "Yes."

"Now, if you had to choose between stopping a monster and saving an innocent woman . . . do you think your decision would be all that hard?"

"Why, no, my son, but—"

"Look at this." The stranger slipped out of one pocket the folded front page of the *Call.* "Here's this morning's paper. This is what it's come to now."

The priest's fingers trembled, opening the news. Then they shook with anger.

6 MORE ZONIES ON THE ROCK!
SAN FRANCISCANS HUNT THEM DOWN
ON THE STREETS & IN THE HOME!

Beneath the headline were six crudely taken photographs, the last on the bottom right circled in red: a remarkably striking young woman, her blond hair swept over one eye.

(Oh, my God . . . I know that one . . .)

"Look familiar, Father?"

"Yes . . ."

"You helped her."

"No . . . I saw her stealing—and I was afraid."

"Then help me now. *Help* me, for the love of God. Help me save one human life."

"Just tell me what—But wait . . . Wait . . . have we met before? I *know* you."

The stranger's lips appeared to move, but the voice was the mulberry bush's.

"Help him, dummy! This is God!"

"You!" The priest laughed breathlessly.

"Me. Come on, we've got work to do."

"But your hair, my son . . . And you're taller. And—"

"Trust me. I'll explain. But you're going to hear my confession. Before you go to Alcatraz."

NIGHT MOVES

It was the ninth of April, dusk, when I left the good Father in Oakland, and sailed back on the ferry for Baghdad.

My original intent had been just to fetch a few things from that wagon. But on the way over, while reading the *Call,* I saw the photo of the six who'd just been hauled off to the Rock. Including the blonde that I knew from the train. Betsy of the Heavy Hands. Then and there I decided I needed a priest.

The length of my confession must have set a record. But the priest hadn't heard one half-like it.

I told him of the *Zephyr* . . . and what had happened with Halley's . . . I answered his questions about '86 and the world according to Wolf . . . I told him of the First World War, the Second, the threat of the Third . . . I answered his questions about drugs and sex . . . I told him the truth about AIDS . . .

The priest said little. When he spoke, it wasn't much more than a whisper. He asked about the—monster. I told him what I knew of Blacke, then told him what I guessed. Father Duffy would have felt more comfortable if we'd been dealing with Satan. And I didn't try to persuade him we wouldn't all be better off if we were.

Blacke . . .

The very name affected him profoundly. And now and then he'd whisper it and I would feel him shivering through the booth's divider. I hadn't been to confession in maybe twenty-five years and the shivering—it was contagious. There I was in nineteen-six, got up in black, with a glued-on mustache and my hair dyed and my nose smashed . . . and

I might have been back in St. Peter's, age ten. I was un-recognizable—taller than ever in heeled boots with lifts—but in the small confessional, I was a boy in Buffalo. A boy whose soul had been shaped with incense . . . dry slivers of wafers on tongue . . . stained glass . . . majestic organs . . .

My guess was that Betsy would be next on Austin's menu. Blood from his own time must still be very sweet. And I couldn't help suspecting that—we tasted *better* over there. The Rock was where the real Austin was at. The Rock was even better than the *California Zephyr*. All it did was sit there, while he came and went as he pleased. The easy kill. Hyena-style.

The priest agreed *he* had to go. A man of the cloth, with a reason to visit, had a far better chance of departing.

Somehow we had to warn her. Even if, as I suspected, the visit would be guarded. We had to deliver a message that might get *through* to Betsy, yet not endanger the priest. Any note was risky. But one warning a woman of vampires, pythons, and hyenas?

We had to give Betsy *some* means of defense . . . which, even if spotted, *might* not be seized. This ruled out silver bullets and enormous pointed stakes. But what were we to bring her? And how to slip it to her?

The plan that we settled on was relatively risk-free, the best that we could figure. He would not visit *just* Betsy. He'd go with a Bible and blessing for each of the six new prisoners. The only difference was: *her* book would be packed with tricks we hoped might cut short Blacke's visit. And tell us more about him and where he really lived.

There was a long silence before the priest asked, "Is there anything . . . that you might like to confess?"

I laughed. A tinny sound. "There isn't time for all my sins."

"Then God forgive you. Peace, my son."

I started to rise, creaky-kneed, from the pew.

"Wait," Father Duffy said. "Tell me . . . Was—will there be nothing of good in the world you come from?"

Well, if I lost, if all was lost, then it seemed important that one person know. Where to begin, though? God, where to begin?

I told him of toasters . . . and microwave ovens . . . and Camelot . . . and the Summer of Love . . . I told him of Martin and Bobby and John . . . I told him of men who had walked on the moon . . . and babies gifted with new hearts . . .

I did not speak of the Earthquake. In the sanctity of the confessional, I still drew the line at that. The Big One would come and it couldn't be stopped. After the Quake, there was a chance that we *would* be the least of their worries. That is, if Austin and Wolf weren't around. I thought that I could handle Wolf. For Austin Blacke, though, I needed an edge. And the Quake was the wild card stashed up my sleeve.

So, I was on the ferry now, standing alone at the rail in the chill. And holding to the misted flashes of the lighthouse on the Rock.

I thought of Betsy in her cell.

Hang on, honey, you hang on . . . This time I'll get it right . . .

The Coast was not the same Coast I'd seen even that morning. And the change since the first night I'd seen it would have broken Patch's heart. Weeks ago, the water cops had had about as much effect as pairs of pink-cheeked altar boys. Now they marched in groups of four and it wasn't their clubs they were swinging, but guns. No one thought twice about stepping aside. A whole troop of Guardsmen, bayonets at ready, marched down the center of East Street. Every now and then I'd hear a quiet catcall. But it would be like a scared schoolboy's, heart thumping as he cried it.

Step too close to an alley, or let down your guard, you might still get split scrotum to sternum. But no one was letting his guard down tonight.

I gave my best *yard look* as I made my way. I walked slow. I walked tall. I did not trip on my new lifts and heels. I hadn't got rid of one clown suit to step inside another.

My eyes were focused dead-ahead on the old Hangdog Saloon. Patch was gone. So was the horn. They were hauling whole boatloads off now to the Rock. And I might just be on the next one. Unless I established myself, here and now: as a serious, serious man.

I was a few yards from the corner when the woman's screams began.

"ZO-NIE!"

The whole block froze cold as water cops streaked by in packs, clearing the walk with fierce sweeps of their guns. And the Guardsmen charged along East Street, sending a couple of cabs into posts.

Presently the air settled a little, each man kicking back on his heels:

It ain't me, boys. I ain't strange.

I took a breath and crossed the street, with only one thought in my mind:

Whatever happens, happens . . . but I am through clowning around. Your move.

Clean, the bald, muscular barman, caught my eye as I swung through the doors. He muttered something or other to one of the boys at the bar. And, before you knew it, heads were turning in a row. First the conversation stopped. Then the can-can girls on stage. Then the piano player, who never failed to find new notes between the keys to play.

I looked the room over and tugged at my Stetson and popped a cheroot in my mouth.

"Evenin', boys." I studied the bar through the blaze of a match. I'd seen most of the faces I saw there tonight. But there was no kidding myself about that. No one knew anyone, not anymore.

Clean scrunched over the bar, biceps bulging.

No one spoke. But everywhere there was the sense of constriction: minds . . . muscles . . . hairy fists . . .

This was the door to Austin, though. I had to be able to *move* in this town. And whatever that cost me, I'd just have to pay. So I sidled, cool and slow, still taking no chances on tripping, to the center of the room. I took a drag from the cheroot and studied the tip through a smoke ring.

I caught a flash of movement from the corner of one eye.

Saw Primo nudge Secondo, who nudged him back and nodded yes.

Secondo snarled, "What have we here?"

Well, I only know what all schoolchildren learn: when
guilty, blame the other guy.

I jabbed the cheroot at Secondo. "You've only got one
ear," I said. "Frankly, friend, that's kind of strange."

Secondo threw the ball right back and asked me, "Where
you from?"

"And you've got a ring in the other. That's *queer*."

Secondo took a giant step. And then another. We squared
off.

"You ain't from around here. Who's—president?" he
cried.

"Roosevelt, you idiot. Supposin' you tell me who's pope."

He raised one fist. It was shaking. "Aw, who cares who's
pope? You tell me, who's—mayor?"

Well, Patch had been a good teacher. And I'd been a
helluva pupil. But I knew Twenty Questions had just taken
a terminal turn.

There was no way out of this one unless I went all the
way.

I blew a smoke ring in his face. "What've you got in your
right pocket, boy."

Secondo looked as if I'd slipped something under his pillow while he'd been sleeping. And he'd just heard it rattling. He didn't know what I was up to. But he knew that it
had to be bad, very bad. The whole room was watching him.

"Who's—I don't know!" he screeched. He started to
reach for his pocket, then howled, pulling his hand back in
shock.

"Empty your pocket," I growled. "Do it *now*."

Secondo was working on staring me down when he spied
something over my shoulder.

"Cops . . . Oh, you bastard! I . . . will . . . kill . . .
youuuu!"

Coppers there behind me.

(Now. Do it. All the way! Do it and you live!)

Secondo swung with all he had. A real turn-of-the-cen-
tury mulekiller blow. I pivoted smoothly inside it—not a

trace of Honkey—slipping the derringer out of my vest. I
had it cocked as he corkscrewed. I didn't blink. It was part
of my hand, a part I slipped under his chin with a squeeze.

I don't know what I'd expected. Maybe a pop and a splatter of blood.

The shot's impact lifted him right off the floor. When he
landed, tables shook. He skidded a couple of feet and then
stopped. The swing doors, quivering, plop-plop-plopped a
heady stew of brains and blood, bone splinters and patches
of hair.

I *felt* the men behind me move.

I lowered the gun to a table, keeping both eyes on the
doors.

I said, "Boys—"

The rest was lost in the thunderous rush of Guardsmen
and cops through the door.

Well, there were cries of "murderer" from all around the
bar. I waited for the commotion to pass, hooking my thumbs
in my vest. While I waited, I passed something silver and
cool into one palm with my thumb.

My heart was thumping crazily. I figured I had a few
seconds before it caught up with my hands.

"Boys," I said, "rest easy now before you start squeezin'
those triggers. Yesterday I saw the bastard slip somethin'
real *strange* in his pocket. So, I followed him here to the
bar."

I raised my hands. I showed my palms. I said a prayer to
Wandini as I knelt beside the stiff.

I slipped my hand in the right pocket, an inch or two
more than I should have. Secondo had died with a hard-on. I
directed my disgust to the *strange* silver coin in my hand.

The Kennedy half-dollar was one of the things I'd retrieved from the wagon before dropping in on the priest. I
tossed it grimly to the cop who had the most stripes on his
sleeve. He took one look and passed it on as if he'd touched
the stiff's hard-on.

I stood up. Nice and slow. I pointed for permission. Then
slipped from my vest's upper pocket one of my new calling
cards.

Stripes studied it. Weeks ago, a card like that, I'd have

been put on the first outbound train. Not tonight, though. Not tonight. I had just bought myself some time to get to Austin Blacke.

Stripes said, "Mister. Don't leave town."

I said, "You know where to find me. Anyone's got any trouble with me pluggin' a *Zonie* with AIDS, just call."

Stripes jerked his chin at the derringer. "Better take that. Times are strange."

I snatched the gun.

I left the room before they changed their minds.

I'd killed a man. He was my first.

And I knew the scene I should play.

At almost any moment, as I walked along the beach, I was going to bawl like a baby. I'd collapse on some rock, in the spray of the surf, just me and the fog and the full silver moon. And I'd be a Better Man. Because I had had a Good Cry.

Well . . .

I must have walked about halfway to the old Presidio when, finally, I just gave up. And turned around and headed back, my eyes fixed, as I walked, on the Rock.

All I could see was the lighthouse, evilly twinkling like some ghostly eye.

Hang on, I begged her. Big blond Betsy. I want you to live, girl. I need you to live.

I need you to tell me *how* to get to Austin Blacke.

Do we reach him through the vampire part?

Or through the hyena?

KEEP THE FAITH

Tuesday morning, when I woke, it was the tenth of April. That left me ample time to kill. And more than enough to get killed in. If Austin got to me before I killed all the time that I needed to kill.

I knew the date of the Big One, I thought. Well, the odds were fifty-fifty. (The twenty-fourth . . . right, Lenny? Caruso's *last performance* . . . right?) But my guess at the time was a crapshoot. There, the odds were a thousand to one. Still, I was taking what odds I could get. There was nothing to do except roll 'em.

That and keep the faith.

Keep the faith in timing.

The Man in Black had bought me time. But the best of covers is like a loaded gun: It has a limited number of rounds. I gave the Man in Black a week before all of the chambers were empty. Or the damn gun went off in my face. (A click behind me on some street . . . Barrel to my temple . . . "What've you got in *your* pockets, eh, pal? . . . Now, you've got ten seconds to tell us where the hell you're *from* . . .")

So, every move had to count.

How neatly had I figured Blacke?

If I knew that *before* we met . . .

But there were no guarantees that our watches were in sync, even if I had him cold.

Austin Blacke's notions of time were not mine.

He might take his sweet time with Betsy, if he troubled with Betsy at all.

No, no. I couldn't wait.

If the gambit worked in time, with Betsy and her Bible, fine.

Meanwhile, there was Wolf.

And there might just *be* a way to rattle Austin's cage but good while taking care of Wolfy.

I spent most of Tuesday lying very low. Trying to remember a few lines of poetry. And thinking hard, very hard, about *Monster Time*.

Keep the faith in motion.

To find Wolf, I had to move. And my moves were limited. I decided, over lunch, to pay the *Call* a visit.

I traveled discreetly by hansom, ignoring the Guardsmen and cops on the street. I figured Wolfy's whereabouts would be kept top secret. Then again . . .

I closed my eyes. I thought: All right, you're a reporter . . . you've been with a paper for twenty-five years . . . and you're good, you're very good . . . But then, one day, out of nowhere, some guy walks in—and he's a *star* . . . How do you like that? . . . You don't, do you? . . . No . . .

I arrived in my tapered gray jacket, frilly white shirt with French cuffs, and black tie. This was the Man in Black by day; the image was clear in my mind. I moved like a man who had business to do, with no time for questions.

There were no guards in the lobby, as there would be in my day. Just a lone receptionist, who hadn't been picked for her looks. Hangdog face and lumpy shape, like a great sackful of doorknobs.

I said I'd come from Washington to speak with Frank McGuane, the ed.

She rolled her eyes. "Who doesn't. Eighth floor. Stand in line."

I was guessing she had two expressions—eyes open and eyes shut—when the two-piece black phone on her desk rang. And she became a girl of twelve.

"Hi!" she cried. "I mean, good day. This *is* the San Francisco Call . . ."

I rode the elevator up. It opened right into the newsroom, where five or six reporters clicketywhacked at their Royals. Two more yelled into brass tubes in the wall for cigarettes and coffee, while three stood in line for the one two-piece phone.

They were working overtime at playing *The Front Page*. I didn't have to ask them why. The voices that came from the rear corner office, the one marked Frank McGuane, weren't soft. There was quite a crowd in there, judging by the volume. Through a small window I caught a few flashes of men in Washington suits.

The editor's visitors wanted to know just where the hell this "Wolf" was. And *he* would be damned if he'd tell them. My guess was the editor would either be making the history books . . . or facing a firing squad soon. Unless I beat them to Wolfy. And Blacke.

I cleared my throat and wondered, in a reverent voice, which of them was Wolfy. I'd come to get his autograph.

The grizzled old vet on the phone snarled "*He* don't show his face in here" and showed me the view of his back.

I started in on the next man in line. "What if I just give you my address. The next time you see him—"

He was maybe half the first one's age, with less than a third of the grizzle. But he liked his job just fine.

He said, "You'd best be leaving, friend. We wouldn't know him to spit on his shoes." Then he joined his back to the first one's.

"Of course," I said. "I understand. Confidentiality!" I swept my gaze through the room. Not a thing. But I hadn't come here for nothing. "Gents," I said, "do me this much. If you see him, tell him—this is all I ask—that one man in San Francisco appreciates his *style*. That, oh *that*, is reporting!"

Nothing again. For three seconds. The two with their backs turned looked over their shoulders. The others simply stared, revulsed, while from the editor's office the volume was cranked up a notch.

I was ready to go when the grizzler snapped. His eyes just crackled with envy and spite.

"Style, is it? Monkey style! You want to find a *monkey*, go . . ."

He said no more.

Whatever he'd told me was all I was going to get. Wolf was a monkey . . . To find him, go where?

I stopped at the reception desk for a last bit of frost from Miss Perky. She was doing her nails, with one eye on the phone.

"I love a woman with polish," I said.

"Hrumph."

"You look like you're bright as a button."

"Pshaw!"

Just then the phone began to ring.

"Wait . . . Let me ask you something. Say you want to find a man—"

"Hrumph! Who wants to find a man?"

"But say you do and someone says, 'You want to find a monkey, go . . .' "

"All men are monkeys," she snapped. Then, sweetly, into the mouthpiece, "Hi! I mean, Good afternoon . . ."

Keep the faith in messages.

You never know when they'll arrive.

It was late.

I was still fine-tuning my plans for *Monster Time* when I heard three light knocks at my door.

"Got a message arrived several hours ago, sir. Day man must've missed it."

I stood by the door, with the derringer cocked.

I said, "Slip it under the door."

And he did, not troubling to whisper his "cheapskate."

Inside the white Palace envelope was one of the world's shortest notes:

4:50
F.D. phoned. Said: "Yes" and "No."
          —The Management

F.D. . . . Father Duffy. The "Yes" meant he'd delivered our loaded Bible to Betsy. The "No" meant that he hadn't had two words alone with her.

That meant it was all up to Betsy and how clever she was with a riddle.

Keep the faith in riddles.

I couldn't sleep. I tossed and turned until I could stand it no longer.

You want to find a monkey, go . . .

Where the hell else would you go but the zoo?

A child's joke? But then, why had he stopped? No, he'd told me something . . .

I phoned the front desk at two-thirty. "I know this may sound foolish, but . . . if you thought a man was a mon—"

The man yawned noisily. "Monkey House," he told me, and hung up the phone.

I rang again. "There could be a gold eagle in this."

"Oh, *yeah*?"

"Sure, sure, that's the word. Say you want to find a man and somebody tells you—"

"The Monkey House. I told you. Hell, dollar to a paper dime that's the oldest darn joke in the world."

"The monkey house."

"The Monkey *Block.*"

"The monkey block?"

"The *Montgomery* Block. See, folks started to call it the Monkey Block first. Then—"

"All right," I said. "I get it."

"Hey, what about the eagle now . . ."

"The oldest joke in the world, eh?" I said.

"Oh, that, you might say, was a figure of speech."

"So was the eagle. A dollar."

I was about all out of Harp cash.

I'd be needing a loan quick from Wolfy.

Keep the faith in faith.

So, the trick was to live to the Big One.

How did Blacke track us?

Through mind vibes? Then I'd give him nothing of Harpo from here. And as little of Dodge as I could.

Did he track, in part, by smell? I ate well and shrewdly— fresh fruit and just-cooked vegetables—changing my scent from the man he had known.

I did hundreds of pushups and situps . . . hours on hours of pivots and moves . . . I'd be needing my strength. All my strength, all my speed.

But I couldn't help thinking this wasn't enough.

THE MONKEY HOUSE

In his waking hours, it had become the Monkey House.

Wolf wondered less when the bars had gone up than why he couldn't seem to leave . . . why he felt as if something were squeezing his mind . . . insisting that this was his home.

He'd come to Papa Coppa's, to his table in the back, and sit for hours troubled by some dreadful sense of loss. His was a great mission, of course; that was clear. And no great style came of age without the spilling of blood. Or the envy of spiteful and envious souls.

He'd outlive the lot of them.

Let them laugh. Let them cackle and giggle.

Like now.

Two tables by the window were filled with drunk Bohemians. Their favorite game, in their cups, was redoing the classics by Wolfy. Tonight, as the Guardsmen and cops roamed the streets, one suggested that they Wolf George Sterling.

"I dunno," a second said. "George is our poet laureate."

"Nonsense!" said another. "Good Lord, man, where's your spirit? Wolfy would ruin anything."

"Sure, sure, that's the word," added a fourth further down. "C'mon, let's give Georgie the Wolf. Rum an' gum to the one who can Wolf this the worst:

> Tho' the dark be cold and blind,
> Yet her sea-fog's touch is kind.
> And her mightier caress ·
>   Is joy and the pain thereof:

And great is thy tenderness,
O cool, grey city of love!

The second man still brooded. "This'll be a sacrilege."

The first man clapped his shoulder. "Naw, the only thing
sacred to Wolf is bad Art. C'mon, you lugs, I'll start you off:
Though the dark be BRRRRRRR! and blind . . ."

Another picked right up on it: "Yet her sea-fog's touch is
—DOTDOTDOT! DOTDOTDOT! EXCLAMATION
POINT!—kind."

The second man, the brooder, roared: "And her KA-
BOOM! KABAM! caress . . ."

Wolf lowered his head in his hands.

That's the way I found him that Wednesday, the eleventh,
when I walked into the Monkey House. The night was
young, as evenings go. But he looked like he hadn't been
sleeping for days. Or had been but wished that he hadn't.

I stood over Wolf's table, black as the night. But I still
hadn't caught his attention.

"Sad excuse for poetry," I said. "Frankly, sounded better
the way those idiots did it."

Without even looking, Wolf snarled, "Aaah, what would
you know about Art?"

"Oh, I know what I like. I take it a little more . . . modern myself. If you know what I mean."

Wolf dropped his hands. Looked up slowly. I had his attention now. And once he took in the sharp hook of the nose
. . . the black pencil line of mustache . . .

"Easy, friend." I urged him. I slipped into a chair kitty-
cornered to his, easing it in right beside him. I put one arm
around his shoulder. With my right hand I patted his chest,
buddy style.

"Who are you?" Wolf asked me. "I—know you."

I slipped one of my cards on the table, while lighting a
cheroot.

Wolf eyed the card. Then looked at me. He couldn't seem
to figure which blew his mind more.

He read, "Have Gun Will Travel . . . Wire Paladin?"

"Heybubbaloobubbawhopbopbop."

"You were on the *train*?"

"Sammy's dead."

Wolf shrugged. "I don't know any Sammy."

"Sammy. *Sam*."

"I don't know any Sam."

"What the hell are you talking about?" I pulled back a couple of inches to get a better look at him.

"I'm telling you, man, I don't know any Sam."

"You're serious," I said. "You are."

Wolf glared at me. I took a puff and brooded about this a second.

"How's Austin?" I said casually.

"I don't know any Austin. Now I'll thank you to get out of here before I start yelling *Zonie*."

My hands had not been empty before when I patted him down. I smiled at him genially. "Better look in your pocket first."

He stared at his pocket in horror; then, in slow motion, he reached. He gawked at the face of the Seiko I'd planted, and slapped it back in in a flash.

"Fuck," he said. "What do you want?"

I took a drag from the cheroot and took my time before answering. "I've decided we ought to be partners. *Monster Time*'s a swell idea. You'll be rich."

Well, he might have been spooked for a second. But that brought out the old Wolf quick.

Monster Time was his, all his. And, go on, let me do my worst. I was just a damned hippie clown cowboy.

"Rich? You bet your ass, I'll be. I've paid my dues. They used to laugh. Laugh at me when I was begging for crumbs, I'm telling you *crumbs* of attention. Well, look who's got the last laugh now? I laugh every week on my way to the bank. I'm gonna live forever. He . . ."

Something had flickered, for only an instant, on the corner of a screen. *(He . . .)* It faded just as quickly, lost in a blizzard of static and snow.

I put my hand on his shoulder. "They're laughing at you now, babe. And they're gonna be laughing for years at your name. When they think of it, they'll remember a second-rate talent who shot for the stars and ended in the Monkey

House with blood and bullshit all over his shoes. Laugh? Hell, they'll be convulsed. They'll giggle from here to Japan."

"No . . . I'm the *first*—I'm—"

"Ah, that'll be the worst of it. Watching them steal from you, pieces and bits. Turning your tricks into real works of art."

"God, no—no, no—anything but that . . ."

I felt almost sorry for Wolfy. But there was work to be done. So, when he clasped my elbow, I placed my hand over his.

"Face it," I said. "You're the Hitler of Art. You're just shorter on humor than he was. They'll all spit on your grave once they've picked your bones clean. Unless . . ."

"Unless?" Wolf cried.

"Well, of course, that is, unless . . ."

"Unless!"

"Unless . . . you left behind, let's say . . . one perfect, perfect masterpiece."

Wolf said "Yes . . ." dreamily . . . then, shrewdly, "What are you saying to me?"

"It really is surprising—I mean, what a man can remember . . . when he feels motivated?"

"Like what?" he said, all business now.

I fed him the line that I knew:

We are the hollow men . . .

I thought he was going to kiss me. He closed his eyes. He stuck out his chin. "I know that," he whispered. "It's—famous."

"Famous, my ass. It's immortal."

"More!"

Well, now came the tricky part. I didn't know the rest, not quite. But I'd once slept with a merry old prof who quoted Auden when I came and Eliot when she did. There are some things a man never forgets, at least not completely. Life was a gamble. I winged it, half making it up as I went.

"Remember this?

> Leaning together
> Our headpieces stuffed with straw.

"Auden!"

"Nope."

"I know. Yeats!"

"Why not start with a T. And the next letter's S.

"Eliot . . . My God, I'm *him* . . ."

"Use your head. He's still a kid. You've got the jump on all of them. Fifteen, twenty years."

"But do you know the rest?" Wolf cried. He gripped my arm, not lightly.

I pried it loose, looking thoroughly hurt. I went a couple more rounds:

> Let us go then, you and me,
> When the night is spread-eagled over the sea
> Like a corpse on a gunmetal table.

"Oh, God, yes, I remember."

"You damn well should," I said. "It's—yours."

"But give me more, a little more. Put some of it together!"

"That's all you'll ever get from me, unless I get something back. I'm working on this Sunday's column."

Wolf slunk back. He looked as if I'd just slipped a noose around his neck. "I—turned it in . . ." he said. "Tonight."

I spread my hands out grandly. "Wolf, start acting like a star. Phone the man tomorrow. Tell him pull it or you walk."

"But when—"

I slid my chair back. Took a stand. "Oh, I'll keep you posted. Maybe I'll phone you tomorrow at six. By the way," I told him, "my cash flow's getting kinda tight."

THE BLUE BLAZER: FINIS

While keeping my room at the Palace, I checked into the Carlton Hotel. Wary of both Wolf and Austin, I'd be moving a lot from here on.

My new room wasn't nearly as spacious. There was no marble bust of a king who had once loved there and gone. The lobby wasn't paved with gleaming silver dollars. No, it wasn't the Palace. It didn't come close. But, if my memory served me right, Paladin had stayed here. So, I wanted to give it a night.

I know what you're thinking: Paladin hadn't existed. A tall, thin man, named Richard Boone, had staged, for a couple of seasons, an illusion that had moved me. And had become, when I was small, a part of my mythical landscape. I never watched *Gunsmoke.* I hated *Will Sonnet. Bonanza* just bored me to tears. I loved the elegant, literate man who waited, in his frilly shirt, warm and wise and charming, for Hey Boy to bring the next wire, the call to arms that transformed him into the Man in Black.

I'd forgotten Paladin, almost absolutely. At gunpoint, I couldn't have told you that night the story of a single show.

I set down my notes for *Monster Time* and puffed at my cheroot. I thought of that last time I saw Richard Boone: pie-eyed and red-nosed and fat and absurd and made stupid by time and defeat.

He, too, had forgotten our beautiful dream.

Time didn't just crush us with bad bloody ends. Coolly

and relentlessly, it wiped away the slate. It left the worst and took the best . . . and then the memory of the best . . . till you were left sitting alone in a room, wondering: Wait a minute . . . Didn't I—yes, I'd forgotten—I used to dream of Paladin. And Sammy—remember that click on the train?—where did she go on me, she was my twin . . . and wasn't there really a Sweet Spot in Time? . . .

By ten I was in a black, bottomless funk.

I decided I needed—

Uh-uh. The wrong word.

I decided I wanted one Blazer.

I'd earned one.

What the hell?

I took one sip and had the sky, fuck Denver's, the sky of the world in my soul. What had possessed me? I must have been mad, playing hide-and-seek with Blacke, putting my life on the line—and for what?

Another sip. I understood: the Sweet Spot had never been lost, it was *here*.

(It was all death and corruption outside . . . futility . . . oblivion . . .)

The Blazer, which I'd thought a nice pup to pet, had just shown its teeth.

I ordered another. Then one after that. That was the sly thing to do. Nice doggy. Good doggy. Made me feel glowy and safe from Bad Thoughts.

(Beyond death and corruption and cancer and Blacke . . .)

The pup, a full-grown dog from hell. I heard it growling, junkyard low. Then it came straight for my throat.

(You will die!)

I don't know how I reached the beach. I might have taken a hansom. Then again, it seemed to me, that I had passed through Babylon and Rome and Greece on the way. Seen the death of whole civilizations—lost, not as they'd said, not in thousands of years . . . no, in mere blinks of Time's eye. Oh yes, the prams kept rolling on. But Time was there to snap them, whole, the instant they came off the line.

Gone, gone, all gone. Gone our sweet particulars. The father's hug . . . the baby's smile . . . the kiss of crisp new linen sheets . . . sugared Christmas cookies . . . sweet cherrywood in the fire . . .

Gone, gone, all of it. All of it and all of us. And then goes the Epoch. And then goes the Age. Only ruins remain . . . and some books, in dead tongues, their covers riddled with spitballs. And then, in good time, goes the Species.

I stumbled and prayed for deliverance, unheard, alone, a doomed drunk on the beach.

Oh, Betsy, what's the point of it? None of us wins, it's all ashes and dust. Not even the ghost of a memory remains. What's the point of one more day, or even one more hour?

I stumbled on. I babbled on. I passed by some golf links, imagining balls that were labeled Egypt . . . Babylon . . . America . . .

I heard a bugle from the fort sound taps for the universe. That, too, would pass. Not even a black hole would remain.

A ways ahead, above the beach, I saw a lifeboat station. Not even a lone candle's flicker inside. They wouldn't be using it this time of year. The tide was low, the Bay as calm as I had ever seen it. This would be a good place to stop the Bad Thoughts.

I had something nice in my pocket. Something much sweeter than candy. Oh boy. I curled my fingers lovingly around its pearly handle. Wow. Who said life was heartless? Who said a man died alone, without friends?

As I walked, I played with it, just the way you do with friends. Stuck the barrel in my mouth. Tasted too metallic. Placed it under my chin. But remembered a man who had done that—and lived on, more or less. I placed it then between my eyes and thought, as I walked, that that felt about right.

And I saw just where I would do it.

I'd never make the station house.

Oh no, my friend was calling now. Tugging at my finger.

But maybe thirty yards ahead I saw the vague shape of a boathouse. I could wrap myself, maybe, around with a flag . . . stretch myself out in a dinghy . . . place my friend between my eyes . . . say, with enormous dignity, something that no one would hear: "My regards to Babylon" . . . or "My checks bounced high, my watch was quick . . ."

I started to run. It was more like a skip. And I was roughly halfway home—when I caught my first whiff of the smell.

It was subtle enough, but alarmingly wrong. A dank flash through the heady kick of the seaweed and the surf.

But it was wrong, undeniably wrong, like the glow from the wheels of the train back in Sparks . . . or Sam's voice in Chinatown . . .

I knew I should turn. I could not.

The smell grew wronger as I advanced. But it was hard to place. A bit riper than it was revolting.

I doubt that it is possible to sober up more quickly.

I made my way around the back.

I saw the broken windows first. Not smashed with stones by truant kids or broken in to climb through. The break was clean and curiously, curiously shaped . . . as if a large bird had crashed through with such speed that it had left its outline.

With every step the smell grew worse.

Until I stood at the window and saw, in the light of the moon, Austin's work. Bits and pieces . . . Bits and pieces . . . and half a skull with the face gone.

I wheeled, doubling over, and puked until I cried.

Then I stood and wiped my mouth and slipped the gun back in my pocket.

I saw the lighthouse twinkling, far and away, in the mist.

"Cocksucker," I muttered. "You want me? You got me. I'll *kick* your Blacke ass. I'll tear your fucking *heart* out!"

STEREOPTICON VI

I

 Austin Blacke could see himself acquiring a small taste for vaudeville. Though men were more amusing, from his own perspective, when they attempted the heights. *Lord* Whittaker's Hamlet, for instance, had been as delicious as his lordship himself would be in a short while.

A man's whole life was mastery—of himself by everything and everyone around him.

But bring on four plump dancing girls he wouldn't spit on elsewhere . . . and his heart was yours for a song.

Bring on a handful of acrobats . . . just bright enough to climb the stairs . . . and every man in the room feels alive. And forgets that he's going to die.

He wished he'd brought the Twelve with him. They would have felt at home here, performing their old, tired tricks.

Austin was prepared to go when the next act was announced.

The twin McGillicuttys were positively guaranteed to reduce the audience to helpless shrieks of laughter.

Suddenly an idea that was uniquely Blacke flickered in his mind.

The iron curtain rose.

The twin McGillicuttys were standing in place, their caps raised.

The audience roared at the sight of the twins in their giant checkered coats.

Austin smiled and waited. He felt certain he could do this thing. Nothing was beyond him now.

Damn shame, though, that Harpo wasn't here to watch. Somehow he'd lost the small clown with the curls. Not a glimpse. Not a whiff. Not a ripple of mind.

Well, Austin had all the time in the world.

The twins took two shuffling steps to the right.

Then two shuffling steps to the left.

They shuffled backward a couple of steps.

Then shuffled quickly forward. And then, without a hitch, did three madcap pirouettes in perfect synchronization.

The first McGillicutty tipped his derby seven times in lightning-quick succession.

The second matched him move for move.

Their voices rose high and away above the screams of laughter . . . as Austin Blacke readied his mind.

"As *I* was going down the street yesterday . . ."

"Ah! As *you* were going down the street—all right!"

"I say, I saw a *girl* at a window!"

"*You* saw a *girl* at a window!"

"And this girl—"

Austin *squeezed.*

"—she had *cancer!*"

The audience, stunned, gasped. The second twin gawked at the first. But Austin, who had never *squeezed* from even half this distance, smiled, chuckled lowly, and gave the second a jolt.

The man jerked back like a marionette. "Ah! As *you* were going down the street yesterday, *you* saw a *girl* at a window, and this *girl,* she had *cancer!* All right!"

"All right!"

"Go on!"

They did, with Austin *squeezing* first one, then the next, while men's and women's voices rose in panic and disgust.

The twin McGillicuttys slapped their knees.

They tipped their caps.

They shuffled left and shuffled right and did more crazy pirouettes.

"—and whole clumpfuls of hair came right out of her head!"

"All right! As *you* were going down the street yesterday, *you* saw a *girl* at a window, and this *girl*, she had *cancer*, the *pain* made her scream, and whole *clumpfuls* of hair came right out of her head!"

"All right!"

"All right!"

"Go on!"

"Go on!"

Blacke fed on their adrenaline. And on the crowd's surge of horror and rage. It was sweet. But not enough.

He *squeezed* the first twin's mind with almost everything he had. The man jerked to attention.

"You there, in the second row! You, the dumpy old bitch in the fright wig! You're gonna get hit by a street car next year! It'll take off both legs at the knees!"

The woman shrieked. Blacke *swept* her mind. A light, almost feathery, tickling rush. She started to giggle like crazy.

The second twin, *squeezed*, jerked exactly like the first.

"You there, the asshole beside her! Your prostate gland is beginning to swell! In six months you're gonna see blood in your piss!"

The man jumped up—and, *swept*, collapsed, prostrated with laughter.

When Blacke *swept*, the feeling was almost like exhaling. OUT.

The energy they gave him back was like breathing. IN.

This was good. And very sweet. But he wanted more tonight.

And so he *squeezed* the two of them, the twin McGillicuttys. They dropped, screaming, to their knees. And began, with a giggle, in sync:

"You there in the seventh row in the salmon jacket! You look kinda strange tonight, so tell us where you're from! All right!"

Blacke *squeezed* to the left. The man leapt, screaming, to his feet. "Hell, I'm the strangest man in town! They oughta put *me* on the Rock!"

Sweep. OUT. The whole damn room. The rush swept through them all at once, erupting in high, manic giggles.

Breathe. IN. Pure energy. The high of their collective force.

Squeeze. The twins, inspired, bolted up. They slapped their knees. They tipped their caps. They did six happy pirouettes.

"All right! All right! Come on! Come on!

"Mirror, mirror, on the wall,

"Who's the strangest of us all!"

Sweep. OUT. A great roar of delight. Then giggles, screams of "Me! It's me!"

Breathe. IN. By the Night, what a rush!

Squeeze. The twin McGillicuttys slapped their knees and tipped their caps. "Who's got cancer? Who's got AIDS?"

Sweep. OUT. The walls shook with roars and whoops of "Me! It's me!"

Breathe. IN.

Blacke continued the skit till the twins had collapsed and the crowd had no more to give.

No . . . They did have one more rush to give him. It really wouldn't do to have the twins around for questioning.

At the back of the hall, Blacke collected himself. He focused all his mastery on one final great, collective

SQUEEZE.

Three hundred people screamed and charged.

Austin quickly lost count of the number of pieces the twins had been reduced to.

Outside, the air was cool and sweet.

And the moon was exceptionally full.

Now and then, on nights like this, it was not possible to stop.

On the Rock was a plump little bonbon. Who would do just wonderfully. Until the small clown with the curls.

(Come on, Harp, where are you?)

II

About suffering, the poem had begun, *the Masters, they were never wrong. . . .*

Betsy knew the words were off. Something to do with a painting. A boy who'd flown too close to the sun and was pictured falling while ships sailed calmly on.

She'd never understood the poem. Miss Wilcox had given her essay an F. *(For heaven's sake, you silly girl, the Masters were painters, not gods. It's right there. Even a child can see it!)* Tonight, though, after all these years, it had come back to her. And still she could not fathom why she had been wrong. Couldn't fate be *like* the gods, and couldn't the gods be *like* painters. Well, maybe not—but, still, an F?

She wished that Clark—well, Billy now—had simply pulled the trigger.

But the Masters couldn't have settled for that. The suffering wouldn't have been . . . right enough.

No, it would begin in the precinct, with five others on the bench with her . . . their captors screaming: *They are strange!*

Ah, but on the ferry—there the Masters found their stride. Five men and women in handcuffs, weeping and telling her they were not strange, while guards jeered and cursed and spat. And gulls flew playfully over the boat. And the island whispered, with its white walls and dazzling red roofs: *Welcome home.*

Perfection of a kind was what they were after.

Later on they'd lose their touch, with concrete cell blocks and massive steel doors. But, here and now, the Masters' touch was subtle, deft, assured. Laughter and the soft chatter of women, out strolling the beautiful brick streets below. The warm thunder of bowled balls down their private alley's lanes. The musical clatter of pins. The tantalizing fragrance of fresh bread from the bakery.

The Masters understood it all.

Between the last bars of her window, on clear nights, a sliver of skyline. Lives still rich with poetry. And what was that but love?

And what was love but loving, not some mirror's obsession with calories and fat. Love began with loving, not with the craving for love. That was the poetry of it. It was what it was, and was simply itself.

(I love you, Mae—I love you—But—

My name is Betsy Atkinson. Now pull the trigger, Billy. It was good to love you.

God help me—what am I to do!

Pull the trigger. And someday remember: I meant what I said. You were worth it. Go on.)

She loved him still. She understood his anger and confusion. Her heart went out to Billy.

But—

Oh God, the Masters knew all there was to know about suffering.

About gulls in the harbor.

And ships sailing on.

And a frightened old priest, with two guards at his side, handing you the Good Book through your cell door's thick-barred window.

About suffering they were not wrong . . . When they brought you a Bible, it was a sad joke. With its center hollowed out and stuffed with trinkets and riddles.

She crossed the room to her hard single cot. Her head just cleared the peaked rise of the ceiling in the center of her cell. From there it sloped dramatically. She stooped, still moving, snatched the Good Book, and sat on the edge of her cot.

She guessed that it was useless, maybe even wrong of her, to read too much into a beautiful joke. But she found herself remembering the urgent look in the priest's eyes. *Read your Bible, for your soul.* And, as he left, almost under his breath, *Call me—if you need to confess.*

(Right, Father. Where's the phone?)

Strange, then. Very strange. And what was she to make of these:

—An ancient black rosary stinking of garlic . . .

—A cheap ring with a sharp glass stone . . .

—A queer note, bizarrely typed:

Prescription for Salvation: Read:

Deuteronomy . . .

Revelation . . .

And

Corinthians

Until

Last of

April . . .

?

(Or: *till letters fall in place.*)

Well, how could she read *anything* with all the pages torn to shit? And why put a question mark after the month? And why the last of April? *Until the letters fall in place* . . . Good Lord, what the devil could *that* mean?

But the note was child's play compared to the verse that came with it:

> If caped angel fly the Bay,
> Let Lord Jesus have his say.
> But oh, if the hyena laugh,
> *Ring* him for his epitaph!
> And if, perchance, the snake you sight—
> It is not love! The head do bite!

Caped angels now . . . Hyenas . . . Snakes . . .

She'd barely finished high school. How could she hope to figure that? Miss Wilcox would just split a gut.

Betsy lay back, closed her eyes. Tomorrow was another day.

Must be the air and the sadness . . . This place just makes a body feel . . .

(5 'SLEEPERS' DEAD ON ROCK!)

(Read the Bible for your soul!)

Betsy forced her eyes open. The lids almost creaked. But suddenly she found she felt exceedingly annoyed.

She glared at the two scraps of paper.

"I am not a dummy, Miss Wilcox," she snapped. "I know how to read."

Prescription for Salvation . . .

Read . . . Colon . . . Read *this* . . .

Deuteronomy . . . Revelation . . . and Corinthians . . . until last of April . . . ?

Right.

(It was what it was, and was simply.)

Wait. If the priest had wanted her to read it that way, in a line . . . then he'd have typed it that way. Right?

But he'd arranged the words just so, in that peculiar fashion. As if he were calling attention not just to the words— which *were* missing pages—but—

(Even a child could read it.)

Not just to *the* words—but to *some* words. See, there! "Last of" had *two* words in it and all the other lines had one. And all of the letters *except* "of" began with a capital letter. So "of" was not important. Right?

"Give *me* an F, Miss Wilcox? Stick it in your ear."

(Until the letters fall in place.)

The real message in the note hit her square between the eyes, sharper than an ice pick:

> *D* euteronomy . . .
> *R* evelation . . .
> *A* nd
> *C* orinthians
> *U* ntil
> *L* ast of
> *A* pril . . .
> ?

Dracula? *Not* Dracula?

If caped angel fly the Bay . . .

Let Lord Jesus . . . Crucifix—rosary scented with garlic . . .

But if the hyena—

WHAT!

She draped the rosary over her neck.

And, on a childish impulse, slipped the enormous fake ring on one finger.

The thing to do was . . . Call a guard . . .

Excuse me, sir, I know I'm strange—*but, you see, there's a vampire coming . . . who may bring a hyena and snake!*

Oh, no. No, you don't. They'd empty the damn poop pan on her for that. The thing to do was close her eyes . . . just for a minute or two . . . feel the lids flutter like butterfly wings as she began to drift . . .

And, wasn't *that* strange? She could hear them:
eyelids fluttering like wings
through the night
to the bars of her cell . . .
and then through.

Lavender-r-r-r-r . . .
She smelled it first, and it was sweeter than love. Then she heard it, very near.

"Come on, get up, you sleepyhead."
The softest and purriest voice in the world.

And talk about romantic glows? The room was veiled in the subtlest, palest of lavender mists.

Now, here was a guy who knew a few things about Romance and Poetry. Sundance, she remembered him, tanned and wholly glorious.

(Picked me right up like a feather . . .)
"Betsy, my beautiful Betsy. Come to me. I need your love."

There. That was the difference between men and boys. A man like that would swim the Bay. Hell, he'd fly across if he had to!

(Wings . . .)
Betsy made a mewling sound.

"If caped angel . . ."
"Eh? What's that?" Sundance smiled. "Well, bless my soul. A rosary."

Betsy gripped its tiny cross. It was barely as large as her pinky. And yet it felt heavy, too heavy too lift.

"Take it off," Sundance said, unbuttoning his spiffy Prince Albert. White satin shirt and tanned chest underneath.

(And what was that sound he had made on the train . . .)
"I said, take it off, girl. It bores me."
Oh God, it was heavy, she hadn't a prayer!

She got it as far as her heart, then her chin, holding it there like a . . .

Joke.

Sundance yawned. Then, with a glance, he reached inside her mind and

squeezed.

"Give me the crucifix . . . That's a girl . . . Just slip it over your neck . . . Yes, like that . . . Good girl, good, that *pleases* me. Now get down on your knees, that will please me a lot. I said, on your knees for me."

"Eat sh—"

Sundance *squeezed* her mind again, much harder this time, and longer. And she fell to her knees as if both of her feet had been swept from beneath with a bat. And then he *swept* her with his mind. But oh, a very different *sweep*. And she felt giggly and vile and wet.

"Dynamite," Sundance purred. "Now, crawl over here like the fat pig you are."

A low growl escaped her throat.

(FAT? Why, you arrogant—)

"Whee!" Sundance cried. "Come on and fight me, I love it!"

He *squeezed*.

Betsy dropped to her elbows, pain stronger than pride. The floor came at her like a wall.

Sundance chuckled lowly. And then he *swept* her. And she was a pig, hopping over on all fours, and hoping he might have some sugary slop.

Sundance took away the beads. Gave them a bored and contemptuous look. And then tossed them onto her cot.

"I hate a chick stinking of garlic. You all smell bad enough as it is."

(You-u-u . . . pig . . .)

"Oh, you're a proud one, aren't you, girl? All I wanted was blood when I came here. But I've got just the thing for you. Yeah, just the thing for a fat, stinking pig."

(FAT!)

Sundance *squeezed* her, unbuckling his belt. Through the crimson haze of pain, she dreamed she saw the rippling of a giant wave.

(Poetry . . . Poetry . . .)

"*Please* me. That's what you're gonna do. *Please* me."

(Train . . . Train . . . His voice went WHOOO-OOPPPPP . . .)

"Bastard—" Betsy started.

Sundance *squeezed.* Purred, "I'm sorry?" Slipped his trousers down a foot. His phallus, the length of a section of hose, snaked out, bounced and quivered, ramrod stiff, before her lips.

Betsy whimpered, "Master . . ."

"Good. Good, that *pleases* me." He laced his fingers in her hair, drawing her in till the head touched her lips. The small fist-sized head with the hole on the tip. "Come on, you know what to do. Enough of this romantic shit."

Sundance *SQUEEZED.* So hard this time she might have brought the house down. But the lavender head, throbbing and growing, slipped through the strained circle of lips.

Sundance held the position a moment, inhumanly pleased with himself.

"Took my time with Sammy. Let me tell you, Chink food is the best."

(Train . . . Train . . . Chinese girl . . . Oh God, she had poetry in her . . . You—)

SQUEEZE.

"But you're just a ton and a half of greased pork. Come on, piggie, Show Time."

She caught a glimmer of something like scales, far and away, by his pendulous balls.

(Poetry . . . POETRY!)

Her jaw popped once. Then twice. Then broke.

(If by chance the snake you sight,
It is not love! The head do . . .)

(BITE!!!)

She sank her teeth into the shaft of the head. Like biting a bagle, a month old, with scales. Her mouth, still stuffed horrendously, suddenly flooded with poetry, blood, and bits and pieces of her teeth.

And then he
SQUEEZED.

The scream was hers as Sundance roared and grabbed her throat and jerked her a foot from the floor in one hand.

"You—cunt!"

Sundance barked. Then he whooped. Then, amazingly, giggled.

(You dummy, Betsy Atkinson, you have no gift for . . .)
(POETRY!)
(But oh, if the hyena laugh,
Ring him for his epitaph!)
(Ring him?)
(Ring him . . .)
(RING him . . .)

From the corner of her eye, a faint glimmer on one finger.
(RING!)

The face before her whirred and popped and snapped and squealed obscenely.

It wasn't strength that moved her hand; she hadn't enough left to breathe.

It was the poetry in her. A transcendent spark of joy. She'd understood, and good for her. And it was the poetry in her that shot the ring up in a swift savage arc . . . to crash on the last patch of tan.

Then she was thrown, and with such force the cell's door was still shaking when she hit the floor. But poetry to see him, still, reeling and clutching his cheek and his cock, his eyes blazing now not with power but pain.

Voices, then.

And footsteps charging down the hall.

Someone pounding on the wall. "Aaa, shut up, I'm tryna sleep!"

The hyena, paralyzed with the pain of losing her.

Betsy smiled, almost out. "Whyn't you come back an' *see* me some time . . ."

The Masters had saved it, the best, for the last—a sudden explosion of form into fog, lavender and swirling . . . and then the flutter of something like wings, out through the bars and back into the night.

That was for Billy, she thought. And Curly, the Chinese girl, and the actor.

And then she was gone.

III

Tonight's performance had left Rod feeling both emptied and filled. And instead of returning direct to his room, he found himself taking some curious turns along streets he had till now avoided.

When it happened, he'd been in the wings waiting for his entrance, for the men to start shaking the stage. What happened was: Rod closed his eyes, only for a second, and somehow felt the presence, the collective energy, of the men and women in the hall. He felt almost—connected by his very strangeness. The sensation passed as quickly as it had come over him. But suddenly he realized: he didn't need the stage to shake . . . or see lavender specks in the dark. He'd felt something better: a direct connection between himself and this world. He raised one hand to Kelley: no tremors or tricks would be needed tonight. From the instant he walked onto stage, he was lost. His hands were beyond him. His eyes were beyond him. He felt just barely conscious of speaking. And when the play had ended, instead of the usual whistles and cheers, a silence of over a minute swelled into the warmest, most loving applause.

Now, at the foot of Chinatown, though the air was exceedingly brisk, Rod felt his mind *swept* with an impulse: to submerge in the ocean of tunics and smoke.

(*Home. We are one. A procession. Dear God. How simple, how beautifully simple life is.*)

Another *sweep*. And then the sense of
lavender-r-r-r
glowing in his mind.

Up ahead, two mah-jongg players nodded at him, smiling. Rod started crossing over, hungry for their company. Not a fear or a care in the world. He was home. And New York was a childish dream of the past.

He made it about halfway there when his mind was *swept* again.

So he followed his heart through the windchimes and mist, through the thick smoke and singaling voices, under a moon that looked ready to burst.

To the alley.

Where he turned.

Feeling, oddly, less *swept* now than
pushed,
what was this, he felt
PUSHED!
What the hell—

Footsteps behind him. A rush of hot breath. Then a hand made of steel on his neck, from behind, snatching him up off the ground like a doll. And they were flying, Jesus, toward the brick wall at the end. At the speed they were going, his face would go through.

But they stopped half a foot before impact.

Rod did what he could to hang loose in that hand, toes straining for the ground.

"She ruined my face," a low voice growled. "That cunt—Goddamn her—strychnine!"

Rod tried, and hard, to breathe. Heard small bones crackling in his neck. And then a dreadful progression of sounds —whirrs, pops, snaps, squeals—that took the heart right out of him.

The hand tossed him up, with a spin on the toss, changing its grip to a frontal. Rod's perspective underwent a horrifying change.

He saw the fangs before anything else, then the jagged red scar through the hair on the cheek. He whispered "Aaa!" before the hand slammed the back of his head at the wall. Surely there had been some breakage inside.

"I need your face! I NEED your blood!"

A slobbering lick of the fangs with its tongue.

Rod's bowels burst. His bladder blew.

But the Voice did not deny him his last majestic line:

"Go fuck—yourself . . . I was a star!"

IV

"Sam? Are you in there, dear?"

Harriet standing again at his door. She'd followed him. Oh, God, the bitch. He'd lost her, he'd thought, but she sure had him now.

And, since he'd met Dodge, the whole town had gone mad.

"Sam, darling? Can't we talk? I—love you, Sam! Please let me in."

Lenny tiptoed to the door. He heard her breathing heavily. Thought he felt her damp need through an inch of hard wood. He had to do something—but what?

"Sam," she cried, "you must be there!"

"Harriet," he said, "that you?"

"Oh, *Sam.* Thank God. I thought—"

"Dear girl, I tremble to think what you must have been—"

"Sam, let me *in,* darling. Open the door!"

"I can't . . . I have—a fever." (God. He'd almost slipped and said the flu. But did they *have* the flu yet?)

"Let me in. I'll help you. I'll—smother you with kisses!"

"No!"

"Oh . . ." There was a second's silence. Then Harriet's voice simply melted with love. "You don't want to give me your fever. Oh, Sam."

"Yes," Lenny cried, "that's it!"

"God bless you, dear. You stay right here. I'm going to fetch you a doctor."

"GOD, NO!" Lenny opened the door, just a couple of inches, bracing the base with his foot. Through the opening her mustache came at him like a squealing bat. Then her fingers, wriggling. Lenny gulped and kissed the tips.

"Sam," she cooed, "when you do that . . ."

"Oh, Harriet." *(Think, man! What!)* "You are my dear, sweet, adorable lamb. But you're ruining . . . my surprise."

"A surprise?" she asked him. "In there, Sam? I don't understand."

"It's nothing," he said. "Come on in." He did not budge his foot, though.

"But no, Sam, not if it's—"

"I'm sure Mother was just being foolish. She used to say it was bad luck for the bride to see—"

"The *bride*," Harriet whispered.

"Come in."

"Why, Sam, I *couldn't*! But . . ." Harriet lowered his eyes. She dared not ask. Yet could not stop. "Have you decided . . ."

"When?" Lenny asked. He smiled, his heart thumping. "In one more week, my darling. The twentieth of April. I've been preparing our—love nest."

"Oh, my. And will I see you—"

"Of course," Lenny said. "We'll have a lot of plans to make. I'll see you Wednesday, the eighteenth. Trust me, my darling. Be patient. I'll have it *all* taken care of by then."

Lenny stood at the window to make sure she'd gone. She blew him a kiss from the walk.

He stayed at the window, surveying the street through a small gap of the shade. He stayed there, brooding, for minutes. Until he heard the angry barks:

"Stop!"

"Halt!"

"Hold fast, or we'll shoot!"

A lone finger, streaking past, whipped something out of his pocket and spun, screaming, "I ain't strange!"

He went down in a volley of bullets.

Lenny stepped back from the window. He paced the room in an agonized funk.

He had to believe he had Time on his side.

He slipped the key from his pocket.

Opened the door to his shrine.

Lit one of the three joints remaining.

And prayed.

He couldn't wait for Halley's. It had to be now, or the dream would be lost.

V

April 12. Thursday.

Wolf was waiting, as instructed, when they paged him to to the phone.

He hadn't slept two hours straight since that fateful meeting. The loss of control over the column seemed fraught with some ghastly potential for ruin.

(We are the hollow men . . .)

If he could remember just one or two more lines, the rest would come; it had to. Then he wouldn't need the man he could not trust, and yet dared not betray.

But for now, at least, Wolf did. And so he scrambled to the phone.

The voice was cool, the message short.

"Eight A.M. Tomorrow. Sharp. Corner of Market and Geary. Alone."

Wolf returned to his table. He lit up a Trophy. The drunks by the window had started their game: this evening, the Wolfing of Shakespeare.

He thought, it's all right. I'll be fine. I'll do this thing, for just one piece. Just one to get me started. My genius will become firmly established. Then I'll leave town. Why shouldn't I? I'll go somewhere. But . . . I don't know. I can't do that. Who'll look after *Monster Time*?

VI

The theater had emptied and all of the actors were gone. About half of the crowd left when it was announced Lord Whittaker had failed to show. The rest straggled steadily through the first two acts, despite the understudy's heroic efforts with the part. Whittaker was Whittaker. And the crowd would not settle for less.

The stage hands left.

The watchman left.

David Francis Kelley had decided to stay for a while, alone.

Lord Whittaker, he thought. That's that. We shall not see his likes again. Some disaster, certainly. Nothing but death or disaster could keep *that* man off stage. But, by the gods, I've never seen a Hamlet like last night's. Everything before that had been mere magnificence. Last night, that was mastery.

Kelley felt a sudden draft rippling from the rear, and looked up from the edge of the stage where he sat.

Far and away, in the very last row, he saw two flickering lavender sparks.

Then he heard the chuckle, low, yet still somehow filling the theater.

"Who is it?" Kelley managed.

"The new Hamlet, asshole," purred a voice the same shade as the eyes.

ZOO STORY

Security precautions. That was what they told the priest in answer to each question.

Why had they waited till well after three to phone Father Duffy in Oakland, when she'd been asking since last night? There'd be scarcely enough time to see her before catching the last ferry out.

Security precautions.

What was she doing, locked up in her cell, when the phone call had said she was injured?

Security precautions. If she was gonna go trippin' all over her cell, leavin' half her teeth on the floor, so it went. The prison doc was quite busy enough with prisoners who weren't *strange.*

And why were they searching him now, head to foot?

Security precautions.

"Besides, Father," one guard said, taking him aside. "Consider yourself lucky." The man, whom he had baptized, slipped from one coat pocket a familiar-looking Bible. "I find this opened in her cell. Kind of a curious Bible . . . wouldn't you say so, now, Father?"

"Jimmy," Father Duffy said.

"Now, don't you Jimmy me. If I didn't know you better, I'd slip you in a cell. And that's where I'll still put you if we see any more of your tricks. She can keep that rosary and that deucin' glass ring she says brings her luck. But they'll be no more notes from you. Not unless we see 'em first." He slipped the first note from his vest. It had been carefully folded. He pressed it in the old man's hand. "She ate the other one before I could see it."

"Forgive me, Jimmy. I'm just an old man. The notes were nothing, just ramblings and prayers."

"Let's go. You've got five minutes. And, Father?"

"Yes, my son."

"If I even hear one word that sounds remotely strange, I swear on the grave of my mother . . ."

Father Duffy nodded. The five minutes they'd allowed him now seemed like an eternity. He wanted to be on the ferry, headed back to Oakland, where the shadow was still spreading but the horror did not live yet.

He was led across the quad to the front of the stockade. A second stockade had just been completed. And the air was heavy with hammer thwacks and hums of saws busily building another.

They took him up one flight of stairs to the cell at the end of the hall. One guard stood on either side, his pistol at the ready.

Through the barred window of her door, he saw her standing at one wall, gazing at the skyline.

"Daughter?" Father Duffy said.

She turned, gave a tiny cry, and ran to the door, smiling. He saw the ruins of her teeth and blinked back the tears.

But her own expression was joyous. She called his name as she reached through the bars.

Father Duffy heard the clicks of hammers to the left and to the right.

He stepped back, just out of reach, and told her, "Easy. Easy, child." Then angrily, to the right, to Jimmy, "I want her put into the hospital now!"

The man looked back unflinchingly, and then looked at his watch. "You're down to four minutes now, Father."

"Then let me hear her confession in peace."

"You'll hear her confession with us standing by. Or you won't hear it at all."

"Father," the woman said. "It's okay. They're only doing their jobs. Let them be my witnesses, before God, that I repent."

Father Duffy nodded. To know she was safe was an excellent thing. Still, clearly, there could be no way for useful words to pass.

But then the woman did something that made the priest wonder if that was quite right. The woman, Betsy, winked, sucked in some air through the fragments of teeth, and began confessing in a loud, clear tone of voice.

"Bless me, Father, for I have sinned. It has been sixteen years since my last confession. I have fornicated with abandon, with about a hundred men . . ."

The guards looked at one another, stunned, then at Father Duffy. "Hey, Father," said Jimmy, "let's . . . keep it down a little."

"But in the past year," the blond woman continued, "I've been especially lustful. I just couldn't get enough. I discovered cucumbers . . . the pleasures of bananas . . . sometimes both at once. I learned a small trick with my fingers that I really must confess . . ."

"All right," cried Jimmy, "there'll be no more of this— this filth! Confession's over." He grabbed the priest's arm fiercely.

Father Duffy broke free of him, roaring, "If I leave without hearing confession, I will damn your soul to hell!"

"It's filthiness!"

"It is *confession,* you fool! It is a confession of *sins.* Now stand back!"

The man did. And a bit further back than he had stood. His partner took a few steps to the right.

"Now," Father Duffy advised her, "a little more softly then, daughter. We mustn't shock the guards."

Betsy winked again. Began. "Well, it was kind of tricky. I had to use certain muscles to hold the cucumber in place . . . and another set of muscles to hold in the banana. Then I'd get a rhythm going with my left second finger . . ."

"For God's sake!" Jimmy cried.

"Madness!" cried his partner.

Each of the men took a half-step away, staring at the flooring.

And Betsy whispered, *"Yes, caped angel flew the Bay,"* before starting up with abandon again.

And that's the way confession went. A full four minutes of obscene, revolting nonsense, with single whispered lines between, her real message to the priest.

When he was put on the ferry, Father Duffy was advised:

"If it's all the same to you, Father, she won't be confessin' again for a while."

The priest nodded sadly. But in his heart he was yowling with joy. He reassembled the lines in his mind, repeating the poem as they sailed:

> Yes, caped angel flew the Bay.
> The Lord Jesus had no say.
> But when the hyena laughed,
> *Ringed* him for his epitaph.
> There's a chance he may go far,
> even with the facial scar.
> But now at night safe sleep I take—
> How sweet it was to bite that snake!

He would phone the man in black, the small man who called himself Paladin now, the instant he got back to Oakland.

Joy now.

Joy and hope.

The ring they'd soaked in strychnine had saved the woman's life.

The creature could be beaten.

And, if any man could do it, Father Duffy had faith in the man with the curls.

But the priest was troubled still by the failure of the cross.

FEAR AND LOATHING ON THE SAN FRANCISCO BAY

It was a beautiful morning that Friday, the thirteenth, and we had the beach, Wolf and I, to ourselves.

I'd phoned the Palace last evening, checking on my messages—and learned I'd had an urgent call from my friend F.D. A few minutes later, the joyous news was mine. But I'd stayed up a long, long time, debating how to play Wolf. I dared not show him the column. There was no way of knowing how close the tabs Austin kept on Wolf were. But Wolf had to have a reason why he must not see the column. A scared Wolf might be useful. But a paranoid Wolf was too risky for me. Besides, for all my cunning, there were questions I still couldn't answer: Was Wolf, in truth, responsible? Did he not deserve a chance? And how could I give him a chance . . . a small chance . . . while using him to my own ends?

Wolf's reaction to the boathouse was much the same as mine had been. We were still, at fifty yards, pretty well downwind of it. But not of that elusive, eerie sense of *badness.*

"Why can't we talk *here*?" Wolf said.

I'd scarcely said three words to him since picking him up at that corner.

"I want to show you something." I gave his sleeve a tug. "Come on."

"I want to know what's going on. I won't take another step." Wolf crossed his arms defiantly. He looked like he meant it.

I lit up a fresh cheroot, took a good long puff, exhaled. "We are the hollow men . . ."

I started off for the boathouse myself. It wasn't long before I heard his scrambling, sandy plops behind.

"Wait."

"Come along, Wolf. Trust me. This is what it's all about."

The sense of badness grew and grew until, with one step very much like another, the first whiff of that godawful *ripeness* kicked in. And that, again, just got worse with each step.

Twenty yards.

"What's going on?"

"Come along, Wolf. Trust me."

Ten yards.

He started babbling. "I don't need this shit . . . No way . . . Fuck the poem . . . I'll be okay . . . I can make it . . . He—He . . . Can't remember . . . It's okay . . ."

"Come along, Wolf." I just walked, eager to have done with this and know where we both stood.

I got him to within five yards without having to threaten to shoot him.

But, there, it was just what things came to.

Wolf put his hands on his hips like a kid. "I'm not going—over there. You can't make me."

"Yes, I can." I slipped out the derringer. Cocked it. Aimed it at one knee.

"But then—"

"I don't get the column in. You'll be on the street with a cup and one knee. Come on, Wolfy, take a look. Immortality isn't for sissies."

"I can't," Wolf cried. "He—He . . ."

I ground out the cheroot with one boot in the sand. Mis-

quoted old Tommy again. "Dare I then to eat a peach . . .
Oh, I grow old, yes, I grow old . . ."

"Yes," Wolf gushed, "I know that—I hear it in my sleep!"

I slipped the gun back in my vest. "Then trust me. Take a
look."

I turned, pointing with one hand to the window in back of
the boat shed.

It took Wolf a little while to get the hang of it, moving his
feet. The smell had grown riper and worse, a lot worse.

He made it, though. He was a trooper.

And I was glad the phaeton was a hundred yards away.

I hope I never live to hear a man scream quite like Wolf
did.

On the way back I had all I could do to keep up with
Wolfy. He moved about half the time on his feet and the
other half, when he tripped, on all fours.

I reasoned with him as we strolled. "Now, I need you.
And you need me. So, trust me when I tell you: you *will* be
paid a visit after Sunday's column."

"Who?" Wolf begged.

"It's better, friend, if you don't know. In fact, the less you
know the better."

"For God's sake—"

"Listen. Your visitor won't like my column one bit. You
mustn't see the column. You mustn't know *what* it's about.
If you do . . ." I jerked my thumb back at the boathouse.

"But—" Wolf was on all fours again, half scrambling up
and then tripping again.

I made my way. Time was short. "You do *not* know. You
must *not* know. Keep what you know in your head. You
submitted the column that *you* wrote. Fact. I threatened to
blow off your kneecap. Fact. You never *saw* the column.
Fact. Don't run. Don't hide. He'll find you. Just stay in your
room. And on Sunday he'll come. Think about nothing except the damn facts. You *didn't* know, you got that? He may
just believe you."

"He . . ." Wolf had a serious block with the word. Nothing on his screen but snow where Austin Blacke or Sam had

been. But, underneath the snow, a speck of nameless, immeasurable dread. Wolf was on his feet, and how.

"What if—*he* doesn't believe me?"

The phaeton was waiting for us where we'd had the driver park.

I stopped. I turned. I studied Wolf and thought about that last *what if.* I set both of my hands on his shoulders.

"If all else fails, then you have this: I know the date of the Big One."

"Dear God . . ."

"April twenty-fourth," I said. "Caruso's last performance."

Wolf babbled incoherently.

"Things get bad, you tell our friend that you know the date of the Quake. He'll like that. It's just his style. But what you're gonna do, see, is feed him the wrong date. You've got to scramble the facts in your mind. *Believe* it when you tell him—that the date of the Quake's the eighteenth."

"But why?"

"Because I want him on edge. The eighteenth is when I take him *out.*"

Wolf grabbed my arm, holding on for dear life. "The twenty-fourth? You're sure of that?"

I focused, hard, practicing what I'd just preached to Wolf. The twenty-fourth, I told myself. *(The twenty-fourth— right, Lenny?)* "You better believe it," I told him. "The twenty-fourth this town rocks to the ground."

We proceeded to the *Call.* I watched Wolf walk into the lobby as if he were crossing Death Row. He handed Miss Perky the envelope, sealed, turned away without a word, and came back to the phaeton. He didn't look at all as if he'd had a reprieve from the chair.

"Relax," I told him. "All is well. As long as that column sees the front page exactly as I wrote it."

I dropped Wolf off at the corner where I'd picked him up before.

"You get what you want Tuesday night. I'll phone you that evening at six."

Wolf closed the door. He clutched at the edge of the

window with two beefy paws. "I swear to God, you fuck with me . . ."

"Hey, you know who I am. You know I'm at the Palace, right? You put my ass on the Rock."

Wolf started to go. Then turned abruptly, a glint of cunning in his eyes.

"The twenty-fourth?" he asked again.

I said, "Absolutely."

"But—on the eighteenth . . ."

"That's the game."

"What—time will you be there?" Wolf asked.

I thought about that glint and said, "He's gonna think it's dawn."

"Ah, but it won't be?"

"Nope. I'll be there at five. But, for God's sake, man, don't tell *him* that!"

"No—I wouldn't. Of course not. He—he . . ."

HAMLET REDUX

 I checked out of the Carlton and moved across town, while keeping my room at the Palace. I holed up in my room at the Cliff House, doing situps and pushups and pivots and whirls. And thinking, *Strychnine . . . That's a start. Way to go, Betsy!*

The madness downtown would get worse by the hour and it was too much to risk. Where there weren't cops, there were Guardsmen. Where there weren't Guardsmen, there was something worse: the sight of men with downcast eyes, walking the streets like scared rats in a maze . . . while kids on passing street cars giggled and screamed:

"STRRRRRAAAAANNNNNGE!"

I kicked back in my room with the paper, after the workout was over. I read:

—Since April 1, when Wolf's column began, thirty-five new prisoners—each reported *strange*—had arrived on Alcatraz.

—A third stockade was being built, and more cells might soon be needed above the original guardhouse.

—Autopsies of the five *Zonies* who'd died had been inconclusive. Specimens of blood and skin, and some internal organs, had been dispatched to Washington.

—Blood and urine samples were now being taken from all on the Rock. Until doctors had determined a method for ID-ing AIDS, citizens were cautioned not to drink from others' glasses . . . or exchange "bodily fluids" . . . Citizens were urged to watch for symptoms of exhaustion . . . a general sense of malaise . . . not just in themselves but in everyone else . . .

—Extensive questioning, by Washington officials, had begun on Alcatraz. While many of the prisoners answered most questions with ease—their powers of adapting growing stronger by the day—all of them evidenced undeniable symptoms of strangeness. Some did not know the president. Some did not know the mayor. Some could not identify the number of states in the Union . . . the capitol of Washington . . . the plot of *Huckleberry Finn* . . .

—Authorities still entertained another possibility: that the *Zonies* were not from the future at all—but had been sent from Russia or Germany or China.

—A blond prisoner, Betsy Atkinson, refused to answer questions. Until she'd "consulted a lawyer." She had been placed last evening into solitary. And there she would remain until authorities determined if *Zonies* had rights under law.

—Frank McGuane, *Call* editor, would not divulge the whereabouts of *Zonie* author Wolf. The courts would soon decide whether he could be compelled under law.

—There had been a riot in a downtown theater: a crowd, driven to madness by the strangeness of two comics, had torn the men to pieces.

—A body had been found, yesterday, in Chinatown, apparently savaged by dogs. Exact details were not given, but the mutilation, according to the *Call*, was "horrid" and "unspeakable."

I flipped ahead, taking all of this in, growing sicker at heart with each page. The town needed the Quake as a desert needs rain.

In the entertainment section, there was a tiny notice: apologies to theatergoers for Lord Whittaker's no-show last evening. His lordship's throat had been ailing. But tonight the actor would return with the best Hamlet ever.

Well, I had bigger worries than whether or not Hamlet showed.

So I lay low, in my room, through the day and into nightfall, figuring, refiguring.

Would the column run on Sunday? That much I could figure on. I'd baited Wolf good and proper.

Would he survive Austin's visit? There was no way to figure that. Any more than I could figure if I was right in using him. But his odds were better than those he'd been dealing the town.

To survive, he'd have to talk. That much I could bank on. He'd feed Blacke the "real" date of the Quake in a hurry *(The twenty-fourth—right, Lenny?)*. Plus the "real" time I'd be there.

I did not begrudge him that.

What bothered me was that last glint in his eyes.

I kept hoping that Wolf would survive our next game. But I dreaded that I'd have to kill him.

So, I had lots to think about besides old Lord Whittaker's no-show.

But the next morning, when breakfast was brought, along with the Saturday *Call*, I found myself thinking of *Hamlet*, all right. Lord Whittaker's latest performance had just made the front page.

A HAMLET FOR THE AGES
LORD WHITTAKER RETURNS, REBORN!

Mere words cannot describe the devastating power of Lord Whittaker's Hamlet last evening. Men and women remained in their seats, exhausted and weeping unstoppable tears.

It was at once Lord Whittaker. And it was not Lord Whittaker.

At intervals, in the first act, the tone seemed almost listless, the gestures somehow empty. But the rhythm was hypnotic; the delivery mesmerizing.

Lord Whittaker seemed somehow—broader.

His rich baritone seldom rose above a low, gruff purr.

The face was undeniably Lord Whittaker's—yet not. The short, but vivid, jagged scar . . .

No need to read any further.

You're a bold one, you, I thought.

After breakfast, I phoned the Majestic and booked myself a tenth row seat for Tuesday, April 17.

And then I set into more pushups and situps and pivots and whirls and techniques.

Now he was out in the open.

He wanted me.

And I would come; in my own time, though, not his.

Me and my beautiful plans for his feet.

Meanwhile, I'd lie low.

Tomorrow morning, in the *Call,* the giggles were on me.

And our friend Austin Blacke wasn't going to like them one bit.

GIGGLES

Sunday morning. The fifteenth.

Austin Blacke, blond and tanned and feeling very Beautiful despite the pink scar on his cheek, was enjoying a breakfast of salmon and eggs. The meal, he would *pass* in a couple of hours. But he would bear forever the final pale reminder of the treachery of women.

The oafish one . . . She'd been prepared. Had somebody—a woman?—finally put it together: That there was only one way off the Rock? A crucifix scented with garlic . . . Of course, that's just the way they'd figure it. But the ring had been coated with strychnine. . . .

Where had that come from?

And how had *she* guessed?

(And where the hell was Harpo?)

"Sir?"

A white-jacketed waiter beside him, silver pot ready to pour.

"Yes," Blacke said. "More coffee. It's sweet."

"It is? I'll get another pot. Must be some sugar in it."

"No, no. Give me more. I always liked my coffee sweet."

"I see . . . Well, here you go."

Blacke asked the waiter as he poured, "Where is everybody?"

The room was empty, except for the table a young man and woman were led to.

The waiter shrugged. "The news, sir. Folks seem to be staying at home."

Austin said, agreeably, "But it's pleasant to watch people reading the news."

At that, the waiter left him, looking once over his shoulder.

Austin returned to his salmon and eggs. He never read Wolf's drivel. He preferred to do exactly what he'd told the waiter: over a meal of sweet coffee and dead food, watch men's eyes widen in horror and fear. That was the right way to read news, he thought.

But all was well, all was well.

(The fucking bitch—she bit my cock!)

There were so many ways to feed, and so many new ways to learn.

(I'll go back—I WILL go—when I'm damn good and ready. . . .)

For now, there was Hamlet, with its alluring vaudeville: mortals dreaming of the heights. It had begun as a lark, that first night: a playful variation of the trick with the two comics. He'd had the Actor's face and blood, and had always hated waste. He'd only half-expected, though, just how amusing it would be. And what had taken Austin Blacke completely by surprise was the surge of energy. The kick of it—the thrill of it!—to *show* them in the Blackest way what their dreams amounted to. It felt like feeding, almost, on the blood from his own heart.

"S.F. *Call!* S.F. *Call!* Anybody, S.F. *Call?*"

Newsboy, perched at the lace-paneled door, a folded paper in hand.

The well-dressed woman, back to Blacke, was sent an agreeable *push* and chirped, "Boy, could we have a paper, please?"

The paper was delivered.

Austin Blacke sat back to wait as the covering comics were peeled from the *Call.*

The woman paused to study the familiar banner:

MONSTER TIME!

And the red letters beneath it:

GIGGLE!
GIGGLE!
GIGGLE!

"What *is* this?" Austin heard her say.

Her companion chuckled. "Come on, honey, turn the page. What's old Wolf up to this time?"

The page was turned.

The woman gawked, leaning in and over. "Good heaven," she said, "a hyena?" The man slid his chair in beside hers. "What the deuce," he said softly. "In love with a *hyena*?"

Blacke was there in five hot steps to snatch the paper from her hands.

"But, sir—" she said.

"See here!" said the man.

But he was off with a scowl and a *squeeze* that doubled both over the table.

He read:

> *Gigglegigglegiggle!*
> *Gather round again, my friends, this time for a break from the horror. This week, Uncle Wolfy will tell you of a Zonie he knew on the train . . . a pathetic, lonely fool . . . who fell in love with a—*
> > *HYENA!*
> *(WHOOOOOOOOOOOOOOOOPPPPPPPPPPPPP!)*
> *Now, I know what you're thinking. You're thinking not even a mother could love the*
> *vilest*
> *and the ugliest*
> *coward of the jungle.*
> *HOW ugly is a hyena? HOW vile? HOW disgusting?*
> *Well-l-l-l-l . . .*

Blacke speed-read the rest of it, in a crazed trot to the street. He'd just closed the door to the hansom when he reached the clincher:

> *But, as bad as things are, there's still hope for our friend.*
> *The Zonie—Mr. Giggles?—has been invited to be cured. The cure will be administered, if Giggles has the*

*nerve, in a sandy setting, beside his favorite "restaurant,"
this Wednesday morning at dawn.*
    (WHOOOOOPPPPP-EEEEE!)

Blacke screamed, "Move this thing!"
The driver cracked the whip.
The horses whinnied and started to race for the Montgomery Block.

LORD HYENA

Wolf was waiting for the end to come the only way he knew: on his knees, before the door.

(You will be paid a visit . . .)

He remembered the bones in the boathouse and cried out, again, in terror. What was the connection, though? What was a hyena to *him*?

(He—)

(I don't know any Aus—I forget . . .)

Three days . . . He could do it . . . It would be all over Wednesday . . . If he could just . . .

(Focus! Focus on the facts! You did not know . . . You do not know . . .)

Wolf was focusing, intently, when the door to his room just exploded.

And, coming at him through the frame, and over the door that had fallen, was—

"WHOOOOOOOPPPPPP!"

—a tanned, absurdly handsome face, already changing obscenely.

Wolf opened his arms in surrender and wailed.

"Master! Lord Hyena!"

"Lord?" The creature stopped and studied him.

"Hear me," Wolf cried. "*Master!* I have things to tell you . . ."

ONE PERFECT DAY

Monday, the sixteenth of April.

And I was alive in the Cliff House, lying low and listening to the surf and sea lions below.

I kept thinking of the train . . . Blacke's leather duster around him like wings . . . me lying there and thinking, Master . . .

Blacke would be there on those golf links, putting balls marked "Babylon," "Egypt," and "America," when all of us and all our dreams were nothing but ashes and dust.

When we looked in his eyes, we were mastered, perhaps, by the power of conviction: his, that he *was* a master of Time . . . ours, that we were Time's fools or its slaves.

But . . . were we slaves *because* we passed?

Or could there be mastery in that?

Lions and hyenas . . .

Where could the lion be in a man's heart . . . if not in his mortality?

Suddenly, I felt an urge, wholly irresistible, for one, just one, perfect day. Before an Age died in the Big One.

It is the poetry in us, this day. The poetry of *being* here, fully here, then passing.

It is my cab driver, wrapped to the waist in a torn-edged blanket, cracking his whip as we clipclop along.

It is the Palace. The Palace will pass. The Palace will pass with its gold cuspidors, its lobby paved with silver, its toilets lidded with Chippendale seats. The Palace will pass into myth, which will pass, until nothing remains of the Palace at all. But today, God's breath has graced the scene. The Palace is blessed by the Sweet Spot in Time.

Yes, the Eighties were good. And the Sixties were good. All Ages pass. And all are good. And this one, in passing, especially good.

The Sweet Spot stops at Les Grenouilles, its window filled with live frogs and turtles . . . soon to be Frog Legs à la Poulette and Terrapin à la Mayfair.

The Sweet Spot loves the Poodle Dog and other "supper bedrooms" . . . where ground-floor respectability strips off another layer with every floor you climb.

The Sweet Spot blesses one and all, not despite but because of the fact: They will pass.

And they are the poetry in us.

The Bridge will come. And the Bridge will be good. But now there is no Bridge and no Bridge is good. Men ferry now across the Bay in lovely ships that too will pass, and with their passing too will pass a way of regarding oneself and one's world.

The Sweet Spot loves the city, always, exactly as it is.

It loves the snorting, magnificent horses that pull our gleaming hansoms.

It loves the crimson cable cars, trundling up and trundling down, and rumbling over the joints of the rails.

The Sweet Spot loves the S.F. Zoo, where I tell the driver to park for a while. I stand before a massive cage, where one lion is stretched out superbly. The lion yawns and studies me, shrewdly yet indifferently. I can see the poetry in its powerful, rippling haunches. But the real poetry comes when I giggle, like Blacke. The king springs to all fours with a ferocious roar. I match it with one of my own. The lion cocks its head and blinks. Clearly, this will take some work. But I know I have one good one in me somewhere. And one is all I'll need for Blacke.

The Sweet Spot is still savoring this perfect, perfect day as we clippityclop along Mason . . . to see Lenny Dirks walking home to his flat.

I call out to the driver.

The carriage is stopped.

I must see Lenny one more time.

THE BIG SPLIT

"What do you want?" Lenny asked me, on guard.

I smiled, still standing by the door. I wouldn't be staying that long. "You know what."

Len, after letting me in—convinced I wasn't Harriet—had taken a seat on the settee. He hadn't looked at me since. Until now.

"You knew," he said. "You knew all along."

"No. Caruso's picture . . . It was like some bell went off, but nothing I could figure."

"So, how then?" Lenny asked me.

"Well . . . that Sunday morning your voice got all excited. It had to be the twenty-fourth—Caruso's *last* performance. You insisted on that. But all the while you were talking . . . you kept looking at your shoe. I thought that was really weird. But, hell, I thought, I'm paranoid."

Lenny groaned. "Jesus. And from that you figured—"

"No. No, it took a while. I just kept remembering you staring at your shoe. And hearing *last performance*. One day I just *knew* that you'd been lying to me. We go back a long, long way. So, I figured you'd lie the way I would. If *I* knew the date of the Quake was Caruso's *first* performance —if I weren't certain what *you* knew and I wanted to mislead you—I'd insist on just the opposite. I'd say I remembered *because* . . ."

Lenny lit a cigarette. He didn't offer me one. Or offer any denials.

"Got something up your sleeve," I said.

"Nope." Lenny stared at his shoe.

I said, "Stop that."

Lenny stopped that and blurted, voice cracking, "Christ!

You've fucked it up here, man, just like you did there. Four more years—I can't wait."

I said, "What the hell are you talking about?"

Len's eyes drifted to his shoe. He pulled them away with a vengeance. "You don't need the comet to go, man! It could be a train wreck or a plane wreck or . . . an earthquake."

"Aw, Jesus, Lenny, say it isn't so," I said.

Len ground out his cigarette. "All you need's a catalyst. Anything works if you're *ready*."

"So, you're . . . checking out in the Big One."

"I'm goin' *back* in the Big One. Let me go, man, will you? Jesus, just get out of here." Len jumped up, started pacing the room. "I don't want any of your negative shit. I tell you, I can pull it off."

I might have said a lot of things. But I had had a perfect day. And so, I said, "Go to it."

Lenny stood, framed in the door to his shrine.

I stood at the main door, one foot in the hall.

He said, "Good-bye."

I said, "Good luck. And say hello to Janis."

I never saw him again.

HEY BOY

Tuesday. April 17. I had had my perfect day. Now it was back to business.

Wolfy and Blacke and the Big One . . . The three together—or bust.

And so I set out after breakfast, traveling discreetly by hansom, to find myself a carpenter who wouldn't ask too many questions.

The length of the stakes was no problem: five feet.

Or the fact that I wanted them tapered, halfway, and sharpened on top down to pinheads.

But two of the requirements raised three pairs of eyebrows. The men didn't mind letting me know this seemed *strange:* wood stakes with the strength of steel . . . and not just round, but *thin*round . . . to the narrowest diameter that could sustain a deadfall of, say, two hundred pounds?

The fourth, though, got into the spirit right off. A problem of logistics.

"How many of 'em will you need?"

"I think thirteen will do it," I said.

"An' how soon do you need 'em?"

"Five."

"That'll cost you extra," he said.

I told him Fine, and asked him if he might know a good gunsmith.

"You mean a discreet sort of gentleman."

"Yeah."

"Well, that'll cost you extra too."

The gunsmith charged me extra too. Not for the Colt—nothing *strange* about that. But for the one silver bullet I'd need . . .

"Reckon this is the right way to stop 'em?" he asked.

"Stop who?"

"You know—*Zonies.*"

"I thought you were discreet," I said.

"Oh, I am. I am that. But if it works, you let me know."

"Will that cost me extra too?"

The old man winked. "That'll be on the house."

Now, you might think a crucifix wouldn't have posed any problem.

But here the obstacle wasn't discretion, or finding a cross in the right size and shape.

(The Lord Jesus had no say . . .)

The problem I encountered was finding a cross that was garish enough. A truly spectacular failure.

It took me a couple of visits. But on my third stop-off I found one.

The cross was fully one-foot high. Aluminum, edged with fool's gold—hysterically and transparently fake. The figure had been so cloddishly done that it was worse than blasphemous: the screaming Jesus was . . . a hoot. It looked like it was singing. Its wounds were the same shade of ruby as the Cracker Jacks-prize stones at each end of the cross.

They didn't charge me extra there. They might have just paid me to take it.

But, with luck, the cross would help keep Austin from spotting the cheesecloth.

Well, of course I needed cheesecloth. The whole point of digging a series of holes that you *expect* to be found . . . is to protect the *other* holes, the ones you *don't* want to be found. Now, if those holes were covered with cheesecloth, and the cheesecloth were properly sprinkled with sand, by moonlight they might not be seen.

I wanted Austin split right up the middle: rattled, even reckless . . . and yet supremely confident. I wanted him thinking he had the game figured down to the last particulars: a clown on the beach with a big, useless gun . . . a joke cross . . . and nine holes that Austin had spotted right off.

The cheesecloth would be for the holes with the stakes that I'd be lacing with strychnine.

With the holes, there were two little problems.

I couldn't dig the holes by day, without risking discovery by Blacke.

From eight o'clock that evening, Austin *ought* to be on stage, allowing a few hours' freedom. But the only way to know for sure would be to keep watch on the theater. And I needed to be in the city to play out the last hand with Wolf.

So, the only perfect time to dig was when I *couldn't* be there on the beach.

I remembered Paladin.

And remembered Hey Boy, who lived, it seemed, to serve him.

I remembered Chan, the newsboy.

I didn't think Chan lived to serve anyone.

But I did think that he might be Hey Boy for a few hours for hire.

"You crazy, hey." Chan tugged his cap and glared at me through the opened cab door. "I gettin' in no cab, hey," Chan jerked his finger at my feet, "with man in high-heel boots."

Whoops.

I smiled, quite still on my seat by the door.

"We'll go around the block one time. I've got a proposition—"

"Hey." Chan's lips were simply quivering with rage. What was he, a pinkieboy?

"Business, boy. It's business. I've got a little job—"

"Aaah, I don't need no job, hey." Chan gave his pockets a jingle beneath the newsboy's apron. From the sounds of it, *Monster Time* had been very good to Chan.

"It'll take you two hours this evening," I said.

"Busy," Chan said. Then, "Hey, that's a *strange* outfit you're wearin'. All black." He smiled shrewdly, looking right. "Cops and Guardsmen down the street. Maybe I call 'em. You gimme an eagle."

I sighed. "Go ahead and call 'em. Maybe one of them—"

"*Hey* . . ." Chan's eyes lit up. "I 'member that. I know you." He pointed across Mason Street to Lenny Dirks' flat. "You live up there, hey? You change face."

Well, I thought, it had been a good plan. But if money didn't move him—

Wait.

"I'll bet I can show you something that'll frighten you out of your wits. You win, I pay three eagles. I win, then you do the job and I will call you Hey Boy."

"Ha! I ain't scared of nothin', hey, and I ain't no Hey Boy."

"Well . . . you're scared to gamble."

"Hey."

"It's all right. You're just a kid."

"I ain't no kid."

"Then get in the cab."

Chan walked right up to the door of the cab as if he might spit in my eye.

"You gimme that gun in your pocket first, hey."

Devious, cunning, and sly little boy!

I slipped Chan the derringer.

He walked around the other side.

He took a seat with the gun on his knee.

"Scary, hey?" he asked me.

"Scary, hey."

"Big scary?"

"Yep."

"I like that, hey. Chan not afraid."

"EEEEEEEEEEEEEEEEEEEEEEE!"

That was Chan coming out of the boathouse.

We'd left the hansom a hundred yards back and he'd done a lot better than Wolf on the way. A few nervous looks at me and pointings of the pistol as the smell got worse and worse. Snatches of some ditty whistled just under his breath. A little slowing of the pace, but no stoppings and no turnings back.

At the door, I'd stopped him, thinking to prepare him. I'd

had just a quick glimpse from the window that night. This was going to be a lot worse. But there had been no stopping Chan, who opened the door with a sneer and walked in.

It had taken him all of five seconds to *see:* the fresh bodies suspended from hooks on the wall, two of them minus their faces . . . bits and pieces of bones on the floor . . . the fraction of skull I had seen that last night . . . and a headless torso split right down the middle, ripe pickings for sandflies and crabs . . .

Now, on the way out, he came barreling, screaming, and swinging his arms like a windmill, taking me down with him onto the sand.

I carried him off, in both arms, round the back, close to the Bay where the air was less ripe.

"I need your help," I told him. "Chan."

I set him down. Forced his head to his knees, waiting while he whooped and gasped, a little like Ghost Boy, for breath.

"Hey—" Chan started. "Hey—"

"Son . . ."

"Chan struggled up. He was fierce-eyed through tears. "Hey—Boy," Chan said. "I—lose."

"No." I put one arm around him. "We win if you help me, Chan."

"Hey—Boy!"

"Hey Boy, then," I told him. "Look, I don't have much money, son . . ."

He knocked me over, crazy-armed, breaking away from my grasp.

"Money?" he screamed. "Pieces! That all it make, hey—*pieces*!"

I had never seen, not in my time, or this, a look of such unbridled fury.

Chan jerked his finger at me as if it were a sword.

"Hey Boy," he said, "dig for free. What your name?"

"Paladin."

"Hey. Paladin and Hey Boy."

"You got it, partner. Let's kick ass."

BUTTERFLIES

So, there I was back in the Cliff House on the eve of an end of an Age.

On the bed, two burlap sacks. The first held nine *untreated* stakes, made to my specifications: five-foot lengths of premium pine, one inch in diameter, tapered from the halfway point to hideously needled tips. The second sack contained four more, except these had been treated with strychnine. A lot. I didn't want Hey Boy confusing the stakes. There was a fifty-fifty chance I'd end in one of the *nine* holes while luring Blacke to the *four*. I might, with luck survive the stake . . . but I didn't relish the strychnine.

On the bed, beside the sacks, was a carpetbag containing: the ludi-cross and my new Colt. The old-time Frontier Six-Shooter, with its twelve-inch barrel, weighed almost as much as my arm. It contained two bullets, each of which, the gunsmith said, might stop a moving train. The third, and last, bullet was silver. I hoped it might stop Austin Blacke if I couldn't get him on one of those stakes.

Butterflies . . . Butterflies . . .

Hey Boy would pick up the two sacks at six at the corner of Mason and Geary. From there he'd lie low for a couple of hours, then stop off at the theater at eight. If I'd learned Blacke was on stage, then Hey Boy got the go-ahead.

He'd have less than three hours to hit the beach, dig the holes, and split. Regardless of whether he'd finished. He was to proceed to the ferry and *wait*, with no explanation why. I remembered people ferrying, after the Big One, to Oakland. What safer place to send him? What other way to warn him . . . without appearing *strange*?

Butterflies . . . Butterflies . . .

The challenge read dawn.

And I'd told Wolfy five.

And so, Austin might get there at four, even three.

But, really, could I *bank* on that?

I'd figured I'd get there at two, maybe one.

But even so . . . Even so . . .

Think: worst-case scenario . . . If Blacke was there and waiting—and caught me with the bag. If I gave the bag to Hey Boy—and anything happened to him . . .

I finished dressing, in evening black, with a clean frilly-white shirt.

While I was doing the studs to my shirt, I made the call to Wolfy. I didn't have to see his face to know he was upset.

"You *bastard*," Wolf barked.

"You're alive."

"Do you have any *idea*, man . . . My God—"

"Relax," I said, "we're almost home. I'll drop off a key to my room at the desk. Eight thirty sharp, tonight. You'll find what you want in my room. But you're not to go in before twelve."

"Are you MAD? I'm going in at eight thirty!"

"Eleven. I'm telling you, I need time—"

"Nine! I want it by nine!"

I said, "Ten." Which had been the game plan all along.

Wolf thought about that for a second. "The key'll be there at eight thirty?"

"Guaranteed. Call the desk."

"Hmm . . . Where will you be?"

"Out."

A brief pause. Then Wolf said, "Oh."

"I want your word," I told him.

"Sure. Absolutely. Ten."

Butterflies . . . Butterflies . . .

Hey Boy was twenty minutes late. He hardly looked Chinese at all, he was so pale. But his small mouth was grim and set. I knew that he'd go through with it. My main worry was he might not understand—

Hey Boy tucked the two sacks under one of his arms. "Hey Boy know what doing, hey. I come by theater. You be there. You tell Hey Boy go to beach. I dig four good holes first, okay? Hide 'em, good, near waterline. Cover up with cheesecloth, sand. Then dig more holes, nine if can, more *in*, maybe thirty feet. Hey Boy leave ten thirty sharp, okay if not finish, hey."

"Good luck," I told him.

"No luck," he replied.

He went his way.

I went mine, to get rid of the cross and the gun on the beach. Oh, I trusted Hey Boy, yes, whatever the demons that drove him. But my instinct urged me to put a limit on the trust.

Worst-case scenario: If all went wrong and the holes were not dug . . . If Blacke was there and waiting . . . If my timing was off and the Quake didn't come . . . my life might depend on the cross and the gun . . .

Butterflies . . . Butterflies . . .

The cabbie couldn't have gone any faster and still kept the wheels on the ground.

There and back.

I arrived at the theater at five after eight. Hey Boy was on time this time and didn't like being kept waiting. He stood by the door of his hansom, pointing sternly at his watch.

I took the steps two at a time . . . charged inside . . . confirmed that his lordship was on, and no sub . . . raced out with a whistle to Hey Boy, who scrambled into his hansom as I half-dove into mine.

Butterflies . . . Butterflies . . .

I arrived at the Palace at eight twenty-five. I had the driver drop a spare key in an envelope marked "Eliot," with neither my name nor my room. If the scene with Wolf really went all the way, I didn't want the deskmen remembering they'd seen me.

Butterflies . . . Butterflies . . .

The cabbie took his sweet time coming back.

It took us six minutes to circle around. Three more for me to catch an elevator inside. And four more to get to the floor I was on, with slow, friendly stops at each floor.

("G'night, there, Mrs. Johnson."

"You, too, dear. And be sure to lock—"

"Pshaw! You don't have to tell *me* that. Say, Mr. Masterton . . . if you don't mind my saying so . . . you look a little *tired.*"

"Me? Why, hellfire, never felt better. No, NEVER felt better!")

It was eight forty-five when I got to my door. I paused in the hallway a moment to think:

What if he's already come here and gone?

What if he's come and found nothing?

It *was* Wolf and Blacke and the Big One, or bust.

I slipped in, observing no signs of disturbance. And, my guess was, if Wolf had come, the room would be in shambles.

I set one of two envelopes onto the desk, the other back in my pocket.

Then I stepped into the closet behind the desk to wait.

It was up to Wolfy now, which message he received.

A SMALL
MISCALCULATION

 8:45.

The way Harriet figured it, Sam had been working too hard. Much too hard. One day he disappeared on her. The next, he'd developed a fever. Well, there was just no telling how some men reacted to marriage.

No doubt the sensible thing was to wait until tomorrow's meeting.

But surely no harm in delivering a loaf of fresh-baked bread, some soup . . . *(making sure that he was there)* . . .

Harriet stood on the street looking up at his silhouette through the shade.

A bride, she thought. I just knew you'd be there.

Len was almost fully packed and ready to leave for the Palace, which should be the right place to be.

The last thing to do was dismantle his shrine. And he was about to, when suddenly the butterflies flew from his gut to his bowels.

At the front door, Lenny hotfooted, while fumbling for his keys. Had he mistakenly packed them?

No time!

He closed the door firmly and raced down the hall.

"Sam? Sam, dear? Are you there?"

Harriet called out discreetly and knocked. She'd put on a shade of lipstick that might set a few tongues wagging. She knocked again and called his name.

Heard someone in the next flat curse.

And, suddenly wishing she could disappear, she tried the handle to Sam's door.

To her surprise, it turned freely.

"Sam?" she cried.

Another curse.

Then a low groan from the bath down the hall.

There you are, my darling. Oh, won't *you* be surprised?

Smiling slyly, she let herself in.

In his pocket, he'd been carrying a folding knife he'd bought that week. He'd been using it to cut the strings with which he'd bundled the papers he'd trash. At the door to his flat, having heard her too well, Lenny unfolded the blade.

You stupid girl, he thought. You fool. Another hour and I'd have been gone. Oh Jesus, I'll do anything if you haven't looked! For God's sake, I just want to go home!

Stealthily, Lenny slipped through the door.

Saw that his prayer hadn't been answered.

And thought he heard Dodge giggling: *You fleabag hippie sack of shit . . . You haven't got it in you . . . A middle-aged goof who'll die slapping his meat . . . Me, I'm checking out as a man, not a clown . . .*

Photographs, certainly. But what kind of photographs? What kind of camera took pictures like these?

Women and children with *paint* round their eyes . . . Men with hair all the way to their shoulders and cigarettes thinner than grass blades . . .

Women's nipples perked through tops littered with lewd little buttons: "Fuck the Pigs" . . . "Make Love not War" . . .

And there in the corner . . . What is that? Let's— EEEEEKKK! Two women dancing—naked!

She backed away in horror, babbling, "Oh, Sam

. . . Sam . . . I loved you . . . But this is—truly—
strange . . ."

She backed, just then, right into Lenny.

Who yanked her head back by the hair in one hand.

And growled, "You bitch, I'm going home!"

Then drew the blade across her throat, before she could
quite finish,

"Zo—
      nie-
          e-
             e-
                e . . ."

TRAPSNAP

9:15. Butterflies. Half asleep on my feet in the closet.

If Wolf held back and kept his word, I might never get to the theater. But I *would* know if he could be trusted. And I still felt I owed him a chance. All I wanted was the smallest hint that *Monster Time* might end.

9:20.

9:25.

I opened the door of the closet, thinking to call the Majestic, when I heard the soft click of the key in the lock.

"Er, Paladin?" Wolf whispered. The room was dark except for the glow of a Tiffany lamp on the desk. "Paladin? It's me . . . There's something I forgot to—Ohhhhh . . ."

He saw it now, the envelope, protruding from under the blotter.

But—

"Paladin?" he whispered. It really was best to be certain. No telling where that psychotic might be.

Wolf padded to the washroom, knocked. "Paladin? You in there?" He swept open the door with the side of one shoe. Stood back and whispered, "Paladin?" turning again to the room. Bed there the size of his own bachelorette. More silk and satin on it than in a goddamn chorus line. Wolf lowered himself to one knee, looked beneath.

Nothing.

Well, of course not. Psychotic maybe, but not all that bright.

Wolf strode boldly to the desk, eased back the chair, lit a

Turkish Trophy, and ran the letter opener under the envelope's flap.

Inside was a lone sheet of paper, which immediately struck him as odd.

He seemed to remember "The Hollow Men" as being rather—longer? Surely immortality required a couple of pages?

Easy . . . Easy does it . . . Little men probably printed real small . . .

With consummate dignity, courage, and hope, Wolf Cotter unfolded the paper to read:

> Mary had a little lamb.
>   Its fleece was white as snow.
> And everywhere that Mary went,
>   The lamb was sure to go!

"Aaaaah! Aaaaah! Aaaaah!" Wolf cried. "I'll get—I'll *get* you—He—HE'LL KILL—"

He heard a click behind him then.

And something cool pressed to one temple.

And a soft, familiar voice: "Well, hi, what's cookin', Wolfy?"

I had Wolf seated at the desk, the derringer behind his ear.

He'd confessed to telling "it" just what I'd expected he would tell. The fake date and time.

But he wouldn't sign the typed disclaimer on the desk. A short, succinct confession that he and the six who had died on the Rock were not from the future, but were—German spies.

"No," Wolf bleated, "He—I can't—"

"Austin who?"

"I don't know any Austin!"

I had no time to play with Wolf. Even after Blacke was gone, Wolf might belong at heart to "He."

I stood there a couple of seconds, staring at his dripping pate, the forlorn hunch of his shoulders.

I said, "You really blew it. Goddamn it, I wanted to trust

you. I had a second envelope. I would've left you that one—
with the real date of the Quake."

"What!"

"Tomorrow morning, asshole."

Wolf turned, horrified, and started to reach for my throat.
I crashed the gun's butt on the top of his skull.

He went down like a sack in the chair.

I slipped the disclaimer, unsigned, in one pocket. Signed
would have been a lot nicer. But I had nothing to work with
to pull off a respectable forgery, and, probably, The S.F.
Call would know his writing fine. I had to hope that this
would do. The editor, at the least, would ID the body. And,
with the note in the cops' hands, there wasn't any danger of
some Son of Wolf writing the column.

I loaded his pants up with *strange* odds and ends: about a
hundred bucks in bills . . . two hundred more in traveler's
checks . . . a New York City subway token . . . a lubri-
cated Trojan . . .

I opened the window and stood there a while, looking
down at the street eight steep stories below.

Then I wheeled Wolf over. Slipped my arms under his
armpits, and hoisted him onto his feet. Grunting, I planted
his butt on the sill. Held him up with one hand on his tie.

There wasn't a chance I could do this, of course . . . Not
really . . . Not go all the way . . .

But I looked at my watch. It was 9:45. And I had to get to
the theater.

Blacke. And Wolf. And the Big One. Or bust.

I closed my eyes. I saw Sam on the train, then heard her
screams in Chinatown.

It was easy after that.

I let go of Wolf's tie. Grabbed both feet and just heaved.

Then I sped off to catch Austin's Hamlet.

STOPWATCH

 His watch had read six after nine for some time, but Hey Boy wasn't worried. As he worked, he just thought of his sister, Hey Moon, all of twenty months old and in pieces. That had been two years ago, but he still heard her screams in his mind.

He'd always had to watch her, lug her around in a pouch on his back while she cried like a demon and tugged at his hair. Some days he'd duck into an alley . . . set her down, say, on top of a crate . . . have a quick smoke . . . pitch some coins at a wall.

She'd been good that afternoon. Hadn't made a sound, just cooed, pointing at the mangy mutt who'd showed at the foot of the alley. He'd chased the dog away real good . . . handed Hey Moon a penny to play with . . . and was just starting to pitch some himself when he heard a raging growl . . . and then, his sister's screams. Bits and pieces . . . arms and legs . . . But how could he have stopped the beast? Three grown men came and all failed, losing their own bits and pieces, until the butcher arrived with his knife.

Hey Boy did not want to know what creature, or what demon, made the pieces in the shed.

It was the dog, in his own mind.

And this time he could stop it, along with her terrible screams in his head.

Would it be 9:30 now? Or 9:45? No, it was probably later than that. He'd just been starting the third hole at nine. Twenty minutes a hole? Twenty-five? Hard to say. The holes, he'd been told, were to be four feet deep; the stakes to be sunk to the marks on their shafts, and then packed very tightly with sand all around. And the cheesecloth had to be cunningly placed, weighted at the corners, and lightly sanded on top. Paladin had told him that these holes were life or death. And he'd worked hard to perfect them.

It was after ten for sure, with still nine more holes to be made.

What to do?

The night was cold and very dark and, yes, he did feel frightened.

But—

"Hey Boy promise—Hey Boy do."

Hey Boy started running to the middle of the beach, the shovel over his shoulder.

The nine to come were to be "sloppy," with the sand he scooped up left all over the beach.

He'd dig six . . . six, at least . . .

He owed his sister that much.

But he wouldn't go to the ferry, no matter what Paladin said. He'd hide someplace safe and remain here to watch.

HYENASPEARE

 10:30. The Majestic. Not a soul to be seen in the lobby, though I've clearly arrived between acts.

Inside, the scene is weirder than a wet dream of Dali's. About five hundred seats are filled—including the one I'd reserved—with men and women in formal attire, all looking as if they are stoned. Ushers, stage hands, and janitors crowd the center aisle steps, their arms around their knees. All eyes are onstage, though it's empty.

There's something in the air here that I cannot finger. Not quite a chill. Not quite a scent.

It's very sweet.

And very strong.

And I'm thinking that I'd like to go close, very close, maybe sit on the very first step near the stage . . . when the wall lights start to dim.

I slip into a space on the step I am on, a couple of yards from the door, as two clowns with spades and mattocks start trading Shakespearean gibberish.

FIRST CLOWN:	*Who builds stronger than a mason, a shipwright, or a carpenter?*
SECOND CLOWN:	*Ay, tell me that, and unyoke.*
FIRST CLOWN:	*Marry, now I can tell.*
SECOND CLOWN:	*To 't.*
FIRST CLOWN:	*Mass, I cannot tell.*

The comatose crowd simply stares. No wonder they look stupefied. They've been through whole acts of this.

I am feeling—not relaxed—but supremely confident . . .
when Austin Blacke appears onstage. And I begin to shiver.

Austin looks magnificent. Though wearing the face of the
Actor, he is, undeniably Blacke. Blacke in those long, loping
strides of his. Blacke in the arrogant shake of his head.
Blacke in the resplendent tan and that somehow victorious
scar on his cheek. Blacke in the unbuttoned white satin
shirt. Blacke in the lavender specks in his eyes.

The first clown, digging, awaits Hamlet's line.

Austin yawns. " 'Has the fellow no feeling of . . .' Aaa,
fuck the rest."

Horatio doesn't miss a beat: " 'Custom hath made it in
him a property of—' *Oh!*" He appears to be speechless with
pain. But Austin gives him a slap on the head. And Horatio,
a trooper continues: "I hate my wife. I hate my kids. Maybe
tonight I'll kill them all and put a bullet through my brain.
Tomorrow and tomorrow creeps this . . . Goddamn moth-
erfucking *life!*"

Austin, Hamlet, shrugs, purrs: " ' 'tis e'en so, the—' blah-
blahblah."

The first clown, still digging, breaks back into song:

" 'But age with his steeling steps
Hath clawed me in his clutch—' "

Austin smiles. And the clown screams, while spinning like
a top:

"I fucked my young wife in the mouth
Until she couldn't swallow
Whee! And now we'll do it her ass
Until her butt is hollow!"

The lion roars inside me. There'll be no waiting for the
beach. I'm just beginning to spring to my feet—when Austin Blacke's real magic hits me.

The clown throws a skull to Blacke, who snatches it and
holds it high, like a star, overhead. He is like some rock star
god, frozen in a pose that dwarfs you with its total mastery.

His eyes appear to sweep the hall without moving in the

least. And if his lips are moving, the moves are too subtle to see as he purrs: " ' That skull had a tongue in it and could sing once. How the knave jowls it to the ground, as if 'twere Cain's jawbone . . .' "

The words themselves begin to fade. I feel the air around me growing heavy now with

lav-en-der-r-r-r . . .

I understand what is happening . . . and yet I am losing the power to want to stop it. The words are not important. He is giving us something far greater: the feel of utter hopelessness . . . the absurd futility of all human life. . . . And, yes, it stings, the knowledge . . . but the

lave-en-der-r-r-r

is sweet.

I feel the protective wall between me and the others fall. I am one of them now.

(Come on, Dodge!)

We are one.

(Where's the lion? Rrrrr. . . .)

This is where we all belong.

Another skull is thrown to Blacke, who holds them both up, lustrous stars. " 'There's another. Why, may not that be the skull of a lawyer? Where be his quidditics now, his quillities, his cases, his tonures and his tricks?' "

(Rrrrrooooo . . .)

This is where the magic is. The man with the tan has the candy: the sound of the dirt on the lid of the coffin . . . the squiggly kisses of maggots and worms. . . .

(Rrrrrooooooaaaaa . . .)

" 'Hm,' " Austin purrs. " 'This fellow might be in 's time a great buyer of land, with his statutes, his recognizances, his fines, his double vouchers. . . .' "

Beautiful. . . . So beautiful. . . .

I hear the sounds of zippers, soft rustlings of dresses, and I do not find it surprising at all when the men on either side begin pumping the meat in their hands. . . . I am having my own party, imagining the maggots in Sister Amelia's snatch, and—

(Rrrrroooooaaaaarrrrr!)

Austin Blacke is still piling it on in his spellbinding lavender way. But I have known one perfect day. And I have been blessed by the Sweet Spot, just once.

I say a short prayer to Wandini—and *throw* a high-pitched, manic giggle several seats down, to the left.

The skull slips out of Blacke's right hand and shatters on the floor. He sweeps the room with a maniacal look, still holding the other skull up. Around me, I begin to hear men and women coming to.

" 'Alas, poor Yorick!' " Austin barks.

I throw two giggles and a whoop—left-right-left, two far, one near, Wandini on my shoulder.

"Who has done this thing?" Blacke screams. "By the power of the Night, I command you!" He holds the second skull higher, ready to do something massive, when—

I throw out four beauties . . . and then, before you know it, mocking whoops and giggles are flying all over the hall.

I have never felt more powerful, more human, more alive . . . until I see Blacke sweep the room, methodically, from left to right, purring one long, prolonged, *"Youuuuu."*

I'm already on my feet before his eyes get to me.

But then they do, get to me.

Austin Blacke says nothing.

He just winks and then tears off the stage through the wings.

My heart is thumping crazily.

Where's he off to? What's he up to?

I check my watch. It's 12:15?

But Hey Boy's long gone—

Hey Boy?

WORST-CASE
SCENARIO

 It would've been easier catching a cab on New Year's Eve in Gotham. No one was *walking* the streets late at night, except for the cops and the Guardsmen. Those who were out had one reason to be out: to beat someone out of a cab.

I scrambled in front of a street car to slip through the door of a hansom approaching a fare at the corner. The top-hatted man poked his head in. He pulled it back out quick enough when I clicked back the derringer's hammer.

"You look a little—tired," I said.

"Never felt better!" the man cried. "Your cab."

At Polk the driver took a right, clipclopping along at six miles an hour. With thickening traffic, the pace slowed about half a mile an hour per block.

Until, at California, we came to an absolute stop.

"What's going on?" I cried.

Above, the driver whistled.

"For God's sake, man! Get a move on, you lug!"

The driver whistled, waited.

In the windows on each side, from out of nowhere, two faces appeared. Neither one looked chipper.

"Out a bit late tonight, there, aren't we, sir?" Beefy, bulb-nosed Irish cop.

"Where might you be headed, sir?" Tall Guardsman with a bayonet.

"Off to the Coast, men," I told them. "Be a bit *strange* to be home in my bed, with them Pretty Waitress Girls."

"How much they chargin'," the cop said, "for a schooner o'beer on the Coast, laddy boy?"

"Hell," I said, "it's robbery. Chargin' a jit at the Hangdog Saloon. And, by deuce, it's only horse's piss."

"What about the Sydney Ducks?" The Guardsmen tapped his bayonet a couple of times on the window.

"Why, strike me straight," I answered. My palms were beginning to drip. "You know as well as I do, ain't seen no Ducks in twenty years. Damn Coast has got all civilized. Scarcely fit for pinkieboys."

"Where you *stayin'*?" barked the cop.

I handed each of them one of my cards, then hooked my right thumb in my vest, around the derringer's butt.

"Paladin?" the Guardsman said.

"Say, wait a minute," said the cop. "Paladin . . . I heard o' you. T'weren't you the fella caught that—"

"HELLLLLPPPPP! HELLLLLPPPPP! ZO-NIEEEE-EEEE!"

There was a high-pitched, piercing scream somewhere high above us. And then the barks of two quick shots. Shattering glass and a scream that trailed off to a melon-type splat on the walk.

I was sent on my way with a word to the wise: not to stay out too late this fine evening.

At about 1:20, we finally crept to the foot of the hill.

The driver called, "End of the line. Ain't drivin', not this late, to no damn Presidio."

I took off at all-out speed, with the derringer snug in the palm of my hand.

Two-ten.

I'd taken the long way around, over the golf links and through the old fort, along the cliffs above the beach.

Fifty yards or so past the lifeboat station, I took a rest to catch my breath. Then dropped like a cat to the bushes below, beginning the dangerous part, the trip back.

I moved slowly, in a crouch, expecting to hear, any second, a manic giggle, above or behind. Or would it be the sound of wings? Or the python's heavy slithering?

What I heard was the rustle of branches instead. And the snappings of twigs underfoot. And the musical lappings of waves on the shore.

And now, as I drew closer, the pounding of my heart.

The beach looked as deserted as the Majestic's stage between acts.

The door to the boathouse was closed.

Not a sign of Hey Boy.

All was well . . . All was well . . .

I crawled out of cover and called out his name. Needing to know, for a fact, he was gone. That that last wink of Austin Blacke's hadn't really meant a thing.

Nothing again was the answer I got. Nothing except for the sounds of the waves and the moon's silent track on the water.

I catfooted to the boathouse, slipping around for a look at the beach.

Slowly, twenty feet ahead, three large spots began to appear, like splashes of blackberry wine.

Three, I thought . . . That's good . . . That's three . . . at least three to play with . . .

A few more steps, and the next row began to come in focus.

Oh, wonderful, wonderful, excellent boy!

That's six, at least . . . You gave me six . . . And I know, I just know, that you started these last . . . You started with the others right? . . . Oh, good God Almighty, look! . . . There's three more . . . a grid of nine, you magnificent, devious, sly, cunning—

BONNNNNGGGGGNNNNNGGGGGGNNNNNGGGGG-NNNNNGGGGG!

I dropped, screaming, to my knees, with both hands over my ears. My head like a cathedral bell that had just been rung with a sledge. Struck so hard, the first spider cracks webbed into a half-hundred more with each ring.

I closed my eyes to stop seeing the cracks.

But it went on, the ringing, even after my face hit the sand.

MIND GAMES

 SLURRRRRPPPPP!
SLURRRRRPPPPP!
SMMMMMMACKKKKKKKKKK!
CRRRRRRUNCHHHHHHHHHH!

I was dreaming, certainly. But there was just no way way around it:

No one could eat like that except Uncle Joe.

Uncle Joe had showed up four or five nights a week, on no particular schedule, to feed . . . talking while he pigged.

Like now:

"Man, oh man, I love Chink food," he said.

The lights had gone out while I slept. The screen the dream was played on was pitch black, tinged with crimson, with millions of infinitesimal cracks.

But I knew it was him, all right. And someone else was with us too. It must've been the dentist . . . though it was hard to figure why he was poking around in my mind, not my mouth. He used his finger ends like picks, and all I could do was try hard to relax.

SLURRRRRPPPPPP!
CRRRRRRUNCHHHHHHHHHHH!

"You idiot. You really thought that—*you*?" Joe said.

I had a fleeting impression that we were seated in a cave, maybe the size of a boathouse. Uncle Joe, at the end, hunched over his bowl like a wolf.

"Shouldn't send a boy," Joe said, "to—"

SMMMMMACKKKKK!

"—do a man's job."

Chink food? That pig—the nerve of him! I clenched my fists and ground my teeth.

Uncle Joe made a sound like a whoop in the dark. And giggled. And cried, "Fight me!"

And then the dentist

SQUEEZED.

(That hurts!)

(Relax, my mother whispered. *Think about a sunny day . . . boats sailing serenely on water . . . white clouds . . . You've got to be foxy with dentists!)*

(In your safe, my father urged. *Remember? In your safe . . .)*

I closed my eyes within the dream. Heard Uncle Joe rise, with a slurp and a crunch, padding over to me.

"C'mon, whatcha *got* in there?"

I felt his fingers on my skull. And through the tips the ripple of a faint

lav-en-der-r-r-r

glow.

(Shut the door! my father said.)

(That ISN'T Uncle Joe! Mom cried.)

Three of us there, small as buttons, in the gray metal safe I'd once had as a boy.

Those fingers poked and prodded, squeezed and rummaged through brain's folds.

"C'mon!" Joe purred. "You're no damn fun at all."

That was when I realized the horrible truth about Joe: he was a dentist of the mind. And he had X-ray eyes in his fingers!

But wait . . . If I'd been brought here to hide something —when he could *see* me hiding it—perhaps the game was really to make sure I hid the right thing . . . And to believe it in my soul . . .

I focused on the twenty-fourth, *convinced* my life depended on the trick I had played with the dates.

Uncle Joe opened the door to my safe. Reached right in and took me out and set me back down on the floor of the cave.

He gave my head a playful whack.

"C'mon, little man, get up. You haven't told me a damn thing that I don't already know."

Joe gave my head another whack. Shook my shoulders.

Whooped, low. "I'm gonna count to three. When I say *now* you'll awaken. And there won't be anything you'd rather have than Chink food."

He set something heavy and wet on my lap. The weight of a medicine ball.

He purred, "One."

(You will awaken and you'll be my boy . . .)

"Two," Uncle Joe said, letting it rip through the floodgates, that glow.

(When you open your eyes, son, you'll know what you see . . .)

"Three," Uncle Joe said.

(Nothing . . . You will give him nothing . . .)

"Now."

I saw Austin Blacke crouched before me, transformed maybe half of the way. He'd sprouted a mouthful of curved scimitars and fat ivories dripping with crimson. The eyes were his, but not the snout. His ears were long and pointy. Beneath the bloodied, gore-soaked shirt, his shoulders and back sloped in powerful arcs.

He smiled at me wolfishly. Nodded at my lap.

I reached.

(Nothing . . . Nothing . . . You're my boy . . .)

I clenched my fingers in the hair. Lifted the weight from my lap with a *plop* and looked right into Hey Boy's eyes.

(Nothing . . . Don't you feed him . . . No!)

I set the head beside me. "Kids are easy," I said softly.

Austin giggled. "Bless my soul, what have we got here?" He leaned over to cuff me again on the ear.

I caught his hand—haired bony steel. "You and me. Man to man."

Like a knife through butter. That was how easily he moved the hand from where I'd caught it to my throat. Then he began to *squeeze*.

(Nothing!)

Throttling me now to an inch of my life.

(Nothing . . . Nothing . . . You know how . . .)

"Haven't . . . got the . . . balls," I rasped.

Another squeeze, or the thought of a squeeze, and the

party would have been over. But Austin Blacke relaxed his grip. His eyes were almost twinkling.

"You want me, boy? You got me. Get your ass out on the beach."

With a bark and a whoop, he was off for the door, the powerful curve of his back leveling out in a series a horrible cracks.

I slipped my watch out of my vest for a look. The hour was 4:58.

I left the watch on the floor beside the derringer he'd wrecked. The barrel looked as twisted as the blade of the shovel he'd used on my head.

Clock time was useless to me now. I'd thought the early morning had been when the Big One had hit. But it would be dawn now in minutes. And for all I knew the Big One was tonight. The Sweet Spot would come or it wouldn't.

I paused before the boathouse wall. I washed it over in a wave that changed it into *my* Wall:

A picture of the Thin Man, gold and tanned and beautiful . . . the Fat Man, defeated by love and by Time . . .

A picture of my mother, smiling, on the day she died . . .

Lenny's picture on the Wall . . .

Sam's picture . . .

Patch's . . .

"C'mon," Blacke called. "Let's do it. It's a beautiful morning to die!"

I scrambled to the tarmac in the corner of the shed. Beneath it, I found the small satchel I'd stashed.

I slipped the long-barreled Colt and the cross under my waistband, smoothing my black jacket over in back.

QUAKE-A-RAMA

It *was* a beautiful morning. Not quite dawn, but nearly. Not light, but fraught with the promise of light. As if the sun were collecting itself to give us a glow to remember.

Austin Blacke sat centered in Hey Boy's grid of holes. Each held a thin, round, five-foot stake, buried two feet underground, tapered to a needled tip. Blacke sat behind the middle hole, on the two-foot sandy stretch between the back two cross-rows. His legs were stretched to the sides in a split. He had his shirt bunched in his left hand, wiping the blood from his chops, while throwing punches that popped with his right. His torso looked like a bronzed marble block, rippling not with muscle, but immeasurable strength in the raw.

Considering what I'd just seen in the shed, he looked obscenely handsome. That thick, rakish mustache. Blond, fingerbrushed hair. And the whitest set of teeth seen this side of La-La Land.

"C'mon over," he drawled. "Don't be shy. Hell, we'll have a high time."

(Show him nothing . . . Nothing yet . . .)

I walked over, faking the spring in my step. I rotated my neck in full circles, hearing the bones creak in protest. I shook out my fingers, rotated my arms.

Blacke tossed the bloodied shirt aside. Stretched his arms out straight on both sides. And doubled over at the waist till one of his eyes almost touched the stake's tip.

"Gee, these sure are scary." Austin sounded real impressed.

I shook out my fingers, rotated my arms, collecting myself

in my *hara*. Sensei George down there somewhere, still trying to get past that hair in the brain.

(Always the brown belt and never the black . . . it's aikido, Dodge, not a system of tricks. Aikido isn't evasion. Size, strength don't count for shit.)

Austin Blacke just smiled and smiled and rose to his feet in a smooth reverse split. Then he crouched before the hole. "There's just one little detail that you ought to know." He moistened the tip of one finger, circled it around the stake's tip, and touched tongue to fingertip. "See, there's this problem with the stakes . . ." He stretched his right palm out over the tip. Held it there a moment as if the stake were a lavender flame and all he was doing was warming his palm. He took a breath, raised the palm to his shoulder . . . then swung it down in a swift, savage arc, impaling his palm on the stake.

Blacke's entire body went into a spasm of pain . . . that melted then, before my eyes, into ecstatic shudderings. He withdrew his palm from the stake with a *plop*. Then held up the ravaged hand.

I was standing just nine feet away. No way around what I saw: the jagged wound in Austin's hand was healing itself as I watched.

(Dodge?

Sensei, Jesus Christ! I think maybe I'm out of my league here!

Relax. For ten years I've been telling you, it has nothing to do with your hands or your feet. It has nothing to do with your height or your weight. The more relaxed, more together mind wins.)

I kicked off my left boot. I kicked off my right. I eased off my socks and then stood at full height.

Austin chuckled, loving it. Me, barefooted with all of the stakes. And five-feet seven inches.

He curled his fingers, calling me.

I advanced to the edge of the grid, stepping in between the long rows on the left, while Austin held position, fists raised before his face.

I catfooted forward, half-turned in a T-stance, leading with my right foot. I had both hands raised in the classic position, open-palmed, as if wielding a sword that I'd lined up with his center.

When I reached the row that Blacke was on, I pivoted, swinging my right foot behind. And, here, I waited for Austin . . . who came bobbing and weaving and feinting. And then threw one *serious* jab.

I brushed it aside with a slap of my palm, returning the hand to position.

(Never box with a boxer, Dodge. Work on his mind. Draw him into your game, don't get suckered into his.)

I slapped the second and the third, top hand returning instantly to keep the line. Not even Austin could cross it.

But Blacke snarled, "What is this shit?" and rocketed the next one through, pure force, Blacke power, two hundred thirty pounds of it collected in one fist.

The blow connected with my jaw and lifted me off the ground half a foot. I landed somewhere outside of the grid and lay back counting stars.

"C'mon, c'mon!" Austin barked. "Get in here and fight like a man."

(Dodge?

Sensei?

I repeat: If you think of the guy as a boxer, you lose. What you do with a boxer is get him so pissed he forgets, for a second, he is one.)

I clambered up, still seeing stars and almost two of Austin Blacke, who was back and waiting near the center of the grid.

"C'mon, Harpo, come to me."

I shuffled in to greet the next volley with more of the soft little slaps.

Pop-slap, pop-slap, pop-slap, pop-slap.

Suddenly, Austin roared and threw a totally wild one, I thought. A left hook that was wrong, dead wrong, but of such ferocity it took my breath away. I panicked and I blocked it hard, not even seeing Austin's right. A dead-on blow that reshattered my nose and set me up, just masterfully, for the sidekick that landed me six feet away.

Austin waited patiently. Purred, "You havin' fun yet?"

I sat, doubled over, gasping and whooping for breath. Whupped. Whupped. Totally whupped.

(Dodge?

Sensei?

Last call. Your mind's the same size his is. Focus absolutely on the man before you. He's not the guy who kicked your ass last year or when you were a kid. Quit running. Quit evading.)

Austin curled his fingers.

Over the horizon, the slowly rising sun threw no light whatsoever on any more holes by the shore.

"The old man was delicious. The Chink bitch, she was heaven. You ever see a woman's head, Harp—I mean when it explodes. You'd be surprised how humbling most women seem to find that. C'mon, c'mon. Come at me. Let's see a little self-respect!"

I made it up to my knees, stopped there a second to spit up a tooth. Looked at the spray of my blood on the sand, and thought, *You're gonna pay for that.*

"C'mon, c'mon, let's get it on!" Austin spread his arms out wide, reveling in his sheer power and bulk.

I clambered up, rotated my neck, and shook my fingers nice and loose.

(Oh, Dodge?

Yes, Sensei?

One more thing. The way things are going, you'll never survive. Not unless you get in straight: You NEVER move back to get out of the way . . . If you step back, or to the side, it's to LEAD him—your mind's moving IN!)

I found another point of entry, near the opposite end of the grid. It was time to get Austin out of his shoes.

I catwalked to the middle hole that Blacke was poised behind. I stood there a sec, in position, then catwalked coolly to the right, to the right vertical row. I stood behind its center hole, well out of reach.

Growling, Austin came for me. I shuffled back, around the hole, and started weaving in and out, around the holes in two cross rows.

"C'mon, c'mon!" Austin roared.

I took a stand and waited, left side of the middle hole, on that two-foot stretch of sand.

Austin Blacke squared off before me again. "You're starting to annoy me, kid."

I spat up another tooth I'd loosened with my tongue and curled my fingers at him.

His hands before his face again, teeth bared between his fists. Thai kickboxer feints below. Feinting jabs with both his fists.

Then—

pop-slap, pop-slap, pop-slap, pop-slap, pop-slap, pop-*snapkick!*

I brushed it away, shuffling in like a shot, on the outside of the kick, almost losing it there on the edge of a hole, but catching my balance from Austin, whose head I had pinned to my shoulder. I whirled IN, pivoting, toes clutching for purchase on sand, as I smashed Blacke's face onto his knee. Then, with a rifle-shot twist of my hip, I sent him flying, spread-eagled, a distance of ten feet.

Blacke fell, screaming, and skidded a ways. Sat up, raging at his shoes.

"Keep 'em on," I told him. "This keeps getting better and better."

Austin kicked them off this time. On his feet, he grinned at me, peeling off his hose.

I settled into his old spot, hands raised again loosely before me.

"All right," he snarled, "no more fooling around."

No boxer shuffle this time.

No all-out furious charge.

Austin Blacke came at me the same way he had on the *Zephyr*, hands loosely at his side, and—though he wasn't wearing one—his black leather duster around him like wings. As he came, his eyes began to change to twin lavender coals. He just kept on coming and every single move he made told me he couldn't be stopped.

(Dodge? Hey, what's happening here?

Sensei, I can't stop him—BIG!)

Blacke stopped two feet before me, beating me down with his mind.

"This next one takes your head clear off. And there's not a damn thing you can do."

He cocked the fist over his shoulder and swung, unstoppable, unbeatable.

(Dodge?

SENSEI!

You mess up again and you're out on the street. You've got it in you. Show me!)

I caught the punch just before impact, deflecting it down and extending it out, taking Austin's balance. I swung in quick, real close to Blacke, my forehead at his shoulder. I locked both hands around his wrist, which I held pinned to my *hara*. I snapped my hip, in, IN, swinging his wrist out before me, a sword. The wrist bone snapped ferociously. Blacke screamed and tensed and teetered on the edges of two holes.

But I was really cooking now. It was all coming together. I had his arm locked, high and straight, and, without a hitch in the flow, I shuffled IN and under it, and snapped my hip again, hard, to the right, bringing his hand back and down to his shoulder in a precise swordlike blow. I heard his elbow shatter and his shoulder pop out of the socket. I shuffled IN. I had him now. Another step, a hard cut down, and he'd land on his back on that stake. And then we could get down to business. After I'd shown who was master.

And I was just about to . . . when the Big One hit. I heard it first, then felt the low rumble. For an instant, I just lost it—a fraction of a second, thin as that hair in the brain. That was all he needed to straighten his arm, broken in three places, and hold me dangling off the ground.

The earth beneath us buckled.

Blacke, grinning, snatched my waist and jerked me over his head.

Without a word, he threw me with everything he had.

I shot my hands out and fell screaming, neatly impaled on the stake.

The Big One began at 5:12:06 on the eighteenth of April, 1906.

About a minute before the Quake struck, birds fell oddly

silent, some veering away, as if puzzled, in flight. Horses whinnied, shifted, snorted, appearing mortally spooked.

But ships on the water were all sailing on. And birds and horses, after all, were only birds and horses. Men went on about their business while the city slept.

One instant there was silence. The next, an orgy of nightmarish sounds that began with an earth-center rumbling. Whole streets began to undulate, first in pondlike ripplings, then in oceanic waves.

Now the birds began to scream.

And autos, with their tires blown, rushed, thumping along on their rim wheels over the capering streets.

The tumult swelled into a roar, the earth shaking like a rat gripped in a terrier's teeth. The shaking topped towers and chimneys . . . felled whole rows of wood-frame houses into splintered kindlings . . . twisted steel railings and bridges and pipelines as if they were made of wet clay.

Whole walls peeled away from fronts of apartment buildings, comically exposing men who were sleeping or taking a dump.

The cupola of the California Hotel crashed through the Bush Street Firehouse . . . carrying Fire Chief Sullivan, already fatally injured, all the way to the first floor.

Pier Three crumbled; sank, whole, in the Bay.

The Ferry Building's tower whipped back and forth like a twig in a gale.

All along the waterfront, East Street bounced and billowed, opening in crazy holes that swallowed cabs and screaming mares.

The Hotel Valencia pitched, teetered, and dropped like a sack. Where there had been four stories, there was now only one. In the wreckage below, eighteen men had been killed. And two lay, crushed, waiting to drown in the flood from a blown water main.

Enrico Caruso, in night clothes, came howling out of the Palace Hotel, vowing he'd never return.

At the Third and Howard Street Station, a fireman sticking his head out the window was decapitated by a falling cornice.

Half of the chimneys in town snapped in two, braining

dozens on the street in raging downpours of bricks. The other half fell through the roofs, killing another three hundred.

Still more were crushed by furniture that slid, by the ton, across floors.

On the twelfth floor of the *Call,* seven Linotype machines suddenly fell through the floor. And then the next. And on. And on. The tonnage paused, for an instant, to collect the editor, and take him with them eight more floors.

The Palace, of course, had been built to outlast anything a Quake could throw. On its roof, Lenny struggled for balance, waiting for his moment, still praying for forgiveness.

I killed her . . . Oh, Jesus . . . I killed her . . . Oh, no . . .

But if a man had saved an Age, could he be damned for one lost life?

Just get me home, I beg you, Lord . . . I'll serve you the rest of my life . . . Get me home . . .

Lenny leaned over the guardrail, watching the carnage below.

He saw the ground open beneath him. Open, close, open, close. Like a giant set of jaws.

He saw something then like a lavender eye, tiny as one of his own eyes, within the churning jaws.

Open, close, open, close.

It was an eye—it winked at him.

Screaming "Home!" he swan-dived over the rail to the lavender eye.

(Dodge?
Sensei?
What I said . . . about hands and feet not mattering? That was metaphorically speaking. This guy's gonna take your head off if you don't get your hand off that stake.)

We were ten seconds into the Big One, and each of them lasted an age. The earth, rumbling, bucking, roaring, pounding the needle-tipped stake through my palm.

Austin Blacke giggled above me. "C'mon!"

(Raphael? That you, honey?

*Mom? Just a minute, Sensei. Got Mom on the other line.
Mom, I can't see so good. I'm seeing red. I'm going blind.*

*Oh, you honey-bunny. Such a baby at the dentist. But—
Good grief, look at that! He's not supposed to drill your
hand. Well, we'll just have to teach him a lesson. Think
about the boats again, sailing serenely across lapping
waves. Now, take the drill out of your hand.)*

"C'mon," Blacke said. "Can't you handle the pain?"

I smiled grimly at him. Thought of clouds and sailing ships
and cotton candy and beautiful girls. And gripped the stake
with my left hand, raising my right in an agonized move.

Blacke grinned and, when I screamed, he breathed as if
inhaling my pain.

(Mom, what's he doin'? It makes me feel so tired . . .)

(Hon, mustn't feed your Uncle Joe . . .)

I'd scrambled halfway to my knees, no particular plan in
my mind, when suddenly the whole beach *kicked*—and I
flew straight into Austin's arms.

"Oh, *yeah*," he drawled. "I like this game."

Over his head again. And, here we go!

(Dodge!

Sensei—look, no hands!)

I took the next stake through the shoulder, twelve inches
through the meaty part and out the other side. Shish kebab
for Austin Blacke.

And the Big One still went on forever, each spasm pounding the stake through my meat.

"Well, look at you," Austin said. "Aren't you a sorry sight?
C'mon."

I craned my head, looking up, up, above Blacke, at the
sky.

"C'mon," I cried. "It's your turn. What do *you* believe
in?"

Blacke's eyes almost twinkled. "Ain't nothin' to believe
in, Harp."

(Raphael? Honey?

*Mom, Mom, help me, Jesus, he's at it again with his drill,
oh, my God!*

Well, hon', white clouds are wonderful. And sailing

*ships. And all of that. But I think your father has some-
thing that he wants to tell you.)*

(Son?

Dad, it hurts! He makes me tired!

*That's my boy . . . That's my boy . . . I'll be god-
damned if I'll sit here and watch some dentist drill my kid
to death. Take both my hands in your hands now. We're
gonna take his drill away and shove it up his ass.*

Daddy—do you mean . . . ?

*I do. You're my boy, you understand? It's time to feed
your Uncle Joe. I mean, REALLY feed him.)*

My father's hands and my hands, then—our four hands
around the stake, pushing up, and pushing up, until the last
sickening *plop.*

More blood than I knew I had in me was pumping out of
my shoulder, as Austin Blacke and I squared off and he
started for me again, and for real.

I fumbled, frantically, with my left hand, yanking out the
ludi-cross. Brandished it before me, in an operatic sweep.

Austin Blacke stopped, stunned. Could not believe his
eyes.

"By the power of Christ, I command you!" I screamed.
"By the lives of the saints and the love of All High!"

Austin shrieked with laughter, snatching the cross from
my hands. "You idiot! There's nothing! You're priceless—
you're a hoot!"

Austin was still giggling, pressing the cross to his crotch,
when the Colt showed in my hand. I braced it, barely, with
the right, cocking back the hammer.

"Wheee! C'mon, Harpo, shoot me!"

The first shot caught him in the gut and sent him splaying
backward, screaming and giggling at once.

I fired the next shot wild, widening my eyes—appropri-
ately horrified—as Austin Blacke, just as cool as could be, sat
up, then rose to his feet.

I watched him coming at me.

(Feed him—Bigger, BIGGER!)

"No!" I screamed. "I shot you!"

Three times I cocked the hammer back, and screamed
when all that came out was a click.

Austin was six feet away and still coming steadily when the earth stopped shaking.

(Feed him, honey—stuff him good!)

"Master!" I shrieked. "MASTER!"

"Yessssss?" Austin stopped, three feet away, amused beyond all get-out.

"I'll serve you!"

"Nawwwww."

"I'll be your slave!"

"Hell, Harp, all mortals are."

"I'll kiss the ground you walk on!"

Blacke jiggled his phallus obscenely.

"I think we'll have you just kiss this instead."

(Dodge?

Sensei?

It's time for Uncle Joe's dessert. And don't screw it up this time, okay?)

"Well," I told Blacke, purring now. "I guess at least one of us won't die pussywhipped."

"WHAT?"

"C'mon, you damned ugly hyena. C'MON!"

I turned, bolting for the Bay, throwing the gun as I ran. The Bay, forty feet ahead, and not a sign of the last row of holes. Hey Boy, come on, Hey Boy, tell me this wasn't for nothing. I know you dug 'em, sure you did!

(Dodge?

Sensei?

Don't look now—)

I didn't have to look to know that Austin Blacke was gaining. I heard the barks and whoops just fine.

Thirty feet and not a sign.

Whispering as I screamed for air, "C'mon, c'mon . . . believe in me!"

Twenty feet. And still no trace. And the Sweet Spot had already come here and gone. My wonderful, wonderful plans for his feet.

WHOOOOOOOOPPPPP!

WHOOOOOOOOPPPPP!

Fifteen feet and I could almost feel his breath.

But something—*something*—up ahead . . . there, just by the shoreline . . . a slight differential of light?

(Dodge?

Sensei!

NOW—MOVE IN! YOUR MIND AGAINST HIS MIND! GO!)

On the spot, I pivoted, Blacke only three of those long lopes away, already reaching for my throat.

But that was then they came:

the roars.

The first was mine. And it contained every name upon the Wall.

Austin *whooped*, backpedaling, absurdly, with his arms.

Just then there was the other roar. And this one came from behind him. The Big One had only been resting a spell. Now it was hitting the beach in full force. Coming at us, from the cliffs, it looked as if some monster were barreling under the sand for the Bay.

The Sweet Spot had come home to me.

I shuffled in and caught Blacke's neck with my left hand, his oversized balls with the right. And, just as we were both thrown high, I pivoted IN, a hard pinwheeling throw. Blacke's head went down, his feet shot up, and still he kept on spinning.

In another second, the holes might not have been there. But, from his screams, I knew they were.

Everything had fallen in place, including Blacke's troublesome feet.

I struggled up, pitched forward, sat, and watched Austin dance on two needly stakes. From behind, he looked like one of those dolls you see stuck to a cake with the pins on their feet. He flopped his arms and cursed and shrieked.

When the Quake finally settled, I picked myself up. Collected the Colt. And moseyed around for a look.

Blacke's chin had fallen to his chest. Strangled sounds came from his throat. His tortured body could no longer swing a single spastic move.

The left stake had made a clean run up his leg, the tip blasting out through the thigh.

The right had shot out through the calf to his groin.

"Strychnine . . ." Austin gasped.

"Bad feet," I told him. "Mixed blood. Lousy circulation. Be one thing or the other."

He lifted his head a few inches. The skin, already blackening, was beginning to bubble and peel from the bones. But his eyes were quite remarkable, looking almost childlike in their wounded innocence.

"You said . . . Fight . . . like . . . man . . ."

I shrugged. Cocked the Colt at his forehead. "That's the kind of man I am."

"Gun—"

"Oh, I know what you're thinking. But there's one thing you should know. There's one more bullet in it. This one's silver, with strychnine."

The shot took the top of his head off.

I sat down and watched the show, until nothing was left but a pile of bones on a couple of stakes on the beach.

A few minutes later, the Big One started up again.

I dressed the wounds in my hand and my shoulder, and started stumbling back to town.

EPILOGUE

I think Patch might have had a grim laugh at the end. The town survived the Big One, as it had all the others before. The fire was what got us, as burning stoves and lanterns met the hiss of shattered gas mains in explosive kisses. Within a few hours there were hundreds of fires all over San Francisco . . . with next to no way to stop them.

The central fire station's alarm system had been knocked out cold.

The fire chief was dead.

Nearly all of the water mains had been destroyed. And time and again, firemen stood with useless, empty hoses while the city burned.

One tinderbox after another went up like so much rice paper: ship chandleries, cheap clothing stores, flophouses, grocerias. The separate fires soon melded together and, fanned by the breeze off the Bay, blazed along.

By noon, hellish sheets of flame had halfway ringed the city.

And smoke rose in towering clouds of black, white, dirty gray, yellow, blue, and red . . . all blending into one dark brownish mass that blotted out the sky.

The night was never darker than a weird red twilight, one that you could read by without so much as a candle.

And now and then the sky would blaze in a giant light show: crackling, spectacular flashes of yellow, blue, green, rose, red, and ultraviolet . . . as if commemorating the loss of the Palace Hotel.

The fire raged for three days and three nights while the dead and the wounded were carted away.

Shattered men and women were seen on every corner lugging baby carriages loaded with possessions. The rasp of trunks across the bricks became as familiar a sound as the blast of dynamite.

My eyes were focused, though, on the resurrection. The town began rebuilding while the ruins were still smoking.

Where a fortune had been lost, a proud sign would be planted: "On this site will be erected a six-story office building to be ready for occupancy in the Fall."

Nine hundred lives had been taken. Seven billion bricks had been dropped. Thirty thousand buildings, wrecked. A total damage of 500 mil.

And yet there *he* was on the corner: some whistling, ruined restaurateur, whipping up eggs on a range he had saved.

For all the horror of it, there was an undeniably exhilarating rush.

Things were simpler now, as Patch might have said. You had your work cut out for you. Your job was the same job as that of the man right beside you: to roll up your sleeves and say not "Where you from?" but "Well, pal, let's get on with it."

In no time, we'd set up camps of tents for 20,000.

By summer, we'd constructed 6,000 "cottages": small wood shacks with eight-foot-high roofs, all packed so closely you couldn't walk between them.

Within a year, we were starting to move these to the owners' new-bought lots.

Two more years, and we'd erected 20,000 *buildings*— bigger, stronger, and better. Suitable for a New Age.

Two fires that no one regretted put a lid on the whole sorry *Zonie* affair.

City Hall and Central Precinct both went up in flames . . . with all related documents reduced to just handfuls of ashes. Birth and immigration records had also been lost in the fires. Suddenly, overnight, it was a little hard to say just who was who. Or what.

And, with Wolf's printed confession and the *Call* editor's death, men started coming forward, reclaiming the loved ones they'd put on the Rock. Next thing you knew, everyone was clamoring: Hey, get them guys off the Rock.

All in all, the expedient thing was to blame it on Wolf and the *Call*.

The town went on.

We all went on and rolled up our sleeves and dug in.

Except . . . folks did get to feeling suspicious about—Germany.

So, I guess if you have to, pin World War I on me.

It's too late to argue now.

Betsy married in the Fall.

I read about the wedding and stood in the back of the chapel to watch. She'd got her man; he looked glad to be caught; they made a handsome couple. She'd put on a few pounds and seemed pleased with the gain. Her smile was simply radiant. Parts, in fact, were solid gold. But, thankfully, that was the style of the day. I was sporting gold myself, bottom front, lower right, which the ladies loved. They said it almost matched my hair.

I passed Betsy once or twice in my remaining years.

But it was wiser, we both knew, to go our own ways.

And we did.

I thought of Lenny often. But never made an effort to learn if he'd died in the Quake.

After all he'd been through, it was nice to think that maybe . . .

That was the reason I owned to, at first.

It came in flashes, now, then, here, there, through the months and years ahead.

Until one day I simply knew: I, too, was *going back*.

And I knew how.

And I knew when.

And I know what you're thinking: Hadn't I learned anything about the Sweet Spot in Time?

But, you see, that was *why* I felt I had to go.

Once the town had been rebuilt . . . I felt as if I'd lost something. From here, it was all history, too many chapters known by heart.

Nor could I bear a middle age spent whistling "Sergeant Pepper's . . ." in Lenny's Golden Age.

What I needed, what I craved, was just what I'd told Lenny: that spirit of adventure . . . that sense of barreling on all eights down an unknown highway. What I needed was to *be* there at the start of something wild. I wanted my goddamn socks back on the floor. I wanted a city of eyes just like Sam's: alert, alive, and hungry for change.

And *that* was why, in 1910, the year of Halley's comet, I left my Pretty Waitress Girl and my new job with Pinkie's. And headed back to Sparks.

I was careful, on the way, to whisper sweet little nothings like these: *Good comet! Nice comet! Noble and wonderful Halley's!*

You can never be too careful, especially when an eastbound train could take you into the future.

At Sparks station, I changed trains to ride the original tracks going west.

Five miles outside of the station, I moseyed along to the front, greeting all along the way with my happiest smile in years.

At the locomotive, I knocked and smiled at the engineer.

When he opened the door I said, "Hi there! I really hate to do this, but—you see, I just have to go *back*."

I showed him my gun.

He remained very calm.

He said, "You wouldn't dare—"

I stuck the barrel in his ear and urged him to listen to reason.

He did. So did his assistant, the burly fireman. The train was brought to a safe, graceful stop and the coupling between the two cars was released.

The two men stood on the platform of the next car, watching. The engineer gave me a sad little wave.

"I sure hope you like it there, wherever it is that you're going," he said. " 'Cause I guarantee you, you won't be there that long."

"Oh, I don't know about that," I replied. "Now, what's this big black lever here—"

"Easy!" he cried.

But too late.

I was *OFF*!

And I wasted no time in letting Halley's have it: "You filthy flying snowball! You garbage heap! You bitch! I know the one place you wouldn't DARE to put me! You couldn't possibly do it—because there won't be any tracks! You lose!"

Ahhhh . . . That's the wonderful thing about comets. Treacherous as hell, if they take you by surprise. But thoroughly predictable if you know how to lead 'em.

There *weren't* any tracks, of course, before 1869. Not to where I was going. But if you ever want to know the meaning of "resourceful," just get a comet riled. We *flew*, and the hell with the tracks. Nothing would stop Halley's from teaching *me* a thing or two.

I sit here now to conclude my report by the soft golden glow of a gas lamp.

The air here is finer, and purer, than any I've known. It is the raw, crude, pungent aroma of new life beginning. It is positively teeming with the mystery of the unknown.

Outside, there are miles of shanties and shacks, thousands and thousands of ships on the Bay.

We'll build a city that men will remember as long as there *are* men to think of such things.

And our dreams and our blood will enrichen its soil.

Long life to San Francisco, the City by the Bay!

And if this record reaches you in the Nineties that I'd had such plans for:

Good luck to you. Long life to you. The Nineties are as good a time as any time you'll see. Forget about the Sweet

Spot. It is there and it will come if you only know how to look.

   This is my report.

                                    Dodge Cunningham
                                    San Franciscan
                                    1849